DATE DUE

MAY 1 4 2016		
JUN 0 2 2016		
SEP 0 9 2016		
NOV 2 7 2017		
		PRINTED IN U.S.A.

BY CURTIS SITTENFELD

Eligible
Sisterland
American Wife
The Man of My Dreams
Prep

Eligible

A NOVEL

CURTIS SITTENFELD

RANDOM HOUSE NEW YORK

Published in the United States by
Random House, an imprint and division of
Penguin Random House LLC, New York.

RANDOM HOUSE and the HOUSE colophon
are registered trademarks of Penguin Random House LLC.

LIBRARY OF CONGRESS CATALOGING-IN-PUBLICATION DATA
Sittenfeld, Curtis.
Eligible: a novel / Curtis Sittenfeld.
pages ; cm
ISBN 978-1-4000-6832-6
International edition ISBN 978-0-3995-8952-2
ebook ISBN 978-0-8129-9761-3
1. Sisters—Fiction.   2. Families—Fiction.   I. Austen, Jane, 1775–1817. Pride and
prejudice.   II. Title.
PS3619.I94E45 2016
813'.6—dc23
2015027778

Printed in the United States of America on acid-free paper

randomhousebooks.com

2 4 6 8 9 7 5 3 1

First Edition

Book design by Elizabeth A. D. Eno

For Samuel Park,
Austen devotee and beloved friend

When the end of the world comes, I want to be in Cincinnati because it's always twenty years behind the times.

—Mark Twain

Part One

Chapter 1

WELL BEFORE HIS arrival in Cincinnati, everyone knew that Chip
Bingley was looking for a wife. Two years earlier, Chip—graduate of
Dartmouth College and Harvard Medical School, scion of the Penn-
sylvania Bingleys, who in the twentieth century had made their fortune
in plumbing fixtures—had, ostensibly with some reluctance, appeared
on the juggernaut reality-television show *Eligible.* Over the course of
eight weeks in the fall of 2011, twenty-five single women had lived
together in a mansion in Rancho Cucamonga, California, and vied for
Chip's heart: accompanying him on dates to play blackjack in Las
Vegas and taste wine at vineyards in Napa Valley, fighting with and
besmirching one another in and out of his presence. At the end of each
episode, every woman received either a kiss on the lips from him, which
meant she would continue to compete, or a kiss on the cheek, which
meant she had to return home immediately. In the final episode, with
only two women remaining—Kara, a wide-eyed, blond-ringleted
twenty-three-year-old former college cheerleader turned second-grade

teacher from Jackson, Mississippi, and Marcy, a duplicitous yet alluring brunette twenty-eight-year-old dental hygienist from Morristown, New Jersey—Chip wept profusely and declined to propose marriage to either. They both were extraordinary, he declared, stunning and intelligent and sophisticated, but toward neither did he feel what he termed "a soul connection." In compliance with FCC regulations, Marcy's subsequent tirade consisted primarily of bleeped-out words that nevertheless did little to conceal her rage.

"It's not because he was on that silly show that I want him to meet our girls," Mrs. Bennet told her husband over breakfast on a morning in late June. The Bennets lived on Grandin Road, in a sprawling eight-bedroom Tudor in Cincinnati's Hyde Park neighborhood. "I never even saw it. But he went to Harvard Medical School, you know."

"So you've mentioned," said Mr. Bennet.

"After all we've been through, I wouldn't mind a doctor in the family," Mrs. Bennet said. "Call that self-serving if you like, but I'd say it's smart."

"Self-serving?" Mr. Bennet repeated. "You?"

Five weeks prior, Mr. Bennet had undergone emergency coronary artery bypass surgery; after a not inconsiderable recuperation, it was just in the last few days that his typically sardonic affect had returned.

"Chip Bingley didn't even want to be on *Eligible*, but his sister nominated him," Mrs. Bennet said.

"A reality show isn't unlike the Nobel Peace Prize, then," Mr. Bennet said. "In that they both require nominations."

"I wonder if Chip's renting or has bought a place," Mrs. Bennet said. "That would tell us something about how long he plans to stay in Cincinnati."

Mr. Bennet set down his slice of toast. "Given that this man is a stranger to us, you seem inordinately interested in the details of his life."

"I'd scarcely say *stranger*. He's in the ER at Christ Hospital, which means Dick Lucas must know him. Chip's very well-spoken, not like those trashy young people who are usually on TV. And very handsome, too."

"I thought you'd never seen the show."

"I only caught a few minutes of it, when the girls were watching." Mrs. Bennet looked peevishly at her husband. "You shouldn't quarrel with me. It's bad for your recovery. Anyway, Chip could have had a whole career on TV but chose to return to medicine. And you can tell that he's from a nice family. Fred, I really believe his moving here right when Jane and Liz are home is the silver lining to our troubles." The eldest and second eldest of the five Bennet sisters had lived in New York for the last decade and a half; it was due to their father's health scare that they had abruptly, if temporarily, returned to Cincinnati.

"My dear," said Mr. Bennet, "if a sock puppet with a trust fund and a Harvard medical degree moved here, you'd think he was meant to marry one of our girls."

"Tease me all you like, but the clock is ticking. No, Jane doesn't look like she'll be forty in November, but any man who knows her age will think long and hard about what that means. And Liz isn't far behind her."

"Plenty of men don't want children." Mr. Bennet took a sip of coffee. "I'm still not sure that I do."

"A woman in her forties *can* give birth," Mrs. Bennet said, "but it isn't as easy as the media would have you believe. Phyllis and Bob's daughter had all sorts of procedures, and what did she end up with but little Ying from Shanghai." As she stood, Mrs. Bennet glanced at her gold oval-faced watch. "I'm going to phone Helen Lucas and see if she can arrange an introduction to Chip."

Chapter 2

MRS. BENNET WAS always the one to say grace at family dinners—
she was fond of the Anglican meal prayer—and hardly had the word
amen passed her lips that evening when, with uncontainable enthusiasm, she announced, "The Lucases have invited us for a Fourth of July
barbecue!"

"What time?" asked Lydia, who at twenty-three was the youngest
Bennet. "Because Kitty and I have plans."

Mary, who was thirty, said, "No fireworks start before dark."

"We're invited to a pre-party in Mount Adams," Kitty said. Kitty
was twenty-six, the closest in both age and temperament to Lydia, yet
contrary to typical sibling patterns, she both tagged after and was led
astray by her younger sister.

"But I haven't told you who'll be at the barbecue." From her end
of the long oak kitchen table, Mrs. Bennet beamed. "Chip Bingley!"

"The *Eligible* crybaby?" Lydia said, and Kitty giggled as Lydia added,
"I've never seen a *woman* cry as hard as he did in the season finale."

"What's an eligible crybaby?" Jane asked.

"Oh, Jane," Liz said. "So innocent and unspoiled. You've heard of the reality show *Eligible*, right?"

Jane squinted. "I think so."

"He was on it a couple years ago. He was the guy being lusted after by twenty-five women."

"I don't suppose that any of you can appreciate the terror a man might feel being so outnumbered," Mr. Bennet said. "I often weep, and there are only six of you."

"*Eligible* is degrading to women," Mary said, and Lydia said, "Of course that's what you think."

"But every other season is one woman and twenty-five guys," Kitty said. "That's equality."

"The women humiliate themselves in a way the men don't," Mary said. "They're so desperate."

"Chip Bingley went to Harvard Medical School," Mrs. Bennet said. "He's not one of those vulgar Hollywood types."

"Mom, his Hollywood vulgarity is the only reason anyone in Cincinnati cares about him," Liz said.

Jane turned to her sister. "You knew he was here?"

"You didn't?"

"Which of us are you hoping he'll go for, Mom?" Lydia asked. "He's old, right? So I assume Jane."

"Thanks, Lydia," Jane said.

"He's thirty-six," Mrs. Bennet said. "That would make him suitable for Jane or Liz."

"Why not for Mary?" Kitty asked.

"He doesn't seem like Mary's type," Mrs. Bennet said.

"Because she's gay," Lydia said. "And he's not a woman."

Mary glared at Lydia. "First of all, I'm not gay. And even if I were, I'd rather be a lesbian than a sociopath."

Lydia smirked. "You don't have to choose."

"Is everyone listening to this?" Mary turned to her mother, at the foot of the table, then her father, at the head. "There's something seriously wrong with Lydia."

"There's nothing wrong with any of you," Mrs. Bennet said. "Jane, what's this vegetable called? It has an unusual flavor."

"It's spinach," Jane said. "I braised it."

"In point of fact," Mr. Bennet said, "there's something wrong with all of you. You're adults, and you ought to be living on your own."

"Dad, we came home to take care of you," Jane said.

"I'm well now. Go back to New York. You too, Lizzy. As the only one who refuses to take a dime and, not coincidentally, the only one with a real job, you're supposed to be setting an example for your sisters. Instead, they're pulling you down with them."

"Jane and Lizzy know how important my luncheon is," Mrs. Bennet said. "That's why they're still here." The event to which Mrs. Bennet was referring was the annual fundraising luncheon for the Cincinnati Women's League, scheduled this year for the second Thursday in September. A member of the league since her twenties, Mrs. Bennet was for the first time the luncheon's planning chair, and, as she often reminded her family members, the enormous pressure and responsibility of the role left her, however lamentably, unavailable to tend to her husband's recovery. "Now, the Lucases' barbecue is called for four," Mrs. Bennet continued. "Lydia and Kitty, that's plenty of time for you to join us and still get to your party before the fireworks. Helen Lucas is inviting some young people from the hospital besides Chip Bingley, so it'd be a shame for you to miss meeting them."

"Mom, unlike our sisters, Kitty and I are capable of getting boyfriends on our own," Lydia said.

Mrs. Bennet looked from her end of the table to her husband's. "If any of our girls marry doctors, it will meet my needs, yes," she said to him. "But, Fred, if it gets them out of the house, I daresay it will meet yours, too."

Chapter 3

IN THE PROFESSIONAL realm, Mr. Bennet had done little while supporting his family with a large but dwindling inheritance, and his observations about his daughters' indolence were more than a little hypocritical. However, he was not wrong. Indeed, an outsider could be forgiven for wondering what it was that the Bennet sisters *did* with themselves from day to day and year to year. It wasn't that they were uneducated: On the contrary, from the ages of three to eighteen, each sister had attended the Seven Hills School, a challenging yet warm coeducational institution where in their younger years they'd memorized songs such as "Fifty Nifty United States" and collaborated—collaboration, at Seven Hills, was paramount—with classmates on massive papier-mâché stegosauruses or triceratops. In later years, they read *The Odyssey,* helped run the annual Harvest Fair, and went on supplemental summer trips to France and China; throughout, they all played soccer and basketball. The cumulative bill for this progressive and wide-ranging education was $800,000. All five girls had then gone on to private colleges before embarking on what could euphemistically be called nonlucrative careers, though in the case of some sisters, nonlucrative noncareers was a more precise descriptor. Kitty and Lydia had never worked longer than a few months at a time, as desultory nannies or salesgirls in the Abercrombie & Fitch or the Banana Republic in Rookwood Pavilion. Similarly, they had lived under roofs other than their parents' for only short stretches, experiments in quasi-independence that had always resulted in dramatic fights with formerly close friends, broken leases, and the huffy transport of possessions, via laundry basket and trash bag, back to the Tudor. Primarily what occupied the younger Bennet sisters was eating lunch at Green Dog Café or Teller's, texting and watching videos on their smartphones, and exercising. About a year before, Kitty and Lydia had embraced Cross-Fit, the intense strength and conditioning regimen that involved weight lifting, kettle bells, battle ropes, obscure acronyms, the eschewal of most foods other than meat, and a derisive attitude toward the weak and unenlightened masses who still believed that jogging was a sufficient workout and a bagel was an acceptable breakfast. Naturally, all Bennets except Kitty and Lydia were among these masses.

Mary, meanwhile, was pursuing her third online master's degree, this one in psychology; the earlier ones had been in criminal justice and business administration. The plainest in appearance of the sisters, Mary considered her decision to live with her parents to be evidence of her commitment to the life of the mind over material acquisitions, and also to reflect her aversion to waste, since her childhood room would go empty were she not its occupant. By this logic, Mary's waste avoidance was truly exemplary, since she hardly decamped from her room from one day to the next and instead sequestered herself with her studies, stayed up late, and slept in. The exception was a standing Tuesday-night excursion, but if asked about this mysterious weekly outing, Mary would bark, "It's none of your business," or that's what she would have said back when her family members still inquired. Also back then, Lydia would have said, "AA meeting? Lesbian book club? Lesbian AA meeting?" .

Jane and Liz had always held jobs, but even for them, a certain awareness of the safety net below had allowed the prioritizing of their personal interests over remuneration. Jane was a yoga instructor, a position that might have let her cover her rent in a city such as Cincinnati but did not do so in Manhattan, and certainly not on the Upper West Side, which she had called home for the last fifteen years. While Liz, too, had spent her twenties and thirties in New York, she had for most of them, until a recent move to Brooklyn's Cobble Hill neighborhood, inhabited dingy walk-ups in the outer boroughs. The exception had been the apartment at Seventy-second and Amsterdam that the sisters had shared shortly after Liz graduated from Barnard College in the late 1990s, just a year after Jane's graduation from the same school. Though they had gotten along well as roommates, the sisters' cohabitation had reached its conclusion when Jane became engaged to an affable hedge-fund analyst named Teddy; Mrs. Bennet's uneasiness with Jane and Teddy living together prior to their marriage was allayed by Teddy's degree from Cornell and his lucrative job. Alas, Teddy's dawning awareness of his attraction to other men ultimately precluded a permanent union with Jane, though Jane and her erstwhile fiancé did part on good terms, and once or twice a year, both Liz and Jane would meet Teddy and his toothsome partner, Patrick, for brunch.

Liz had spent her entire professional life working at magazines, having been hired out of college as a fact-checker at a weekly publication known for its incisive coverage of politics and culture. From there, she had jumped to *Mascara,* a monthly women's magazine she had subscribed to since the age of fourteen, drawn equally to its feminist stances and its unapologetic embrace of shoes and cosmetics. First she was an assistant editor, then an associate editor, then a features editor; but at the age of thirty-one, realizing that her passion was telling stories rather than editing them, Liz had become *Mascara*'s writer-at-large, a position she still occupied. Though writing tended to pay less than editing, Liz believed she had a dream job: She traveled regularly and interviewed accomplished and sometimes famous individuals. However, her achievements did not impress her own family. Her father still, after all this time, pretended not to remember *Mascara*'s name. "How's everything at *Nail Polish*?" he'd ask or "Any new developments at *Lipstick*?" Mary often told Liz that *Mascara* reinforced oppressive and exclusionary standards of beauty; even Lydia and Kitty, who had no problem with oppressive and exclusionary standards of beauty, were uninterested in the publication, likely because they were fans of neither magazines nor books and confined their reading to the screens of their phones.

And yet, if Liz's job underwhelmed those close to her, its flexible nature was what had allowed her to remain at home during her father's convalescence, and the situation was similar for Jane, who had taken a leave of absence from the yoga studio where she was employed. Five weeks earlier, the two sisters had traveled to Cincinnati unsure of the outcome of, and greatly rattled by, Mr. Bennet's surgery. By the time it was clear that he would make a full recovery, Liz and Jane were deeply involved in both his recuperation and the day-to-day proceedings of the household: They grocery shopped and prepared cardiac-friendly meals for the entire family; they took turns transporting Mr. Bennet to his doctors' appointments, including to the orthopedist treating the arm Mr. Bennet had broken when he'd lost consciousness during his original heart incident and had fallen at the top of the stairs in the second-floor hall. (Because he still wore a cast on his right arm, Mr. Bennet was unable to drive himself.) Additionally, though they had made little progress so far, Liz and Jane intended to address the cluttered and dusty condition into which the Tudor had deteriorated.

While their sisters could in theory have performed all such tasks, the younger women appeared disinclined. Though also clearly rattled by their father's heart incident, they weren't rattled in a way that caused them to alter their daily schedules: Lydia and Kitty carried on with CrossFit and leisurely restaurant lunches, while Mary emerged from her room erratically to attempt to engage family members in discussions of mortality. In the kitchen, observing her father drinking the powdered-psyllium-seed-husk-based liquid meant to offset the constipating effects of his pain medication, Mary had announced that she considered the Native American view of life and death as cyclical to be far more advanced than the Western proclivity for heroic measures, at which point Mr. Bennet had poured the remainder of his beverage down the sink, said, "For Christ's sake, Mary, put a sock in it," and left the room.

Mrs. Bennet expressed great concern about her husband's plight—indeed, she could hardly speak of the evening on which he'd been hospitalized without sobbing at the recollection of the fright it had caused her—but she could not act as his nurse or chauffeur because of her many Women's League luncheon duties. "What if you ask somebody else on the committee to take over and you're the chair next year instead?" Liz had inquired one day when Mr. Bennet was still in the hospital. Her mother had looked at her in horror.

"Why, I'd never hear the end of it," Mrs. Bennet said. "Lizzy, all those items being solicited for the silent auction—*I'm* the one keeping track of them."

"Then how about creating an online spreadsheet that everyone can see?" Because Mrs. Bennet wasn't proficient with a computer, Liz added, "I can help you."

"It's out of the question," Mrs. Bennet said. "I'm also the one who's been talking to the florist, and I'm the one who had the idea to do napkins with the league's insignia. You can't pass off things like that in midstream."

"Does Mom secretly hate Dad?" Liz asked Jane the next morning when the two sisters were out for a run. "Because she's acting really unsupportive."

"I think she just doesn't want to face how serious things could have been," Jane said.

After Mr. Bennet's return home, however, Liz wondered if she'd been wrong not about her mother's antipathy for her father but only about its being secret. Although her parents resumed their regular lunches together at the Cincinnati Country Club as soon as Mr. Bennet possessed the energy, the couple led largely separate lives within the Tudor. In fact, her father no longer shared the master bedroom, instead sleeping in a narrow sleigh bed in his second-floor study, a setup that predated his hospital stay. When Liz asked Mary how long the arrangement had existed, Mary squinted and said, "Five years? Or, I don't know, ten?"

Reinforcing Liz's dismay was the fact that, although Dr. Morelock had explicitly talked about the importance of Mr. Bennet embarking on a diet low in red meat, salt, and alcohol, Mrs. Bennet had welcomed her husband home with a cocktail hour of Scotch and Cheetos followed by a steak dinner. When the subsequent night's entrée was roast beef, Liz discreetly asked her mother afterward if she might consider making chicken or salmon. "But Kitty and Lydia like beef because it's caveman food," Mrs. Bennet protested.

"But Dad had a heart attack," Liz said.

For all the nights since, she and Jane had taken turns preparing dinner. They had also agreed to stay in Cincinnati until the weekend after the Women's League luncheon. Liz had little confidence that her mother would step in and provide care for her father at that point; rather, with his cast off by then, his physical therapy well under way if not complete, and his ability to drive likely restored, she hoped he'd be able to care for himself.

Chapter 4

"HONK SO YOUR mother knows we're waiting," Mr. Bennet said. In the large circular driveway of the Tudor, waiting to depart for the Lucases' barbecue, Liz sat in the driver's seat of her mother's Lexus sedan, with Mr. Bennet in the passenger seat and Jane in back.

"She already knows," Liz said, and Mr. Bennet leaned over and, using his left arm, which was the one not in a cast, pressed the horn himself.

"Jesus, Dad," Liz said. "Show a little patience."

The Bennets would transport themselves to the Lucases' in no fewer than three cars: Lydia and Kitty would drive out in Kitty's Mini Cooper, and Mary insisted she'd take her own Honda hybrid. "This way, it won't be a problem if Dad is tired and needs to leave early," Mrs. Bennet had said as she, Liz, and Jane conferred in the kitchen about the slightly droopy strawberry-and-blueberry-bedecked sponge cake Jane had made.

In the driveway, Liz turned to her father. "Are you eager to meet the famous Chip Bingley?"

"Unlike your mother, I don't care whom any of you marries or, frankly, if you marry," Mr. Bennet said. "The institution hasn't done much for me, Lord knows."

"That's a nice sentiment." Liz patted her father's knee. "Thank you for sharing."

Mrs. Bennet appeared at the back door, looking flustered, and called out, "I just need another minute." Before they could respond, she vanished again.

Liz glanced at Jane in the rearview mirror. "Jane, are *you* excited to meet Chip?" Jane was gazing out the window; so placid was she in demeanor that at times it was difficult to discern whether she was upset or simply reflective. In any case, she had never participated with much gusto in the banter her father and sisters enjoyed.

"I suppose," Jane said as Mrs. Bennet emerged from the house.

"How lovely of you to join us!" Mr. Bennet called out his open window.

Liz started the engine as her mother climbed into the backseat. "The phone rang, and it was Ginger Drossman inviting us for brunch," Mrs. Bennet said. "That's what took so long." As she leaned forward into the front seat, a look of concern pinched Mrs. Bennet's features. "Lizzy, I'm sure there's time for you to run in and put on a skirt."

In her teens or early twenties, such a remark would have irritated Liz, but at thirty-eight, having wardrobe fights with her mother felt preposterous. Cheerfully, she said, "Nope, I'm comfortable." Even if her mother couldn't recognize it, the shorts she had on were extremely stylish, as were her sleeveless white blouse and straw sandals.

Jane spoke as they pulled out of the driveway. She said, "I think Lizzy looks pretty."

Chapter 5

WHILE IT WAS technically accurate that both Liz and Jane were single, this fact did not for either woman convey the full story. After Jane's fruitless early engagement, she had met a man named Jean-Pierre Babineaux, a courtly French financier, and they had become a couple for the better part of a decade. Though Jane had assumed she and Jean-Pierre would marry, their conversations on the subject were always marked by a bittersweetness she recognized in retrospect as a kind of warning. It was not that either of them lacked affection for the other but, rather, that the circumstances of their lives were incompatible: He was fifteen years older than she, divorced, and the father of twins who were, when Jane met him, twelve. He traveled back to Paris frequently, and while Jane could hardly complain about her visits there, staying at the apartment he maintained in the Sixth Arrondissement, she did not wish to live so far from her family and certainly not permanently; yet Jean-Pierre's ultimate plan was to return to his birthplace. Further, while Jane unequivocally wished to bear children, Jean-Pierre had had a vasectomy when the twins were two.

Jane and Jean-Pierre's eventual breakup was no less devastating for being both protracted and decorous. At thirty-seven, she was single once more and remained so for the next two years. Shortly after her thirty-ninth birthday, following the painstaking consideration of a multitude of anonymous candidates, Jane lay on her back in a hospital gown at a clinic on East Fifty-seventh Street, awaiting the insertion of donor semen into her cervix via needleless syringe. Though Jane followed all the recommendations for creating conditions favorable to pregnancy—she stopped drinking alcohol, slept eight hours a night, and meditated daily—fertilization didn't occur during that cycle or in any of the next several rounds. While not statistically anomalous—few women attempting to become pregnant via donor insemination were immediately successful—this lack of progress was discouraging as well as expensive, and Jane's insurance covered none of the monthly $1,000 charge. Anticipating her parents' disapproval, she hadn't disclosed her pursuit to them and thus was receiving no extra money beyond the rent, which Mr. Bennet paid directly on her behalf. Thus, for the first time in her adult life, Jane found herself bypassing restaurants, forgoing haircuts, and shunning the street on which her favorite clothing boutique, with its elegantly tailored $400 pencil skirts and luxurious $300 sweaters, was located. Such sacrifices would not, she recognized, count by most people's standards as hardships, but she was privately conscious of a new austerity.

With no one other than Liz did Jane discuss her efforts to become a mother. Her gynecologist had suggested that she tell her parents even before the first insemination, but Jane thought that if she wasn't able to become pregnant, then she'd have courted the double punishment of what she assumed would be her mother's histrionics and no baby. And Jane still hoped to marry eventually, though marriage was no longer her immediate goal.

Unlike Jane, Liz wished to avoid motherhood. That she was dating a married man made such avoidance logical, though whether these circumstances had occurred by chance or subconscious design even Liz herself couldn't say. In the late nineties, Liz and Jasper Wick had immediately hit it off as new hires in the fact-checking department of the same prestigious magazine: They bit back smiles when the books editor, who was from Delaware, pronounced the word "memoir" *memwah;* they got lunch together several times a week at a cheap Thai restaurant; and they routinely divided the work between them when checking facts on onerous articles. (They had started their jobs using computers with spotty Internet connections, back when fact-checking meant visiting the public library or waiting anxiously for the return of phone calls.)

When Liz and Jasper met, he had a girlfriend, which was unsurprising: He had deep brown eyes and tousled blond curls and was at once smart and irreverent, boyish and thoughtful, with, in Liz's assessment, the perfect quantities of neuroses and prurience to make him interesting to talk to, receptive to gossip, and game for analyzing the behavior and personalities of others without tipping over into seeming unmasculine. Indeed, Jasper's sole flaw, in Liz's opinion, apart from his girlfriend, was that he wore a gold ring from Stanford University, his alma mater; Liz did not care for either jewelry on men or academic ostentatiousness. But she actually was glad to have identified the one thing about Jasper she'd change, because it was similar to realizing what you'd forgotten to take on a trip, and if it was only perfume, as opposed to your driver's license, you were relieved.

Initially, Liz had believed that a union with Jasper was just a matter of time; such was Jasper's tendency to confide in her about the multitude of challenges he and his girlfriend, Serena, were experiencing that Liz imagined *she* need not persuade him of anything. While still together with Serena, Jasper had dropped conversational bombshells on Liz that included "I mean, I talk way more openly with you than I do with her" and "Sometimes I think you and I would be a good couple. Do you ever think that?" Liz knew for certain he had said these things because, although she no longer kept a journal, she'd written them down verbatim, along with their date of utterance, on an unlined sheet of computer paper she kept in her nightstand. Also, after she mentioned to Jasper that as a toddler she'd referred to herself as Ninny or Nin, he began calling her by the latter pet name.

Eight months into knowing Jasper, meaning seven months and

three weeks into being thoroughly smitten with him, during a blizzard that occurred on a Saturday in February, Liz went running with him in Central Park in five inches of snow, while flakes were still falling. Jasper's pace combined with the snow on the ground made this outing the most grueling physical exertion Liz had ever experienced, and by the second mile, she could take it no more. She stopped, leaned over, pressed her palms to her knees, and said while panting, "I give up. You win."

"Really?" Jasper was a few feet in front of her, looking over his shoulder, grinning under a black fleece cap. "What's my prize?"

Your prize is me, Liz thought. "Bragging rights," she said. "And a hot drink from any bar that's open." Then she knelt and let herself collapse backward into the snow.

Jasper retraced his steps and lay down beside her. They were quiet as the flakes fluttered and spun in the air above, the sky a dirty white, the snow beneath them a chilly cushion. Jasper stuck out his tongue, catching a flake, and Liz did the same. All the usual noises of Manhattan were muted by the storm, and she felt completely happy. Then Jasper looked over at her. "So I broke up with Serena last night," he said.

The joy that flared in Liz's heart—it was almost too much. She hoped she sounded calm as she said, "I guess that makes sense."

"You think so?"

"It just seems like you guys have had a lot of issues."

"She's furious, though. She claims I ambushed her." Though no prettier than Liz, Serena was far more confidently difficult, more expectant of appeasement and conciliation.

Liz said, "Do you still feel like going to Alex's thing tonight or you think you'll skip it?" This was an anti-Valentine's party a co-worker of theirs was throwing, but if Jasper wanted to forgo it, Liz thought, they could order takeout, watch a movie, and have a mellow night.

"I'll probably go."

Liz was then assaulted by something wet and lumpy, a substance that broke upon contact with her nose and dispersed into her eyes and nostrils.

"Ouch!" she cried. "What the hell?" But by the time she asked, she knew. While she didn't really have the impulse to throw a snowball back, Jasper was smiling with anticipation. When her snowball glanced off the shoulder of his waterproof jacket, he said, "Oh, Nin, I have so much to teach you."

How long, on that day, did Liz imagine it would take for them to become romantically involved? Six or eight weeks perhaps—long enough for him to process his breakup with Serena, *process* being a word Jasper himself, unlike either of her college boyfriends, actually used in reference to his own emotions. But apparently little processing was necessary. Liz felt no compulsion to keep a close eye on Jasper at the party, which made it all the more soul crushing when he left with the host's sister Natalie, who was a junior at NYU.

A rebound, Liz told herself. Natural enough, and perhaps even best to get it out of his system. Surely what was obvious to Liz—and to others, too, there'd even been an older female editor at the magazine who'd murmured to her, "You and Jasper Wick would be so *cute* together"—would soon become visible to Jasper as well.

Alas, Jasper and Natalie were a couple for two years, and it took only a few weeks of their courtship for Liz to revert to her Serena-era patterns with Jasper: She was his lunch companion, intermittently his jogging partner, his professional sounding board—she would copyedit and proofread the pitches he was crafting in the hope of getting a front-of-the-book piece in the magazine—and she was also his confidante, helping to parse his concerns about Natalie's immaturity or his irritation at his roommate, who would, while stoned, consume Jasper's tortillas and peanut butter. Once when Natalie was at her parents' house in Phoenix, Liz and Jasper drank many beers together on a Wednesday night at a dive bar near Times Square, and, unable to bear it any longer, Liz blurted out, "But what about *us*? I thought you pictured *us* as a couple!"

Jasper seemed startled. "That's what you want?" he said.

"Of course it's what I want!" Liz said.

"Part of me wants it, too." Jasper's tone was pained rather than flirtatious. "But we'd be the real thing, and I don't know if I'm ready for that. You're such an important friend that I don't want to risk losing you."

When they left the bar, before parting ways in Port Authority, they stood on the corner of Forty-second Street and Seventh Avenue and continued talking; there were between them always an infinite number of subjects to be addressed and dissected, mulled over and mocked and revisited. It was a windy March night, and the wisps of Liz's brown hair that had slipped from her ponytail blew around her forehead and cheeks.

Abruptly, Jasper said, "Your hair is all crazy tonight." He stepped toward her, his hand out. But at the same time, Liz raised her own arm and pushed away her hair, and as she did so, Jasper withdrew his hand and took a step back. There were countless hours—or maybe more than hours, maybe weeks and days—that Liz devoted to replaying this nonaction, this absence of contact. Because her hair hadn't been *that* crazy, it was frequently slipping from a rubber band, so obviously he had been about to touch her, about to kiss her even and perhaps to become her boyfriend and the love of her life. Had she intercepted him out of habit, because it was her hair and her head? Because she didn't believe in kissing the boyfriends of other girls? Or because she was, in some instinctive way, intent on wrecking her own destiny?

On the night he didn't touch her, Liz and Jasper both were twenty-four years old. For the next six years, they never kissed; they even slept in the same bed twice, at a friend's aunt's house in Sag Harbor and another time on a road trip to visit Jasper's sister at the University of Virginia. Meanwhile, Jasper cycled through additional girlfriends—after Natalie there was Gretchen, and after Gretchen there was Elise, and after Elise there was Katherine—and Liz halfheartedly went out with other guys but never for longer than a few months. Jasper would ask about such men in great detail, and once, when Liz was first giving online dating a whirl, they arranged that he and Elise would have drinks at the same bar where Liz was meeting her online prospect so that Jasper and Liz could debrief in mid-date; this seemed a terribly amusing idea in advance that was plainly fucked up in its execution.

Jasper, of course, hadn't told Elise and, thus, pretended that seeing Liz was a coincidence, and Liz wasn't sure if it made matters better or worse that Elise appeared to believe the farce.

By this point, neither Jasper nor Liz was employed by the magazine where they'd met, but Liz still worked in the same building, and Jasper would return for lunch in the cafeteria, which had been designed by a famous architect and was reminiscent, with its blue-tinted glass partitions, of a series of aquariums. For all these years, Liz's attraction to Jasper, and Jasper's apparently lesser but not nonexistent attraction to Liz, was something they'd allude to jokingly—for instance, after visiting the Guggenheim together, she held up the ticket stub and said, with what she hoped was unmistakable sarcasm, "Maybe if I sleep with this under my pillow tonight, you'll fall in love with me," and he grinned and said, "Maybe so." They'd less often but still regularly have emotional, alcohol-fueled confrontations, always initiated by Liz. "It's ridiculous we're not together," she said once. "In most ways, I basically am your girlfriend."

"I hate that I'm causing you grief," Jasper replied.

"I'm an idiot," Liz said. "Anyone looking at me would think I'm an idiot."

"You're not an idiot," Jasper said. "You're my best friend."

If only she had let him smooth back her hair!

At intervals, Liz swore off Jasper—she'd say, "Our friendship is unhealthy," and she'd briefly embrace yoga, which, loyalty to Jane aside, she hated—but Liz's and Jasper's social circles overlapped enough that within a week or a month, they'd run into each other at a party or a Frisbee game and then they'd talk and talk about all the things they'd both been saving up to share with the other.

When they were thirty-one, Jasper announced his engagement to a pert and friendly associate at a white-shoe law firm, a woman named Susan about whom he seemed to Liz no less equivocal than he had toward earlier girlfriends. After a run together, he asked Liz if she'd be a groomsman; seeing her expression, he added, "Or a groomswoman, whatever." When Liz began to sob, he said, "What? What?" and she sprinted away and didn't speak to him for five years; though she still laid eyes on him at media events, she did not attend Jasper's wedding, let alone participate in the ceremony.

One Saturday in the spring of 2011, Liz and an oboist she'd met for a blind date ran into Jasper and Susan on the High Line, Jasper pushing a stroller in which a toddler slept. Susan greeted Liz warmly—like Elise, Susan had always seemed improbably unsuspicious of Liz, causing Liz to wonder exactly how Jasper explained their friendship—and the five of them ended up sharing brunch, during which the toddler, a boy named Aidan, awoke and shrieked so relentlessly that Liz forgave Jasper just a little. That Monday morning, Jasper emailed Liz: *It was great to see you. Really miss our friendship.*

After an exchange of messages, they met for a weekday lunch at which they discussed recent articles they'd either loved or been outraged by, and then Jasper confided the financial pressure he felt now that Susan had decided she wanted to quit law and remain at home with Aidan. The last few years had, apparently, been rough: as a newborn, Aidan had had colic; Susan had initially struggled with breastfeeding though now was unwilling to give it up; and she was spending enormous quantities of time online trying to determine which potentially toxic chemicals were contained in the cleaning agent used on the carpeting in the halls of their building. Meanwhile, Jasper was spinning his wheels at work. He knew he was capable of running a magazine—he was still a senior editor rather than an executive editor, which was the usual jumping-off point for being an editor in chief—and welcomed Liz's thoughts about what publication might be most suitable for his continued ascent up the professional ladder. Jasper's great respect for Liz's ideas and opinions, his wish for feedback from her on every subject, even the subject of whether it was weird that his wife was still breast-feeding a nineteen-month-old, was simultaneously the most flattering and the most insulting dynamic she had ever experienced. She thought that if the option were available, he would run a cord between her brain and his, or perhaps simply download the contents of her cerebral cortex.

The next time she and Jasper met after the five-year hiatus, it was for drinks, and after the third round, Jasper said that he and Susan had together reached the painful conclusion that their marriage had run its course and that while both of them had had the best of intentions, they agreed they'd made a mistake choosing each other. The catch was that if Susan or any of her siblings divorced, Susan's deeply Catholic grandmother, a rich, spiteful, and surprisingly hale ninety-eight-year-old living on the Upper East Side, would cut them out of her will, and Aidan wouldn't get to attend private school. Thus, although Jasper and Susan had each other's blessings to pursue extramarital relationships, they would continue to live together until Susan's grandmother died. After conveying this information, Jasper swallowed, and there were tears in his brown eyes as he said, "It was always you, Nin. I messed up so badly, but it was always you."

At points during their five-year silence, Liz had indulged in the fantasy that Jasper would show up at her office or apartment—possibly, as in a movie, having run through the rain—to urgently declare his love. He might even, in such scenarios, have said, *It was always you.* But he would not have still been legally wed to Susan; certainly, he would not be the father of a nineteen-month-old. And yet, through the shimmery softness of the three gins she'd consumed, Liz thought that these compromising circumstances gave the situation a certain credibility: It *wasn't* too good to be true. She *didn't* need to feel unsettled by getting everything she'd always hoped for.

Back at her apartment, the consummation of their whatever-it-was also was not a dream come true—certainly fourteen years of buildup and more than a half dozen cocktails between them didn't help matters—but it was adequate, and afterward, when Jasper fell asleep holding her, she wished that her twenty-two-year-old self could know that it would, in the end, happen for them. Her twenty-two-year-old self might have been less charmed when Jasper woke up forty minutes later, took a hasty shower, and hurried home to his wife and child; despite Jasper and Susan's conjugal agreement, it was Jasper's turn the next morning to get up with Aidan at five A.M.

Within a week, Jasper had made three more visits to Liz's apartment and in two cases slept over; patterns had been established. The drawbacks to this version of a relationship were so glaringly obvious—

because members of Susan's extended family loyal to her grandmother lived in Manhattan, discretion was necessary, and Liz and Jasper therefore didn't dine together in restaurants, nor were they each other's dates for work-related functions—that they hardly seemed worth dwelling on. On the other hand, she was able to enjoy genuine closeness, as well as physical intimacy, with someone she knew well and cared for deeply, while still having time to work and run and read and see friends—perhaps, in fact, more time than when she'd been scouring dating websites or spending three hours at a stretch analyzing her singleness with Jane or other women. A few friends knew about Jasper, as did her older sister, and their skeptical reactions were for Liz sufficient deterrent to discuss the unusual arrangement further; it was too easy for it to sound like Jasper was doing nothing more than cheating.

One Friday evening in late May, two years into Liz's reconciliation with Jasper, Liz was at Jane's apartment; Jane chopped kale for a salad while Liz opened the bottle of red wine she'd brought. "Are you really making me drink alone again?" Liz said.

"I'm fostering a hospitable uterine environment," Jane replied.

"Meaning, yes, I'm on my own."

"Sorry." Jane frowned.

"Don't apologize." Liz pulled a glass from Jane's shelf. "And any fetus would be lucky to inhabit your womb. I bet you have the Ritz of uteruses. Uteri?" Liz held her filled glass aloft. "To Latinate nouns and to reproduction." Jane tapped her water glass against Liz's as Liz added, "Remember Sandra at my office who took three years to get pregnant? She said she went to this acupuncturist who—" In her pocket, Liz's phone buzzed, and she wondered if it was Jasper; apparently, Jane wondered the same thing because she said, with not entirely concealed disapproval, "Is that him?"

But it wasn't; it was their sister Kitty. Liz held up the phone so Jane could see the screen before saying, "Hey, Kitty. I'm here with Jane."

"It's Dad," Kitty said, and she was clearly crying. "He's in the hospital."

Chapter 6

HALF AN HOUR after complaining to Mrs. Bennet of heartburn that he attributed to the veal cacciatore she'd made for dinner, Mr. Bennet had climbed the staircase from the entry hall on the first floor of the Tudor to the second floor and collapsed, gasping for breath. Lydia had heard him fall, Mary had called 911, and he'd been transported by ambulance to Christ Hospital.

Upon receiving Kitty's phone call at Jane's apartment, Liz had immediately begun trying to find flights while Jane put away the food; as it turned out, the evening's final flights to Cincinnati out of both LaGuardia and JFK had already departed. With reservations for the early morning, Liz returned to her apartment, tossed clothes into a suitcase, slept fitfully for a couple hours, and met Jane again beyond LaGuardia's Terminal D security checkpoint at six A.M. By then, their father was out of a six-hour surgery, intubated, and unconscious in the intensive care unit.

Though he was awake and his breathing tube had been removed

when Liz and Jane arrived at the hospital straight from the airport, he was alarmingly subdued and appeared much smaller in his hospital gown than in his usual uniform of khakis, dress shirt, and navy blazer. At the sight of him, Liz bit back tears, while Jane wept openly. "My dear Jane—" Mr. Bennet said, but he spoke no more; he offered no drollery to reassure them. The many wires monitoring his vital signs beeped indifferently.

He remained in the hospital for a week. But on his second day after surgery, he'd moved from intensive care to the step-down unit, and his health had improved consistently. In increments that were less steadily apparent than manifest in sudden moments, his coloring brightened, his energy increased, his mordant humor returned, and it seemed then that he really would be all right.

In the meantime, the eldest Bennet sisters fell quickly into certain patterns. They slept in twin beds in the third-floor room that, when they were growing up, had belonged to Liz. She'd set the alarm on her cellphone for seven o'clock, and they'd rise and run together before the day grew too hot: around the curve of Grandin Road, past the bulge of the Cincinnati Country Club, right on Madison Road and again on Observatory, then up the long incline of Edwards Road's first hill, which was gently graded but endless, and its second hill, which was short and steep. Back at home, they'd eat cereal, take turns showering, then determine what needed to be accomplished that day.

Originally overshadowed by their father's ill health, but asserting itself with increasing insistence as Mr. Bennet improved, was the sisters' realization that the Tudor, built in 1903, was in a state of profound disrepair. For the last twenty years, Liz and Jane had made three-day visits home, usually around the holidays, and Liz realized in retrospect that her mother had likely spent weeks preparing for their arrival. This time, when Mrs. Bennet hadn't prepared at all, mail lay in stacks on the marble table in the entry hall; mold grew in the basin of the third-floor toilet; spiderwebs clung to light fixtures and the corners of ceilings; and Jane and Liz were sharing a room because the bed and most of the floor in the adjacent room that had once belonged to Jane were blocked by an assortment of boxes, some empty save for bubble wrap but some as yet unopened, addressed by various high-end retailers to Mrs. Frederick M. Bennet. The day before her father had been discharged from the hospital, Liz had used the blade of a scissors to open three packages, which contained, respectively, a plush cream-colored throw pillow overlaid by an embroidered pineapple; a set of royal blue bath towels featuring Mrs. Bennet's monogram; and twelve dessert plates with Yorkshire terriers on them (the Bennets had never owned a Yorkshire terrier—or, for that matter, any other breed of dog).

That her mother devoted extensive attention to housewares was not news; the usual impetus for Mrs. Bennet to call Liz in New York was to ask whether she was in need of, say, a porcelain teapot with an ivy motif that normally cost $260 but was on sale for $230. Invariably, without broaching the topic of who might pay for the teapot in question, Liz ruefully declined; it sounded charming, but she had such limited space, and also, she'd remind her mother, she wasn't a huge tea drinker. Once, years before, Liz had been talked into accepting as a gift a large gold-rimmed platter—"For your dinner parties!" Mrs. Bennet had said brightly—but upon learning eighteen months later that Liz had during that time held no dinner parties, Mrs. Bennet had insisted that Liz give the platter back. Shipping it had cost $55. So no, it wasn't a secret that her mother fetishized all manner of domestic décor, but the sheer quantity in Jane's former bedroom, plus the fact of so many boxes being unopened, raised for Liz the question of whether some type of pathology might be involved.

Meanwhile, on an almost daily basis, the Tudor revealed its failures: dripping faucets, splintering floorboards, obscurely sized sconce light-bulbs that had burned out. In many instances, it was unclear to Liz whether a particular predicament, such as the eight-foot-square water-stained patch on the eastern side of the living room wall, was new or whether her parents and sisters had simply been turning a blind eye to it for months or years.

The three acres of land surrounding the Tudor presented its own set of complications, including an extensive growth of poison ivy behind the house and a fungus on the large sycamore tree under which Liz had once held picnics for her dolls. As far as she could tell, her father had for quite some time done no more outside than mow the grass and, since getting sick, had not even done that. It occurred to Liz one day, as she waited on hold for an estimate from a yard service, that her parents' home was like an extremely obese person who could no longer see, touch, or maintain jurisdiction over all of his body; there was simply too much of it, and he—they—had grown weary and inflexible.

During the hours she'd allotted each day for work, Liz would open her laptop on the pink Formica desk her parents had purchased for her in 1987 and respond to queries from *Mascara* editors about a recent article she'd turned in, schedule or conduct interviews, fend off or follow up with publicists. In addition to features on varying topics, Liz wrote three mini-profiles each month for *Mascara*'s long-running "Women Who Dare" column—for example, a corporal in Iraq, a blind aerobics instructor, or a principal in Wichita who'd saved her students from a tornado. Although Liz privately thought of the subjects as "Attractive, Well-Groomed Women Who Dare," finding and interviewing such individuals was her favorite part of her job.

Jane, by contrast, was not attempting to work from Cincinnati. A few times a week, she'd attend a yoga class at a studio in Clifton, but in the capacity of student rather than teacher. Yet still, for both women, the days passed surprisingly quickly, a cycle of morning runs, doctors' appointments, errands, meal preparation, and family dinners. May had soon turned into June and June into July.

Jasper and Liz texted each other frequently, sometimes hourly. From him, accompanying a photo of the turbaned breakfast sandwich vendor at the corner of Fifty-fifth and Sixth: *Pretty sure this guy misses u.*

Liz had returned to New York for one night after her father was discharged from the hospital, a trip that allowed her to meet with her editor, collect additional clothes from her own and Jane's apartments, discard the open containers of yogurt in their refrigerators, give away her bamboo plant, and provide copies of keys to an assistant in Barnard College's Residential Life & Housing Office, a woman who had on late notice and with surprising good humor procured undergraduates who would until August 31 be Liz's and Jane's respective subletters.

Once these tasks were accomplished but before riding back to the airport, Liz met Jasper at his apartment at eleven A.M. on a Tuesday; as she arrived, Susan and Aidan were leaving for a gymnastics class. Though they hadn't seen one another since their encounter on the High Line two years before—in the interval, Aidan had transformed from an overgrown baby to a miniature person—Susan said in as ordinary a way as she might greet a neighbor, "Hey, Liz."

But once Susan and Aidan were gone, as Liz and Jasper removed their own clothes in the bedroom—they didn't have a great deal of time and, in any case, were well beyond the stage of effortful seduction—Liz experienced a disquiet that was both unanticipated and unsurprising. She said, "Do you and Susan still sleep in this bed together?"

"When we do, it's like brother and sister," Jasper said. "And it's only because our couch is so uncomfortable. Don't forget, she has a boyfriend."

Naked, Jasper climbed onto the bed, which was unmade, its beige sheets and lavender-colored cotton blanket pushed toward the foot of the mattress. There was a moment when Liz almost couldn't continue—the sight of Aidan, along with this setting of Jasper and Susan's ongoing domesticity, no matter what their agreement, was just too awkward. But there Jasper was, the physiological evidence of his readiness already apparent; and he was a good-looking man; and she needed to get to the airport; and the reality was that she, too, wanted to have sex—it had been and would be a while. She unfastened and shrugged off her bra, which was her last remaining article of clothing, and joined him in the bed. Five hours later, her plane landed in Cincinnati.

Chapter 7

MRS. BENNET HAD not, as it turned out, needed to lean on Mrs. Lucas excessively in order to convince the latter to facilitate a meeting between the Bennet daughters and Chip Bingley. Upon receiving Mrs. Bennet's phone call, Mrs. Lucas had declared that nothing could bring her greater pleasure, or reflect more flatteringly on Cincinnati, than the attendance of the beautiful Bennet girls and their parents at the barbecue that the Lucases were hosting for several recent arrivals to Christ Hospital, where Dr. Lucas was both a physician and a high-ranking executive.

Mrs. Lucas shared with Mrs. Bennet the affliction of an unmarried adult daughter, though in Mrs. Lucas's case the disappointment was embodied just once rather than multiplied five-fold. Charlotte Lucas, who had been Liz's classmate and closest friend at Seven Hills for fifteen years, was also single, a bright and poised human resources manager at Procter & Gamble who since graduating from college had been about seventy-five pounds overweight. To Mrs. Bennet's mind, this fact placed Mrs. Lucas's misfortune in a separate, albeit equally frustrating, category from the one in which her own daughters fell. Obviously, Charlotte wasn't married because she was heavy; therefore, she simply needed to go on a diet. Mrs. Bennet's own daughters, however, possessing no discernible physical or personal flaws (except for poor homely Mary), had no clear means of remediation.

Mrs. Bennet, who herself was not a stranger to rotundity, had wondered if Mrs. Lucas considered Charlotte a candidate for Chip's affections, but Mrs. Lucas's unhesitating inclusion of the Bennets at the barbecue reassured Mrs. Bennet that her friend harbored no unrealistic expectations where Charlotte was concerned. Thus, despite having failed to pair off any of her daughters in the two decades she'd been actively trying, Mrs. Bennet's hopes for the barbecue were high indeed.

The Lucases lived in Indian Hill, a suburb fifteen miles from downtown and home to the sort of Cincinnatians who enjoyed owning horses or at least purebred dogs who could roam on multi-acre properties. The Lucases' house was a vast brick colonial with a balcony over the front door and a slate roof. In the kitchen, various Bennets embraced various Lucases, Jane passed off her sponge cake, and Liz walked to the window to survey the dozen or so guests already chatting on the flagstone patio in the backyard. "Jane, come see your future husband," she called merrily.

Jane joined her. "I take it Chip Bingley is the tall, dark, and handsome one?"

Charlotte Lucas said, "No, Chip is the guy in the seersucker shorts. The tall, dark, and handsome one is his friend Fitzwilliam Darcy, who joined the stroke center at the University of Cincinnati last year as a neurosurgeon. The rumor is he's also single, but he's kind of standoffish. He and Chip went to medical school together." Charlotte turned to Jane. "Did you really never watch *Eligible* when Chip was on?"

"She's never watched any of *Eligible*," Liz said. "She's like a unicorn."

"Oh, Chip's season was fantastic," Charlotte said. "There was an actual physical fight involving ripped-out hair extensions."

Mary, who had caught up to her mother's car on the drive out, said, "I find *Eligible* degrading to women."

"So you've mentioned." Liz glanced at Charlotte. "Did you say Chip's friend's name is Fitzwilliam, and if so, did he just sail over on the *Mayflower*?"

"He goes by his last name." Charlotte grinned. "Though I'm not sure Darcy is much better."

In recent years, Charlotte and Liz hadn't spent time together beyond Christmas parties or lunches scheduled during Liz's trips home from New York, but they still took immense pleasure in each other's company. Indeed, it had been one of the highlights of Liz's longer-term return to Cincinnati to resume her friendship with Charlotte in a genuine fashion, as adults, and to find that her enjoyment of the woman was no less than it had been of the girl. They only half-jokingly speculated about whether they were the last two single people from their high school class, though Liz wondered if Charlotte suffered from this distinction more acutely—Charlotte lived in Cincinnati, where her mother could nag her at closer proximity; she didn't have the buffer of an older sister who was, ostensibly, even more overdue to marry; she did wish to have children; and she didn't have a secret boyfriend.

"Chip is shorter than he looks on TV, right?" Charlotte said. "But definitely cute. And that guy in the V-neck, Keith, is another new emergency doctor"—the man in question was black, the only nonwhite person at the party—"and the woman in the striped dress is an intern. The man next to her is her husband, and that toddler is theirs." In addition to these guests were an attractive blond woman Liz didn't recognize and two older couples Liz had previously met at the Lucases' New Year's Day open house; the men in both couples also worked as doctors at Christ Hospital.

"Is Keith single, too?" Liz asked. "Because if he is, Jane, there's basically a man buffet for you to pick from."

"I might remind you," Mr. Bennet said as he blithely fixed himself a gin and tonic at the nearby wet bar, "that you're not observing those gentlemen from behind a two-way mirror." Mr. Bennet held up his hand, and Dr. Lucas waved back.

"I doubt they read lips," Liz said.

Jane turned to Charlotte. "Is the blond woman a doctor?"

"That's Caroline Bingley, Chip's sister. She lives in L.A., but she's helping him get settled here."

"Chip *is* handsome," Jane said, and Liz and Charlotte exchanged an amused look.

"Then let's go out and I'll introduce you," Charlotte said.

Chapter 8

AFTER THE FLURRY of greetings, Liz found herself talking to Keith, who was congenial and, she quickly discovered, engaged to a woman finishing her medical residency in San Diego. By the time the chicken breasts had been grilled, and the potato salad, coleslaw, and rolls set out, Liz and Keith had covered the topics of San Diego's climate, Cincinnati's climate, and Cincinnati's famous chili, which Keith had not yet sampled. As Liz and Keith moved on to Keith's interest in golf, Liz was gratified to observe that Jane appeared to be deep in conversation with Chip Bingley; that conversation continued as Jane and Chip procured food and took seats side by side on a mortared stone retaining wall, soon joined by Chip's sister Caroline.

When Liz had prepared her own plate of food, she walked to the four-person patio table where Fitzwilliam Darcy was sitting with the husband of the intern and one of the older doctors. The older doctor and the husband were discussing how the Reds were faring this season, and, addressing Fitzwilliam Darcy (or, Liz reminded herself, just Darcy), Liz pointed to the empty chair. "Is this seat taken?"

"It is," Darcy said. He didn't temper his rebuff with any apology, and Liz assumed he must have misheard her; he must have thought she'd asked if the seat was free.

She said, "It *is* taken?"

"Yes," Darcy said, and he remained unapologetic. "It is."

In spite of Charlotte's warning about Darcy seeming standoffish, Liz was so disconcerted that she was tempted to say, *Forgive me for imagining I was worthy of sharing your table.* So he had gone to Harvard Medical School; so he was a neurosurgeon—neither fact gave him carte blanche to be rude. Before moving away, she smiled in a manner she hoped he understood was fake.

Spying Kitty and Lydia nearby, Liz walked to them and perched on the cushioned ottoman by Kitty's knees. Her younger sisters were debating the ideal time to arrive at their next gathering, which apparently would be hosted by the owner of their CrossFit gym. Lydia pointed toward the roll on Liz's plate. "Don't carbs make you feel sluggish?"

"Everything in moderation," Liz said. There were many reasons she found her sisters' enthusiasm for CrossFit and the Paleo Diet irritating, including that Liz herself had been familiar with both long before they had, having written an article about CrossFit back in 2007. Another source of irritation was that her sisters looked fantastic; they had always been attractive, but since taking up CrossFit, they were practically glowing with energy and strength.

When Liz's phone vibrated in her pocket, she was almost finished eating and even more insulted by Darcy's snub than she'd been at first, because the chair beside him had remained empty all this time. She took the opportunity to go inside, wash the barbecue sauce from her hands at the kitchen sink, and check the message.

Southampton biggest clusterfuck of all time, read the text from Jasper, and she typed back, *Hang in there. When fireworks?*

God knows but none will b as bright as u, Jasper texted.

A reference to my sparkling personality or sequined nipple pasties? Liz typed.

Yowza, Jasper replied.

Standing just inside the back door, looking down at her phone, Liz gradually became aware of a conversation occurring on the screen door's other side; after focusing for a few seconds, she realized the speakers were Chip Bingley and Fitzwilliam Darcy.

"—much better than I expected," Chip was saying. "When I told people I was moving to Cincinnati, I was practically getting condolences, but it's not bad at all."

"Said like a man who's just spent an hour talking to the only good-looking woman at the party," Darcy replied. "Not counting your sister, of course." Liz could hear the rattle of ice cubes, then Darcy added, "I'm sure they do their best, but Cincinnatians are painfully provincial." Inside the kitchen, Liz smiled. It was oddly satisfying to receive confirmation of Darcy's snobbishness.

In a friendly tone, Chip said, "In your first year here, you didn't find any lady Buckeyes who met your exacting standards?"

"I can hardly think of anything less tempting," Darcy said.

Chip chuckled. "Someone told me Jane's sister Liz is single, too."

"I suppose it would be unchivalrous to say I'm not surprised."

Liz's jaw dropped; abruptly, the eavesdropping had ceased to be satisfying. Who did this man think he was, and what did he have against her personally? When being introduced, they hadn't exchanged more than ten words.

"Here's what I've learned about the people in this city," Darcy was saying. "They grade their women on a curve. If someone is described as sophisticated, it means once during college she visited Paris, and if someone is described as beautiful, it means she's fifteen pounds overweight instead of forty. And they're obsessed with matchmaking. They act like they're doing you a favor by conscripting you to have coffee with the elementary school teacher from their church during the two free hours you might have in an entire week. I've lost count of how many of my colleagues' wives have tried to set me up. With your having been on TV, they must be licking their chops."

"You know what?" Chip said. "I'm making it my mission to get you a social life in Cincinnati, and don't try to tell me that's an oxymoron. If all you have is two hours a week, let's make them a great two hours." His affectionate tone was, Liz thought, no particular credit to him— not only was Chip apparently unmoved to defend her from Darcy's aspersions, but it hadn't even seemed to occur to the former that his friend's words were offensive.

"Good for you if you like it here now," Darcy said. "And I don't mean that facetiously. But I'll be curious what you think this time next year."

As Chip began speaking, Liz pushed open the screen door and, in an emphatically friendly tone, said, "Hi!" She glanced from Chip's face to Darcy's and, making eye contact with Darcy, held his gaze for an extra beat. "I was just inside thinking what grade I'd give myself," she said. "I realized it would be an A-plus, but I've heard we grade on a curve here, so I'm probably what—more like a B for the coasts? Or a B-minus? If you have a minute to figure it out, be sure to let me know." Without waiting for either to respond, she walked past them, eager to repeat Darcy's comments as widely and quickly as she could.

Chapter 9

LIZ AND JANE went for their usual run the next morning, and they had just passed Edwards Road when Jane said, "So Chip texted after we went to bed to see if I want to get dinner tomorrow night."

"He already texted? For dinner? On a Saturday night? Jane, he's smitten with you."

"I don't know," Jane said.

"What do you not know? You guys practically had to be pried apart when we left the Lucases'."

"He's really nice," Jane said. "And attractive, obviously. But the situation is so contrived—his having been on TV, Mom scheming to get us introduced. Doesn't that make it seem ridiculous?"

"There's not the tiniest shred of doubt in my mind that you'll find your dream man sooner or later. If it happens to be someone Mom pushed you toward, well, even a stopped clock is right twice a day."

"It's made life simpler that since I started the IUI, I haven't met anyone I've wanted to go out with," Jane said. "Because what would I say on a date? 'I like you, but by the way, once a month I get anonymous sperm shot into my uterus? Hope that won't put a damper on things!'"

"You're getting ahead of yourself," Liz said. "Just go out to dinner with him."

Jane was quiet, and Liz said, "I can hear you ruminating. What?"

"I know I shouldn't make a big deal out of one date," Jane said slowly. "But I can't help doing the math. What if we start dating, we go out for three months or six months or eighteen months, and *then* we break up? By that point, I'm forty or forty-one."

"You're not having IUI while you're here, right?" Liz looked at Jane, who nodded.

"Starting the process again at a new clinic is too complicated," Jane said.

"In that case, give Chip a chance while we're in Cincinnati. Have a summer fling. You did like him."

They were passing Corbin Drive, and Jane said softly, almost so softly Liz couldn't hear, "That's true. I liked him a lot."

Chapter 10

"THE THING I'M confused about," Liz said to Mary, "is what day does Mervetta come? Because the house is getting gross." A twice-monthly fixture at the Tudor since Liz's childhood, Mervetta cleaned the Bennets' toilets, vacuumed their rugs, and changed their sheets; once, when Liz was ten, Mervetta had told her that the Bennets were the only white people she'd ever known who ate grits.

Mary's expression was both uncomfortable and amused, as if Liz had made an offensive joke that Mary wished she didn't find funny. She said, "Mervetta died."

"Oh, God," Liz said. "No one told me."

"Maybe because before that, Mom fired her. She caught her sitting on Lydia's bed watching TV."

Liz winced. "So who cleans the house now?"

Mary shrugged. "Nobody."

The two sisters were standing in the kitchen; Liz had just returned from lunch with Charlotte Lucas.

Liz said, "Did anyone go to Mervetta's funeral?"

Mary shrugged again. "I didn't."

Chapter 11

"YOUR MOTHER HAS shared a tragic piece of news about Cousin Willie with me," Mr. Bennet said when the family was assembled for dinner. "He's coming to visit."

"Really, Fred," Mrs. Bennet said, and Jane said, "Dad, that's an awful way to set us up."

Mr. Bennet smiled as if he'd been doubly complimented. "As you all know, my sister is flying out next week, to check if I still have a pulse and, in the event that I don't, to take possession of our mother's silver. For reasons that elude me, her stepson has decided to accompany her."

Liz swallowed a spoonful of the gazpacho Jane had prepared and said, "I know you all find this hard to believe, but Cousin Willie is kind of a big deal."

"And if I were an insomniac," Mr. Bennet replied, "I'd like nothing better than to hear him explain why."

"Maybe he can tell us why the Internet in this house is so slow," Kitty said.

"Or teach Mom to use her cellphone," Lydia suggested.

"His start-ups have made millions of dollars," Liz said, and Mr. Bennet said, "Yet he doesn't know how to put on a pair of trousers."

"That was 1986," Jane said.

Which indeed it had been—the summer before Liz had started sixth grade, the Bennets had made a trip to California to visit Mr. Bennet's sister, Margo, and to meet the man to whom she had just become engaged, a widower with a three-year-old son. Someone (Mr. and Mrs. Bennet each vehemently denied responsibility) had decided it would be a lark to make the journey by car. Thus the Bennet family had set out from Cincinnati in their minivan, driving roughly five hundred miles a day for five days in a row; at the time, Jane was twelve, Liz eleven, Mary three, Kitty in utero, and Lydia not yet conceived. In Liz's memory, the trip was a blur of rolling hills becoming flattened prairies, flattened prairies becoming sprawling ranchlands, and ranchlands becoming scrubby desert. In Utah, a detour to see the red rock region had been scuttled due to increasing familial tensions; the minivan's backseats had become a mayhem of hair-pulling, girl farts, and toddler squalls that distracted Liz from her powerful wish to reach the end of the tawdry romance she was reading in which a brooding Cheyenne loner inserted his fingers into the most private cavity of a young British heiress while they rode upon the same horse. Liz's utter thrall to Colt and Jocelyn's story compelled her to ignore a building nausea that eventually asserted itself with her crying out, "I'm going to be sick!" and vomiting an Egg McMuffin, hash browns, and ketchup onto Mary fifty miles northeast of Sacramento. Liz did sometimes wonder if their relationship had ever properly recovered, and insofar as it hadn't, she couldn't blame her sister.

By the time the Bennets pulled into the driveway of the home belonging to Aunt Margo's new fiancé in Sausalito, the minivan was strewn with food wrappers and socks and discarded Mad Libs books, not only reeking of vomit but also making an unaccountable scraping noise on the rear right side of the undercarriage; the Bennets' antipathy for one another was of such an intimate variety it was almost like affection. They spilled out of the car and walked up the brick path of a well-tended bungalow, but before they could ring the bell, the front door opened and a small red-haired boy stood before them completely naked. "Dad!" the boy yelled. "They're here!" His limbs were alabaster, his penis minuscule and, particularly to Mary, bewildering. "Look away, girls!" Mrs. Bennet cried, prompting in Liz and Jane a fit of giggles. This was Cousin Willie and also, obviously, Cousin Willie's willy.

Over the years, the Bennets and the Collinses saw one another intermittently, and at some point it became apparent that Cousin Willie was a bit of a technology savant. He taught himself to code at thirteen, began advising local businesses on how to bolster their Web presences at fifteen, and dropped out of UCLA during his sophomore year, after selling a company that had developed a proprietary format for transmitting data between servers and Web applications—which was to say, a company no Bennet understood whatsoever—for a rumored $20 million. Now a man of thirty, Willie was running his third or fourth software development start-up. And yet all of the Bennets except Liz and her mother refused to see him as anything other than a naked three-year-old. Mrs. Bennet was clearly intrigued by his money and had once asked Liz a series of probing questions about how he'd received the payment for his first company, questions to which Liz didn't know the answers. And Liz herself had some years back run into Willie at a technology conference in Las Vegas that she was attending as a journalist and had shared a surprisingly pleasant lunch with him; although the conversation had essentially been a monologue on his part, it had been an interesting monologue, and he was the person who had first told her about Twitter.

At the dinner table, Mrs. Bennet said, "Jane, I imagine you'll be busy with Chip Bingley, but Liz can entertain Willie when he's here."

"Why will Jane be busy with Chip Bingley?" Kitty asked.

With relish, Mrs. Bennet said, "They're having dinner tomorrow night at Orchids."

Uncertainly, Jane said, "Mom, you haven't been reading my texts, have you?"

Merrily, Lydia said, "She doesn't know how!"

Mrs. Bennet appeared uncontrite. "Helen Lucas mentioned it."

Jane furrowed her eyebrows, which for her reflected genuine pique. "How would Mrs. Lucas know?"

Liz cleared her throat. "I think I told Charlotte. But just in passing."

"Chip and I might never see each other again after Saturday." Jane's cheeks were flushed. "So please, can everyone not make a big deal out of this? Mom, I'll have plenty of time to spend with Cousin Willie."

"It was obvious that Chip found you absolutely charming, Jane," Mrs. Bennet said. "And so he should have. But you'll have to ask why he didn't go into private practice. Working in an emergency room, he must see very unattractive people."

Liz, who felt some responsibility for displeasing her sister, said, "I wonder if Willie is interested in visiting the Freedom Center."

"Just so you all know, I have a paper due at the end of next week," Mary said. "I won't have much time for Willie or Aunt Margo."

"That's so heartbreaking," Lydia said. "I wonder if they'll ever recover from the devastation."

"Well, I look forward to seeing both of them," Jane said.

From the head of the table, Mr. Bennet said, "That makes one of us."

Chapter 12

AFTER DINNER, LIZ followed the scent of nail polish to its source, which turned out, as was often the case, to be Kitty; she sat on the counter in the bathroom she and Lydia shared, the door open, painting a rather impressive pattern on her toenails of cream-colored polish with sparkly gold dots.

Liz turned on the overhead fan. "You know how Dad sleeps in his study?" she said. "Is it because of the Jewish thing?"

Without looking up, Kitty said, "Maybe."

"Do you think it is?"

At last, Kitty met Liz's eyes. "Ask them."

Liz had no intention of doing so. Mr. Bennet's two great and overlapping interests were genealogy and history—when capable of driving himself, he whiled away many afternoons in the stacks of the Mercantile Library downtown—and at some point about a decade prior, he'd announced with amusement his discovery that Mrs. Bennet's maternal grandmother had been Jewish; indeed, prior to her marriage, Ida Conner had been Ida Rosenbluth. While not an overt anti-Semite, Mrs. Bennet was prone to making declarations about almost all religious and ethnic minorities that were often uncomfortable for her listeners. "Jews are very fond of dried fruit," she'd told Liz on more than one occasion, and when Liz had been in fifth grade, Mrs. Bennet had refused to purchase a party dress for her that had a black sequined bodice and a black velvet skirt, on the grounds that it was "Jewish-looking."

Unsurprisingly, Mrs. Bennet wasn't receptive to Mr. Bennet's pronouncement about her religious ancestry. Adding insult to injury, Lydia and Kitty took to referring to their mother, in and out of her presence, as the Jewess; in fact, Lydia once reduced Mrs. Bennet to tears by recommending that she have a late-in-life bat mitzvah. This teasing had faded over time, possibly replaced with Lydia's badgering of Mary about her sexual orientation. But perhaps, Liz thought, the consequences of the genealogical discovery lingered still.

In the bathroom, Liz said to Kitty, "You don't think Mom and Dad would ever get divorced, do you?" The more pointed question, which Liz didn't ask, was *Do you think they should?*

Kitty made a scoffing sound. "They're too lazy," she said.

Chapter 13

ON SATURDAY EVENING, just before being picked up by Chip Bingley, Jane stood in front of the mirror that hung over Liz's bureau, applying blush. As she glanced at Liz's reflection, Jane said, "Should I have watched his season of *Eligible*? Are there things everyone else knows about him that I don't?"

Liz sat at her desk, where she planned to spend the next few hours working—her parents were having dinner at the country club with neighbors, Lydia and Kitty were headed out, Mary was in her own room with the door closed—although already, both quite accidentally and quite horribly, Liz had found herself on a webpage featuring cannibal lemurs. Given that she was researching an upcoming *Mascara* feature on how to ask for a raise, it was difficult to say exactly how this had happened.

Liz pushed her chair back and set her feet on the edge of her desk in a way her mother had been objecting to for three decades. "Did you tell him at the Lucases' you've never seen the show?" she asked.

Jane nodded.

"Then that might be part of your charm," Liz said. "He came off like a good guy, I promise. He did his share of on-air smooching, but he wasn't sleazy."

"He told me that patients sometimes ask for his autograph." Jane appeared troubled rather than gratified. "Can you imagine?"

"Here's my one hesitation about him," Liz said. "And it's not huge, but for what it's worth—there's this idea that he didn't want to be on *Eligible* and his sister talked him into it. I call bullshit on that. People only do reality TV because *they* want to. I read somewhere that everyone on those shows is trying to make it in Hollywood."

Jane set down her blush container and turned to face Liz. "You think?"

Liz shrugged. "He wouldn't be the first."

"Aren't you the one who encouraged me to go out with him tonight?"

"It could be that he saw *Eligible* as a lark and thought, *Why not?* I didn't get an egomaniacal vibe when I talked to him. I just don't totally buy his backstory."

"I'm almost afraid to tell you this now," Jane said, "but you know how his sister Caroline is here for a few weeks from L.A.?"

"I saw her at the Lucases', but we hardly talked."

"She's his manager," Jane said.

Liz squinted. "Meaning what?"

"I guess ever since *Eligible,* he gets approached about product endorsements or doing charity events. She handles all of that for him."

Liz struggled not to form an expression of distaste; Caroline Bingley had on the Fourth of July revealed herself to Liz to be almost as unappealing as Fitzwilliam Darcy. As Caroline, her brother, and Darcy had been about to depart together, Caroline had first told Liz that she kept forgetting whether she was in Cleveland, Cincinnati, or Columbus, then she'd lamented the local dearth of decent sushi or yoga. Liz had considered recommending Modo Yoga, which was the studio Jane frequented, but decided instead to withhold the kindness.

Liz had by that point in the party shared Darcy's remarks with other attendees, animated as she did so by a giddy and outraged fervor. Charlotte Lucas had laughed, Mrs. Bennet had been deeply insulted, and Jane had speculated that Darcy had known she was eavesdropping and had been joking, which Liz thought gave Darcy far too much credit.

In her bedroom, Liz said to Jane, "Maybe you and Chip can get paid to show up together at nightclubs. That would be funny."

"You're sending very mixed messages right now, Lizzy."

Liz grinned. "I contain multitudes." She added, "Sorry. Just enjoy yourself tonight, and forget I said anything."

Chapter 14

LIZ WAS STILL at her desk, though actually doing work—she was reading a commencement speech delivered by Kathy de Bourgh, a famous feminist whom she hoped to interview for her pay-raise article—when Lydia entered the room and said, "Have you seen my phone?"

Liz shook her head.

"Fuck," Lydia said. "I need to text Ham to see what time we're meeting, but my phone is the only place I have his number."

"Who's Ham?"

"Ham Ryan."

"Am I supposed to know who that is?" Liz asked.

"He owns the box we go to."

Box, to Liz's annoyance, was the preferred CrossFit term for its gyms. She said, "Is he your boyfriend?"

Lydia's expression was disdainful. Sarcastically, she said, "Are we going steady? Do you think he'll give me his varsity jacket?"

"Excuse me for daring to make conversation with you after you came into my room."

"There's a spider on your wall."

At first, Liz wondered if this was some coded insult used by millennials, but when she turned, she saw a real spider, brown and quarter-sized. She stood to grab a sandal, and when she whacked the shoe against the wall, a chip of paint flaked off.

"Gross," Lydia said. "Tell me if you find my phone." She hadn't yet left the room when Liz opened a new window on her Web browser and typed in *Ham Ryan CrossFit Cincinnati*.

He was handsome, of course: short light brown hair coaxed by product into a sort of glistening spikiness, as well as blue eyes and a tidy goatee. His real name was Hamilton, apparently, and he was from Seattle.

Liz cared little about either CrossFit or Lydia's paramours (their turnover was too frequent to justify investing much attention) while finding Kathy de Bourgh's commencement address genuinely interesting; yet somehow, she spent the next forty minutes exploring the nooks and crannies of the website for Ham Ryan's "box," and even came away half-tempted to try a recipe for Paleo crab cakes, if only doing so wouldn't please her sisters.

Chapter 15

CLOSE TO MIDNIGHT, as Liz was shutting down her computer, she heard someone ascending the staircase to the third floor; to her surprise, it was Mary rather than Jane. On Mary's face was an unconcealed smirk. "Look." She passed her phone to Liz.

The small screen showed an item on a celebrity gossip website that Liz thought of as holding greater appeal for Kitty and Lydia than Mary, with a headline that read, "Flunky Hunky: Did Eligible Bachelor Almost Fail Out of Harvard Medical School?" Below was a photo of Chip Bingley in a tuxedo, clinking champagne flutes with one of the comely female finalists from his season. Liz skimmed the entry, which was only a paragraph ("Former classmates say Bingley was known more for hitting the bike trails than the books . . ."), then gave back the phone. "So?" she said. "He passed his boards, obviously."

"If you cut off your finger, would you want him to be the one to stitch it on?"

"The fact that he wasn't first in his class doesn't mean he's incompetent."

Mary raised her eyebrows dubiously. "I knew there was something fishy about a graduate of Harvard Medical School ending up in an ER in Cincinnati. It was probably the only job he could get."

This seemed a rather presumptuous judgment from someone who herself had never been employed. "Don't show that to anyone," Liz said. "Even if it's true, it's irrelevant."

Chapter 16

AT FIVE-THIRTY IN the morning, Liz awoke to the rustling of Jane slipping into the twin bed across from hers.

"Yikes," Liz mumbled. "I guess it was a successful date."

"Oh, Lizzy," Jane said. "Chip's amazing."

Chapter 17

AFTER DINNER AT Orchids, Jane and Chip had moved on to Bakersfield for drinks. (Liz didn't learn any of this until the afternoon, because Jane not only slept through their morning run but also skipped the eleven A.M. service at Knox Presbyterian Church that Mary and Mrs. Bennet attended every Sunday, Liz and Jane attended when in town, and all other Bennets eschewed except at Christmas.) Following drinks ("Did you actually drink or were you fostering a hospitable uterus again?" Liz asked, and Jane said she'd had one glass of wine at dinner and another at the bar), Jane and Chip had returned to his apartment in Oakley, where they'd taken the opportunity to discover that they were a couple truly compatible in all ways. "Do you think I'm slutty?" Jane asked.

"You're thirty-nine years old," Liz said. "You should do what you want. Was it weird with his sister there?"

Jane shook her head. "The room she's staying in is at the opposite end of the apartment." Jane was still lying in bed as she relayed these facts, and Liz sat on the other twin bed. "It wasn't awkward with Chip at all, and neither of us was drunk," Jane added. "I really like him. I just—I felt a way I hadn't for so long. And it barely had to do with how good-looking he is. He *is* good-looking, but I was just so comfortable with him. He's genuinely nice and not self-centered. I really don't think he's an aspiring actor. He told me the *Eligible* producers got in touch recently asking him to be on a reunion show, and he said no."

"Then I stand corrected."

"He also was mortified you'd overheard him and Darcy talking at the Lucases'. He wanted me to tell you how sorry he is, and how he doesn't share Darcy's view of Cincinnati at all."

Liz smiled. "At least when it comes to the women here, I'd say that's obvious."

"Really, though." Jane's expression was serious. "Chip says Darcy can be kind of brusque, but he's a really good person and a world-class surgeon."

"With a world-class ego, apparently. Just to warn you, Mom's downstairs practically salivating. She knows you were out late."

"You didn't tell her how late, did you?"

"No, but I can't promise she wasn't looking out the window when Chip dropped you off."

"It's funny, isn't it?" Jane said. "Because think how much trouble I'd have gotten in back in high school for coming home from a date at five in the morning. But I just had to wait twenty years, and now Mom's probably thrilled."

Chapter 18

"I'VE GOT A question that you need not repeat to any of your sisters," Mr. Bennet said. He and Liz sat in an exam room at the orthopedist's office, waiting for the removal of the cast on his arm, a duty Jane had told Liz she didn't think she could sit through. "I'm afraid I'll throw up," Jane had said, and Liz had said, "Because of the saw?" Jane had shook her head and said, "Because of the smell."

"This business about Mary being homosexual," Mr. Bennet continued. "Do you think there's anything to it?"

Surprised, Liz said, "Why?"

"Your mother wouldn't like it, of course. But what's the old saying about people going about their business as long as they don't do it in the street and frighten the horses?"

"Wow, Dad," Liz said. "Have you become a Democrat?"

Her father shuddered. "Scarcely. But where *does* Mary go on Tuesday nights?"

"You could ask her. Where she goes, I mean, not if she's gay. Well, you could ask her that, too, although I don't know if I would." Liz had concluded some years earlier that Mary wasn't interesting enough to be gay. All the gay people Liz knew in New York, both men and women, were a little more something than average—a little more thoughtful or stylish or funny—though perhaps, Liz reflected, it was New York itself rather than gayness that accounted for their extra appeal.

"If Mary has a friend she doesn't think she can bring to dinner, that'd be rather a shame," Mr. Bennet said. "Her significant other deserves to suffer as much as the rest of us." He was looking at Liz directly, and she tried not to squirm. Was he talking about Mary, or was he actually alluding to her and Jasper?

"She must have her reasons," Liz said. "You did just say yourself that Mom would be horrified."

"Your mother is horrified many times a day."

"At least now Mom has Chip Bingley to pin her hopes on. Did you know he and Jane went out for the second time last night? They went to a movie."

Before Mr. Bennet could answer, the door opened, and there appeared a male nurse in aqua-colored scrubs, carrying the plastic saw with its round blade at one end; the entire contraption wasn't much larger than an electric toothbrush. "Fred!" the nurse said, though they had never met. "How are we today?"

Reading the nurse's name tag, Mr. Bennet replied with fake enthusiasm, "Bernard! We're mourning the death of manners and the rise of overly familiar discourse. How are you?"

Chapter 19

"REMEMBER ALLEN BAUSCH?" Mrs. Bennet said as Liz sat by herself at the kitchen table eating lunch.

Liz looked at her mother with curiosity. "Mary's prom date?"

"You should find him on the computer and send him a message from Mary. That's something that happens a lot now. Couples find each other on their computer after losing touch, and then they get married."

"He's probably married to someone else."

"He isn't. His aunt is in the Women's League."

"Either way, why would I reach out to him? Shouldn't Mary do it?"

"She can be so stubborn."

"Were Mary and Allen even a couple? They might have just gone to prom as friends."

"He's a lawyer in Atlanta, and he's very active in his church," Mrs. Bennet said. "If that's not the description of a man looking for a wife, I don't know what is."

Chapter 20

CHARLOTTE LUCAS CALLED Liz midweek. "I'm organizing a game night for Friday," she said. "Can you come, and can you tell your sisters?"

"Do you remember that Lydia cheats?"

"Is it possible to cheat at Charades?"

"Oh, she'll find a way," Liz said. "I think Jane's going out with Chip again Friday—for the third time, if you can believe it. But I'm definitely in, and I'll try to round up Mary or Kitty."

"Jane should bring Chip. Or should I invite him myself?"

Liz hesitated. On the one hand, the chance to observe her sister and Chip together was tempting. On the other hand, if Chip attended game night—and Liz nerdily, unabashedly adored game nights—he might bring his sister or, worse, Fitzwilliam Darcy. But who was she to exclude others? "Sure," she said to Charlotte. "Call Chip."

Chapter 21

SO DEPRESSING AND uncomfortable had Liz found the update about Mervetta that in searching for new housecleaners, she sought agencies that would send rotating crews of three rather than an individual, with whom Mrs. Bennet might have a falling-out.

With estimates in hand for both cleaning and yard services, Liz knocked on the door of her father's study. When he called, "There's no one home," she pushed the door open.

Mr. Bennet's desk, which he sat behind, faced into the room, so that Liz saw the back rather than the front of his computer. Aside from this computer, her father's study looked as it had when his parents had sold the house to him in 1982 for the sum of one dollar, the same year they sold their summer home in Petoskey, Michigan, to his sister, Margo, for the same price. Indeed, it was quite possible that Mr. Bennet's study, with its sleigh bed, brown velvet curtains, leather-topped writing desk (the leather was burnt red and had a border of gold-leaf embossing), and porcelain desk lamp with fringed shade, was unchanged since Liz's grandparents had first moved into the Tudor in 1927.

In her youth, Liz had understood her father to be an important businessman, an investor—he had driven each morning to a two-room office on Hyde Park Square, where he'd employed a secretary named Mrs. Lupshaw—and it was only with the passage of time that Liz realized that the investments he oversaw were solely those belonging to his immediate family and that, further, their oversight accounted for the entirety of his job. This realization had been so gradual that it was not until her junior year of college, when a friend of Liz's said of the wealthy older guy the friend was dating, "He pretends to work, but I think he's one of those men who push around piles of his family's money," that Liz felt an unwelcome sense of recognition. A decade earlier, when her father had "retired," Liz had wished she did not have the cruel thought *From what?*

Liz entered the study. "I've found people to clean up the house and the yard," she said. She glanced at the reporter's notebook in her hand. "I'm thinking I'll have them both come every two weeks, though obviously you'll need the yard people less after the summer. When Mrs. Bildeier dropped off banana bread, she gave me the name of the cleaning service she uses, and she said they're great."

Her father's eyes were focused on the computer screen as he said, "Your mother cleans the house, and I mow the lawn."

"In theory, maybe. But you still don't have full mobility, and Mom is so focused on her Women's League luncheon." Following the removal of his cast the day before, Mr. Bennet's right arm was pale, shrunken, scabby, and, even after a shower, not entirely free of the rotten odor Jane had predicted; when Liz had asked Dr. Facciano how long it would be before her father could drive, the doctor had said four to six weeks.

"Nor is Nancy Bildeier's house an advertisement for anything," Mr. Bennet said. "If she owns a piece of furniture not covered by dog hair, I've never noticed it."

Liz hadn't expected resistance. Uncertainly, she said, "What if I pay for the first visits?" At present, she had $13,000 in her savings account, an amount that reassured her in comparison to the nonexistent nest eggs of her sisters but that also appeared inexplicably low given that her annual income was $105,000, she had no dependents, and, apart from living in New York, she wasn't profligate.

"That's not a good use of your money," Mr. Bennet said. "Nor of mine. The answer is no."

"But don't you think the house is kind of a mess? And the yard, too?"

Mr. Bennet sounded untroubled as he said, "Everything tends toward entropy, my dear. It's the second law of thermodynamics."

Chapter 22

TO LIZ'S SURPRISE, both Lydia and Kitty exclaimed with delight on hearing at dinner of Charlotte's Charades invitation. "I hope you know I'll kick your asses," Lydia said, and Mary said, "By cheating, you mean?"

"What if we're on the same team?" Liz asked. "Is your ass kicking restricted to your opponents or is it indiscriminate?"

"Do you ever pass up a chance to use a big word?" Lydia replied. "Or do you find that circumlocution always magnifies life's conviviality?"

"That wasn't bad," Liz said. "Especially for someone who scored as low as you did on the verbal part of the SATs."

"Stop quarreling, girls," Mrs. Bennet said. "It's unbecoming."

"They'd never speak to one another otherwise," Mr. Bennet said.

"Chip and I are going out Friday," Jane said. "But if we weren't, I'd love to come."

"Charlotte's inviting him, too," Liz said, and Mrs. Bennet said,

"I'm sure Chip would rather spend time alone with Jane. A new couple needs space."

Lydia turned to her eldest sister, her voice merry. "Jane, do you think Chip will be the one you lose your virginity to?"

Mr. Bennet stood, dropping his napkin on the table. "As interesting as I find this conversation, an urgent matter has come up. I need a hamburger."

Simultaneously, Liz said, "Dad, you can't drive," and Jane said, "Dad, you can't eat red meat."

Mr. Bennet gestured toward his plate, atop which sat moderate portions of lentil stew prepared by Jane and salad prepared by Liz. "This is unacceptable," he said. "I'm not a small woodland creature. Lizzy, we're going to Zip's."

"Dad, Dr. Morelock is the one who recommended a plant-based diet," Jane said. "It wasn't us."

"The iron in a hamburger will *help* Dad," Kitty said. "Just don't eat the bun."

"That'd be like watching a burlesque show with one's eyes closed," Mr. Bennet said.

"Yuck," Mary said.

Mr. Bennet pointed toward the back door. "Hop to, Lizzy."

Liz glanced at Jane, who sighed audibly. This Liz took as tacit permission, and she, too, stood; the truth, unfortunately, was that the lentils *were* almost flavorless. "Does anyone else want anything?" she asked.

Everyone did except for Jane—they requested hamburgers and cheeseburgers and french fries—though at the last minute, just before Mr. Bennet and Liz walked out the back door, Jane called after them, "Fine. I'll take an order of onion rings."

Chapter 23

"ARE YOU STILL planning to stay in Cincy until September?" Jasper said to Liz over the phone. "Because I don't know if I can wait that long for you to get back."

"I was thinking we should meet somewhere for a weekend in August," Liz said. "Maybe Cape Cod?"

"Here's my question," Jasper said. "I realize your mom's shindig is the biggest thing ever to happen in her life. But when she claims to be spending her days on nonstop planning, what's she literally doing? Isn't the event at a hotel that's making the food and taking care of the setup?"

While Liz had wondered the same thing, she wasn't sure Jasper knew Mrs. Bennet well enough—they'd met only once, years before—to have earned the right to ask. "She and the other women are trying to get donations for the silent auction," Liz said. "And the proceeds from the auction go to a shelter for homeless teenagers. It's not total society-lady fluffiness."

"Okay, now you're making me feel like a bad person. But doesn't your mother know I need my Nin?"

Liz smiled. "You know I'm here for my dad, not my mom. Besides, you kept me waiting fourteen years. Surely you can wait two more months."

"What kind of jackass would keep Liz Bennet waiting for fourteen years?" Jasper said. "If I ever met that guy, I'd punch his lights out."

Chapter 24

WHEN CAROLINE BINGLEY and Fitzwilliam Darcy walked through
the door of Charlotte's downtown apartment, the sight of Darcy rattled Liz more than she wished to admit.

"Sorry," Jane murmured to Liz—Chip and Jane had indeed decided to start their evening at Charlotte's—as the newest arrivals
headed into the kitchen to obtain drinks. "Are you okay?"

Liz squared her shoulders. "Of course."

But Darcy's comment at the Lucases' barbecue about Liz's ostensibly single status—*I suppose it would be unchivalrous to say I'm not
surprised*—had echoed unpleasantly in Liz's head during the last week.
Could it have been his spontaneous attempt at wit? Or in their brief
encounter, had he taken note of some off-putting feature of her
presentation—disgustingly bad breath, say—that no one, even Jane,
had ever felt comfortable mentioning? In New York, Liz rarely dwelled
on the contours of her romantic life, but in Cincinnati, the irregularity
of her arrangement with Jasper had come into sharper focus. Depend-

ing on how long Susan's grandmother took to die, it could be several more years before Jasper and Susan officially divorced and, Liz imagined, she and Jasper moved in together. Eventually, in some low-key ceremony, they would marry. It seemed plausible she'd be the last of her sisters to wed, but Liz didn't share her mother's view of matrimony as a race. After all, she already had a companion to reliably talk things over with and another body in the bed to reliably curl against, and weren't those marriage's truest perquisites?

And yet, with regard to Jasper, Liz wasn't impervious to self-doubt. At a co-worker's wedding, when filling out a form that required her to declare her marital status or identify an emergency contact (she always wrote Jane's name), or if otherwise confronted with evidence of choices she'd made without necessarily having recognized them as such in the moment—these circumstances all gave her pause. In recent weeks, as she'd repeatedly bumped into former classmates or old family friends, the proof was ample that other people's choices had been different. A few days before, she had met Charlotte for a drink at Don Pablo's, which had once been their favorite restaurant, and as Liz took a sip of her pomegranate margarita, she realized that at the adjacent table, standing up to leave, was their Seven Hills classmate Vanessa Krager, as well as a bald man who appeared to be Vanessa's husband and four children between the ages of five and twelve who appeared to be their offspring. How was this mathematically possible? And wasn't there, in Vanessa's avid reproduction, something unseemly, some announcement of narcissism or aggression? It was generally less shocking to Liz that twenty years after high school she was still her essential self, the self she'd grown up as, unencumbered by spouse or child, than that nearly everyone else had changed, moved on, and multiplied. After moderately warm greetings, introductions, and updates (Vanessa was working part-time doing billing for a chiropractor, the family was soon due at the ten-year-old's piano recital), Vanessa said, "Liz, I read your interview with Jillian Northcutt. Do you think Hudson Blaise cheated on her?"

Five years earlier, after the dissolution of one of Hollywood's then-most-famous marriages, Liz had been the first journalist to interview the actress Jillian Northcutt post-split. That this remained Liz's best-known article was slightly embarrassing—the entirety of the interview, which had happened in a hotel suite, had lasted eighteen minutes and occurred in the presence of not only Jillian Northcutt's publicist and personal assistant but also the publicist's assistant, a silent manicurist, and an equally silent pedicurist. While the encounter had paid dividends in subsequent cocktail party conversations, and had even landed Liz on several entertainment talk shows, she actually felt sorry for Jillian Northcutt because of the degree of prurience she inspired.

To Vanessa, Liz said, "I think the only people who really know what went wrong are the two of them."

Insistently, Vanessa said, "But he and Roxanne DeLorenzo were together like a month later!" At this point, Vanessa's husband said, "V, we gotta go," and Charlotte said, "Great to see you, Vanessa," and then the family departed in a commotion that included spilled rice from a polystyrene take-home container, tears, and intersibling violence.

When they were gone, Charlotte and Liz looked at each other, and at exactly the same time, Liz said, "There but for the grace of God go I," and Charlotte said, "Should I freeze my eggs?"

"Jinx?" Liz said.

When Charlotte laughed—Liz hadn't been sure she would—Liz was reminded once again of how much she liked her friend.

But if Liz's aversion to having children was clear to her, she was less certain about her romantic status. At times, she wondered why no one besides Jasper had ever truly captured her heart or, perhaps more to the point, why she hadn't captured anyone else's. Because even the half dozen men she'd dated casually—they had ended things as often as she had or had seemed less than devastated when she initiated the breakup.

These were the unsettling thoughts swirling in Liz's mind as the various guests at Charlotte's apartment procured drinks and greeted one another. In addition to the Bennet sisters and the Bingley contingent, Charlotte had invited a friend of hers from Procter & Gamble whose name was Nathan; he'd brought along his boyfriend, Stephen. Initially, Liz managed to talk exclusively to Nathan and Stephen, whom she hadn't previously met, but after a twenty-minute stretch in which she didn't even glance in Darcy's direction, she found herself right beside Caroline Bingley.

Caroline was regarding Liz with what the latter woman took to be a rude scrutiny; given that Caroline was the sister of Jane's new beau, Liz suppressed her own impulse to rudely stare back. Smiling, she said, "Liz Bennet. Jane's sister. We met on the Fourth of July."

Caroline's pretty features (blue eyes, the lightest smattering of freckles, a delicate and just barely upturned nose) contorted slightly. She said, "Did we?"

Oh, for Christ's sake, Liz thought. *No wonder you and Darcy are friends.* "Just briefly," Liz said. "When you told me you were having trouble remembering if you're in Cincinnati, Cleveland, or Columbus. You're in Cincinnati, by the way."

In an unfriendly tone, Caroline said, "Yes, I've figured that out."

A pause ensued, and then Liz said, "I hear you're Chip's manager. Do you have other clients or do you just work with him?"

"I'm really selective about who I take on," Caroline said. "There's an amazingly talented nineteen-year-old actress who's been in some indie films, and now one of the networks is interested in creating a sitcom for her. That's the kind of person I work with—not, like, whatever random dude is juggling puppies on TV this week."

Liz said, "So reality-TV stars, but only of the finest quality."

Caroline blinked, saying nothing, and Liz added, "What's her name?"

Caroline seemed confused.

"The nineteen-year-old," Liz said. "What's her name? I sometimes write about celebrities, so I might know who she is."

"Oh. Ella Brandy."

"And what has she been in?"

Caroline shook her head, and it was unclear to Liz whether the gesture contained condescension or evasiveness. "The one that's getting a ton of buzz has shown at festivals, but it's not in theaters yet." Caroline didn't ask about the context in which Liz wrote about celebrities. Instead, Caroline said, "Yeah, when I tell people in Cincinnati I'm a manager, they assume I work at a fast-food restaurant."

"Oh, I doubt that," Liz said. "Although I have always wondered what a manager does. I get what the agent does, and I get what the publicist does, but the manager seems, I don't know—like an advice giver? A glorified friend?" Caroline narrowed her eyes suspiciously, and it occurred to Liz that she might have overstepped the bounds of feigned politeness. She added, "I was in L.A. last spring for a—" but at that moment, Charlotte tapped a fork against her wineglass and the room quieted.

"There's been a motion to divide Charades teams into sisters versus everyone else," Charlotte said.

People chuckled, and Mary said, "That doesn't seem fair."

"But unfair in your favor, presumably," Darcy said. He was standing about ten feet from Liz, where he'd been talking to Chip and Jane. "Since families have their own shorthand."

It wasn't that he was wrong but, rather, that he spoke in such an obnoxious tone. Loudly, Liz said, "I'm up for Bennets against the rest of you."

Charlotte grinned. "Game on."

Chapter 25

AFTER CHARLOTTE HAD distributed paper and pens, the newly assembled teams retreated to separate corners of the living room to gen-
erate their phrases in hushed tones.

"*Eligible,*" Kitty suggested immediately, and Liz shook her head.
"Too easy. Tom Cruise?"

This time it was Lydia who gave Liz a withering look. "Tom Cruise
is old and creepy."

"Frida Kahlo?" Mary said.

Lydia said, "Is that a lesbian?"

"Maybe we should do a movie," Jane said.

"*Dirty Dancing,*" Kitty said, and Liz said, "Definitely." It would be
truly gratifying, she thought, if Darcy was the person forced to act it
out. After Jane ripped the place where she'd written *Dirty Dancing*
from the larger sheet of paper, they were able to decide on additional
phrases with less dispute.

The other team wasn't as efficient, though as Darcy had pointed out, they did not all know one another well. In addition to Darcy himself, the team was composed of Caroline, Chip, Charlotte, Nathan, and Stephen.

When the teams convened around the living room table, they determined through a coin flipped by Chip that Team Bennet would go first. Mary selected a scrap of folded paper from the pile on the table, read it, and frowned. "I barely know what this is."

"No talking," Caroline said, and Liz said, "Just start, Mary. The clock's ticking."

Mary held up one palm and with the other fist mimed cranking a silent-film camera.

"Movie!" Kitty and Lydia shouted together.

Mary held up four fingers.

"Four words," Jane said. "You're doing great."

Mary paused and thought.

"For God's sake, Mary," Lydia said. "Get over yourself."

Mary held up four fingers again, and Liz said, "Fourth word."

Mary flung her hands out from her waist as if shooing away a swarm of insects. "A grass skirt?" Liz ventured. "Elvis Presley? *Blue Hawaii?*"

Mary shook her head and repeated the gesture.

"Going pee!" Kitty shouted. "Peeing everywhere! Shitting in your pants!"

"Exploding with diarrhea!" Lydia cried. "Pepto-Bismol! Having your period!" As Mary shook her head sternly and the two youngest sisters giggled, Liz abruptly understood the nature of the discomfort that had been thrumming within her since Caroline Bingley and Fitzwilliam Darcy had entered Charlotte's apartment: What would have been a night of inconsequential silliness was now unfolding before the judgmental gaze of outsiders. Thus, the game resembled an audition in which Darcy and Caroline's negative impressions of Cincinnati would either be confirmed or contradicted. But why did the duo deserve, simply by reason of their imperiousness, for everyone present to strive to win their favorable opinion? Or no, not everyone—certainly not Lydia and Kitty—and if the youngest sisters' indifference to the outsiders humiliated Liz, it was her own humiliation that she found infuriating. Let Caroline and Darcy think badly of Cincinnati and its inhabitants! Why should she care? But, unaccountably, she did.

Mary waved one hand back and forth, as if attempting to erase the previous gestures, then held up a finger.

"First word," Jane said.

Mary held up two fingers.

"Two syllables," Liz said.

Mary again held up one finger.

"First syllable," Liz said.

Mary cupped her hand around her right ear.

"Sounds like," Jane and Liz both said.

Mary tapped her knee. "Bee's knees," Jane said at the same time Liz said, "I need you." Mary was shaking her head. She patted her leg, this time higher, and Kitty said, "Thigh meat. Dark meat. Chicken breast."

"Tits and ass!" Lydia yelled.

Thankfully, this was when the timer went off, and in a tone indicating that she felt the failure was her sisters' rather than her own, Mary said, *"Legends of the Fall."*

"What the fuck is that?" Lydia said.

"It's a movie," Liz said. "Actually, a book, too, but Brad Pitt was in the movie."

"Then why didn't you do that?" Kitty said to Mary. "It's not like you don't have an armpit."

"No, that was hard," Jane said. "Even if we'd had more time, I don't think I could have gotten it."

"I still don't understand why you were pretending to have diarrhea," Lydia said, and Mary said with impatience, "It was *fall* like *waterfall.*"

Liz avoided looking at either Darcy or Caroline as Nathan from Procter & Gamble stood and took a scrap of paper from his team's pile. When he'd unfolded it, he made the same camera-cranking gesture Mary had.

"Movie," Charlotte said.

Nathan raised a finger.

"One word," Chip said.

Nathan closed his eyes, balled his hands into fists that he shook by his ears, opened his mouth, and pretended to scream.

Flatly, Darcy said, *"Psycho."*

"Hey," Nathan said. "Not bad."

Chip chuckled. "Are you sure you're not a ringer, Darcy?"

"Seriously?" Caroline said with delight. "That's it?"

"That's it," Nathan said. "All hail—what's our team name anyway?"

"The Conquistadors," Charlotte suggested. "Booyah, Bennet sisters!"

Liz didn't mind Charlotte's competitive spirit—she knew the affection underlying it—but Caroline Bingley caught Liz's eye, and Caroline's demeanor contained no similar warmth. "So much for family shorthand, I guess," Caroline said.

The game proceeded much the way it had begun, with Lydia and Kitty making guesses that were as off-color as they were inaccurate; when the answer was *The Sound of Music,* they shouted, "Hemorrhoids!" and "Blow job!"; for Dwight Eisenhower, "Dildo!" and "Threesome!" Her younger sisters' vulgarity was not a surprise to Liz; indeed, she herself, more than Jane or Mary, could enjoy a dirty joke. However, the difference between Liz and her youngest sisters was their lack of deference to context. Among near strangers, Liz would never have been so artlessly, fearlessly crude. But Kitty and Lydia were always themselves, in a way Liz found both appalling and admirable. They would discuss pubic hair at the dinner table, text in church, refer as unabashedly to their hangovers as Liz would have to a stubbed toe. Perhaps, Liz thought, their nonchalance about judgment or consequence reflected the greater leniency Mr. and Mrs. Bennet had shown them; their parents had, when Liz and Jane were children and teenagers, still been concerned with bedtimes and then curfews, with grades and chores and thank-you notes. Whereas on a recent afternoon, when Liz had asked Lydia if she had any stationery Liz could use to belatedly write to a publicist who'd taken her to lunch in New York the week Mr. Bennet had fallen ill, Lydia had said she didn't own stationery. "Then how do you thank people?" Liz asked, and Lydia said, "For what?"

But the aspect of Lydia and Kitty's crassness most noteworthy to Liz was their lack of concern that it would adhere to them. They were such pretty girls, with long blond hair, like Jane's—Liz and Mary were brunettes—and their bodies, per their dedication to CrossFit, were superbly toned. Plus, they were *young* still, their skin creamy, their eyes bright, no matter how late they returned home on how many nights. Did they not wonder if shouting about dingleberries might in some way detract from their dewy beauty, conjuring an incompatibly, uncomplimentarily vivid image in audiences' heads? It appeared they did not.

Yet even as Liz felt gripped by embarrassment, she also felt embarrassment's opposite, a liberating kind of resignation. Her sisters were people who never passed up an opportunity to talk about sex, shit, or combinations thereof; if her family horrified Darcy and Caroline, so be it. It was mostly for Jane that she felt regret, should the evening compromise Chip's impression of her.

It was during the third round of the game, on Jane's turn, when the indecency reached its apotheosis. The clue, as it turned out, was "Jingle Bells," yet, with great enthusiasm, Lydia kept repeating, "Alabama Hot Pocket! Alabama Hot Pocket!" Liz ignored her, and together she and Mary ultimately guessed the answer, but after the turn was finished, Stephen said, "I'm almost afraid to ask."

Lydia and Kitty dissolved into laughter. Liz stood. "Does anyone need another drink?"

Stephen said to Lydia, "Whisper it in my ear?"

"Oh, please," Charlotte said. "No secrets. Just say it."

Liz rolled her eyes at Lydia and Kitty as she passed them en route to the kitchen; once there, after opening a new bottle of wine and refilling her glass, she checked her phone. She'd received no interesting emails and no texts at all. *Sporty* was shipping on Monday, so she knew Jasper would be working most of the weekend.

"I think Caroline is having the cabernet," a male voice said. "Does that sound right?"

When Liz looked up, Darcy had entered the kitchen and was standing at the counter holding two open bottles side by side.

"I have no idea." Liz watched as he poured, then she said, "Actually, she must have been drinking the other one, because I just opened that. Here." Liz took a step forward and reached for the glass Darcy was holding; in one long slug, she finished its contents. When the maroon liquid was gone, she returned the glass to the counter. "Problem solved."

"That glass was mine," Darcy said.

"Oops," Liz said. "Are you worried about my B-minus Cincinnati germs?"

After Darcy refilled the same glass, he looked at her, took a sip, and said, without smiling, "I have confidence in my immune system." As he poured from the other bottle into Caroline's glass, he said, "You might recall that it was you yourself, not I, who assigned you a grade of B-minus."

"I was empathizing with your plight—looking at the world from your perspective."

"I see." Everything about him—every inflection of his voice, every expression he made—oozed superciliousness.

"For what it's worth, my sisters aren't representative of all people from Cincinnati," Liz said. "Lydia and Kitty happen to have exceptionally bad manners."

"I'm well aware that your sisters have exceptionally bad manners," Darcy said, and Liz immediately regretted her quasi-apology.

She said, "So where are you from that's so superior to here?"

"I grew up outside San Francisco. Though again, you're putting words in my mouth—I never said *superior*."

"Close enough," Liz said. "And, you know, just for the record, whatever it is you think about the people here, your opinion says more about you than the city. Because I'm not sure what you think other places have that we don't, but fifteen-dollar cocktails made with locally grown ingredients? We've got them. Indie bands? Got them. Reiki healers? We've got those, too. Maybe you have to search a little harder, but all that's here, and so is lots of other stuff, like beautiful old houses that are completely affordable and an awesome riverfront park and nationally ranked sports teams and easy commutes and a mix of races and ethnicities. You can have a really high quality of life in Cincinnati."

This was without question the most passionate paean to her hometown Liz had ever delivered—in fact, she wasn't certain she believed all of it—but Darcy simply said, "You're lucky to be so enthusiastic about the place you live."

"Oh, I don't live here," Liz said. "I live in New York."

At this, Darcy did something she hadn't previously seen: He smiled.

"It's not that I *wouldn't* live here," she said quickly, though she wasn't sure this was true, either. "It's just that it doesn't make sense with my job. I'm a writer for *Mascara* magazine, but I came back because my dad had heart surgery."

"A bypass?"

Liz nodded. "He's doing well." Reflexively, she knocked on a wooden cabinet.

"Did he have it done at Christ?" Liz nodded again, and Darcy said, "Their cardiothoracic department is good."

"Are you fermenting the grapes yourself?" someone said then, and both Liz and Darcy turned to see Caroline. "You've seriously been in here for twenty minutes," Caroline said, and beneath her breezy tone, Liz heard an unmistakable territoriality. How convenient, Liz thought, that Caroline's managerial obligations had brought her to Cincinnati.

"Liz was just telling me that she's a writer for a magazine," Darcy said. "*Mascara*, you said?"

"Oh, that's funny," Caroline said. "Do you write articles like 'Twenty Tips to Be a Tiger in the Sack'?"

"That's not *Mascara*," Liz said.

"I'm over Charades," Caroline said to Darcy. "Want to get out of here?"

More loudly, Liz said, "I know what magazine you're thinking of, and it's not *Mascara*. We write about sex, of course, but not in a cheesy way."

Caroline glanced at Liz. "You what?"

"*Mascara* focuses on serious issues," Liz said. "I went to Saudi Arabia last year for a feature on gender relations in the Middle East."

There was something challenging, or weirdly accusatory, in Caroline's tone as she said, "Did you have to cover your hair?"

"I wore an *abaya* and a head scarf in public," Liz said.

Caroline smiled faintly. "Aren't you the world traveler." Her focus reverted to Darcy as she said, "Charlotte is talking about ordering food, but I'd rather just leave."

"We can go," Darcy said.

Charades hadn't concluded, Liz was pretty sure, though she wasn't about to insist on extending the game.

Darcy turned toward her. "I'd suggest that the Cincinnati Chamber of Commerce hire you, but I guess it'd be a long commute."

He and Caroline were almost out of the kitchen when Liz said, "Did you just make a joke? I hadn't realized you had a sense of humor."

Chapter 26

NEITHER MR. NOR Mrs. Bennet visited the third floor with any regularity, which was why Liz was mildly surprised, while working at her desk, to see her mother standing in the threshold of her room. Mrs. Bennet held out a small cardboard box, its top flaps sticking up. Her tone was unapologetic as she said, "I thought this was for me."

Several times a day, the doorbell of the Tudor rang, and it was usually either a family friend bearing a casserole or baked goods intended to bring comfort during Mr. Bennet's recovery or else a FedEx or UPS delivery. About three-quarters of the deliveries were intended for Mrs. Bennet—they accumulated, often unopened, in the front hall and the dining room—and the rest were assorted products and media kits sent to Liz at *Mascara* by publicists and forwarded by the magazine: diet protein powder and samples from celebrity sock lines, forthcoming tell-alls, new kinds of lip gloss.

"Thanks." Liz stood and took the box.

With a certain ostentatiousness, Mrs. Bennet said, "I have no idea who it's from." As her mother turned and walked away, Liz saw that the label featured the logo of and address for *Sporty*, with Jasper's first and last names above the logo in entirely legible handwriting. Reaching into the box, Liz pushed aside tissue paper to reveal a piece of stationery with the *Sporty* letterhead on which Jasper had scrawled *THINKING OF YOU!* Beneath the paper were a bright red sheer teddy and thong underwear in a matching hue. The items, which presumably would have been flimsy even if well-made, were clearly cheap, which didn't preclude them from holding a semi-ridiculous allure offset by the humiliating possibility that they had been examined by her mother. Or, thought Liz, the humiliating certainty. But if Mrs. Bennet was not going to ask Liz about the gift, Liz would not offer any explanation.

She called Jasper on her cellphone, and when he answered, she said, "My mom opened your package. She said to compliment you on your discretion and elegant taste."

Jasper laughed. "You think she knows that opening someone else's mail is a federal offense? Hey, word on the street is that Noah Trager is being shit-canned later this week. Don't you think I'd make a good editor in chief of *Dude*?"

"Actually, you would."

"Edward van Pallandt is co-hosting that benefit tonight for the Burmese dissident. The tickets are sold out, but I'll bet I can get in. You think I'm jumping the gun if I go and mention my interest in *Dude* to van Pallandt?"

Noah Trager was the current editor in chief of *Dude*, a men's magazine; Edward van Pallandt was its publisher's creative director, a bon vivant who had, in one of the great moments of Liz's entire life, complimented her shoes as they were riding the elevator together. (The shoes were beige suede caged booties, and, most gloriously of all, Liz had purchased them for thirty dollars at TJ Maxx in Cincinnati.) As for the Burmese dissident, Liz didn't know who that was.

She said, "How certain is it that Noah is being fired? Who told you?"

"I've heard it from a couple people."

"I think it's fine to go to the benefit and talk to Edward van Pallandt, to remind him who you are, but I wouldn't mention *Dude* specifically. That seems vulturish. Is your résumé updated?"

"I'll send it to you, and you can take a gander. You know what you should send me? A picture of you in the lingerie."

"With or without my mom in the background?"

Jasper chuckled. "She knows you're an adult, Nin."

"I wouldn't be so sure." Liz propped her feet on her desk and leaned her chair back on two legs. "Who's the Burmese dissident?" she asked. "An artist?"

"Hmm," Jasper said. "Maybe I should learn the answer to that question before I go tonight."

Chapter 27

AUNT MARGO AND Cousin Willie arrived at the Tudor in time for cocktails on Tuesday; also, unprecedentedly, Chip Bingley would be joining the Bennets for dinner. "I think it's good Aunt Margo and Willie are here, because they'll distract Mom," Liz said to Jane in the kitchen as she poured almonds into a bowl. "Maybe she won't get in Chip's face as much."

"Shouldn't it take the pressure off that Dad and Mom both met him at the Lucases'?" Jane said. "That's what I've been telling myself."

"Oh, the question isn't whether *they'll* approve of *him*. But if he wasn't scared off by Lydia and Kitty at Charades, then I bet you're in the clear." Liz folded over the top of the almond bag and clipped it shut. "By the way, I feel like Willie has hired a stylist. He looks a lot better."

Jane smiled. "You don't think he could have spruced up on his own?"

"Not to be uncharitable, but no. Those are extremely trendy pants he has on." And yet—even more uncharitably—from the moment of their clumsy hug outside the airport terminal, where she'd picked up the visitors, Liz had also been sure that, wardrobe notwithstanding, Willie's essential awkwardness remained intact. In her head, Liz thought of him as either the most confident awkward person she'd ever known or the awkwardest confident person. Of medium height, with a chubby build and puffy red hair, he continued to show a fondness for speaking at length about his professional pursuits that was tempered only slightly by his listeners' inability to follow.

When Liz and Jane entered the living room where their sisters, parents, aunt, and cousin were gathered, Willie appeared to be in midmonologue. "We get thirty million unique visitors per month," he was saying, and as Liz made eye contact with her father, who was seated just a few feet from Willie, Mr. Bennet let his eyelids droop. Liz looked away. "If you want to compare that to the competition, it's not even close," Willie said. "Jig-Jig gets ten million, *maybe* twelve. Once the kinks are worked out, we'll leave everyone else in the dust."

"I don't suppose you have cheese and crackers," Aunt Margo said.

Simultaneously, Mrs. Bennet said, "Mary, put out the Vermont cheddar," and Lydia said, "The casomorphins in cheese are as addictive as opium."

In a peevish tone, Mrs. Bennet said, "Everyone has very strong opinions about what we eat these days."

"Lizzy," Willie said, "I saw in the airport that they're still printing dead-tree issues of your magazine."

"That's how some people prefer to read," Liz said. "I realize you're not one of them."

Mrs. Bennet said, "Willie, if there's anything special you'd like to do in Cincinnati, Liz has the most open schedule. Jane is tied up now with her new beau, who'll be joining us for dinner." Mrs. Bennet turned to her sister-in-law. "His name is Chip Bingley, and he moved here to work at Christ Hospital. He went to Harvard Medical School."

"Bingley, did you say?" Willie squinted. "That name sounds familiar."

With pleasure, Mrs. Bennet said, "It was his great-great-grandfather who started Bingley Manufacturing, which of course has made sinks and such for years and years."

"And by sinks, Mom means toilets," Lydia said. "We're all crossing our fingers that Jane becomes the crapper queen."

Mildly, Jane said, "Chip and I have only gone out a few times."

"He's very serious about you," Mrs. Bennet said. "Now, does his family still own Bingley Manufacturing or did they sell it?"

"That hasn't come up," Jane said.

"If only there were a global computer network where you could find that kind of information," Willie said, and he chuckled as he pulled out his phone.

Liz said, "Willie, do you watch *Eligible*? Because Chip was on it a couple years ago."

"That was just a little silliness," Mrs. Bennet said. "Just blowing off steam after his residency."

But Willie looked up from his phone with recognition. "He was the one who cried in the finale!" Willie said. "I knew I'd heard his name."

"I didn't know you watch *Eligible*," Aunt Margo said to Willie, and Liz said, "Don't we all? Besides Jane."

"He was under a lot of pressure." Jane cleared her throat, then spoke more loudly. "The crying thing—a producer had told him that one of the women was suicidal because he didn't propose to her, and he felt awful. It's not like he cries more than the average man."

It wasn't so much the content of Jane's comments as their knowing and protective tone that caught Liz's attention. Maybe, as improbable as it seemed, Chip Bingley really was Jane's happy ending. How wonderful this would be, and how deserving Jane was.

Cousin Willie scrolled down the screen of his phone. "In 1986, the Bingley family sold Bingley Manufacturing to multinational industrial company L. M. Clarkson. Doesn't say for how much, but, Jane, it's safe to assume your guy has a nice cushion under him if he ever gets sued for malpractice." Willie glanced up. "Lizzy, I'd love a tour of the city. Margo and I figured out on the plane that I haven't been here since I was fourteen. All these years, Dad and I were planning to come back when one of you got married." He spoke warmly, without apparent awareness of the topic's sensitivity, then added, "According to the Twitter hive, the zoo and the Underground Railroad museum are Cincinnati's must-see destinations."

Mr. Bennet said, "Or if you'd like a recommendation, you could ask someone who's lived here for sixty-four years."

"Dad, *you've* never been to the Freedom Center," Kitty said.

"No, but I did used to date Harriet Tubman."

Liz said, "Dad, I'm taking you to physical therapy tomorrow at nine, right? Then I have to do a phone interview at eleven. But, Willie, I could give you a tour after that. Or, I don't know, Mary, would you want to?"

"I have too much work." As Mary shook her head without even feigning regret, Liz was reminded of her theory that, because Mary wasn't very pretty, she received credit for being intelligent or virtuous in ways that, as far as Liz could discern, her sister was not. In fact, Liz disliked Mary more than she disliked Lydia, and certainly more than Kitty, all of whom, of course, out of obligation and habit, she loved. But if you assumed that accompanying Mary's supposedly scholarly interests was an open-minded acceptance of others, or that accompanying her homeliness was compassion, you'd be wrong; Mary was proof, Liz had concluded, of how easy it was to be unattractive *and* unpleasant.

"I have loads of meetings tomorrow for my Women's League luncheon," Mrs. Bennet was saying to Aunt Margo and Willie. "The girls will tell you I've been working myself to the bone. But we'll all have dinner at the country club." She leaned forward, as if to divulge a bit of confidential information, and whispered, "Margo, I'm sure you remember how delicious their Caesar salad is."

"Is that water damage on the wall?" Aunt Margo stood and crossed the living room. "My God, Fred, you're lucky the house hasn't crumbled around you."

"I'm still hoping it might," Mr. Bennet replied.

"That happened during a rainstorm last week," Mrs. Bennet said, and though Liz didn't consider her mother a particularly faithful adherent to the truth, the fib, occurring in front of no fewer than six people who could have contradicted it, was unusually bold. "But now that you've reminded me, Margo," Mrs. Bennet added cheerfully, "I'll be sure to call the handyman."

Chapter 28

THEY ATE IN the dining room instead of the kitchen. Prior to Willie and Aunt Margo's arrival, Lydia and Kitty had been tasked with moving boxes from the front hall and the dining room table to Jane's old room (CrossFit notwithstanding, this was the first time since Liz's return home that she had seen her youngest sisters exert themselves), and, along with her most elegant china, Mrs. Bennet had put out place cards, presumably to ensure that Chip Bingley sat next to her. He had arrived bearing both a bottle of wine and a bouquet of flowers, and though a vase of purple hydrangea had already occupied the table's center, Mrs. Bennet had instructed Liz to whisk them away and display Chip's arrangement instead, as if he'd interpret the existence of another bouquet as a personal affront.

After much discussion between Jane and Mrs. Bennet, the menu consisted of cold poached salmon, roasted potatoes, a green salad, and a berry tart. Because of the supreme importance of the evening, Mrs. Bennet had set aside her Women's League responsibilities, and mother and daughter had spent the entire day tidying the first floor and preparing the meal.

It was only a minute or two after they'd all sat down that Kitty asked, "Chip, did they pay you to be on *Eligible?*"

"I was wondering the same thing," Cousin Willie said, and Mrs. Bennet said, "Goodness gracious, Chip doesn't want to talk about that. Tell me, Chip, is it Philadelphia where your parents live?"

Chip, who had recently taken a bite, chewed, then patted his mouth with a white linen napkin. "They live on the Main Line," he said. "So the suburbs, though I've tried to talk them into buying an apartment downtown. Center City has really experienced a renaissance in recent years." He glanced at Kitty, who was across the table from him. "I don't mind talking about the show." He turned back toward Mrs. Bennet. "If you don't mind, that is. I wouldn't want to offend your sense of propriety."

Had sweeter words ever been spoken to Mrs. Bennet? And by a wealthy suitor courting her eldest daughter, no less! Practically purring, Mrs. Bennet set her hand on Chip's forearm and said, "Go right ahead."

Looking around the table, Chip said, "I trust that this conversation is off the record. But, yes, the star of each season gets paid. I think the amount varies based on negotiations by one's lawyer or agent—in my case, it was an entertainment lawyer, because I didn't have an agent—but it's a respectable amount."

"Six figures?" Lydia asked, and Mrs. Bennet said, "Heavens, Lydia, where are your manners?"

Chip smiled gamely. "Let's leave it at *respectable.*"

"Are you saying you got paid and the women didn't?" Mary asked.

"I fear that might be the case," Chip said, "though it's not because of sexism. The same is true when the star of the cast is female and the contestants are men. Either way, I think everyone at least gets a per diem."

"How long was the shoot?" Liz asked. She was at the far end of the table from Chip, between Cousin Willie and her father.

"Shorter than you'd think," Chip said. "Eight weeks."

"It's all scripted, right?" Mary said. "Everyone knows it is."

"Yes and no," Chip said. "Sure, the producers nudge you in certain directions. Or something happens spontaneously, but the cameras didn't catch it just right, or maybe somebody was sneezing in the background, so they do three more takes. And obviously the great majority of footage never makes it on the air. They have a few hundred hours to whittle down for each eighty-minute episode. But I still think people's essential personalities come through. A lot of those girls were a bit outrageous to begin with." He glanced around the table. "Have I put you to sleep yet, Mr. Bennet?"

"No more so than our dinners usually do. Carry on."

Chip grinned. "The other reason things could get dramatic was that the alcohol was flowing, and not just at night. They'd serve booze from lunch on, and if there was a justifiable way of offering it earlier, like a Bloody Mary at brunch, they'd do that."

"Now it's actually starting to sound civilized," Mr. Bennet said.

"Too bad you're married, huh, Dad?" Kitty said.

"You're being filmed, and you're mic'd, from the time you wake up in the morning until you go to sleep at night." Chip was still holding his fork above his plate, not biting. "They've taken away your cellphone and forbidden computers, music, even books and magazines—partly to avoid copyright issues, but also because none of that makes for good television. Who wants to watch people read? Or if you were listening to music, it'd be hard for the editor to cut the scene. But that means you're bored, you have no privacy, and you're separated from your normal support system. It's a perfect storm for acting out. I guess I'd say people *are* themselves, but they're also not themselves, if that makes sense."

"Are you mic'd when you're taking a dump?" Lydia asked.

"Lydia," Jane said.

Chip seemed unfazed. "That's the one place you do get privacy."

"What's Rick Price like?" The question came from, of all people, Aunt Margo. For the past eleven years, which in TV math was somehow the equivalent of eighteen seasons, Rick Price had been the host: an affable-seeming fellow from Phoenix, Arizona, who had gotten his start as a meteorologist.

"He was a good guy," Chip said. "The same off-camera as on. It must be a strange job, because on a typical day, I'd guess he was on-set four or five hours, but then some of the challenges and ceremonies would literally last all night. Or he'd travel with us to Barcelona. One thing I had to remind myself was that even though he was nice, part of his job description was to stir the pot. He and the producers were like town gossips. They'd tell me, 'Such-and-such girl told so-and-so that you said this to her.' "

"It's your sister who convinced you to do the show, isn't it?" Mrs. Bennet said. "It wasn't your idea." From their separate ends of the table, Liz and Jane made eye contact.

"I hadn't seen *Eligible* when Caroline suggested I apply. She shot a video of me, just chatting for a few minutes. But I filled out the forms. I thought it was silly, but I did it to humor her."

"I knew it!" Mrs. Bennet said.

"Now, I must admit," Chip added, "that before you're selected, they subject you to a very intense background check. There's a battery of psychological and physical exams that must be as thorough as what a vice-presidential candidate goes through. The producers aren't messing around. So it would be disingenuous to pretend I just woke up one day and found myself on TV. I could have opted out along the way."

In a warm voice, Cousin Willie asked, "Any skeletons in your closet they uncovered?"

Chip shook his head. "For better or worse, I'm a pretty dull fellow. But they called my college roommates, my former employers, my parents—who were, by the way, none too thrilled to hear about my plans. Mr. and Mrs. Bennet, I suspect they felt the way you would if any of your lovely daughters announced they were appearing on reality TV."

"Being on *Eligible* just sounds annoying," Liz said. "As a journalist, I've seen how the sausage gets made in the entertainment world, and it's actually not glamorous."

"I've interviewed *so* many famous people," Lydia said in what was apparently her Liz imitation, and Kitty, following suit, added, "Did you guys know I've been on TV three times?"

To Chip, Liz explained, "I interviewed Jillian Northcutt after she and Hudson Blaise split up. I certainly hope that's not the crowning achievement of my career, but I did go on some shows to talk about her, and my impression of the producers I dealt with was that they were smart, friendly, and completely ruthless about getting you to say what they want you to on-camera."

"No argument here," Chip said.

Liz hoped she didn't sound confrontational as she said, "So why'd you do it?"

Chip's expression was strange, or perhaps it seemed so only because Liz didn't know him well; she wasn't sure if he was embarrassed or proud, but when he spoke, it was clear he was utterly sincere. He looked at Jane before saying, "I did it to find love."

Chapter 29

AFTER DINNER, JANE returned with Chip to his apartment, and he dropped her off back at the Tudor just before six in the morning, when he was due at the hospital. Though Liz could tell Jane was trying to be quiet as she entered the bathroom on the third floor, Liz was glad for the opportunity to talk with her sister. They decided to set out early for their run—the temperature was expected to reach the mid-nineties by noon—and they descended through the quiet and semi-dark house, where the rest of their family slept.

In the driveway, they stretched. "You don't think Mom's trying to pimp me to Cousin Willie, do you?" Liz asked as she extended her left leg, her heel balanced against the asphalt. "Even as desperate as she is on my behalf, I hope she'd draw the line at incest."

"Since he's our step-cousin, it's not technically incest."

"No," Liz said. "But it's still technically gross." She pointed toward the street. "Ready?"

As they jogged out of the driveway, Jane said, "If you don't want people to treat you like you're single, whether it's Mom or anyone else, you could tell them you're not." This wasn't a new conversation; Jane thought that at least their parents should know about Jasper, especially since it was possible that Mrs. Bennet might feel sympathy for the delicate circumstances surrounding Jasper's wealthy grandmother-in-law.

Liz said, "You mean the way you've been so open about your IUI?" When she glanced at her sister, Jane's expression was somber. "You know I'm kidding, right?" Liz said. "So I thought last night with Chip went really well."

Both women were quiet as three SUVs in varying hues of silver drove by, then Jane said, "Maybe Chip's the right guy at the wrong time. Would you ever live in Cincinnati? Like, permanently."

Liz chortled. "Wait, are you planning to break up with him or to stay here forever and become his wife?"

"There are reasons to live in Cincinnati besides Chip."

"Name one. And don't say Cincinnati is cheaper, because every-where is cheaper than New York."

Jane smiled. "Yet you were outraged that Darcy doesn't like it here." They were approaching the country club, and Jane continued: "Everything in New York is such an uphill battle. And even though I used to feel like I couldn't live in Cincinnati because I wouldn't have my own identity—I could only be Fred and Sally's daughter, or 'one of the Bennet sisters'—maybe I was wrong. Talking to Dad's nurses in the hospital, or that night I went to the lecture at the Hindu temple—I can see now that there are a lot of different Cincinnatis. This sounds dumb to even say, because it's so obvious, but most of the city has nothing to do with Seven Hills or Hyde Park or"—Jane gestured to her right—"the country club."

"So where would you live? Over-the-Rhine?"

Jane's expression became sheepish. "Oh, I'd definitely want to live in Hyde Park. Not next door to Mom and Dad, but maybe a bungalow around Erie Avenue."

Had Jane been looking online at real estate? Would it be a betrayal for Liz to check the search history on her own laptop, which Jane occasionally used? Liz said, "If I moved back, I'm sure I'd find some great place to live. I wouldn't have to make a reservation to take a spin class or wait in line just to get into the grocery store. But then I'd look up one day and be like, 'What the fuck have I done?'"

"You still sound like Darcy," Jane said. "Speaking of which, Chip is planning a dinner party, and he wants you to come. But just to warn you, Darcy will be there, and so will Caroline, of course."

"I'd be delighted to attend. I'm willing to overlook Chip's horrible taste in friends and sisters because of his wisdom in falling for you."

"Caroline is actually nice when we hang out at the apartment."

"Yeah, I'll bet."

"The only night Darcy's free this week is Sunday. Can I tell Chip you'll be there?"

"Not only will I be there," Liz said, "but I'll be impersonating a pleasant woman with great manners."

Chapter 30

"COME HERE," KITTY whispered. Standing in front of the open door of the second-floor guest room, she crooked her finger.

"What?" Liz said at a normal volume, and Kitty whispered, "Shh!"

As she got closer to her sister, Liz could hear a rhythmic whirring, like that of a fan. On reaching the guest room's threshold, she was greeted with the sight of Cousin Willie sprawled on his back on one of the twin beds, the covers kicked off and Willie clad in tighty-whitey underpants and nothing else. His mouth was open, and he was snoring extremely loudly. Beside Liz, Kitty convulsed with silent laughter.

It was then that Lydia appeared behind them in the hall, apparently having gone to retrieve her smartphone. She held it in the air, its camera trained on Willie's form, or at least this was what she did until Liz grabbed the phone away and jammed it under her left armpit. "No," Liz said, also at a normal volume.

"Give it back," Lydia hissed, lunging toward Liz.

"Only if you leave him alone." Liz's preference at this juncture in adulthood was to avoid physical fights with her sisters, yet the longer she'd been in Cincinnati, the less remote the possibility had come to seem.

"Give it to me," Lydia said.

"He doesn't even know," Kitty said.

"Exactly," Liz said. "If I catch either of you filming him again, I'll drop both your phones in the toilet."

"Fuck you," Lydia said, but when she grabbed for the phone again, Liz let her take it. Lydia and Kitty strode away, and Liz glanced inside the guest room. She'd expected that the commotion would awaken Willie, but he continued to snore undisturbed. Gently, Liz shut the door.

Chapter 31

HER ARTICLE ABOUT asking for a raise was due by the end of the week, and Liz still hadn't succeeded in interviewing Kathy de Bourgh, the famous feminist. To Kathy de Bourgh's publicist, Liz had sent emails that were, in various iterations, lighthearted and casual, stern, obsequious, and desperate. She'd been rereading *Revolutions and Rebellions,* the classic work in which Kathy de Bourgh chronicled her time in the women's movement from the early sixties on: the marches and sit-ins and arrests, her testimony before the Senate Judiciary Committee on behalf of the Equal Rights Amendment, which had occurred (this detail had titillated Liz when she'd first read the book as a college freshman) on the same day that Kathy de Bourgh called off her wedding to the smolderingly handsome attorney general of New York. However, as much as Liz was enjoying *Revolutions and Rebellions* this time around, she knew that her editor wouldn't be pleased if she used decades-old book quotations in lieu of fresh remarks from an interview.

So cognizant of Ms. de Bourgh's jam-packed schedule, Liz wrote in her latest email to the publicist, *but if I could get her on the phone for even five minutes, I know our readers would be thrilled to hear her perspective. And just as a reminder, we at* Mascara *still proudly consider Ms. de Bourgh "family."* Prior to becoming a professional activist, Kathy de Bourgh had herself been a reporter and had worked for two years at *Mascara;* it had been Liz's employer that in 1961 published the still-legendary article about the week Kathy de Bourgh had gone undercover as a dancer at a Times Square nightclub.

Liz had just hit Send when her mother entered the room. Mrs. Bennet glanced around, as if for spies, before whispering, "Is Lydia dating a bodybuilder?"

Uncertainly, Liz said, "Do you mean that guy Ham?"

Mrs. Bennet appeared distressed. "Gyms can be very dirty places. There are lots of germs on the equipment."

"Kitty and Lydia seem pretty healthy to me."

Mrs. Bennet took a step forward. "Can you find the bodybuilder on the computer?"

Liz looked at her watch. "I'm leaving in a minute to take Willie on his tour."

"Just quickly," Mrs. Bennet said. "It won't take long."

Liz sighed and pulled up the same webpage with the photo of Ham she'd found before. Her mother bent toward the screen.

"Oh, he's very handsome." Mrs. Bennet sounded surprised and pleased. "And look, he *did* go to college."

So that had been the source of concern. "How do you even know about him?" Liz asked.

"I just heard some talk. Oh, dear." Mrs. Bennet was again reading from the computer screen. "Does ROTC mean his family couldn't afford tuition?"

"Either way, CrossFit is very popular," Liz said. "I bet he's financially stable now."

"I hope he doesn't take steroids. They shrink the testes, you know."

Trying to ignore the unappealing sound of her mother using the word *testes,* Liz said, "I don't think steroids are a CrossFit thing."

"Your friend Jasper," Mrs. Bennet said. "Is he married or not married?"

Liz tensed. Had she been lured into a trap with this talk of gym germs and Ham's testicles? Looking straight ahead, not at her mother, Liz said, "He's married."

"I was trying to remember," Mrs. Bennet said, and Liz thought, *Yeah, right.*

She put her computer to sleep and closed it. "Want to come on the tour with Willie and me?"

"Oh, I'd just be a third wheel," Mrs. Bennet said confidently. "I'm sure the two of you have loads to catch up on."

Chapter 32

IT WAS COUSIN Willie who kept Liz waiting; still apparently on Pacific time, he had slept in, and at noon, their agreed-upon hour of departure, he was in the shower.

Even though it was hot, Liz went outside, sat on the Tudor's front steps, and pulled out her smartphone; checking it only worsened her mood as she saw an email from Kathy de Bourgh's publicist saying that Kathy de Bourgh would be available for the next ten minutes. Which wasn't completely impossible to take advantage of, though Liz would have preferred that it were—she wished she hadn't known about the publicist's message until it was too late. Because although she *could* dash upstairs, turn on her digital recorder, and ask earnest questions while hoping Kathy de Bourgh couldn't hear her panting, Liz didn't, in this moment, possess the will. She didn't feel like a grown-up professional journalist; sitting in the heat in a T-shirt, not-so-stylish shorts, and flip-flops, waiting for her dorky cousin, she felt instead like a sweaty, grumpy teenager. *So sorry but about to enter a meeting,* she typed on her phone to the publicist. *VERY disappointed and really ap-*

preciative that Ms. de Bourgh has made time for our conversation. Any way to reschedule for late this afternoon?

Churlish as her mood was, Liz recognized that Cousin Willie was not at fault, and once he was in the passenger seat of her father's Cadillac, she made an effort to sound chipper. "I thought we'd start by going to the riverfront," she said. "It's kind of nice to walk along Bicentennial Commons, even though it's sweltering. And then we can go to the Freedom Center, and after that a late lunch at Skyline Chili."

"Great," Willie said. "I always enjoy spending time with you, Lizzy."

"Remind me what you're working on now," Liz said, and after that, little more was required of her because Willie proceeded to deliver a monologue that took them all the way to their destination: He spoke of load balancing, scaling strategy, CPU usage, SSL certificates, and maintenance windows, or lack thereof. Finally, as they were pulling into the parking lot off Pete Rose Way, Liz interrupted and said, "So tell me about the coolest women in Silicon Valley that I've never heard of."

Willie seemed confused. "Cool how?"

"The movers and shakers," Liz said. "The up-and-comers. Who'll be a household name two years from now?"

"If you're trying to write an affirmative action piece about female entrepreneurs, you have a better chance of finding a field full of four-leaf clovers."

Slightly taken aback, Liz said, "Well, who's the next Nancy Nelson?" Nelson was the CEO of one of the world's largest software companies.

"My point exactly," Willie said. "She was hired for that job two years after the IPO. She's a suit, not a visionary."

"I realize she isn't a coder, but she has an impressive track record." Then, to change the subject, Liz said, "Have you been seeing a stylist?"

She'd meant it as a factual inquiry, but Willie seemed pleased. "A woman at Nordstrom named Yvette has been helping me. It means a lot that you noticed, Lizzy, with where you work."

"Well, I'm not in the fashion department. But you're welcome."

After a brief silence, Willie said, "You don't have a boyfriend, do you? I'm assuming I'd have heard about it if you did."

Liz hesitated before saying, "Not exactly."

"Do you want children?" It was strange but not offensive—certainly less offensive than his remark about female entrepreneurs—to be asked so straightforwardly. With her family, such questions were usually alluded to rather than openly discussed. Somehow the fact that all five sisters were unmarried made them a phenomenon, an amusing or appalling one, depending on your perspective, though in either case there was rarely recognition of each woman's individuality.

Yet still Liz knew better than to answer honestly. She said, "I'm not sure. Do you?"

"Of course," Willie said. "And, Liz, you'd be a great mom. For someone like you, with your quality of genes, not to have kids would be a real waste." Clearly, he believed himself to be complimenting her.

"Are *you* seeing anyone?" she asked.

"Frankly, a lot of the women I meet are gold diggers. I recently thought I was taking a girl out for dinner, and it turns out she was a lady of the night." Willie hadn't relayed the information in a humorous tone, so Liz tried not to laugh.

She said, "How'd you figure it out?"

"She eventually mentioned a fee."

Liz pressed the back of her hand to her mouth, which didn't adequately conceal a snort. "Sorry," she said. "I'm not—you must have been horrified. But how did—did she say, 'Okay, now you have to pay me'?"

"We'd gone out for dinner, and I thought we were having a good time. I asked if she'd like to have a glass of wine at my house, and she said, 'Okay, for a thousand bucks.'"

"Jesus. I'm in the wrong line of work."

Liz had parked, and they climbed from the car and followed the path toward the river.

"There was no penetration," Willie said. "Just a BJ. I hope that doesn't make you think less of me, Lizzy."

They were walking side by side, which Liz hoped meant Willie didn't see the revulsion that passed over her face. It hadn't occurred to her that he'd accepted the prostitute's offer in any capacity. But Liz couldn't deny that she had helped lead them to this point in the conversation. She said, "I'm sure there are lots of women who'd love to date you free of charge."

"Liz." He touched her elbow. "Paying for sex—I had never done anything like that. But I just—I'm not very experienced. I'm not still a virgin, but I was till I was twenty-three."

"You don't owe me an explanation. Seriously."

"Please don't mention this to Margo."

"Of course not," Liz said. "Let's never speak of it again."

Chapter 33

THE OAKLEY SKYLINE Chili wasn't the closest one to the Freedom Center, but it was Liz's favorite, the location the Bennets had frequented during her childhood, long before she'd realized the famous combination of spaghetti, cinnamon-and-cocoa-infused ground beef, shredded cheddar cheese, and crumbled oyster crackers was actually fast food. It was after two o'clock and the restaurant was mostly empty when Liz and Willie entered. Right away, Liz noticed him: Sitting at the counter, apparently alone, was Fitzwilliam Darcy. He wore a navy polo shirt and seemed to be eating a three-way, so named for its noodles, chili, and cheese; a four-way would include either beans or raw onions as a topping, and a five-way would include both.

She pretended not to see him. Willie ordered two cheese coneys and Liz a four-way with beans, and as Willie commenced a lengthy analysis of Bitcoin, Liz was grateful to remember that among Skyline's attractions was the efficiency of its service; no more than five minutes had passed when the waitress delivered their loaded-up oval plates.

"Admittedly, the client isn't where it needs to be vis-à-vis user-interface," Willie was saying as Liz crushed oyster crackers and sprinkled the crumbs over her chili. "But it's not that far away. Why are you doing that?"

"You just do. It's part of Skyline."

"Is it mandatory?"

"Yes, and the chili police will arrest you if you fail to comply." Willie looked confused, and Liz said, "I'm teasing, Willie. Do whatever you want."

He took an individual cracker and pinched it between his thumb and forefinger.

"Go like this." Liz scooped up a handful, smashed them in her fist, and dropped the cracker dust onto his chili. "Don't overthink it."

"I had no idea that you offer private tutorials," a voice said, and Liz knew without looking up, though she did look, that it was Darcy.

Gesturing across the table, Liz said, "My cousin Willie is in from out of town."

"Fitzwilliam Darcy," Darcy said, and extended his hand.

Willie stood and, as they shook, said, "Will Collins."

Semi-sarcastically, Liz asked Darcy, "Are you a regular here?"

"I try not to come more than once a week." He patted his abdominal region, which was flat. "Everything in moderation."

"I wouldn't have guessed you for a Skyline fan," Liz said. "We have to make sure visitors try it, but usually people who didn't grow up in Cincinnati don't like it."

Darcy's expression was haughty. "I believe we've established that there's a lot you don't know about me." Nodding once at Willie, Darcy said, "Enjoy." A moment later, he was gone.

Chapter 34

ON MOST NIGHTS after dinner, Mrs. Bennet and varying combinations of her daughters gathered in the den behind the first-floor staircase to watch television. On this particular night, the family matriarch was joined by Liz, Mary, and also Aunt Margo; Jane had gone to Chip's apartment, and Kitty and Lydia were at a birthday party for one of the members of their gym. (The cake—Liz had not been able to resist asking—would be made with almond flour and coconut oil frosting.)

Just as some people enjoy knitting in front of the television, Mrs. Bennet was fond of perusing housewares catalogs; indeed, the sound of pages turning, that quick flap when no item caught her eye and the pauses when something did, the occasional businesslike lick of the index finger, was one of the essential sounds of Liz's childhood. This habit was also, apparently, what allowed Mrs. Bennet to maintain a belief that she had not actually "watched" a wide variety of shows even though she had been in the room for the duration of entire episodes and, in some cases, entire seasons.

They were midway through a reality cooking show when Willie popped his head into the room. He said, "I was wondering, Liz, if you'd like to go for a walk."

"Me?"

"It seems like a nice night."

Liz was slouched on the floor, her back against an ottoman, and she glanced over her shoulder, first at her mother, then at Aunt Margo. How irritating, Liz thought, that rather than fulfilling her obligation to Willie, giving him a tour had instead made him see her as his special pal.

"Liz and Jane run in the morning," Mrs. Bennet said. "You should go with them tomorrow, Willie."

"Running with three people is kind of awkward," Liz said, then immediately felt mean. "But we can go for a quick walk. Want to come, Mary?"

Unapologetically, Mary shook her head.

Liz feared that Willie wanted to bring up the conversation they'd had about the prostitute—perhaps he wished for further reassurance that she wouldn't repeat it—but once they got outside, he seemed to have no particular agenda.

"I hope you're not bored being here," she said as they turned left on Grandin Road. "I'm afraid Cincinnati is better to live in than visit."

"I can see that," Willie said, and since he was simply agreeing with her, Liz tried not to again feel offended. "I need to do some work tomorrow, and I wonder if there's a café you recommend. Your parents' bandwidth is a joke."

"There's a place called Awakenings on Hyde Park Square." The heat of the day had dissipated, and it was actually pleasant to be outside; around them, invisibly, cicadas buzzed. She said, "The summer I graduated from college, I was back here for a few months before I moved in with Jane in New York. Mary and I played Twenty Questions one time when we were waiting for takeout at a Chinese restaurant. This was before any of us had cellphones. Anyway, I was guessing, and it was a person who lived in Cincinnati. I got to the twentieth question and still didn't know who it was. And I'm *good* at Twenty Questions."

Liz laughed a little at her own impulse to brag about something unimpressive, and Willie didn't. "Mary told me it was me," Liz continued. "I was the person she was thinking of, but I hadn't guessed myself. And I was all outraged, like, 'I don't live in Cincinnati! I live in New York.' She said, 'You could have fooled me.'" Liz and Willie were passing a miniature château—even in its modified version, it was seven or eight thousand square feet—and Liz said, "I guess I'm a Cincinnati opportunist. In New York, I play the wholesome-midwesterner card, but when I'm back here, I consider myself to be a chic outsider." Even before Willie replied, Liz felt the loneliness of having confided something true in a person who didn't care. Still, when he spoke, it was more disappointing than she'd expected.

He said, "That chili we had—I liked it okay, but I keep burping up the taste of it."

"That happens to everyone," Liz said. "It's called repeating on you."

Chapter 35

NEITHER LIZ NOR Jane carried their phones on their morning run, so Liz didn't receive the texts from Jasper until after she'd eaten breakfast and gone upstairs to shower. *I had a great idea call me,* read the first, followed by a second: *Don't u want to know why I'm a genius?* She walked into the bathroom and sat on the edge of the tub, still in her perspiration-ridden tank top and shorts.

Jasper answered on the second ring. "Cincinnati is like the world headquarters of squash, right?" he said without prior greeting. "The sport, not the food."

"Yep, I was with you."

"They send an insane number of kids to play in Ivy League schools every year. But why Cincinnati?"

"Good question," Liz said.

"Don't you think it's crying out for an article?"

In under two seconds, Liz thought, *But I need to write the next "Women Who Dare" as soon as I finish my asking-for-a-raise piece,* then thought, *But it would be fun and random to report an article in Cincinnati,* then thought, *And since I've barely written about sports, that could be a cool challenge.* Growing up, she hadn't played squash herself but had known kids at Seven Hills who did.

Jasper said, "Mainly, though, it'll give me an excuse to come out there and bang you in a hotel room that I get to expense. Win-win-win, right?"

"Oh," Liz said. "Right." Already it seemed a bit embarrassing that she'd imagined he wanted to assign the piece to her rather than himself.

"Plus I can drop by for one of the famous Bennet family dinners," Jasper said. "And see your ancestral home."

Years earlier, Jasper had met Mr. and Mrs. Bennet and an adolescent Kitty and Lydia on a trip they'd made to New York for the lighting of the Christmas tree at Rockefeller Center. To Liz's alarm, fourteen-year-old Kitty had seemed more interested in finding out from her older sisters how one procured a prescription for the Pill than in seeing the Rockettes; Lydia, who was still comparatively innocent, was focused on acquiring underwear from Bloomingdale's that said BLOOM-IE'S across the back. As had happened often with Jasper over the years, the experience of introducing him to her family at brunch had felt to Liz like an enticing yet unsatisfactory facsimile: *Here's the guy who's almost my boyfriend.* That hadn't been what she'd said, of course, and to her mother's prying questions, she'd insisted that Jasper was simply a friend.

On the phone, she said, "Well, you could have dropped in for a family dinner before sending me skanky lingerie."

"You gotta get over that, Nin," Jasper said. "Have you ever heard of a kid named Cheng Zhou?"

"No."

"He's a prodigy. This eleven-year-old kid of Chinese immigrants who's racking up insane squash titles."

"Interesting—I mainly associate the sport with rich white people."

"See?" Jasper said. "I already know more about your hometown than you do."

Chapter 36

LIZ ENTERED HER father's study. "Do you think Mom has a shopping addiction?"

"Without question." From behind his desk, her father's tone was equanimous.

"I'm not kidding," Liz said.

"Nor am I."

"Do you think anything should be done about it?"

"Like what?"

"I don't know. Like having her see a shrink."

"Do you imagine your mother would consent to such a thing?"

Liz sighed and folded her arms. Years before Jane's embrace of yoga, had her father quietly achieved some Zen state that buffered him from the disturbances of daily life? Or was it just that he couldn't be bothered to exert himself, so bored was he by his family members' shortcomings?

Aunt Margo's voice became audible from the first floor. "Fred, what happened to the mirror of Mummy's that used to hang in the dining room?"

"Leave and shut the door behind you," Mr. Bennet hissed. "Quick. Tell her you don't know where I am."

Chapter 37

AT THE LAST minute, Jane had asked Chip if Cousin Willie could be included in his dinner party. Willie and Aunt Margo were returning to California the next morning, and Liz suspected that Jane felt guilty for hardly having spent time with him.

Chip lived on the eighth floor of a recently completed building in Oakley, not far from Skyline Chili; its décor, Liz thought upon entry, was so much like that of an upscale airport hotel—geometric-patterned carpet, inoffensive prints hanging from the wall, sleek and not particularly comfortable-looking sofas and chairs—that she wondered if he had rented it furnished.

"Come in, come in," Chip said as he greeted Liz by kissing her cheek, and there was something downright brother-in-lawish about the gesture. Then he heartily shook Willie's hand. "Thrilled you could make it," Chip said to Willie, and Liz liked Chip in this moment the most she ever had. "Can I get you drinks?" Chip said. "Caroline made some of her signature sangria, and don't be deceived by the sweetness. It's lethal."

"Some people say the same about Caroline herself," Liz murmured to Jane. Noting Jane's perturbed expression, Liz added, "Sorry."

In the dining room, a glass table was set for nine—two places shared the head, presumably reflecting the addition of Willie—and from a bar assembled atop a credenza, Caroline was handing drinks to Charlotte Lucas, as well as to Keith, the other new emergency room doctor Liz had met at the Lucases' barbecue, and to an attractive woman, also black, whom Liz guessed to be Keith's San Diego–dwelling fiancée. This supposition was confirmed with introductions, during which, through a closed sliding glass door that led to a small concrete balcony, Liz made unexpected and forceful eye contact with Fitzwilliam Darcy.

Darcy's back was to the street below, his elbows balanced on the balcony railing and a glass of sangria in his right hand. He looked, Liz thought, like a model in a local department store newspaper insert: handsome, yes, but moody in a rather preposterous and unnecessary way. Neither of them smiled, nor did either of them immediately look away. She realized he was on the balcony alone. What a strange man he was.

Something, though she couldn't have said whether it was a compassionate impulse to rescue a person standing by himself at a party or an urge with a more antagonistic origin, impelled her toward him; she opened the sliding door and stepped outside. The balcony's only furniture consisted of two slender, black wrought iron chairs.

"Are you enjoying the refreshing summer evening?" she asked. Though it was after seven o'clock, it was still thickly humid. Darcy blinked at her, and she added, "Believe it or not, there's something I've always liked about summer in the Midwest. I even like the sound of the cicadas."

Darcy took a sip of sangria. "Of course you do."

"Here's a nugget about Cincinnati for you," Liz said. "We produce a weirdly disproportionate number of champion squash players. Did you know that?"

"Yes," Darcy said. "I did."

"Really?" She looked at him quizzically.

"I played squash at boarding school."

Unable to restrain a smirk, Liz said, "Of course you did. What boarding school did you go to?"

"It's called Exeter."

With some pique, Liz said, "Yes, I've heard of it. And then where'd you go to college?"

After a pause, he said, "I went to college back in the Bay Area."

"Berkeley? Stanford."

"Stanford."

"I've never understood why people do that," Liz said. "Like, 'I went to college in New Haven,' or, 'I went to college in Boston.' Do you think if you reveal your elite education, I'll be so intimidated that I'll faint?"

Darcy shrugged. "It seems less pretentious."

"It's *more* pretentious! You know what? I can handle your Stanford degree. I went to Barnard. And you know what else? I've lived for the last twenty years in New York, and so has Jane."

"Yes, you mentioned that at Charlotte's," Darcy said calmly. "During the same conversation when we discussed *Mascara* sending you to Saudi Arabia, where you wore an *abaya* and a head scarf."

His recall was somewhat unsettling. "Oh," Liz said. "I guess we did talk about it."

"Perhaps you didn't realize I was paying attention."

"You know," Liz said, "what year did you graduate? I'll bet we're close in age."

"I graduated from college in ninety-seven."

"Then you were in the same class as a good friend of mine. Did you know Jasper Wick?"

"Yes." Darcy seemed unimpressed by the coincidence.

"You don't think that's noteworthy?" Liz said.

"Not especially."

"Really? That here we are in Cincinnati in 2013, and you went to college in California in the mid-nineties with basically my closest friend?"

"That's how socioeconomic stratification works. I'm sure you and I know other people in common, too, though personally, I find the name game tedious."

"Well," Liz said, "my apologies for boring you."

Darcy didn't say she hadn't bored him; he said nothing.

"Jasper's coming to Cincinnati soon to write an article about squash players," Liz said. "Maybe you two should have a reunion."

"I doubt my schedule will allow it."

"Do you not like him or something?"

"We weren't friends." Darcy's disinclination to elaborate, his apparent belief that he needn't explain or excuse himself, was enormously irritating. And his eschewal of convention was even more bothersome than it would have been if he were unaware of etiquette, which, obviously, he was not.

"Were you both in love with the same girl?" Liz asked.

"Caroline mentioned your fondness for interrogation."

"Some people think asking questions is friendly and polite. Plus, I'm a journalist."

"Maybe the reason you're a journalist is that it gives you a professional justification for being nosy." Darcy took another sip of sangria, and very briefly, before he licked it off, a trace of purple liquid clung to his lips. Then he said, "Excuse me," bowed his head, and walked inside, leaving Liz alone on the balcony.

Chapter 38

DINNER WAS TO be individual pizzas that the guests would prepare to their own liking, with an array of thoughtfully selected toppings: sun-dried tomatoes, fresh basil, artisanal salami. While Liz appreciated the casually festive menu, it soon became clear that Chip had, by the time of his guests' arrival, not yet made the dough, apparently unaware that it would need to sit for an hour after he'd mixed the ingredients. In addition, his oven could fit no more than four pizzas at a time. Thus, it was ten o'clock when they sat to eat, and half the pizzas were cool.

Liz ended up between Willie and Jane; somehow, on Jane's other side, sat Darcy rather than Chip. It was not clear to Liz that she had, in her earlier exchange with Darcy, embarrassed herself, but it also wasn't clear that she hadn't. Thus, she decided to abstain from initiating further conversation with him.

"You look very pretty tonight," Willie said to Liz at one point, and she was just tipsy enough—the sangria was indeed strong—to find the comment endearing rather than weird.

"Thank you, Cousin Willie," she said. "You look very handsome."

At the conclusion of the main course, Jane, Liz, and Charlotte cleared the plates, and when Charlotte and Liz were standing by the kitchen sink, Charlotte said, "Were you and Darcy flirting on the balcony?"

"Oh, God, no," Liz said. "The opposite. And I'm pretty sure he's dating Caroline."

"Really?" Charlotte said. "I didn't know that."

At the table, Caroline was on Darcy's other side and had spent most of the meal curled toward him in conversation like a poisonous weed. As a dessert of brownies and Graeter's ice cream appeared, Jane murmured to Liz, "Chip bought me a mountain bike." She didn't seem pleased.

Liz looked at Jane. "That was nice of him." While at the Tudor for dinner, Chip had mentioned that he'd already explored several area trails.

Jane shook her head. "I think it was expensive."

"Well, I'm sure he wouldn't have bought it if he couldn't afford it. Sorry, Jane, but he's into you."

"Maybe that's the problem," Jane said. "Maybe his expectations are too high."

Liz laughed. "You think if he gives you a fancy bike, you're obligated to put out? Because if I'm not mistaken, you've been doing that for weeks."

"It just seems soon for such an extravagant present."

"Will you relax and enjoy being courted?" Liz said. "It's not a diamond ring."

"Well, I definitely wouldn't accept *that*," Jane said. After a pause—on the other side of the table, Keith, his fiancée, and Chip were discussing a "hot" appendix Keith had seen the previous day—Jane added, "You think I should keep the bike?"

"Yes," Liz said. "Go riding with him. Have fun."

Willie, who had been in the bathroom, rejoined them then and gestured toward a pint of ice cream on the table. "The famous black raspberry chip, I take it?"

Liz passed the pint to him. "When in Cincinnati," she said.

In spite of her plan not to initiate conversation with Darcy again—certainly not on this evening, and possibly not ever—Chip and all eight of his guests ended up back out on the balcony, and Liz found herself standing just inches from the person she'd sought to avoid. For better or worse, she was someone who filled silences and smiled at strangers. Thus she said to Darcy, "How was your pizza?"

"That cicada sound you like so much," Darcy said. "It's the males contracting their abdominal muscles."

The sound was audible at that moment, beneath the simultaneous balcony conversations. She said, "Did you learn that in medical school?"

He dispensed one of his infrequent smiles. "I just looked it up on Wikipedia. It's a mating call."

"How romantic," Liz said.

"For what it's worth, I don't wish Jasper Wick ill," Darcy said. "Everyone should have the right to move on from their past."

Liz looked at him sharply. "What's that supposed to mean?"

"I assume you know he was kicked out of Stanford."

What? Liz thought. She said nothing, and Darcy, who appeared genuinely surprised, added, "Did you not know that?"

"It actually isn't something we've discussed."

In the shadowy summer night, they watched each other. "Didn't you say he's your best friend?" Darcy said.

"Why did he get kicked out?"

"I shouldn't speak for him," Darcy said. "But it's not as if it was a secret. It caused a campus-wide stir."

"Was it drugs?" Liz asked. "Or cheating on a test?"

Darcy's expression had grown impatient; if an unspoken détente had occurred between them, it was no longer in effect. "Those are questions for you to ask Jasper," he said.

Chapter 39

"LIZZY, I CAME to say goodbye," Cousin Willie said. "It's been great to reconnect with you."

Liz was at her desk, writing an email to Kathy de Bourgh's publicist, who had ignored Liz's entreaties since her failure to call during Kathy de Bourgh's ten-minute window of availability several days before. "You, too," Liz said to her cousin. Miraculously, Mary had agreed to drive Aunt Margo and Willie to the airport, and their imminent departure made Liz generous toward her cousin.

Willie stopped just a few feet from Liz's chair; his countenance was serious, and he seemed agitated.

"Is something wrong?" Liz asked.

Instead of speaking, he swiftly bent down and pressed his lips to hers. The surprise of the kiss was exacerbated when it became evident that he did not mean for it to be brief; he proceeded to open his mouth, and with the intrusion of his tongue, Liz pulled back her head in horror.

"Oh, Willie—" She was shocked but not entirely; she was appalled but also amused; she felt, already, cruel and distant, as if this were a moment she was comically describing to Jane or Jasper rather than currently experiencing. Still, she needed to focus in order to extricate herself with dignity or grace.

"I realize I'm not a prince in a fairy tale," Willie said. "But we get along. We're known quantities to each other. And you're almost forty."

"*Jane* is almost forty. I'm thirty-eight. But, Willie, my God, we're cousins."

"Not by blood. It isn't like our kids would face a stigma." These hypothetical children that she didn't want with any man, least of all Willie—she resented him for conjuring them up. "Look," Willie said. "You and I are practical people. I've never been able to see the point of roses and chocolates, and I'm guessing you haven't, either. But I'll be faithful to you. I'll respect your work, and I know you'll respect mine—I don't want a woman who gives me a hard time about my long hours. I think we owe it to ourselves to give a relationship a try."

"Just out of curiosity," Liz said, "did you come to Cincinnati with the idea of hitting on me?"

"You and I have always been compatible. Margo and your mom both think we make a great couple." Willie set his hand on her shoulder; immediately, she lifted it away, stood, and folded her arms.

"We're *not* a couple," she said. "And if you're under the impression that I want us to be one, you're mistaken." Softening her tone, she added, "When you meet some awesome woman in a year or two, you'll be so glad you didn't end up with me."

"How can you be certain I'll meet someone when you haven't?"

Ignoring the question's sting, Liz said, "There's a lot you don't know about my life."

Willie sighed; he seemed irritated rather than wounded. "Does the cousin thing bother you that much? Growing up, we hardly spent time together."

"Yes, it does bother me."

"I'm open to giving you a few days to think it over," Willie said. "I'll call you later this week, after I'm back in California."

"No, Willie. And I can tell you now that it's a waste of time to try this with any of my sisters."

Willie set his hands on his hips. "Do you know how much I'm worth?"

"You need to go." She would not give him a farewell hug; his obstinacy had become offensive.

He looked at her curiously. Perhaps, Liz thought, he was for the first time realizing that she had an identity, an agency, other than those he'd invented for her. At last, he said, "It's funny you think there's such a big difference between being thirty-eight and being forty."

Chapter 40

JANE, WHO WAS the first person with whom Liz wished to discuss what had just transpired, was at a yoga class. Jasper was the second person, except that Liz remained unsettled by the information she'd learned the previous night about his alleged expulsion from Stanford. And so, having barricaded herself in the third-floor bathroom because Cousin Willie was, at least for a few more minutes, still on the Tudor's premises, it was to Charlotte Lucas that Liz sent a text while sitting on the tile floor: *Cousin Willie just kissed me eek!!!!!!*

Less than a minute later, Charlotte's return text pinged: *Wait like KISSED kissed??*

Yes what's wrong w him? Or me?

That's VERY weird. Willie's cute in a nerd way but um, cousins?!? An additional text from Charlotte arrived a few seconds later: *Headed into meeting have a drink tonight?*

Yes!! Liz wrote back. *Zula? Somewhere else? U name time.*

Then she called Jasper.

"Should I stay at the Cincinnatian or 21c?" he asked. "Fiona's booking my ticket to Cincinnati right now."

"You know how my cousin Willie the Silicon Valley whiz kid is visiting?" Liz said. "He just came on to me!"

Jasper laughed. "Incest is best, huh? You can be like the Egyptian pharaohs."

"I'm not joking. He stuck his tongue in my mouth."

"Did you like it?"

Liz hadn't been planning to blurt out what she said next; somehow, it simply emerged. She said, "You didn't get expelled from Stanford, did you?"

There was a long silence, an immediately sour silence, and finally, Jasper said, "What the fuck? Where's *this* coming from?"

"I'm sorry." Until now, Liz really hadn't believed it; she'd imagined Darcy was confusing Jasper with someone else. "I shouldn't have—there's this guy here named Fitzwilliam Darcy, and I guess you guys—"

Before she could finish, Jasper said, "*Darcy* lives in Cincinnati? What the hell is he doing there?"

"There's a big stroke center where he's a surgeon."

Jasper laughed bitterly. "Of course he is. The dude has had a god complex since he was twenty years old. What a wanker." Rarely was Jasper this undilutedly aggrieved; though he was a frequent complainer, his complaints tended to contain some degree of levity, even charm. He said, "I'll bet I never told you that a lot of what went down at Stanford was Darcy's fault."

This was correct, in part because she and Jasper had never spoken of what had gone down at Stanford, period; Liz was sure of it. Indeed, she had always been under the impression that the school and his time there were a kind of emotional lodestar. In addition to his gold Stanford ring, he sometimes, on fall weekends, wore a much-faded red Stanford sweatshirt; he kept in his living room a framed photograph of him with several fraternity brothers, a row of handsome, athletic-looking men-children in ties and blue blazers, though it struck Liz for the first time that she had never actually met any of the other people in the photo. New York was crawling with her Barnard classmates, but it had seemed unsurprising that his college friends lived on the West Coast.

"I'll tell you the whole saga in Cincinnati," Jasper was saying. "It puts me in a bad fucking mood just thinking about it."

"You should stay at 21c," Liz said. "I've never been, but it's supposed to be very hip."

"I hope you're not friends with Darcy," Jasper said. "I wouldn't let that dude lick my shoe."

It was a relief to be united with rather than divided from Jasper. "Don't worry," Liz said. "I feel the same way."

Chapter 41

THE ONE SOLACE to the unpleasant direction Liz's conversation with Jasper had taken was that it had distracted her from her encounter with Willie. After she'd ended the call, however, that encounter combined with the confirmation of Jasper's Stanford expulsion created in her an even higher level of turmoil. Without asking permission and with no particular destination in mind, she left the house in her mother's car; a few minutes later, she was pulling into the parking lot of Rookwood Pavilion with the idea of getting a manicure and pedicure, and she emerged from the salon after more than an hour also missing four inches of hair, with the remainder layered in a way she was almost certain her colleagues at *Mascara* would be unimpressed by.

Lydia and Kitty sat at the kitchen table wearing workout clothes and eating cashews and organic beef jerky. When Liz entered the house through the back door, Lydia said, "Did you enter the Witness Protection Program to escape from the lust of Cousin Willie?"

"I like your haircut," Kitty said. "You couldn't have pulled that off a few years ago, but your cheekbones are showing more as you get older."

Liz looked at Lydia. "Who told you about Willie?"

"Mom is flipping her shit," Lydia said. "FYI."

As Lydia spoke, Mrs. Bennet's voice became audible from the other side of the closed swinging door between the kitchen and dining room. "Is that Lizzy? Is Lizzy back?"

The door swung into the kitchen, and Mrs. Bennet appeared, flushed and bustling. "Lizzy, what on earth were you thinking? Why, you probably hurt his feelings terribly."

"Mom, please don't tell me you think I should date Cousin Willie."

"He's smart, he's successful, and it's late in the game for you to be picky."

"He's my—"

"He's your step-cousin, Elizabeth. Don't try to tell me you're related, because you aren't."

"It's not legal in Ohio to marry your first cousin," Liz said. During her pedicure, she had checked this information on her phone, hoping to bolster her dismay with facts; she didn't mention that such a marriage actually was legal in California. "So let's say we fell madly in love, which would never happen. If we wanted to make it official, we'd need to hire a lawyer."

"That'd be awesome if you went to prison for marrying Willie," Lydia said. "I'd laugh so hard."

"Is someone else pursuing you?" Mrs. Bennet asked, and her accusatory tone made Liz immediately think of the red teddy. "Because if there is, I'd like to know who."

Chapter 42

"OKAY, DON'T KILL me," Charlotte said to Liz at Zula, "but I was thinking about it, and I can see Willie being a good boyfriend."

"Have you ever had a conversation with him?"

"I talked to him for a while at Chip's dinner party. He was nice."

"Putting aside the cousin stuff, which there's no way I can do, he's incredibly pompous. And even though he's smart, he isn't very interesting, because he's not interested in other people. In retrospect, I realize that the only questions he asked were when he was evaluating me as girlfriend material."

Charlotte looked carefully at Liz. "Are you sure there's no ST between you and Darcy?"

"I'm totally sure." ST, an abbreviation the two friends had been using since their high school days, stood for sexual tension. Liz leaned forward. "Although it turns out Jasper and Darcy went to college together and don't like each other." She thought of mentioning Jasper's expulsion from Stanford, but without yet knowing the circumstances, she was hesitant. Instead, she said, "Jasper's coming to Cincinnati to write an article about squash. Want to meet him when he's here?"

"Of course I do. Wait, did you just say he's coming to write an article?" Charlotte rolled her eyes. "Please."

Liz laughed. "And because I'm irresistible and he can't stay away from me," she said. "Also because of that."

"Is he really writing an article, or is that just the excuse he's giving people?"

Liz took a sip of wine. "It's both."

Chapter 43

RETURNING TO THE Tudor at ten o'clock, Liz saw in the driveway an unfamiliar navy blue SUV and therefore, knowing she wasn't the last one awake, left the kitchen light on. She'd passed through the dining room and reached the front hall when she heard from the den hushed but unmistakably flirtatious voices that halted just before Lydia appeared in the den's doorway. "Are you suffering from PTSD after Willie kissed you?" Lydia asked.

"Probably," Liz said.

"Come in here." Lydia's tone was uncharacteristically warm. "I'll introduce you to Ham."

He was, as Liz had discerned from his website, fit and handsome in a rather conventional way, though when he stood as she entered the room, she saw that he was significantly shorter than she'd have imagined. Ham extended his arm. "Hamilton Ryan. Or Ham, if you prefer, just like the lunch meat."

"Liz Bennet."

"One of the New York sisters, if I'm not mistaken," he said.

"Not bad," Liz said. "There are a lot of us to keep track of." She gestured to the television screen, which was frozen on the opening credits of a popular cable series about FBI agents, and asked, "Which season?"

"First season, first episode," Ham said, and Liz said, "Then you guys have a lot to look forward to. Or at least until season three, when it comes unraveled. Ham, you own a gym?"

"I do."

"Liz thinks CrossFit is 'culty.'" Lydia made air quotes.

Good-naturedly, Ham said, "It is."

"I never said that," Liz protested. "It just wasn't for me."

"Because she tried it once six years ago, for an article she was writing."

"I did it more than once," Liz said.

"That's right," Ham said. "You work for a magazine. That sounds like a cool job."

"Depending on the day," Liz said.

"Liz, Ham is old like you," Lydia said. "He was born in the seventies."

Liz and Ham made eye contact and laughed. "I thought you seemed kind of geriatric," Liz said. "What year?"

"Seventy-nine."

"Oh, you're a spring chicken. I was born in seventy-five. You're from Seattle, aren't you?" Ham nodded, and Liz realized that she had just mentioned information she'd learned from her online investigation rather than from Lydia. "So how'd you end up in Cincinnati?" Liz asked.

"The short version is, I followed an ex here."

"That's enough interviewing," Lydia said to Liz. "You can leave now." Both she and Ham were sitting on the couch by this point, their bodies nestled together.

"Wow, Lydia," Ham said. "No mincing words for you, huh?" But he set his arm around her as he spoke, and Liz had the bewildering thought that perhaps Lydia had met a nice, normal, down-to-earth guy. What she'd have in common with such a person was difficult to fathom.

"Lydia is known in the family for her subtlety," Liz said, and in reply, Lydia raised her middle finger. "Nice to meet you, Ham," Liz said.

Chapter 44

IT WAS AGAIN Liz's turn to drive her father to physical therapy, and no sooner had they pulled out of the driveway of the Tudor than Mr. Bennet said, "The reason your mother wants you to give Cousin Willie a chance is that she thinks his money will save us. Don't listen to her."

"Save you how?"

"It turns out my time in the hospital was frightfully expensive."

"How much?"

"It's hardly your concern, but since you asked, let's see. The surgery was a hundred and twenty-two thousand, not counting the anesthesia. It was three thousand a day to stay at that elegant five-star hotel known as Christ Hospital. Then there's a little something called a doctor fee, and that was another seven thousand. Shall I go on?"

"Isn't most of it covered by health insurance?"

"Your mother and I don't have health insurance. Neither of us has had a serious ailment before now."

"Oh my God, you don't have health insurance?" Liz was truly astonished, and it occurred to her to pull over, but then what? Nothing would change, *and* they'd be late for physical therapy.

"Let me be clear," Mr. Bennet said. "If Willie offered to pay all our bills this instant, it wouldn't be incentive enough for you to endure his company." Despite Liz's growing panic, Mr. Bennet sounded practically nonchalant.

"Lydia and Kitty and Mary must not have health insurance, either, right?" Liz said. "I always assumed they were on yours." Though, as she considered it, she realized that both Mary and Kitty were probably too old for this to be true. As she merged from Dana Avenue onto Interstate 71, Liz said, "Maybe you should take out a mortgage on the house."

"My dear, the house *is* mortgaged."

"I thought Pop-pop and Granny sold it to you for a dollar."

"That was thirty years ago, and there are seven of us in this family. I've indulged your sisters and mother for far too long."

"When did you get the mortgage?"

"Eight years? Ten?" Mr. Bennet invoked the number as neutrally as if he were trying to recall how much time had elapsed since he'd last visited Europe.

"Do you and Mom have an investment advisor?"

"*I'm* our investment advisor."

"What does Mr. Meyer do?"

"Our taxes, and none too adeptly, but we've put up with his incompetence for so long that it seems disloyal to go elsewhere."

"Then at least you've been paying taxes?"

"Through the nose."

"How much is your mortgage payment each month, and how much do you have in savings?"

"You need not worry about that, Lizzy."

"Yet Mom thinks I should bail out the family by, like, whoring myself to Willie? Just for the sake of argument, if I called him and said I'd changed my mind, then what? Would I say, 'And by the way, do you mind transferring a hundred thousand dollars, or four hundred thousand, or however much it is, into my parents' bank account?'"

"I'm not sure your mother's thought it through that clearly. It's the general proximity to Willie's money that appeals to her."

"Is this a plan Mom and Aunt Margo hatched together?"

"Margo doesn't know about our financial predicament, nor do any of your sisters, and you mustn't mention it to them. I'm in no mood for histrionics. But, yes, Margo does like the idea of you and Willie. My protests fell on deaf ears."

"So what will you do about the bills?"

"When you're as old as I am, you know that situations have a way of sorting themselves out."

"Wait, when does your Medicare kick in?"

"On my sixty-fifth birthday," Mr. Bennet said. "It's a shame I didn't think to schedule my myocardial infarction for six months from now, isn't it?"

Liz sighed. "I hate to even suggest this, but you could take out a second mortgage."

"We have one." Again, her father delivered the information matter-of-factly; when she looked across the front seat, he appeared less sheepish than she might have anticipated.

"Jesus, Dad," she said.

"I'd volunteer to have a hit man off me, but our life insurance policies have lapsed, so I'd be of no more use dead than I am living."

"There must be someone at the hospital we can talk to," Liz said. "There's no way you're the first person to be treated there without insurance." Her father said nothing, and Liz added, "Because correct me if I'm wrong, but aren't you basically headed for foreclosure on the house?"

"Let's not borrow problems."

"This is almost making me think I *should* date Willie."

With certainty, Mr. Bennet said, "Not even if we become paupers begging in the street."

Chapter 45

ACCORDING TO JANE, Caroline Bingley had at last discovered a sushi restaurant in Cincinnati that met her standards and had invited Jane to join her there for lunch. *Just us 2, none of your sisters,* Caroline had specified in a text to Jane that morning that Liz had seen while Jane was in the shower, and Liz had tried not to experience the doubly insulting sting of being excluded by a person she didn't care for.

"I wonder if she's sniffing you out as a sister-in-law," Liz said as she passed off her father's car keys to Jane. If Caroline was, Liz thought without true optimism, perhaps Chip could be the one to save the Bennet family from financial ruin. Although Liz was still rattled by the conversation with her father, and didn't realistically see how she could honor his wish to keep its contents private even from Jane, this didn't seem like the moment to repeat them.

"I'm pretty sure Caroline just wants to hang out," Jane said. The sisters' eyes met, and Jane whispered, "Lizzy, he told me last night that he loves me."

"Oh my God," Liz said. "I knew it! Did you say it back?"

Jane seemed bashful but very pleased. She nodded. Still whispering, she said, "It's crazy, right? We've only known each other a few weeks."

Beneath her pleasure for Jane, Liz felt a stab of envy; she and Jasper did not say it, after sixteen years. Once, more than a decade before, during an overwrought conversation following a few months of not speaking, Jasper had said to her, "I love you in my life," and she'd replied, "I love you in mine." It had been a triumphant and horrible moment, never replicated.

Trying to sound lighthearted, Liz said to Jane, "When you know, you know."

Chapter 46

TALIA GOLDFARB, THE executive editor of *Mascara*, had sent Liz an email that read, *Woman who dares?* A link led Liz to an article mentioning the first female Chinese astronaut—apparently known as a taikonaut—and below the link, Talia had written, *Also how was interview w/ K. de Bourgh?*

After sending yet another email to Kathy de Bourgh's publicist, Liz looked up the cost of various medical procedures and calculated that her father's hospital bill was roughly $240,000. The next tasks, she thought, were to find a mortgage statement; to determine how much her parents had in savings; and to make an appointment with someone in Christ Hospital's billing department. She was walking down the steps from her bedroom to the second floor to see if it might be an opportune time to root around in her father's study when her cellphone rang. She hurried back upstairs to where she'd left the phone on her desk, saw that the caller was Jane, and answered by asking, "How was lunch?"

"Oh, Lizzy." Jane's voice was tremulous. "I fainted at the restaurant, and they've brought me to the ER."

"Wait, are you okay? What happened."

There was a long silence. Then, so quietly Liz almost couldn't hear her, Jane said, "I'm pregnant."

Chapter 47

LIZ HAD FIRST been made aware of her older sister's exceptional goodness in 1982, when Jane was in second grade and Liz in first. May Fete, which was an annual celebration for the elementary school students at Seven Hills, was to occur on a Friday afternoon early in the month, and Liz was ecstatic with anticipation at the thought of the Cakewalk, Balloon Pop, and Goldfish Toss.

Jane fell ill with chicken pox a full week before the festivities. Due to the length of time necessary for symptoms to develop, it was impossible that she transmitted the virus to Liz, but *someone* did, and on the day of May Fete itself, Liz was febrile and profoundly itchy. Most of Jane's lesions had healed by then, and since she was back in school, there was no medical reason for her to skip the event. That she did so was entirely voluntary, an act of solidarity that even at the time Liz regarded with wonder. Were the situation reversed, Liz would without question have attended May Fete. But Jane was calmly insistent, saying to their befuddled mother, "If Lizzy is staying home, I am, too." She added, "Next year, we can go together."

That evening, Jane and Liz ate mugs of peppermint ice cream sitting side by side in Liz's bed while Liz wore white cotton gloves meant to discourage scratching; then Jane read aloud from *Frog and Toad Together*, and they went to sleep at eight o'clock. Despite the frenzy of excitement May Fete continued to provoke in Liz for several more years, when she recalled it in adulthood, what she remembered more than any bounce house she'd jumped inside or trinket she'd acquired was the kindness of her sister.

Chapter 48

REVELATORY AS IT was, Jane's news had not been shared in a way that invited further questioning. She merely told Liz she had passed out for just a minute or two and, although she was sure that she was fine, the doctors wanted to run a few tests before releasing her. She was at Christ Hospital, she said, and had seen Chip briefly, before he got summoned to another patient, but he was not the one treating her. Caroline was still with her. And Liz mustn't tell anyone else in the family.

"I'll be there as fast as I can," Liz said.

It was only upon hanging up that Liz realized she was both alone in the house and without a car: Jane had taken their father's Cadillac to meet Caroline, their parents were having lunch at the country club, and their sisters were God knew where. Liz considered texting Mary, Kitty, or Lydia but decided against it because of their unreliability and indiscretion. She next considered taking a bus, but she was entirely unfamiliar with the routes, and finally, she considered calling a taxi, which was something she had never done in Cincinnati and therefore was uncertain could be accomplished with efficiency. Then, decisively, she changed into running shorts, a sports bra, and a tank top. She laced up her turquoise-and-orange sneakers, found her sunglasses, grabbed a baseball cap from Kitty's room, chugged a glass of water as she stood by the kitchen sink, and hurried outside. It was just after one o'clock and ninety-six degrees; Christ Hospital was four and a half miles away, according to the directions on her phone, so she estimated it should take her thirty-five minutes to get there.

Unlike when she ran with Jane, Liz took her phone; she stuck it between her underwear and hip, but even before she reached the street, it fell onto the driveway. So she clutched it, heading west on Grandin Road, which was the same route she took each morning with Jane; she even passed the country club, where, presumably, her parents were midway through their pseudo-healthy Caesar salads. How much, Liz wondered for the first time, were the country club's annual fees?

At Madison Road, instead of turning right, she made a left toward O'Bryonville, passing the antiques stores and clothing boutiques. The air was thick, and the sun felt aggressive, possibly malevolent.

So Jane was pregnant; Jane was *pregnant.* The most immediate question, of course, was whether this development was attributable to the sperm donor or Chip. If it was the sperm donor, Liz thought, Jane would have conceived eight weeks earlier, in which case wouldn't she have known? Then Liz recalled Jane's hesitation about Chip, in spite of her obvious attraction to him—*had* she known? And her comments about moving to Cincinnati—those, too, could have been hints at her condition, though it was equally likely she'd want to stay in town in order to raise a child with Chip or, if she was a single mother, to avoid the expense and hassle of New York. Either way, between Chip and an anonymous donor, Liz couldn't say which was preferable. Complications were sure to arise from both.

Passing the Gothic church of Saint Francis de Sales, where Liz went south on Woodburn Avenue, she was sweating more than she ever had in her entire life. The potential irony of fainting on the way to see Jane after Jane had fainted didn't escape Liz; and yet, despite the heat and the fatigue in her muscles from already having run that morning, adrenaline kept her focused. A baby—after all this time, Jane was to be the mother of a baby!

East McMillan, which was the widest and busiest thoroughfare on Liz's run thus far—there were few pedestrians and many cars— shimmered in the sun. Kitty's baseball cap was royal blue, with a University of Kentucky logo, though UK was a school no one in their family had attended, and Liz wondered if the cap was making her head warmer. Removing it didn't seem to help matters, however, and on the Reading Road overpass, she donned it again. She considered slowing to a walk, but Auburn Avenue wasn't far off, and once she reached it, she was practically there.

By the time the enormous brick edifice of Christ Hospital came into view, Liz felt that time had collapsed and she had been running for several years through a stasis of heat. Behind her sunglasses, perspiration fell into her eyes, making it difficult to see. Glancing at the map on her phone, she followed Auburn Avenue to Mason Street and curved toward Eleanor Place and the entrance of the emergency room. Just outside its automatic door, beneath the porte cochere, she stopped and bent, setting her hands on her knees, to catch her breath.

"Liz?" said a male voice, and Liz stood up straight. Sweat was dripping from all the usual places, her temples and the back of her neck and her armpits, but also from a range of body parts less commonly associated with thermoregulation, including her kneecaps. She removed her sunglasses to wipe her eyes with the heels of her hands, and a droplet of sweat flew through the air and landed on the forearm of Fitzwilliam Darcy's white coat; she saw it happen, and she was certain that he did, too. In a tone that fell somewhere between confusion and disapproval, he said, "What are you doing here?"

Only at this moment did her choice to run to the hospital appear strange as opposed to merely uncomfortable. It seemed difficult to avoid the truth, though surely the entire truth wasn't necessary. Still breathing unevenly, she said, "Jane fainted, and they brought her to the ER. But I think she's fine. What are *you* doing here?"

"Seeing a patient. Does Jane have a history of syncope?"

"If that's the same as fainting, then no."

"It *is* a very hot day. And not the time most people would choose to go running."

"Only mad dogs and Englishmen, I hear," Liz said. "But there were no cars at our house. Do I go through there?" She gestured toward the automatic door.

"I'll go with you," Darcy said, and as they walked inside, he added "Jane's thirty-nine?"

"Yes." In spite of the other subjects preoccupying her, Liz couldn't help noting that her sister's age must have been a topic of discussion between Chip and Darcy.

"If she's generally in good health, I suspect it's heat syncope," Darcy said. They paused at a reception desk, and Darcy said, "I'm Dr. Fitzwilliam Darcy, and I need to find a patient named Jane Bennet."

The receptionist typed briefly on her keyboard before saying, "Room 108." Neither Liz nor Darcy spoke as they continued walking. At a set of double doors, Darcy held a badge on a lanyard around his neck up to a sensor, and the doors opened toward them. They were in a wide hall and had no sooner rounded a corner than they saw Caroline Bingley, who wore such a peculiar expression—it seemed to be a combination of mirth and fury, but was that even possible?—that Liz had the hysterical thought that Jane might have died. "Is she okay?" Liz asked with alarm.

Caroline's eyes narrowed. Glaring, she said, "Congratulations, Auntie Liz."

Chapter 49

WHEN LIZ PULLED back the curtain at the entrance to Jane's small room, she saw her sister in a bed whose mattress was set at a semi-reclined angle. Jane wore a hospital gown (Liz hadn't expected the change of clothes, which somehow made Jane's status as a patient official), and a tube inserted into a vein at her left inner elbow delivered clear liquid. Quietly, almost silently, Jane was crying. The sisters' eyes met, and Jane brought a tissue to her nose. "Oh, Lizzy," she said. "What have I done?"

Liz climbed onto the bed beside Jane and set an arm around her. "I stink," Liz said. "Just to warn you."

Briefly, Jane appeared to forget her distress. "Did you go to Cross-Fit?"

"I ran here," Liz said. "There were no cars at home. Are you okay?"

Jane's lower lip quivered.

"Not to put you on the spot, but is it Chip's or from IUI?"

A few seconds passed, then Jane shook her head, unable to speak.

After another interval of silence followed by an enormous sniff, Jane said, "Everything was so chaotic with Dad's surgery. I kept meaning to buy a test, to see if the last round at the clinic had worked. Then I met Chip, and we were having such a good time that suddenly it seemed like maybe it'd be better if I wasn't pregnant."

"So it's not Chip's?" Liz said.

"They're going to do an ultrasound to figure out how far along I am. Anything is possible, I guess, but we've been using condoms."

"Does he know you're pregnant?"

Jane sighed. "At the restaurant, the EMT asked if I could be, and I said maybe, but I didn't mention the donor stuff. Of course, Caroline heard, and she told Chip before I had a chance. I think she called him from her car as I was riding in the ambulance. So he found me, and he was very sweet and worried. I wasn't even sure I *was* pregnant at that point because they hadn't done the blood test. But I felt like I had to explain to him about the IUI, and he was a little shocked, and then he got called away for a stab wound before we could finish the conversation. That was an hour ago."

"Wow," Liz said.

Jane wiped her nose with the back of her hand, and Liz stood to pluck a tissue from a box on the nearby counter. "At least I wasn't just stabbed," Jane said. "It could be worse."

"True," Liz said. "But you're still allowed to be upset."

"It was so strange at the restaurant, Lizzy. I thought—I never think this—I thought, 'Maybe instead of sushi, I'll order teriyaki.' Raw fish seemed disgusting. But Caroline suggested splitting a few rolls, and I said okay. When the food came, I looked at it and just the smell—I was sure I would throw up. Instead, the next thing I knew, I was lying on the floor with a bunch of waiters staring at me."

After procuring the tissue, Liz had perched at the foot of Jane's bed. "So—" Liz hesitated. "Do you *want* to be pregnant?"

"I did." Jane's voice quavered. "Before meeting Chip, I wanted it a lot."

Chapter 50

INCLUDING THE TIME since Jane's most recent period, the technician who completed the ultrasound placed the pregnancy at between nine and ten weeks; because Jane knew to the hour when the final round of insemination she'd undergone prior to leaving New York had occurred, she could confirm the estimate. "So a late February due date," Liz said. "A snow baby."

She didn't mention Chip's name, and neither did Jane. Notably, Chip hadn't reappeared in Jane's hospital room during Liz's time there, nor had Caroline or Darcy; Liz had no recollection of bidding farewell to either of them after seeing Caroline in the hall.

Two hours had passed since Liz's arrival at the hospital, and Jane's emergency room doctor had just stopped in for a final consultation, inquiring as to whether Jane had an ob-gyn and encouraging her to take prenatal vitamins; Jane informed the doctor that she had been taking them daily for more than ten months. After she was discharged as a patient, it occurred to her and Liz simultaneously that they were without a car.

"Let's start with Mary," Liz said. "She's likelier than Lydia or Kitty to keep her mouth shut."

"We aren't calling any of them." Jane's voice brooked no argument. "I'm not ready for them to know."

After a few seconds' hesitation, Liz asked, "Could Chip give us a ride?"

"He doesn't get off until seven," Jane said. "And then he has to do charts." She was changing from her hospital gown into her clothes as she added, "We'll take a taxi back to the sushi restaurant and get Dad's car. And don't say a word to anyone. Seriously, Lizzy—not even to Dad, in one of those heart-to-hearts you two like to have. Do you swear?"

"Do you have health insurance?" Liz asked.

Jane nodded. "Of course. Do you swear?"

On the one hand, Liz was enormously relieved; on the other hand, there was still a secret bankruptcy *and* a secret pregnancy to contend with. How exactly had her family members found themselves in such circumstances? "My lips are sealed," she said.

Chapter 51

"CHIP'S PARENTS HAVE a summer house in Maine," Mrs. Bennet said as Liz chopped cauliflower on a cutting board by the kitchen sink. "In Boothbay Harbor, which is supposed to be stunning. Suzy Hickman's sister and brother-in-law go there, and Suzy says the views are divine."

"If you want to help, you can wash the cilantro," Liz said, and Mrs. Bennet didn't move from the spot where she stood.

"Obviously, a wedding is usually held where the woman grew up," she continued, "but if Maine is meaningful to Chip, I'm sure one of you other girls will get married at Knox Church."

"Has anything specific led you to believe that Chip and Jane are planning their wedding?" Liz asked. "Because that's not my impression."

Mrs. Bennet appeared offended. "Well, they're head over heels!"

"I think they like each other," Liz said, "but it's still early."

"I prefer when a man officiates," Mrs. Bennet said. "It's more natural. A lady did Allie Carnes's wedding, and she had the oddest little squeaky voice."

Liz had finished chopping the second of two cauliflowers; she lifted the cutting board and dumped its contents into a roasting pan. "I noticed some boxes in Jane's old room that haven't been opened," she said. "What's in them?"

"Those are presents I'm saving for Christmas."

It was tempting, but surely ill-advised, to ask which future recipient of the monogrammed royal blue bath towels happened to share Mrs. Bennet's initials.

"I've started thinking about what will happen when you and Dad sell this house," Liz said. "I wonder if you and I should do some decluttering."

"We wouldn't dream of selling the house." Mrs. Bennet laughed. "We'll be carried from here feet-first."

Liz opened the refrigerator, pulled out a bag of cilantro, and turned on the faucet. Avoiding eye contact, she said, "You realize shopping can be an addiction just like alcohol, right? I don't know if you've ever thought of talking to someone."

"What a preposterous thing to say! Do I appreciate a bargain? I certainly do."

"What if I take some stuff over to the Resale Shop?" Liz said. "Just dishes we never use, or maybe the furniture in the basement from Granny. You don't have to be involved."

"Granny's furniture is very valuable. Do you know what you ought to be doing, instead of meddling?"

"This is just a guess, but dating my cousin?"

"I'd like to see you do better than Willie."

Since Liz's adolescence, when viewing television commercials that celebrated the ostensibly unconditional love of mothers for their children, or on spotting merchandise in stores that honored this unique bond with poems or effusive declarations—picture frames, magnets, oven mitts—she had felt like a foreign exchange student observing the customs of another country. But if Liz wasn't close to her mother, neither was she consumed with the maternal resentment she had observed in some friends. Her mother had been adequate—often annoying, far from abusive.

Liz turned off the faucet and shook the water from the cilantro. With as little emotion as possible, she said, "As a reminder, not everyone gets married, and bringing it up all the time won't increase the chances for any of us. I'm definitely not interested in Willie."

Mrs. Bennet's tone was thoughtful rather than intentionally cruel. She said, "You have no idea how lucky you are that someone like him would settle for you."

Chapter 52

JANE USUALLY LEFT for Chip's apartment after dinner, but that night she joined Liz, Kitty, and their mother to watch television in the den. When Jane entered the room, Mrs. Bennet looked up from the catalog she was paging through and said, "Is Chip working tonight, honey?"

Jane nodded, and even if Liz hadn't known that Chip's shift finished at seven, she'd have been able to tell that her sister was lying.

Several minutes later, when Kitty and Mrs. Bennet were discussing whether the throat of the prostitute on the legal drama was likelier to have been slit by her ex-husband or her john, Liz murmured to Jane, "Any word from him?"

Somberly, and also quietly, Jane said, "He just called."

"And?"

"We're having dinner the day after tomorrow."

This plan did not sound promising to Liz—the formality of it, the delay. She said, "Did you tell him how far along you are?"

Jane nodded.

So he was aware the baby wasn't his, Liz thought. And he wasn't planning to talk about it with Jane for forty-eight hours.

Jane stayed in the den for no more than twenty minutes and went up to bed before the show's conclusion; apparently, she was unmotivated to find out that the crime had, as Mrs. Bennet had suspected, been committed by the prostitute's ex-husband.

Chapter 53

IN THE MORNING, when Liz's phone alarm sounded, Jane said with what Liz suspected was feigned bleariness, "I'm going to skip the run today." Though for all Liz knew, her sister was in the grip of morning sickness; furthermore, Liz had no idea how far into pregnancy vigorous exercise was recommended.

After using the bathroom and changing, Liz paused in the door of her childhood bedroom and looked at her sister. The curtains still were closed, but sunrise had occurred, and the room was more light than dark. Liz thought of asking if Jane needed anything, but Jane's breathing was as deep and steady as if she really were asleep again.

Chapter 54

LIZ FOUND Mr. Bennet in his study. With his computer screen obscured, as usual, from her view, it struck Liz that she had always given her father the benefit of the doubt, assuming him when in his study to be immersed in matters that were tedious but necessary, his attention to the welfare of the family steadfast and somehow masculine.

She closed the door behind herself and said, "You need to sell the house. I saw online that the Ellebrechts sold theirs for $1.8 million in March. Do you know if they'd renovated their kitchen?"

Mr. Bennet looked at her with amusement. "You've been busy."

"Let's say you get $1.2 million for this house, which is obviously a very rough guess. You pay off your hospital bills, buy a condo in the three hundred thousand range—I think you can get two to three bedrooms for that in Hyde Park—and you draw up a budget for living expenses and stick to it. Oh, and whatever you think of Obama and his healthcare, you and Mom both need to get insurance through open enrollment, which should start October first."

"Your mother wouldn't stand for me selling this house."

"I don't see how you have a choice. Do you own your cars or lease them?"

"And what will become of your wastrel sisters?"

"You're the one who keeps saying they need to leave the nest, and you're right. There's no reason for them not to have jobs. How much are the country club's annual fees?"

"Your mother would rather drink strychnine than not belong to the Cincinnati Country Club." Mr. Bennet's expression grew mischievous. "Shall we offer her some?"

"Are there other major expenses I'm not thinking of?" Liz asked. "Mom's jewelry must be worth something, right? And there's that portrait in the front hall of whoever it is."

Seeming impressed, Mr. Bennet said, "My dear, you're positively cold-blooded."

"I bet you guys will feel relieved to live somewhere smaller, without so much stuff. Do you prefer a real estate agent you already know or someone outside your social circle?"

"If your mother and I lived somewhere smaller, we might have to actually see each other."

"The bills you've gotten from the hospital," Liz said. "Have you done anything about them? Have you called anyone?"

For a few seconds, they watched each other silently.

"Give them to me, and I'll make an appointment and go in with you," Liz said. "The situation won't get better by ignoring it."

Chapter 55

JANE'S CONVERSATION WITH Chip had not gone well. Although he hadn't explicitly accused her of dishonesty, he'd questioned her assertion that she was pregnant via donor insemination rather than through an encounter in New York of the more traditional kind, which was almost the same thing. It wasn't, Jane told Liz, that he showed a heretofore concealed cruelty; he still seemed like himself, just no longer besotted. "I'm not an idiot," he'd said. "It's not like I thought you were a virgin before we met."

When Jane had insisted that there was absolutely no chance her pregnancy had resulted from anything other than the IUI procedure, he'd said, "Then I don't understand why you never told me you were trying to have a baby on your own. How could you keep such a huge secret?" And this question, Jane had to concede, was a fair one.

The exchange had taken place at a restaurant downtown, where Jane had driven herself, which, she said to Liz, had been an intimation about the way things would go: Rather than picking her up, Chip had met her in public to break up with her.

"And did he?" Liz asked.

"Not in so many words," Jane said. "But he claimed it wasn't a good night for me to come over because he and Caroline needed to talk about some business stuff. And when we said goodbye, he kissed me on the forehead." Liz could tell that her sister was fighting tears. "He said the news was a lot to digest, and he'd probably need a few days. But, Lizzy, I'm sure it's over, and I don't blame him."

As Jane spoke, it was just after nine P.M., and the two sisters were standing in the Tudor's basement. Instead of watching television in the den, Liz had decided to investigate this subterranean wilderness to which she normally did not descend except to do laundry or retrieve food from an extra refrigerator; the room containing these appliances was reasonably clear, but three additional rooms were nearly impenetrable storage units for all manner of familial detritus. It was in the largest of the three overstuffed rooms that Jane had found her.

"I should have told him from the beginning," Jane said. "But I guess I was waiting for things to not work out or else for him to fall for me so completely that he wouldn't care I was knocked up."

"He's a good guy," Liz said. "I bet he'll realize this isn't insurmountable."

"Maybe." Jane pointed to a witch's hat encircled by a dusty orange velvet ribbon. "Isn't that from my fourth-grade Halloween costume?"

"And check this out." Liz lifted the hat to reveal a high, narrow marble table with curved legs ending in deer hooves that had once occupied their maternal grandmother's living room. "Remember how this used to scare Mary?"

"Why are you down here?" Jane asked.

"Oh, you know," Liz said. "Memory lane."

Chapter 56

LIZ STAYED IN the basement until past midnight, though as fatigue overtook her, she was chagrined to look around and realize that her efforts had, if anything, made the room look worse. She'd been trying to sort items into broad categories—dishware, sports equipment, holiday decorations—and she'd partially succeeded, while also eliminating already-scarce floor space. Plus, she'd encountered at least a dozen spiders, not all of them dead. She'd deal with the mess later, she thought, and she flicked off three light switches and climbed the steps to the kitchen. She didn't, until it was too late, realize that Lydia and Ham Ryan were kissing avidly by the stove. They noticed her at the same time she noticed them, and they sprang apart, Lydia saying in an accusatory tone, "What the hell?"

"Sorry," Liz said. "I was in the basement."

"Hi, Liz," Ham said.

Lydia scowled. "Doing what?"

Oh, to be twenty-three, Liz thought, to make out in that way that left your lips swollen and your skin blotchy. Not that Lydia was by any means an innocent, but still—something about her kissing her new boyfriend in their parents' kitchen while everyone else in the house was asleep made Liz wistful.

"I was trying to sort through some junk, and now I'm going up to bed," Liz said. "Hi, Ham."

"I read some of your articles online," Ham said. "The one about Saudi Arabia was fascinating."

"You don't need to butter her up," Lydia said.

Ham laughed. "You think because you don't care what happens in the Middle East, no one else should?" Looking at Liz, he said, "How long were you over there?"

"Ten days," Liz said. "And thank you."

"Don't bother hitting on her," Lydia said. "She has some married boyfriend she thinks none of us know about."

Ham grinned at Liz—his good nature almost made Lydia's alarming statement seem like no big deal—and then he leaned in and kissed Lydia's nose. He said, "At the risk of encouraging you, your jealousy is kind of cute."

Chapter 57

POKING AROUND ON websites for local real estate agencies, Liz discovered that a former Seven Hills classmate named Shane Williams was, by all appearances, successfully selling houses to and for Cincinnatians, among them several professional athletes; Bengals and Reds players both offered written testimonies of Shane's aptitude. While Hyde Park didn't seem to be the main area where Shane conducted business, he had nevertheless sold a handful of properties within a few miles of the Tudor. Liz remembered Shane fondly; he had been warm and outgoing not only in high school but also the three or four times they'd crossed paths in their twenties, when their classmates had gathered at bars the night before Thanksgiving.

However, in spite of Shane's professional credentials and personal charm, Liz wasn't certain she should contact him. The reason she wasn't certain was that Shane was black and her mother was racist. As with her anti-Semitism, Mrs. Bennet's racism was of the conversational, innuendo-laden variety. She would never be so ignorant as to announce that black people were less intelligent or moral than their white counterparts, but without compunction she'd tell Liz not to shop at the Kroger in Walnut Hills because it was "dirty," and once at Christmas when Liz had suggested giving Mervetta a cashmere sweater, Mrs. Bennet had said, "For heaven's sake, Lizzy, Mervetta wouldn't appreciate cashmere."

Liz was pretty sure a black adult had never visited her parents' house in a social capacity. Over the years, black men had fixed the Bennets' balking dishwasher and overburdened air-conditioning pumps, had removed their garbage and repaved their driveway; and for more than a decade, Mervetta had arrived at the Tudor every other Friday at eight A.M. to vacuum their carpets and scrub their toilets. But it was only ever black girls, Seven Hills classmates, who, in attending birthday parties and sleepovers, had been invited into the Tudor simply to enjoy themselves. And whether or not Liz contacted Shane wouldn't change this fact; he, too, would be an employee.

Yet surely hiring the kind of white, female, middle-aged real estate agent her parents might run into at the country club was a bad idea, and likely to spread gossip about the financial situation in which the Bennets had found themselves. There was, of course, such an abundance of white, female, middle-aged real estate agents that Liz certainly could find one who didn't belong to the country club and whom her parents didn't know. But she liked the idea of working with someone familiar.

Was it delusional to hope that her mother's potential discomfort about Shane's race would be eclipsed by her far greater discomfort about needing to move? *Be the change you wish to see in the world,* Liz thought, and she emailed her former classmate.

Chapter 58

FOR SEVERAL MORE mornings, Jane didn't run with Liz, and on the fourth day, when Liz came back upstairs after eating breakfast, Jane still lay in bed. Liz crossed through the bedroom to take a shower and, after she emerged from the bathroom, dressed quietly. When Jane spoke, however, it sounded as if she had been awake for some time. She said, "Will you hate me if I go back to New York early?"

Liz turned around. "Of course not. You probably need to see your obstetrician, right?"

"They don't actually test much before the end of the first trimester, although they might because of my age."

"You're not thinking—" Liz paused and rephrased the question. "Are you considering, ah, terminating?"

"I keep waiting for a text from Chip," Jane said. "I have this idea he'll invite me to come over."

"I think you'll hear from him," Liz said, though as the days had passed, her optimism about what more he'd have to say had diminished.

"I really, really wanted a baby," Jane said. "It was what I wanted most in the world. And now—" She didn't finish.

Liz said, "But you know Chip, and you don't know the baby yet. I'm sure we'll find your baby totally delightful, but it's hard for an abstract idea to compete with someone you've been hanging out with." Lifting a beaded bracelet from the top of the bureau, Liz added, "I keep meaning to tell you I found a website for this organization called Alone But Together. It's for women who choose to have kids on their own."

Jane smiled sadly. "I've been a paid member for two years. You haven't said anything to Mom, have you?"

"God, no." That Jane wouldn't be able to hide her secret indefinitely was a fact that Liz assumed she didn't need to convey. And Jane's wish to leave Cincinnati was wholly understandable to Liz, even if the idea of staying behind without Jane was disheartening. As Liz slid the bracelet over her left hand, she thought of the year Jane had skipped May Fete because she, Liz, had chicken pox. Liz meant it when she said, "Whatever you want to do, you have my support."

Chapter 59

ONCE AGAIN, THE scent of nail polish led Liz to Kitty; this time, Kitty was creating on her fingers an intricate tiger pattern of black stripes over a reddish-orange background.

"Lydia and Ham seem kind of serious," Liz said. "Are they?"

As she dipped the brush back into the bottle of black polish, Kitty said, "Ask her."

"Will you suggest that she invite him to a family dinner? I think Jane and Chip might be done, and meeting Ham could soften the blow for Mom."

Still focused on her fingers, Kitty said, "If you want to make Mom happy, marry Willie."

"Ham seems like a good guy, but if I tell Lydia to invite him, she'll refuse just to spite me."

Kitty glanced up. "Do you know Ham?"

"I've talked to him a few times. Why?"

"There are things about him that might surprise you." The smug and coy expression on Kitty's face—Liz didn't care for it.

Nevertheless, she said, "Like what?"

Kitty shrugged. "Just things."

"Is he actually a jerk?"

"No." Really, Kitty looked irritatingly pleased with herself. Partly to change the subject and partly because it was true, Liz gestured at Kitty's nails and said, "Have you ever considered doing that professionally? You're really good at it."

Kitty's expression turned sour. "You're so condescending."

"Kitty, I work in an industry where the best makeup artists and stylists are treated like rock stars. Not that those kinds of careers are the norm, but I bet a regular person can make a decent salary." Or a regular person could make a salary that compared favorably, Liz thought, to no income at all.

Kitty was watching Liz with doubt. "Why did Chip and Jane break up?"

"I'm not sure if they want the same things."

"He dumped her?"

"They're still not officially finished, but I think it's mutual." Briefly, Liz was tempted to ask if what Lydia had declared several nights prior in the kitchen was true—that everyone in the family knew about Jasper. He was due to arrive in Cincinnati the following week, and as the date approached, Liz had become increasingly conscious of the oddness of hiding his visit from her family. Yet surely the oddness of his entering the Tudor, which she had no plans for, would be even greater. At least he'd meet Charlotte; for the second of Jasper's two nights in town, Liz had made a dinner reservation at Boca, for which Jane also would join them, assuming she was still around.

In any case, asking Kitty about Jasper would eliminate all doubt, and whether because of age difference, geography, or temperament, Liz had never spoken openly to her younger sisters. In certain ways, they knew one another well, they recognized one another's habits and preferences; yet years could pass without a conversation of real substance occurring between them.

"Chip once had a patient who'd stuck a lime up his butt," Kitty said. "Did you know that?"

"I can only imagine what questions you asked to elicit that information."

Kitty grinned. "Maybe Chip's proud that he got it out."

Chapter 60

AS LIZ AND Mr. Bennet left the rehabilitation center after his physical therapy appointment, her phone buzzed with a confusing and unpunctuated text from Jane: *Chip gone*

Calling Jane in front of their father was impossible; then, as they headed south on 71, Mr. Bennet said, "Stop by the fish market, will you? I'd like some oysters."

She knew he meant the smoked kind, and Liz tried to remember whether smoked oysters were healthy. She said, "A Seven Hills classmate of mine is a real estate agent now, and he can come over and discreetly look at the house. What do you think?"

"Supposing I say no—in that case, what time will this fellow show up?"

If the situation were not so dire, Liz might have felt abashed. She said, "He's free tomorrow at the same time Mom has a Women's League meeting."

"Of course he is."

In the fish market parking lot, Liz said, "Are you okay going in alone?"

"For heaven's sake," Mr. Bennet said. "I'm not a boy in short pants."

"I didn't know if you'd need help carrying stuff."

As Liz watched him walk in the rear entrance of the store, she called Jane and said, "Gone where?"

"To Los Angeles." Jane sounded more confused than upset. "Remember when I told you *Eligible* is doing a reunion show? He decided to be on it after all."

"Did the hospital let him take a leave?" Liz asked.

"I don't know. He only sent a text."

An unpleasant recognition was spreading within Liz that Jane's worst fears about Chip were wholly justified. "What a flake," Liz said. "I'm sorry, but who bails on their job—their job as an ER doctor—after less than three months? Will you forward me the text?"

"Hang on."

A few seconds later, the gray bubble appeared on the screen of Liz's phone: *Hi want to let u know I'm headed to LA today 4 eligible fan favorites reunion show. Been wondering if dr right fit. Great getting to know u, u r really special person.*

Raising the phone back to her ear, Liz said, "Is this a joke?"

"He must have been in a hurry," Jane said.

"I don't care if his hair was on fire. This is appalling."

"I want to feel compassion for him." Jane's voice was firmer. "I don't like being angry."

"Jane, even a yogi can be pissed when her boyfriend turns out to lack basic communication skills." Liz could see their father emerge from the store carrying a plastic bag.

"I know I can," Jane said. "I just don't want to."

"Well, you're definitely better off without him." How rapidly Liz's once-favorable opinion was curdling, what unflattering details, previously ignored, could be marshaled as evidence for a contrary view: Chip had been nice enough, yes, but clearly narcissistic and immature; he had never been serious about medicine or her sister. "Dad and I will be home in five minutes," Liz said. "Want to go to Graeter's and drown our sorrows in mocha chip ice cream?"

As Mr. Bennet opened the passenger-side door, Jane said, "I hope you know how much I appreciate your support, Lizzy. But now I think it really is time for me to leave Cincinnati."

Chapter 61

LIZ HAD SCHEDULED Shane Williams's visit to the Tudor for one o'clock; meanwhile, her father had, albeit without good humor, agreed to ask Mary to drive him to the Mercantile Library; and under the guise of sisterly thoughtfulness, Liz had scheduled a prenatal massage for Jane. Though Lydia and Kitty were unaccounted for, they were the least likely to be home in the middle of the day.

Shane remained much as Liz remembered him: fit, preppy, cheerful, and loquacious. After she opened the front door of the Tudor and he leaned in to hug her, she stole a glance at his ring finger and noted that it was bare. In light of Shane's profession, there was a decent chance he was gay. Yes, he'd been the prom date of her friend Rachel in 1993, but back then, even at progressive Seven Hills, students hadn't exactly been bursting out of the closet.

"If anyone comes home, we can pretend we're just catching up," Liz said. "I know I mentioned this on the phone, but my dad hasn't told my mom they need to move." Such candor about her family's financial predicament would, Liz knew, particularly displease her mother, but Liz didn't see how she had the luxury of discretion.

"It's a beautiful house," Shane said.

As Liz led him into the living room, she said, "How have the last twenty years treated you?"

Shane laughed. "Can't complain." He gestured toward the large water stain on the wall. "What's up with that?"

"It looks awful, doesn't it? I keep meaning to call a contractor and figure out the problem."

"As long as you're at it, you could think about painting this room. If you went a few shades lighter, it would really brighten things up. Maybe a pale gray or ecru."

As he spoke, Liz noted—how had this fact never registered with her?—that the walls were an uninviting mustard shade.

"If you replace the painting over the mantel with a mirror, that'll also help lightwise," Shane was saying.

Liz pulled her phone from her pocket and typed in his suggestions as they moved from the living room back through the front hall to the den, then the dining room. In the kitchen, Liz said, "Unfortunately, since the goal is to sell quickly, I can't see them doing a full renovation here."

"At least this is really open," Shane said. "Buyers like that now."

Upstairs, his suggestions were similar: painting the walls, removing clutter, fixing anything conspicuously broken (such as the pocket door on the tiny bathroom in Mary's room, which had for at least a decade closed no more than halfway). In Kitty's room, Liz said, "In case this isn't obvious, my three younger sisters still live here. I'm not sure if it's the boomerang generation thing or just their personal immaturity, but they basically—"

Before she could complete the thought, a form rose from the swirl of sheets and pillows on the double bed and took the shape of Kitty herself. Bleary-eyed and messy-haired, yet still displaying her unconcealable native beauty, Kitty squinted at Liz and her guest. "Why are you in my room?" She pointed to Shane. "Who are you?"

Uneasily, Liz said, "This is my friend Shane. I didn't realize you were here."

"Shane Williams," Shane said warmly, and he waved. "A pleasure to meet you."

Kitty stood, apparently unself-conscious about wearing a T-shirt, a pair of pink-striped underwear, and nothing else. She glared at Liz. "I'm not immature."

"I didn't mean you," Liz said. "You know what? We'll give you privacy."

Hastily, Liz led Shane to the third floor and then to the basement. "Steel yourself for the worst," she said as they descended to the Tudor's lowest level, and Shane said, "You'd be surprised what I've seen."

In the front hall again, Liz said, "Be totally honest. How much do you think my parents can get?"

"Hyde Park is always desirable, and this is one of the premier streets. But I can't lie: Your folks will see better offers if they do some updating."

"But it's still worth at least a million, right?" Liz said. "Even in the condition it's in?"

"Let's say you declutter like crazy," Shane said. "Because you're just shooting yourself in the foot otherwise. But if that's it and you do nothing else, yeah, I'd say asking a million is reasonable. Or maybe we price it at 1.1 million with the hope of grossing a million even."

"You're trying to *sell* our house?" Kitty said, and Liz looked up to see her sister on the stairs; though fifteen minutes had elapsed since their last encounter, Kitty still wore nothing other than the T-shirt and underpants. "Do Mom and Dad know?"

Liz exchanged a look with Shane. "They're getting old, Kitty. They can't stay here forever."

"We won't do anything without your parents' blessing," Shane said. "Here—" He walked up a few steps and passed Kitty a business card. "Any questions I can answer for you, anything you want to talk about, call me twenty-four/seven."

Kitty glanced at the card, then looked between Shane and Liz. "Shane and I went to Seven Hills together," Liz said. "I didn't just meet him for the first time today."

"I've got a showing now out in Sycamore," Shane said, "but, Kitty, really, don't be shy." Was he, Liz wondered, hitting on her sister? To Liz, he said, "You and I can touch base later today or tomorrow."

"Please don't say anything to anyone else," Liz said to Kitty after Shane left. "I'm only doing due diligence."

"But we're happy living here." Kitty's expression was petulant. "It's not fair for you to kick us out, then go back to New York."

Chapter 62

NEED TO TALK *to u,* the text from Charlotte read. *Got a min?*

"What's up?" Liz said after she'd called her friend.

"I hope you won't be weirded out," Charlotte said, and Liz detected in Charlotte's tone both pleasure and genuine nervousness. "I'm pretty surprised myself. But here goes: After you and I had drinks last week, I sent an email to Willie. Just like, *Hey, heard your trip to Cincinnati may have ended on a strange note, hope you're taking care.* He emails back right away and wants to know if he can call me, and I say sure. We end up talking till four in the morning. Then the next night, the same thing. To make a long story short, he's invited me to visit him this weekend."

"We're talking about Cousin Willie, right?" Liz said. "That Willie?"

"Yes," Charlotte said. "That Willie."

"You shouldn't feel sorry for him," Liz said. "Willie's a big boy."

Some retracting on Charlotte's part occurred. "I don't feel sorry for him."

As if she were unaware of the retracting, as if this conversation had not become deeply strange, Liz said, "How did you have his email?"

"We'd exchanged cards at Chip's dinner party."

Which in itself, in light of subsequent developments, seemed suddenly suspicious. There was something displeasing to Liz about this unexpected association between Charlotte and Willie, and an additionally displeasing awareness of her own displeasure. If Charlotte was happy, and indeed this was how she sounded, shouldn't Liz be happy for her?

"Obviously, you can do whatever you want," Liz said. "But you don't think he's, like, a tech doofus?"

Coldly, Charlotte said, "No, I don't."

"I don't mean doofus like he's an idiot. He's very smart. He's just, I don't know—he's so awkward. You don't think?" She was making things worse, not better, and she could hear herself doing it, but Charlotte and Willie? Really?

"I've got to get ready for a meeting," Charlotte said. "I'd appreciate if you don't mention this to your family."

Why was Liz the repository for everyone's confidences? She wanted to say something complimentary about Willie, but it was hard to figure out what. When the call had ended, Liz winced, balled her right hand into a fist, and bit her own knuckle.

Chapter 63

ON THE THIRD floor, Jane stood in warrior pose, her left leg extended behind her and her arms outstretched. As Liz entered the bedroom, Jane gracefully let her arms return to her sides and said, "Amanda and Prisha want to hire me as their private yoga instructor, and they told me I can live with them for as long as I want, even after the baby comes."

Though Liz felt some dismay, the plan made sense: Amanda was a college friend of Jane's, a Barnard graduate who'd made a fortune at a hedge fund before trading corporate life in Manhattan for recreational beekeeping and lucrative, long-distance, part-time consulting from the Hudson Valley. Amanda's wife, Prisha, was a high school English teacher, and they lived with their eight-year-old son, Gideon, on a bucolic five-acre spread two hours from the city.

"Do you think you'll tell Mom and Dad you're pregnant before you leave?" Liz asked.

Jane shook her head. "I want to sit with it a while longer."

Liz sighed. "Well, there's something I have to tell you. It turns out Mom and Dad are hugely in debt." Jane looked aghast, and Liz said, "I know. But it is what it is, and their only choice is to sell the house. You shouldn't worry, but if you were planning to borrow money from them in the next little while, borrow it from me instead. Just focus on taking care of yourself. The reason I'm telling you is that this could be the last time you're in the house."

"I feel terrible. I had no idea."

"Because you weren't supposed to. None of us were. Have you bought your plane ticket to New York?"

"For a week from today. Does that mean I'll miss Jasper?"

"Sorry, but no such luck. He gets to town Wednesday." Liz leaned against her desk and folded her arms. "So you won't believe this, but Charlotte and Cousin Willie have been talking on the phone, and now they think they're in love and she's going to visit him."

Liz expected Jane to react with either disgust or amusement, but her sister was serene.

"I can see them as a couple," Jane said.

Chapter 64

AFTER PARKING IN the P3 Garage at Christ Hospital, Liz and her father took the skywalk to Level A, whereupon Mr. Bennet asked the young woman at the information desk for the location of the administrative suite.

"The billing department is that way." Liz pointed.

"We're going to see Dick Lucas."

"But we have an appointment with a financial counselor named Chad Thompson."

Mr. Bennet's expression was thoughtful. "Men named Chad make me uneasy."

"Is Dr. Lucas expecting us?" He held, Liz knew, some sort of executive position at the hospital, though Liz wasn't sure precisely what it was. She wondered if he was aware of Charlotte's trip to Palo Alto to see Cousin Willie.

"I assure you Dick won't turn us away," Mr. Bennet said.

This turned out to be accurate. In the administrative suite, Mr.

Bennet gave his name to the woman at the reception desk, and no more than a minute later, Dr. Lucas appeared in the seating area in a gray suit, a yellow tie dotted with a pattern of tiny blue hummingbirds, and a white coat. "Fred and Liz!" he said in a voice that implied he couldn't imagine a more pleasurable surprise. "To what do I owe the honor?"

"If we might have a word in private." Mr. Bennet nodded toward the receptionist.

In Dr. Lucas's office, Liz and her father sat in chairs facing a massive cherry desk on which rested a gold nameplate that read RICHARD G. LUCAS, VICE PRESIDENT AND CHIEF CLINICAL OFFICER.

"Sally and I have gotten ourselves in a bit of a pickle," Mr. Bennet said. "Apparently, my stay here earlier in the summer wasn't all-expenses-paid."

"Would that it had been," Dr. Lucas said warmly.

"We're having a liquidity issue, and Liz here is convinced that if we don't pay up on time, a shady character will find us and break our kneecaps."

Dr. Lucas chuckled. "We can't have that, can we?"

Liz cleared her throat and said, "My dad doesn't have health insurance."

Dr. Lucas winced, but still somehow affably. "Tsk, tsk, Fred. I'm no more a fan of our president than you are, but when open enrollment starts, I'd urge you to sign up."

Liz said, "I'm under the impression that sometimes hospitals have flexibility in terms of payment plans." She'd anticipated marshaling her shaky, Internet-gleaned knowledge to bargain with Chad Thompson, a stranger, and she found it more rather than less uncomfortable to do so with a man who, in her youth, had prepared pancakes that she and Charlotte ate in their pajamas after sleepovers. Still, Liz tried to sound mature and professional as she added, "I know that the cost of procedures can vary from hospital to hospital, and also that lots of medical bills contain mistakes. I'm wondering—"

"Easy there, Liz," Mr. Bennet interrupted.

"No, she's quite right," Dr. Lucas said. "Mistakes happen, and there's nothing wrong with using a fine-tooth comb to go over the figures. Here's what I recommend. We have a crackerjack team down in our billing department, and there's a fellow by the name of Chad Thompson. I'll call him now, tell him my good friends are on their way, and I'm certain we can figure out a payment plan that works for the Bennet family and for the hospital. How does that sound?"

Although there was some vindication in hearing Chad Thompson's name, the vagueness of Dr. Lucas's plan failed to entirely reassure Liz. She blurted out, "My parents are selling their house, so that should help with cash flow."

Mr. Bennet leaned forward. *"Entre nous,"* he said to Dr. Lucas.

"Absolutely, Fred, absolutely. Life is complicated. I'm just relieved you're sitting across from me now looking hale and hearty." He glanced at Liz. "Your father gave us quite a scare, didn't he?"

"And thank you for everything you did—everything everyone here did—to take care of him," Liz said. "I hope it doesn't seem like I'm not grateful."

"She shows her gratitude by accusing the people who saved my life of malfeasance," Mr. Bennet said to Dr. Lucas. "As you can imagine, her mother and I are very proud."

Chapter 65

LIZ WOULD HAVE estimated that there were twenty boxes in Jane's former bedroom; when she counted, there were sixty-one. She looked at the dates of the packing receipts for the boxes she'd already opened, and the pineapple throw pillow was from 2008.

Online, she had found a so-called eBay valet, a woman who lived ten miles away in Terrace Park and would resell these items and return to Liz 70 percent of their sale price. Kathy de Bourgh was a believer that it was better to ask for forgiveness than permission—in *Revolutions and Rebellions,* she had described learning this lesson during the 1970 Women's Strike for Equality—and it was in a de Bourghian spirit that, after taking inventory of all of the boxes' contents, Liz loaded up her father's Cadillac and made two trips to the valet's house. Fortuitously, Liz didn't encounter anyone while carrying boxes from the third floor to the driveway. One of the virtues of the Tudor was the privacy offered by its capacious dimensions, and though Liz suspected that this fact reflected poorly on her, she was at times most able to enjoy her family members when she could sense their presence nearby without actually interacting with them.

At the conclusion of her second round trip to Terrace Park, Liz called the number for a general contractor, whose receptionist scheduled a water-stain evaluation for two days hence. After the call, Liz felt a sense of achievement that she realized wasn't commensurate with the day's modest progress. The meetings with Dr. Lucas and Chad Thompson, the drop-offs to the valet, and the appointment with the contractor were steps in the right direction; but to see them as true resolution could only be folly.

Chapter 66

"I'VE BEEN OFFERED a position as a private yoga instructor by some friends in upstate New York," Jane said at dinner. "It's been wonderful being home, but I'm moving there next week."

"Bravo," Mr. Bennet said, just as Mrs. Bennet, with great distress, asked, "But what about my luncheon? And for God's sake, Jane, what about Chip? He'll be devastated."

"As a matter of fact," Jane said, "Chip is in Los Angeles now, shooting an *Eligible* reunion."

A silence followed, then several family members spoke at once.

"When did this happen?" said Mrs. Bennet.

"Is he hanging out in hot tubs with other girls?" said Kitty.

"Why would he sign on for that all over again?" said Mary.

"Hmm," said Lydia. "Maybe so he can hang out in hot tubs with other girls?"

"How long will he be gone?" Mrs. Bennet asked Jane. "You'll have to get back here by the time he returns."

Jane's eyes met Liz's, and Liz was tempted to announce herself that Jane and Chip had broken up. What did postponing the news achieve?

"I don't know if Chip is coming back," Jane said.

"But the hospital must be counting on him," Mrs. Bennet said.

"It's obvious he's always been torn between Hollywood and medicine," Liz said.

Mrs. Bennet looked suspiciously at Jane. "Are the friends you're staying with those ladies?" *Those ladies* was how Mrs. Bennet had referred to Amanda and Prisha ever since Jane had told her mother of their marriage years earlier. Having met Amanda during Jane's undergraduate years, Mrs. Bennet had said, "I did always think she had very manly posture."

"Yes," Jane said. "And I'm really looking forward to working with them."

"If Chip wants you to move out to California, you're a fool to tell him no," Mrs. Bennet said. "A man with his background and education can't be expected to wait around while you dillydally."

"Mary, maybe you should be the one to move in with those ladies," Lydia said. "I think you guys have something in common."

"Lydia, when do Mom and Dad get to meet Ham?" Liz asked.

"When I feel like it," Lydia said.

"Who, pray tell, is Ham?" Mr. Bennet said.

"He went to the University of Washington out in Seattle," Mrs. Bennet said, and Lydia glared and said, "Have you been stalking him?"

Mrs. Bennet looked affronted. "Lizzy told me." She turned to Jane. "I saw some place settings in the Gump's catalog that are very elegant. You should start thinking about what you want to register for so you're ready when the time comes."

Chapter 67

THE DEADLINE FOR Liz's pay-raise article had come and gone, and Liz still hadn't heard back from Kathy de Bourgh's publicist; feeling un-Kathy-de-Bourgh-ishly defeated, Liz emailed the article to her editor, Talia.

So sorry the interview didn't come through, Liz typed. *Good news is I have solid quotes from high-ranking woman at IBM. Maybe reconnect w/ de Bourgh in the future?*

Chapter 68

THE NIGHT BEFORE Jasper's arrival in Cincinnati, while watching television in the den with Jane, Kitty, and Mrs. Bennet, Liz said during a commercial, "Kitty, will you give me a pedicure?"

Kitty looked at her with confusion. "Why?"

"Because you're good at it and I need one." Liz extended her legs and wiggled her toes.

"Fine, but I'm not touching your calluses," Kitty said.

"It's a deal," Liz said.

"The calluses are because you run too much," Mrs. Bennet said without glancing up from her catalog. "All that jostling is bad for your ovaries, too."

In Kitty's bathroom, which was where she and Liz adjourned to, Kitty was thoroughly professional in demeanor as she applied the layers of polish, focused and serious in a way Liz had never seen. Perhaps most impressive of all, Kitty owned pale pink disposable foam toe separators, which she inserted and told Liz to wear for the next forty-five minutes while the polish dried. "I've never waited that long in my entire life," Liz said, and Kitty said, "I put four coats on. Trust me."

With the separators in, Liz walked on her heels down the hall to Mary's room and knocked on the door. After a minute, Mary opened it just a few inches, as if concerned about intruders.

"How's it going?" Liz said.

"What do you want?" Mary asked.

"I'm just coming to say hi." It was shortly after eleven P.M., and during her pedicure, Liz had heard Mary climb the stairs, apparently returning from wherever she'd been. "Did you have a good night?" Liz asked.

"You're acting weird," Mary said.

Trying to maintain a casual tone, Liz said, "Where do you go on Tuesdays, anyway?" Really, the omertà surrounding Mary's night life made no sense.

"Nowhere," Mary said.

Warmly, Liz said, "Well, obviously, you go *somewhere*."

"I'm not gay, if that's what you're asking."

The inquiry was going less well than Liz had hoped. "I wasn't," she said, which may not have been entirely true. "In fact, I was wondering if it had ever occurred to you to find out what happened to Allen Bausch."

Mary squinted. "My prom date? That guy was such a loser."

Switching tacks, Liz said, "Of all the degrees you have, which one do you think you're most interested in pursuing for a career?"

"I won't finish this one until December."

"It's a master's in psychology, right?" Liz said, and Mary nodded. "Would you like to be a therapist?" Liz asked. The notion seemed at best ill-advised and at worst harmful to others. To her relief, Mary shook her head.

"I'm studying applied psychology, not clinical."

"Remind me what people do with applied psychology degrees?"

Mary shrugged. "Employee training. Product testing."

"You should work for Procter & Gamble!" Liz exclaimed. Seeing that her zeal seemed to repel Mary, Liz added more calmly, "I'm sure

Charlotte would be happy to talk with you." Presumably, Liz thought, her own awkward last encounter with Charlotte wouldn't make an entreaty from Mary unwelcome. Liz then wondered how Charlotte's visit to see Cousin Willie had gone.

"Are you asking me this stuff for an article you're writing?" Mary said, and Liz said, "Can't I just be interested in your life?"

"Yeah, right." Mary nodded with her chin toward the floor, where Liz's toes were five different candy colors on each foot. She said, "That looks ridiculous."

Chapter 69

THE CINCINNATI AIRPORT, while indeed an airport, was not actually in Cincinnati; rather, it was located across the river in Hebron, Kentucky, and this was where Liz picked up Jasper Wick just before noon. He'd texted her after his plane landed, as she was pulling off the highway, and by the time he emerged from the terminal, Liz was waiting by the curb. She climbed from the car to wave, and when Jasper smiled, he looked exceptionally handsome.

His curly blond hair was thinner than it had once been but still abundant enough to be windblown, and his brown eyes remained mirthful. He kissed her on the mouth—this was a bolder display of affection than they partook of in New York and that even in Cincinnati did not feel risk-free—and Liz said, "Welcome to the 'Nati."

"You didn't tell me the airport's a ghost town. I think a tumbleweed just blew by."

"It used to be a Delta hub, but that was a while ago." Jasper set his suitcase in the trunk, which Liz closed. Inside the Cadillac, she said,

"Should we eat first or just go straight to your hotel?" In case her meaning wasn't clear, she wiggled her eyebrows exaggeratedly.

"Actually, I need you to drop me at Avis. You know where that is?"

Liz looked at him in confusion. "Why did I pick you up if you're renting a car?"

"I didn't know if this was one of those airports where the rentals are a million miles from the terminal. Plus—" He smiled at her. "I wanted to see you."

"Jasper, I could have been working."

"I thought we were about to go have a nooner. Don't be mad, Nin. I didn't rent the car till yesterday because I didn't realize how far apart my hotel and the sports mall are."

Sighing, she started the car and followed the signs to Avis, which was under a mile from the terminal. As Jasper stepped from the car, he said, "I'll text you my room number when I check in."

She shook her head. "Let's just go get lunch. Meet me at the Skyline Chili on Madison Road in Oakley."

Jasper laughed. "Making me work for it now, huh?" he said. "Okay. I'll play."

Chapter 70

"BIG NEWS," JASPER said as the waitress at Skyline set down their dishes of oyster crackers. "I had a drink with Brett Yankowitz yesterday." This was, Liz knew, a powerful literary agent, though she had never met him. "He digs my book idea about that Idaho fly-fishing family," Jasper continued. "If he sells it, I'll take a leave in the spring."

"Will *Sporty* let you?" Contrary to the rumors Jasper had previously shared with Liz, no announcement had occurred about the firing of the editor in chief of *Dude*.

Jasper said, "If they want to keep me, they will. How long you think it'd take me to write a book—three months? Four?"

"Don't you need to finish the first fifty pages for Yankowitz to sell it?"

"Presumably."

"So keep track of your average daily word count. I bet you—" At that moment, Liz glanced at a person passing her and Jasper's table and was startled to make eye contact with Fitzwilliam Darcy. He was approaching from the rear of the restaurant and was no more than three feet away; to pretend she hadn't noticed him would be preposterous.

"You really are a regular here," she said, and Darcy said, "I'm a man of my word."

"Wait a second," Liz said. "You guys know each other."

If she hadn't been aware of Jasper and Darcy's mutual antipathy, she'd have immediately intuited it; Jasper did not stand to greet his former college classmate. Instead, coolly, Jasper said, "Fitzwilliam Darcy. It's been a while."

Equally coolly, Darcy said, "It has."

Liz wondered if he'd eaten alone again.

"I wouldn't have expected you to wash up in Cincinnati," Jasper said. To Liz, he added, "No offense."

"I'm a physician at a stroke center here," Darcy said.

"I'm in town from New York to write about squash for *Sporty*, where I'm a senior editor. Also about to sign a contract for a book about the royal family of American fly-fishing."

"Congratulations," Darcy said, and surely the word had never been uttered with less enthusiasm. Darcy looked between her and Jasper. "I won't keep you." He nodded. "Liz."

When he'd moved on, Liz said, "Remember Chip, the *Eligible* guy Jane was dating? Darcy's good friends with him. Oh my God, have I not told you that Jane's pregnant?"

"No shit—from the mail-order sperm or the old-fashioned way?"

"The sperm, which seems to have sent Chip running. He didn't know she'd been trying to get pregnant on her own, so I get that it's shocking, but still—he's fled all the way back to L.A. to be on an *Eligible* reunion. Don't mention any of this when we have dinner with Jane."

Jasper looked intently at Liz. "You're not banging Darcy, are you?"

"Are you kidding?"

"I could swear he was giving off a territorial vibe."

Liz made an expression of distaste. "You're imagining things. Anyway, I'm pretty sure he's going out with Chip's sister."

"Is *Eligible* the one where the dude kisses the girl on the cheek when he wants to kick her to the curb?"

"You don't need to pretend you're unfamiliar with it, Jasper. We watched the entire first season together."

Jasper smiled then, and in spite of certain contraindications, Liz had always found his boyish smile irresistible. "We did, didn't we?" he said. "Okay, busted. But I haven't seen it since."

Liz smiled back at him. "A likely story."

Chapter 71

LIZ HADN'T YET left the parking lot of Skyline when her phone buzzed with an incoming call from Shane Williams. "A colleague of mine has clients who are very interested in your parents' house," he said. "What's the soonest you'll be ready to show it?"

"How spruced up does it have to be?" Liz asked. "I've been working on the basement, but it's, you know, a large project."

"What if you take the weekend to address the most pressing stuff and they come over Monday?"

Which meant five days, two of which were while Jasper was in town, to not only make the house look its finest but also to break the news of the impending sale to her sisters and mother. Liz winced, then said, "That seems doable."

"Sometimes it's simplest just to rent a storage unit, load it up, and sort things later," Shane said. "I'd also make fixing the water stain in the living room a priority."

"I'm following up," Liz said. "How does pricing work if the house isn't officially on the market yet?"

"This is what's known as a pocket listing, which in some cases can drive up offers. You're still asking the same amount, but it never enters the MLS. My gut tells me 1.1 million if you and your parents are cool with that."

"That sounds good." Where in Cincinnati, Liz wondered, were storage units located, and how much did they cost to rent? She had a vague memory of driving past some en route to her father's physical therapy appointments, but maybe she was imagining it. To Shane, she said, "The people who are interested in the house—do they have kids?"

"I'll ask." Shane's voice was cheerful. "But I assume so because it's a perfect house for a family."

Chapter 72

CHARLOTTE LUCAS TEXTED in the afternoon, asking Liz if she'd be free for a drink that evening. Because Liz already had plans to meet Jasper in the bar of the 21c hotel at nine o'clock, when he finished his reporting for the day, she suggested to Charlotte convening in the same place at seven. Prior to this outing, Liz went online to rent a ten-by-fifteen-foot storage locker on East Kemper Road, and also arranged to rent a truck over the weekend.

It was only when Liz and Charlotte were seated at a table, wineglasses in front of them, and Charlotte stated the opposite of what Liz had anticipated that Liz realized how confident she'd been that the trip to California would be a failure.

"Willie and I are moving in together," Charlotte said. "I wanted you to hear it from me."

"*You're* moving in with Cousin Willie?" Liz could not conceal her astonishment.

"He isn't my cousin." Charlotte seemed businesslike—if her demeanor wasn't ecstatic, neither was it at all dejected.

"But you hardly know each other."

Charlotte shrugged. "Living together should fix that pretty quickly."

"Have I ever told you how cool I think it is that you've stayed in Cincinnati on your own terms? You're this smart, attractive person with a high-power job, and you didn't even have to leave town to make a life for yourself."

"I'm not sure what you're trying to convince me of."

Liz dropped her voice. "Did you sleep with him?"

"If you really want the answer, try not to look so grossed out. And yes, I know all about the prostitute who gave him a blow job, if that's what you were planning to tell me next."

It hadn't occurred to Liz to divulge this bit of information; she forced her lips to relax from their curl of distaste. "So you'll go out to California? I don't see how he could live in Cincinnati, with his—"

"I'm moving there," Charlotte interrupted. "Silicon Valley has great opportunities for someone with my résumé. And in spite of my supposedly awesome life here, I'm ready for a new adventure. Listen, Liz—I'm not asking for your permission. I'm just doing you the courtesy of telling you." Charlotte flagged a waiter who was passing by. Though he wasn't the same person who'd brought their drinks, she said, "We're ready for the check."

Chapter 73

IT WASN'T YET seven-thirty when Charlotte left the bar—the two women had spent less than fifteen minutes together—so Liz texted Jasper to see if he'd be returning any earlier than nine o'clock from his interviews. When Jasper didn't respond, she texted again saying she was already at the hotel and needed him to call the front desk and authorize them to give her a key to his room. Another twenty minutes passed without a reply, at which point Liz finished off the last of the second glass of wine she'd ordered and irritably walked to Seventh Street, where she'd parked her father's car.

Back on Grandin Road, as she pulled into the driveway of the Tudor, she could see through the large kitchen windows that her sisters and parents were eating dinner, a shrimp salad Liz herself had prepared. Rather than join them, and without deference to the two drinks she'd recently imbibed, Liz entered the house through the front door, dashed up to the third floor, changed into her running clothes, and hurried back out the front.

She took off at a sprint and slowed only slightly when she reached Madison Road. So Jane was pregnant and Chip was no longer interested in her; Charlotte Lucas and Cousin Willie were a couple; Mr. and Mrs. Bennet were broke, as, by extension, were all four of Liz's sisters. She needed to extract herself, she thought. She needed to go back to New York. It crossed her mind to make her own reservation on Jasper's return flight, but with Jane leaving, Liz had no faith in her other family members' abilities to fend for themselves.

She was passing the pharmacy and then the animal hospital and was deep in thought when someone said, "Twice in one day—you're everywhere." Liz blinked, and just a few feet away, coming toward her, she saw a tall, dark-haired man who also was running; he wore navy shorts, a plain gray T-shirt, and earbuds that he withdrew as he said, "I wonder if I'm following you or you're following me."

So preoccupied had Liz been that even though she recognized Darcy, she had trouble forming a coherent response. Finally, querulously, she said, "I'm not following you. I usually run in the morning." They both were by this point jogging in place, and Liz heard herself announce, "And anyway, Charlotte Lucas is moving to Palo Alto to live with my cousin Willie."

Even in her agitated state, it occurred to Liz that Darcy might consider the divulgence a kind of village gossip on which he'd frown, yet the animosity between them was also strangely liberating; offending each other had never posed a hypothetical threat but, rather, was the basis of their relationship. And in any case, his expression when he spoke was more pensive than judgmental. He said, "I didn't realize they were a couple."

"They're not. At least they weren't. I mean, literally, less than three weeks ago, Willie tried to kiss *me*. After he left Cincinnati, he and Charlotte had a bunch of phone conversations, she went to Palo Alto for the weekend, and now supposedly they're in love. Which is insane, right?"

After a few seconds' consideration, Darcy said, "I'll turn around and run with you. I live near Rookwood Commons, so it's not out of my way."

"I was never dating Willie," Liz said. "He's my step-cousin, but still, it was so weird that he kissed me. And I'm not jealous of Charlotte. I'm only worried about how miserable she'll be as his girlfriend."

Darcy said in a level tone, "Though jealousy would be understandable—not of Willie per se but of Charlotte finding a partner she wants to be with."

"Is she that desperate to have kids? Because they don't know each other at all."

"They met when he was in Cincinnati?" Darcy glanced over, and Liz nodded.

"Then she went to visit him, and that's the sum total of their interactions. I've always thought of Charlotte as down-to-earth, but this is just batshit."

"I take it you don't believe in love at first sight."

"Does anyone over the age of thirteen? Do you?"

"*I* don't, no," Darcy said. "But I don't rule out for others what I haven't experienced firsthand."

"Oh, please," Liz said. "Don't pretend to be more-open-minded-than-thou. If they're so sure their destiny is to be together, why not date long-distance for a few months? Or, hell, Charlotte can move out there and get her own place." She turned her head to look at Darcy. "By the way, you know how you think my family is a trashy mess? You haven't heard the least of it. Apparently, my dad has burned through all the money he inherited, he has huge bills from his time in the hospital, and no one except Jane and me has health insurance or a job. My mom was hoping Willie would become my boyfriend and bail us out of debt. Oh, and I think she's a compulsive shopper."

"I'm sorry to hear all that." Darcy was somber.

"Chip really dodged a bullet, huh?" They had reached the intersection of Madison Road and Observatory Avenue, and without discussion, they cut right onto Observatory. Liz didn't attempt to conceal her resentment as she added, "Is he enjoying himself in L.A.?"

"I haven't been in touch with him since he left. I'm under the impression that the show doesn't let people communicate with the outside world." Darcy sounded as if he were discussing a subject no more fraught than the weather.

"Isn't the Christ ER furious with Chip? How can they not be?"

"I doubt they're happy."

"Would you ditch your job like that?"

"I don't know that medicine has ever been the right fit for Chip. Good people can go into it for the wrong reasons."

Liz snorted. "And Chip's *such* a good guy. It must be nice to get to walk all over people and then be let off the hook because of how sensitive and confused you are."

Darcy appeared unfazed. "Speaking of moral paragons," he said, "how's Jasper?"

"I'm not sure he liked Skyline as much as you do."

"He's enlightened you, I take it, about his undergraduate transgressions?"

Liz didn't want to admit that she and Jasper still hadn't talked about what had occurred at Stanford. Instead, she said, "You seem really fixated on something that happened a long time ago."

"As a professional storyteller, you must admit it's a vivid tale."

Vivid? Liz thought uneasily. They were almost to Edwards Road, and she said, "You said you live near Rookwood Pavilion, right? I'm going this way." She gestured to the right, and as she did, she felt for the first time a peculiar awareness of the fact that she had just confided in Darcy (in *Darcy*) and he had listened, mostly with respect. The awareness was not entirely agreeable, and was perhaps part of why she said what she did before peeling away. She called, "Have a good night in the shithole that's Cincinnati!"

Chapter 74

AT THE TUDOR, Ham and Lydia were in the driveway, walking toward Ham's navy SUV. "Since when have you run twice a day?" Lydia said. "Are you anorexic?"

"Do I look anorexic?" With both hands, Liz pinched her belly; though the flesh there was not inordinate, neither was it nonexistent.

"I like an evening run," Ham said. "Think about life while the sun goes down."

"You sound like an old man," Lydia said.

Genially, Ham said, "Compared to you, I *am* an old man."

Lydia snickered. "Just so you know, that makes Liz an old woman. Not that you'll get any argument from me."

"You grew up in Seattle, right?" Liz said to Ham. "Where'd you go to high school?"

"Seriously?" Lydia said.

As in other midwestern cities, the question was considered both a local cliché and a method by which residents not-so-surreptitiously ascertained one another's social status.

"If he's not from here, obviously I didn't mean it that way," Liz said. "I was just wondering because my boss at *Mascara* is from Seattle."

Briefly—so briefly that Liz almost didn't notice—Ham and Lydia exchanged a look. "I grew up in the uncool burbs," Ham said, and Lydia tugged on Ham's arm and said, "We have to go."

Ham said to Liz, "It seems right now isn't the moment, but someday soon I'll explain my complicated and tormented adolescence, when I'm not being physically pulled away by your sister."

"Did you just have dinner with my parents?" Liz asked.

Ham shook his head. "Although I met them, and Jane and Mary. Thumbs-up all around."

"Next time you should come earlier and eat with us."

Lydia said, "Liz, sorry to break your heart, but Aunt Margo just called and told Mom that Charlotte Lucas is moving to California to live with Cousin Willie."

Liz hadn't expected the news to remain secret for long, but still—immediately upon leaving 21c, Charlotte must have given Willie the okay to spread the word.

Ham clicked his key, and the SUV made a pinging noise. He opened the passenger-side door—*Ah, chivalry,* Liz thought—and as Lydia climbed in, she said to Liz, "I guess if Willie's a chubby chaser, you really aren't anorexic."

Chapter 75

LIZ'S GOAL HAD been to sneak back upstairs for a shower, but she was intercepted in the entry hall by her mother, whose countenance reflected a kind of outraged relish. "I'll bet you're having second thoughts about Willie now," Mrs. Bennet said.

"Actually not," Liz replied.

"Charlotte won't have to work another day in her life."

"Charlotte likes her job."

Mrs. Bennet pursed her lips. "Well, she certainly didn't need to think long before giving notice to Procter & Gamble."

Chapter 76

"YOU NEED TO tell me what happened at Stanford," Liz said to Jasper. "I get that you don't like to think about it, but not knowing is weirding me out."

She was back in the bar of 21c, and they were waiting for a salad for her and french fries to share. Though Liz still hadn't eaten—Jasper had ended up returning to the home of a squash coach for dinner—it was nine-thirty.

"I'll tell you," Jasper said. "But your buddy Darcy doesn't come out looking good."

"All the better."

Jasper exhaled deeply. "It's spring of senior year. What should be the pinnacle of college, a time to chill with your friends before facing the real world. I'm taking creative writing with this woman who has a graduate fellowship. So one, she's not a real professor, and two, she isn't even a fiction writer. She's a black poet named Tricia Randolph, and by the way, I don't think she ever published a book before or since, so God knows how she was teaching at Stanford. As my final assignment, I turn in a story about guys at a frat party. It's satire, and I totally mean to make these guys douchebags, but Tricia Randolph calls me into her office and says, 'Jasper, how do you think your female classmates will feel about your objectification of women?'"

Experiencing a prickle of uncertainty, Liz said, "Why did she ask that?"

"The main character and his friends are saying which girls they'd fuck, but, again, it's satire. And yes, that *is* how guys in college talk. Don't kill the messenger." Jasper's face twisted with bitterness. "Tricia Randolph says unless I rewrite it, it can't be workshopped. I say fine, then it can't be workshopped. But the story's already out there, everyone in the class has a copy, and they make more copies for their friends. It becomes this total samizdat phenomenon." Liz could tell that Jasper had been transported back—he was far from her, Cincinnati, and his own adulthood.

"When the story's an underground hit, Tricia Randolph is humiliated," he continued. "She decides to seek revenge. Pretty soon, I'm sitting in front of the judicial affairs board, and who's one of only three undergrads on it but good old Fitzwilliam Darcy. He'd been tapped to be a student representative by the administration. I seriously think he's one of those dudes where, his whole life, he's gotten credit for being smart and moral for no reason other than he's tall. Anyway, it's 1997, Stanford and campuses everywhere are in the grip of political correctness bullshit, Tricia Randolph suddenly decides that she's offended by my story not just as a woman but as a *black* woman, and suddenly I'm caught in the middle of a racial controversy. And I swear to you the story had not one thing to do with skin color. But Darcy, who could have been the voice of reason—he was the only person on the board I actually knew, including faculty—he throws me under the bus. The next thing I know, I've been expelled." Jasper's expression was both so sour and so expectant that it crossed Liz's mind that he hoped she'd challenge him, except that her specific presence hardly seemed to register.

She said, "But what were the charges against you?"

"Some very vague violation of school policy. Obviously, the university was afraid Tricia Randolph would sue."

"It seems like she should just, at the most, have given you an F."

"After she offered to let me rewrite the paper and I said no, I was fucked. It was double jeopardy."

Liz was fairly sure the situation in question wasn't double jeopardy, but this hardly seemed the moment to point it out. She said, "Did you attend graduation?"

He shook his head. "I got my degree on the condition that I left campus immediately."

How had Liz not known about this episode? She had met him a few months after its conclusion. She thought again of never having been introduced to anyone with whom he'd attended Stanford.

After the food arrived, they spoke only intermittently, which was unusual for them; she was tired and suspected he was, too. Interviewing people, paying close attention—it always wore her out. As they rode the elevator upstairs, she said, "You're meeting the coach again for breakfast tomorrow?"

"Yeah, at nine-thirty at a pancake place near his house."

In the hotel room, she used the bathroom first, and as she brushed her teeth, she wished, sex-wise, that she'd eaten fewer fries. But when she emerged from the bathroom, she found him sound asleep, still in his clothes. The TV was on, as were several lights. She didn't wake him. Instead, after turning off the lights and the television, she slipped under the covers, listening to his steady breathing. He hadn't offered to let her read his story from college, and if he had, she wouldn't have wanted to. In fact, as she turned on her side and closed her eyes, she very much hoped that no copies still existed.

Chapter 77

"YOU!" MRS. BENNET shouted as she hustled from the front door of the Tudor toward the Cadillac Liz was driving. "You have some nerve, young lady! Telling your sisters that Dad and I are selling this house just because you've decided it's time."

It was shortly after eight A.M. Having set her phone alarm for six o'clock, Liz had sleepily turned off the ringer and not awakened for another hour and forty-five minutes, at which point sunlight was flooding Jasper's hotel room. As she'd driven along Columbia Parkway, she had rehearsed possible excuses for her whereabouts; to her right, the languid Ohio River had seemed to mock Liz's agitation.

The moment she pulled into the driveway, Liz's fears were confirmed: She saw her mother, who wore a cream-colored satin bathrobe and slippers; behind her mother was Jane (looking, Liz noticed for the first time, rather curvy); behind Jane was Mary; and behind Mary were Kitty and Lydia.

Liz pressed her foot against the brake and turned off the engine;

surely the way to make a bad situation worse would be by running her mother over. As Liz opened the car door, her mother shouted, "This is *not* your decision! Do you understand that, Elizabeth? If and when the time comes, it will be your father and I who choose to sell the house."

To Kitty, Liz said, "Why did you tell her?"

"I didn't tell her anything," Kitty retorted.

"It wasn't Kitty," Jane said. "I thought Mom knew."

"You don't get to waltz in and tell us what to do!" Mrs. Bennet's face had become scarlet.

"Where am *I* supposed to live?" Mary asked.

"You'll live here!" Mrs. Bennet said. "You'll live just where you always have."

"Get on the Internet and find an apartment, Mary," Liz said. "It's 2013. That's what people do."

"I know you and Jane think you've been terribly helpful with your organic vegetables and your opinions about how we can all improve ourselves," Mrs. Bennet said. "But who do you think was making dinner for the last twenty years while you were enjoying yourselves in New York? Do you imagine I let your father and sisters go hungry?"

"We've been trying to make your life easier," Liz said.

"We never meant to step on your toes, Mom," Jane added. "We wanted to free up your time so you can focus on the Women's League luncheon."

"Everyone likes Mom's food better than yours," Kitty said to her older sisters.

"Do you know how you can make my life easier?" Mrs. Bennet, who was three inches shorter than Liz, drew herself up, scowling. "You can stop meddling in matters that are none of your business."

It was at this point that Mr. Bennet, whose emergence from the Tudor had gone unnoticed, cleared his throat. "Lizzy's not wrong about the house, and you know it, Sally," he said. "We do need to sell. Girls, clear out your rooms and start looking for other living arrangements."

Mrs. Bennet looked aghast. "You can't be serious."

"We don't have a choice," Mr. Bennet said. "Tempora mutantur, my dears."

Mrs. Bennet appeared to be gasping for air. "I thought one of the girls would eventually live in the house with her own family."

"Me," Lydia said. "I'm going to."

Mr. Bennet seemed defeated as he said, "Then I suggest you find a leprechaun and abscond with his pot of gold."

Gently, Jane asked her sisters, "Have you guys ever thought of temping?"

"What do you care?" Lydia said to Jane. "You're about to skip town." She looked at Liz. "And you don't really live here, either. You two are carpetbaggers."

Mrs. Bennet's tone was newly hopeful as she said, "Jane, maybe you and Chip can buy the house."

An uncomfortable expression passed over Jane's face, then she squared her shoulders. "Chip and I have broken up," she said.

"Really?" Mary said. "You mean you're no longer going out with the guy who's shooting a dating show right now in California? I'm shocked."

"Oh, Jane." Mrs. Bennet sounded bereft. "Now you'll never have children."

Chapter 78

IN THE BASEMENT, keeping in mind Shane's advice to skip a true reckoning in favor of efficiency, Liz shoved Christmas lights into a file cabinet and a badminton set into an old suitcase with a broken zipper. She vowed as she worked to immediately recycle the magazines she'd let accumulate in her apartment the minute she returned to New York, as well as to sort through her closet and donate to Goodwill everything she hadn't worn in the last year.

She'd been in the basement for close to two hours and had encountered what she suspected was an extended family of spiders—energetic youngsters, weary parents, deceased great-aunts—when she heard someone descending the steps. Lydia appeared, carrying a bottle of coconut water that Liz imagined, until Lydia took a long swig from it, was for her. "I can't believe you talked Dad into this," Lydia said. "You're being really selfish."

"It isn't my decision, Lydia. Do you have any idea how much it costs to maintain a house this size?"

"It isn't like there's a mortgage."

Rather than correcting her sister, Liz said, "How much do you think property taxes are?"

Lydia shrugged.

"They're more than twenty thousand a year. Let's say the boiler goes out—how much would you guess it costs to buy a new one?"

Lydia closed her eyes and made a snoring noise.

"I know you don't believe it, but getting a job and a place of your own will be the best thing that's ever happened to you," Liz said. "You'll feel so grown-up and independent."

"You sound like a tampon commercial. Anyway, I'm moving in with Ham."

"And not chipping in on rent?"

"He owns his place."

"Do you really want to rely on a man to support you?"

"Spare me your feminist propaganda, Liz. You know, you should get Ham to help you down here. He's the most organized person I've ever met. He only uses one kind of hanger, and they all have to hang the same way."

"Great," Liz said. "Send him over."

Lydia took another sip of coconut water. "Kitty and Mary are talking about becoming roommates. Wouldn't that be hilarious?"

"It's not a bad idea."

"I'd never live with Mary. She's so annoying."

"You *do* live with Mary," Liz said.

Lydia laughed. A certain preemptive aura of departure indicated that she was about to go back upstairs—what must it be like, Liz wondered, to observe another person in the midst of a major task that was no more her obligation than yours and to feel not the slightest compulsion to assist?—and Liz said, "Do you even have a résumé?"

Lydia grinned. "Some of us are able to get by on our looks."

Chapter 79

WHEN U FINISHED today? Liz texted Jasper from the basement. *Moving a million pounds of junk from parents house to storage locker, can't wait to see you!*

At sports mall til 7ish, Jasper texted back. *Still on for dinner w/ Jane and your friend?*

She hadn't formally canceled with Charlotte, Liz realized, though doing so didn't seem necessary.

Just us & Jane now, she texted. *Lets meet 21c lobby 7:45.*

Less than half an hour later, when she heard her name being called from the kitchen, there were a few seconds when she thought Jasper had ignored her prohibitions about visiting the Tudor and come to rescue her, and she was touched. "Down here!" she called back, though even by then, she knew it wasn't him.

"There's a rumor going around that you could use some help," Ham said as he entered the room.

"Really?" she said. "Wow. Thanks."

He shrugged. "Slow day at the office. What's our strategy here?"

Though Mary had accompanied Liz to pick up the rental truck and trailer, Liz had otherwise been feeling like the little red hen in the fable, planting and harvesting the wheat while the animals around her played. Now, at last, she had an ally, and if she weren't so sweaty, she'd have hugged him.

"The storage locker is about ten minutes away," she said. "If you're really game, we could make the first trip now."

This was what they did; up the steep, unfinished basement stairs, through the kitchen, and into the driveway, they carried suitcases and end tables and boxes full of decades-old files to the truck. "You don't want to just dump this?" Ham asked about a stack of faded Easter baskets, fake grass still nestled inside them, when they'd made the first drop-off and were loading the trailer for the second time.

"I know it seems crazy, but if my mom asks if I got rid of anything, I want to be able to say no," Liz said. "I mean, I have gotten rid of stuff since I've been home, but it was before today."

"You sure you never got a law degree?" Ham said. They climbed into the trailer to stow the latest deposits, and as he hopped out, Ham said, "Random question: Do you think your parents are Republicans?"

"My dad, yes, with maybe a libertarian streak. My mom has the views of a Republican, but I'm not sure she votes. Why?"

"That was the impression I got from Lydia, but I was just wondering. You think your parents have any gay friends?"

"As Lydia may have mentioned, there's speculation that they might have a gay daughter."

"Lydia did share that theory." They had reached the basement again.

"Is your family conservative?" Liz asked.

"Very. My mom moved to Florida after my dad died, to a retirement community I'm pretty sure is a Tea Party training camp. Unfortunately, she and I aren't close."

"You're not conservative?"

"I'd call myself a centrist."

"I think of CrossFit being conservative—is that wrong?"

"No, it's right, although I'd say my box has a different vibe than some."

"And you were in the military?"

"Yeah, the army. I spent some time in Korea and did a tour in Afghanistan."

"Wow," Mary said. "I can see the floor in here." Liz hadn't realized her sister was in the vicinity and hoped Mary hadn't heard the recent comment about her.

"Want to give us a hand?" Liz gestured toward a brown corduroy beanbag chair with a split seam through which small bits of polystyrene were spilling.

"I'm sorry," Ham said, "but that's definitely garbage. Seriously, Liz."

"Of course it's garbage," Mary said. "Did Liz tell you it's not?"

"I don't want Mom to get pissed at me for throwing things out," Liz said.

"Then I'll do it," Mary said. "Where's the trash pile?"

"It's your lucky day," Liz said. "You get the privilege of starting it."

Chapter 80

AT BOCA, JASPER ordered a seventy-five-dollar bottle of wine—especially since Jane wasn't drinking, Liz hoped he planned to let *Sporty* cover the bill—and after the sommelier had delivered it, Jasper said, "If you guys are the scullery maids at your house for the summer, who's making dinner tonight?"

Liz, who didn't recall having used the words *scullery maid* with Jasper, said, "Actually, Jane made them some chicken and cold soup."

Jasper grinned. "God forbid they fend for themselves, right? Hey, Jane, Lizzy mentioned you're with child—mazel tov."

Somberly, Jane said, "Thank you."

"How you feeling?"

"All right," Jane said.

"That's great. I swear Susan was puking her guts out from conception to delivery."

Liz could feel Jane glance at her, and it was with an air of overcompensatory cheer that Liz raised her glass. "Bon appétit," she said. "Please, Jasper, tell us more."

What Jasper really wanted to talk about, clearly, were his interviews with the squash players and coach, and he proceeded to do so over appetizers (oysters for him, beet salad for both Jane and Liz), entrées (pasta for Jane, scallops for Liz, filet for Jasper), and into dessert (crème brûlée for Jasper and Jane, nothing for Liz). Again, his long-windedness bothered Liz less than Jane's observation of it; Liz suspected the evening was reinforcing Jane's impression of Jasper as self-centered. He'd been describing the rather intense father of eleven-year-old Cheng Zhou when Liz said, "Did I tell you Jane's going to be the private yoga instructor for a family in Rhinebeck?"

"Oh, yeah?" Jasper swallowed a spoonful of crème brûlée. "Who?"

"I went to college with one of them," Jane said.

"So is it a real job or a pity thing?"

"Jesus, Jasper," Liz said, and, in a jovial tone, Jasper said, "Well, she *is* pregnant and single."

"Yeah, on purpose," Liz said. "And she could go back to her job in the city if she wanted. This is just a change of scenery."

"I thought you two had a leave-no-man-behind deal," Jasper said.

Liz glared at him. "Things have changed, and you know what? I'm a big girl. I can handle being in Cincinnati without Jane."

Calmly, Jane said, "I hope my friends haven't hired me out of pity, but maybe I'll never know." Turning toward Liz, she said, "And of course I'm very appreciative that Lizzy's staying here until our mom's lunch event."

"Speaking of which," Jasper said, "I trust Sally Bennet and the gals are still having lots of productive three-martini meetings?" As he mimed pouring liquid into his mouth, Liz sensed that Jane, too, was bristling.

"Jasper," Jane said. "Tell us more about the squash players."

Chapter 81

JASPER ORDERED ANOTHER bottle of wine from room service, and after it had been delivered, along with two glasses and a fruit and cheese platter, he made a toast. "To Cincinnati," he said. "Which doesn't suck nearly as much as you'd led me to believe."

They were side by side on the bed, fully clothed on top of the covers, with the platter between them. Liz tapped her glass against his and said, "Wow, don't give me a swelled head." But she was already in a better mood; she was relieved not only that the dinner was finished but that Jasper had indeed paid for it.

"What were you moving to a storage locker this afternoon?" Jasper asked.

"I was clearing out the basement so the house doesn't look like it should be condemned when the realtor shows it."

"Your folks are selling their place?" Jasper reached for a slice of Gouda. "When my parents downsized, all I could think about was if it was the first step toward me feeding them creamed corn and changing their diapers."

Liz squinted at Jasper. Hadn't they discussed her family's financial problems? And then it occurred to her that the conversation she'd had about selling the Tudor hadn't been with Jasper; it had been with Darcy.

"My parents aren't selling by choice," she said. "They're deep in debt."

"That's a bummer." Jasper popped a strawberry between his lips and said while chewing, "Because I'd much rather you be an heiress."

"Isn't that what Susan is for?" Liz said.

"Good point. Hey, I got an email from Brett Yankowitz saying if I write up my fly-fishing proposal, he'll be more than happy to take a gander. Which is awesome, but after today, I'm like, maybe I should write a book about squash prodigies instead. As backward as the Cincinnati airport is, it's still a hell of a lot easier to get to than Idaho."

"Fly-fishing is more romantic than squash," Liz said. "Wouldn't you rather do your reporting standing in a beautiful stream instead of under fluorescent lights?"

"True."

"Speaking of romance—" Theatrically, because she was incapable of not mocking herself when initiating sex, Liz winked at Jasper.

"Come here," he said, and he reached out with both arms to help her over the cheese platter.

The kissing was fun; he was in a good mood, too. All of which made it surprising that once they were actually naked and recumbent, technical difficulties presented themselves. While not entirely flaccid, neither was the relevant part of Jasper's anatomy sufficiently stiff to move on to the next stage of activity, and the more directly Liz attempted to improve the situation, the less promising the outlook became. They were facing each other, and at last, Jasper lifted away Liz's hand. "I don't know what's going on," he said with frustration.

"It's not a big deal," Liz said, while trying to shove from her mind the thought that the whole squash article had been a pretext for him to fly to Cincinnati so they could have sex. "We'll try again later."

"You don't want me to just get you off, do you?" Jasper said, which seemed a far less gallant question than *Do you want me to get you off?*

After a few seconds, she said, "Let's try in a little bit." She rolled over and reached for the remote control on the nightstand.

They landed on a political talk show, and the longer they watched, the more incredulous Liz felt. After not seeing each other for almost two months, how could this happen? Just purely as a physiological matter—shouldn't he have been struggling not to finish too fast rather than to get started?

"Do you and Susan have sex?" she asked. She hadn't planned to say this; the same moment the question had occurred to her, she'd uttered it.

"Are you kidding?" Jasper said. "Susan hates me."

"Does she still have that boyfriend?"

"Where's all this coming from?" Jasper said. "Yes, she and Bob are still together."

"I'm feeling confused about what just happened," Liz said.

After a beat, Jasper said, "Sorry for not being able to satisfy your insatiable sexual appetite."

"This is *not* about me being sexually insatiable." Liz sat up, folding her arms over her bare chest. "Are you sleeping with someone else?"

"The other woman is asking if there are other women? Please tell me you see the irony."

"Are you?"

"Liz, what the fuck?"

"That's not an answer."

Jasper was looking up at the ceiling, not at her, and his tone had reverted to being sincere and conciliatory when he said, "You're really important to me. The conversations we have, the way we talk—there's no one else I have that with."

She had been such a fool, such a preposterous, unmitigated idiot; how could she have been this foolish?

She said, "Who else are you sleeping with?"

The expression on his face was oddly compassionate as he said, "You really want me to tell you?"

"Yes."

"Fiona."

"The editorial assistant?"

He nodded. Liz didn't know how old Fiona was, but definitely under twenty-five; also, red-haired and gorgeous. All this time, Liz had understood that her relationship with Jasper closely resembled a distasteful cliché; she hadn't understood that it actually *was* a separate, equally distasteful cliché.

"Anyone else?" Liz asked. When she and Jasper made eye contact, he didn't do anything—he didn't nod again, or shake his head, or speak. Then he pulled her toward him and she let him; she lay with her face pressed to the warm skin of his shoulder.

"You're like my life coach," he said softly, and she was pretty sure this was his ultimate compliment.

So many years—her entire adulthood thus far!—wasted on this man. And she was more to blame than he was. Would extricating herself be difficult or not difficult?

She still thought they might have sex, either later that night or the next morning before he flew back to New York. But they didn't, and he had to leave for the airport early in order to return his rental car.

Chapter 82

KDB GIVING A speech in Houston on Thurs, Aug 29 to Nat'l Society of Women in Finance, read an unexpected email to Liz from Kathy de Bourgh's publicist. *20 minutes available after for sit-down interview, assuming mention in your article of speech/organization.*

In theory, *Mascara* frowned on agreeing to conditions of coverage, but in practice, it happened constantly. Also, twenty minutes with Kathy de Bourgh, modest as it might sound to a nonjournalist, was enough of a coup that it would result in a full profile rather than a few remarks tucked into an article on a different subject. Thus, without checking in with her editor at *Mascara*, without doing further research on the event, Liz wrote back, *I definitely will attend.*

Chapter 83

"I KNOW THIS isn't your cup of tea, so thank you," Jane said. She and Liz stood in the backyard, beneath the fungus-afflicted sycamore tree.

"Just, not to sound disrespectful, but we should leave for the airport eight minutes from now," Liz said.

Jane had invited Liz to join her as she bid a ceremonial farewell to the Tudor, which Liz superstitiously thought but did not tell Jane increased the likelihood that the prospective buyers wouldn't like the house after all.

Jane closed her eyes, took a deep breath, exhaled, then said, "Om." Liz didn't close her eyes and wondered if their parents or sisters were watching from a window. "Thank you for sheltering our family all these years," Jane said. "For keeping us warm in the winter and cool in the summer"—both claims, Liz thought, were rather generous, given the draftiness that kicked in around November and the erratic functionality of the third-floor air-conditioning—"and thank you for being a place where we celebrated holidays and played games and ate delicious meals. Even our challenges here have made our lives richer and deepened our ability to feel. Our family has been very lucky to live somewhere beautiful."

At the mention of games, Liz had remembered a specific round of gin rummy she and Mary had played in the eighties, when Liz had gotten a perfect hand and ginned before she drew for the first time; in spite of herself, she felt genuine sadness. But it wouldn't have been honest to attribute the sadness entirely to the Tudor's impending sale. It also was attached to her disappointment with Jasper, a disappointment that abruptly and retroactively colored the past: All those years growing up here, she'd unknowingly been headed toward a selfish, dishonest man.

Jane said "Om" once more and opened her eyes. "Do you want to add anything?"

Liz shook her head. "I'm okay. I'll put your suitcase in the car while you say goodbye to everyone."

Chapter 84

MR. BENNET BID farewell to Jane indoors, but the female members of the family all followed her to the driveway, where Mrs. Bennet continued to offer miscellaneous advice, as if Jane were leaving for her freshman year of college. "Get a little single-serve coffeemaker so you're not dependent on those ladies in the morning," she called into Jane's unrolled window. "They're only about thirty dollars."

"Mom, I don't drink coffee," Jane said, and from the driver's side, Liz said, "We need to go so she doesn't miss her plane."

"I love you all," Jane said. "And I'm only a phone call away."

"A nice hostess gift is a cheese board," Mrs. Bennet said. "But if you get one that's bamboo, tell them not to put it in the dishwasher."

"Jane won't be their guest," Lydia said. "She'll be their servant."

"Bye," Liz called, but she hadn't begun accelerating when, entirely audibly, Mrs. Bennet said to Kitty, "I just wish Chip hadn't gone back to California."

As Liz turned out of the driveway, she said to Jane, "Did you decide what you're doing with your apartment after September first?"

"I guess if I'm not going back, I should end my lease, but the idea of moving—well, I shouldn't complain after you and Ham cleaned out the entire basement yesterday. You were heroic, Lizzy."

"You wouldn't say that if you saw the storage locker. Ham did his best, but it looks like the town dump."

"I have this fantasy of getting rid of almost everything I own and replacing it with minimalist baby gear. Just a car seat, some onesies, and some cloth diapers."

"Is there any such thing as minimalist baby gear?" Liz asked as she made a left onto Torrence Parkway. "In other news, I think maybe I'm finished with Jasper."

"What happened?"

"Besides me finally seeing what's been in front of my face all along?" Liz tried to smile, and without warning, tears came to her eyes.

"Oh, Lizzy," Jane said. "I'm sorry."

"He was awful at dinner," Liz said. "Don't you think?"

Sympathetically, gently, Jane said, "He was just being himself."

Chapter 85

THE GRASMOOR, WHICH was located on Madison Road—Liz passed it on her jogs—consisted of two handsome, three-story, cream-colored brick buildings with green awnings. The unit Liz and her parents viewed, which was for sale for $239,000, had three bedrooms, two and a half bathrooms, two terraces, and a view of the fountain in the court-yard. For the duration of the tour, which was conducted by Shane, Mrs. Bennet wept, a fact that seemed to cause greater consternation for Shane than for Liz or her father.

"Seriously," Liz said as the tour concluded, "getting this much space for this amount of money is incredible."

"My dear," Mr. Bennet said, "your coastal affectations are in imminent danger of becoming tedious."

"For comparison, I'd love to show you a unit down the street," Shane said, and Mrs. Bennet said, "I don't have the energy."

Liz said, "Mom, let's keep going a little longer."

"You have absolutely no idea what this is like for me," Mrs. Bennet said.

"Losing a house can be like losing a member of the family," Shane said. "Am I right, Mrs. Bennet?"

She looked at him vaguely—Liz had decided against mentioning Shane's race in advance of his meeting her mother, saying only that he'd been a Seven Hills classmate—then, as if Shane hadn't spoken, Mrs. Bennet turned back to Liz. "I'm sure you can't understand now," Mrs. Bennet said. "But someday you'll learn what it's like to be treated with utter callousness by your own children."

Chapter 86

IN THE EARLY evening, Liz left for a run. It was a muggy day on which rain didn't seem impossible, and though she certainly hadn't timed her run in the hope of crossing paths with Fitzwilliam Darcy—their other encounter had happened a bit later—she was oddly unsurprised, on reaching Easthill Avenue, to spot a tall man in navy shorts and a red T-shirt. "I thought you said you run in the morning," he said by way of greeting, and already, without any discussion, he had reversed direction and was keeping pace alongside her.

"I do," Liz replied. "Or I used to, with Jane, but now that—actually, I took her to the airport earlier today. She's gone to stay with friends in the Hudson Valley."

"That's a very civilized way to spend the month of August."

"Oh, really? You think it's a scenic place to mend a broken heart?"

After a pause, Darcy said, "I get the impression you see Chip as some sort of cad for leaving town, but it's clear that he and your sister are at very different points in their lives."

"And you're the authority?"

"You can't argue that using a sperm donor is typical behavior for a woman hoping to enter a relationship."

"I assume you're aware she got pregnant before she and Chip met. Life doesn't always happen in the ideal order, but the proof that she wanted to be in a relationship is that she *was* in one."

"She seemed to have serious reservations."

"You hardly know my sister!" Darcy didn't refute the statement, and Liz added, "So is Caroline Bingley still here or has she gone back to L.A., too?"

"She's gone back to L.A."

"Are you devastated?"

Darcy was facing straight ahead as he said, "Why would I be?"

"Aren't you and Caroline a couple?"

"What's led you to believe that?"

"Besides my powers of observation?"

"Your faith in those powers is misplaced. Caroline and I dated briefly, when Chip and I were in medical school, but that was years ago."

"Not that I care, but it's obvious she still has a thing for you."

"I wonder if the man she's seeing in L.A. knows that."

"Is that what she tells you to make you jealous? And it looks like you're falling for it, too."

Darcy seemed amused. "Yet you accuse *me* of presuming to understand more than I really do."

As they turned onto Observatory Avenue, Liz said, "Then who's your love interest? There must be someone."

"You might not be aware of this, but surgeons work extremely long hours."

"And enjoy boasting about it, too, I hear. Okay, here's my guess: a waify, aristocratic investment banker–slash–social worker–slash–ballerina who lives in—I'll say Boston. Or maybe London. Just not Cincinnati, of course, because we all know about the subpar quality of Cincinnati women."

"What I said at the Lucases'—and I hope you know that you're an exceptionally brazen eavesdropper—is that I don't want to be set up on blind dates at the whims of my supervisors' wives. That's hardly putting a moratorium on all Cincinnati women." As they passed Menlo Avenue, Darcy added, "I rarely date waifs, by the way. Or ballerinas, though the category of waifs would seem to subsume the category of ballerinas. Aristocrats, investment bankers, and social workers I'm all fine with."

"When you and Caroline dated, why'd you break up?"

"Why does any couple break up? We weren't compatible."

"Have you ever been married?"

"No. Have you?"

"No, but here's the thing," Liz said. "You're—pardon the word choice—very eligible. You don't have to feign modesty, because I'm sure you know it. I personally would never go out with you, but you're tall, you went to fancy schools, and you're a doctor. To the general public, which has no idea what a condescending elitist you are, you're a catch. You could be married if you wanted, or at least have a girl-friend. And don't give excuses about your schedule, because people make time for what they want to make time for."

"Are *you* single right now?"

It was a strange question; just a few days before, she'd have said no. "I am," she said, "but it's recent. Anyway, everyone knows it's com-pletely different for a woman. You could stand on a street corner, an-nounce you want a wife, and be engaged fifteen minutes later. I have to convince people to overlook my rapidly approaching expiration date." But Liz did not feel, in this moment, like a dusty can of soup on the grocery store shelf; she felt practically gleeful. She was strong and healthy and not pregnant, sweating happily in her tank top and shorts, fleet in her turquoise-and-orange shoes; the gray clouds had dissipated without rain, and beside her was a man who, obnoxious though he might have been, didn't bore her in the slightest. She said, "When we get to Edwards, want to race up the hill?"

"You know those little dogs who get up in the faces of German shepherds and bark at them?" he said. "That's what you remind me of."

"Are you scared you'll lose?"

"Apparently, growing up with Title IX gave you quite a sense of self-esteem."

"All right, then," Liz said. "It's on." Though they still were fifty yards from Edwards Road, she began sprinting; she was flying up the sidewalk, past the houses and trees, the cars on Observatory Road a peripheral blur. No more than a few seconds had passed when he caught up to her, but they both were running too fast to speak; she simultaneously felt wild and breathless and like she was about to laugh. For a few more seconds, they were neck and neck, until he pulled ahead. She was pushing herself as hard as she could, and, turning onto Edwards, he was only a few feet in front of her, then more than a few, and before long they were separated by half a block. Still, she propelled herself forward; if she was to lose to Darcy, it wouldn't be by a centimeter more than necessary.

He was waiting for her at the top of the hill, and she was gratified to see that he was still panting; she slowed down, staggering a little, incapable of speech. She rested both hands atop her head, then removed them and bent at the waist. After a minute, she heard him say, "That was respectable."

She raised her torso, shaking her head. "Don't patronize me." Her limbs burned, her heart pounded; she was exhausted, possibly nauseated, but also giddy. As they faced each other, there was between them such a profusion of vitality that it was hard to know what to do with it; they kept making eye contact, looking away, and making eye contact again. At last—surely he was thinking something similar and she was simply the one giving voice to the sentiment—she said, "Want to go to your place and have hate sex?"

Darcy squinted. "Is that a thing?"

The bravado filling Liz—it wasn't infinite, it could dissipate quickly. But while it still existed, she said grandly, "Of course it's a thing."

"Is it like fuck buddies?"

"This isn't a sociology class. A simple yes or no will do." She added, "It's similar, but without the buddy part."

"I take it you mean right now." He didn't seem flustered or even all that surprised.

"Yes," Liz said. "I mean now." This was his last chance to accept the offer, though she didn't plan to tell him so. But perhaps he sensed the door closing, because he said, "Okay. Sure."

Chapter 87

CINCINNATI WAS THE city where Liz and sex had made each other's acquaintance—in a rather festive cliché, she had lost her virginity to her prom date, whose name was Phillip Haley, and she'd subsequently brought home her two college boyfriends for visits, during which surreptitious intra-Tudor romps occurred—but all of that had been quite some time before. And Jasper's visit had, of course, been unexpectedly fruitless.

As she followed Darcy through the main entrance of a bland three-story brick building and up to the second floor, she experienced a sense of mischief reminiscent of her youthful encounters. Outside his door, Darcy used the front of one running shoe to pry off the heel of the other, then repeated the gesture in reverse with his socked toes, and Liz did the same. Inside the apartment, nothing hung on the walls, and no rugs covered the hardwood floors. The living room held only a long couch, a flat-screen TV, and a low table with a closed laptop computer on it. He led her to the kitchen, which was small and windowless but looked recently renovated; between the counters and the cabinets, the walls were lined with a pattern of black, white, and green tiles. He filled two glasses with tap water and passed her one. They drank in silence, then he said, "I suppose either we both take showers or neither of us does."

Feeling a minor appreciation for his willingness to assume the role of host, she shook her head. "I need to be back at my parents' house before dinner. I will pee, though. Do you have a condom?"

He nodded.

In the modern, clean bathroom, after urinating, Liz washed her hands and splashed water on her face, though more to cool off than establish hygiene. In the bedroom, which contained a king-sized bed covered with a gray cotton spread, a nightstand, and a lamp, Darcy was seated on the floor, still in his shirt and shorts, with one leg stretched out and his torso extended over it. Liz walked to him and held out a hand, and he took it and stood. Uncertainty then presented itself, and no doubt if she had been eighteen, or probably even if she'd been twenty-eight, she'd have looked to him to banish this confusion; but she was thirty-eight, she had orchestrated the encounter, and so she said, "I'm thinking it's more efficient if we both take off our own clothes. Do you care about getting sweat on your sheets?"

He seemed to find the question funny. "They're washable."

Thus, standing a few feet apart, they stripped. She avoided looking at him, except that she snuck a few glances. He was hairier than she'd have guessed, though not in a bad way, and while she'd known he was fit, he was practically sculpted; if she'd previously realized just how perfectly muscled he was, she might have been too intimidated to make this overture.

Then his body was pressed up against hers, they were kissing—never having participated in hate sex, she was glad to learn kissing was part of it—and the naked standing-up kissing went on for a while, accompanied by roaming hands, and at some point, an air conditioner kicked on with a forceful whirring, and after another interval, a cacophony of car horns was audible through the apartment's closed windows, out in the sunny evening populated by people who weren't, for the most part, kissing each other while standing up naked. Then either he nudged her toward the bed or she pulled him, and soon after that he removed the condom from the drawer of his nightstand. All in all, the experience was highly satisfying, certainly for her, and judging by external clues, it seemed reasonable to conclude for him as well; without question, it was far more enjoyable than prom night with Phillip Haley or most other couplings she'd partaken of in the twenty years following. Indeed, one sign of just how agreeable she found the interaction was that she was only vaguely aware of the identity of the person with whom she was sharing it. At the beginning, the preposterousness of this proximity to Darcy—Fitzwilliam Darcy!—had distracted her and then again at the end, as she emerged from the delirious haze in which they'd mutually collapsed. It was as she returned to herself that it occurred to her to wonder whether what they were doing counted as cuddling; surely, even if hate sex permitted kissing, cuddling was a violation. She rolled away and sat up, reaching to find her clothes on the floor.

She could feel his gaze but waited to look at him until she was fully dressed in her damp and reeking shirt and shorts. Finally making eye contact, she said, "I'll let myself out."

As it happened, they had never made it under the bedspread but instead conducted their entire transaction atop it. In that moment, both his hands were set behind his head, and his long, hairy, muscular body was exposed. There was on his face an expression difficult to read, and she felt determined not to blush. "See you around," she said.

Was he amused? Perturbed? Bewildered? It was impossible to know. "Indeed," he replied.

Chapter 88

LIZ WAS WRITING a check from her bank account to the contractor when she received the text from Jasper. The contractor had scraped away the bubbling, flaking paint from the water stain in the living room, then covered the wall with primer and a coat of mustard-colored paint from the can Liz had, to her surprise and delight, unearthed during her basement excavations. The source of the water stain, the contractor informed her with such reticence that it occurred to Liz he feared offending her by drawing attention to her stupidity, was that the roof gutters were all overflowing with leaves, which created flooding during rainstorms. "Keeping your gutters clean is a good thing to do," he said gently.

In its entirety, Jasper's text said *Awesome!* and provided a link to an article about a man in Nebraska who had unsuccessfully tried to shoplift a snake from a pet store. Jasper was taking her temperature, Liz knew. He wanted to see where things stood between them. She didn't respond.

Chapter 89

SHANE'S COLLEAGUE'S CLIENTS were scheduled to visit the Tudor between two and three on Monday afternoon, which meant the house's inhabitants needed to be elsewhere. After arranging for Mary to take their father to the Mercantile Library ("I already did that last week," Mary said, and Liz said, "Exactly. It's called pulling your weight"), Liz had requested that Lydia, Kitty, and Mrs. Bennet accompany her to the Kenwood mall to help her select an outfit in which to interview Kathy de Bourgh. This seemed to Liz such a transparently obvious excuse that she was surprised by how readily they agreed to it.

She was inside a dressing room, wearing a blue wraparound dress, when, at two twenty-five, which was far earlier than she'd expected, she received a call from Shane. "They love it," he said. "They're making an offer tonight, which obviously will be contingent on the inspection."

Looking at herself in the mirror—her dark hair, the expensive dress that didn't belong to her, her bare legs and feet—Liz actually smiled. "Thank you, Shane," she said. "This is such great news."

Chapter 90

IT WASN'T THAT Liz had changed her mind about Darcy's essentially disagreeable nature; rather, she had concluded that a romp or two in his bed would neither diminish nor exacerbate his disagreeability, especially if she discussed it with no one, even Jane.

Twenty-four hours after their initial coital encounter, she went for another run fully prepared to see him; so prepared, in fact, that she was surprised not to see his imposing figure at Easthill Avenue, then surprised at Observatory Avenue, at Menlo Avenue, at Stettinius Avenue, and by Edwards, she had to admit to herself that the chances of crossing paths with him had grown slim. Really, she had little idea of either his work schedule or his exercise routine.

The question then was how deliberate to be—whether to dispense altogether with pretenses of coincidence, track down his email or phone number, and arrange another meeting using the same specificity she'd employ to make a dentist appointment. The antipathy she and Darcy felt for each other meant the sacrifice of pride such a plan would entail was simultaneously more and less consequential than if they shared mutual fondness and respect.

She returned to the Tudor without either laying eyes on him or coming to a conclusion about what her course of action ought to be; and thus, in more than one way, she was deeply frustrated.

Chapter 91

THE NAMES OF the prospective buyers were Jacqueline and Adam Whitman, and they offered the Bennets $915,000 for the Tudor, which offended Mrs. Bennet so keenly that she took to her bed immediately upon hearing the figure. Shane had emailed a scanned copy of the offer to Liz as dinner was concluding, and the amount had left Mrs. Bennet unable even to watch television in the den; she needed to manage her distress from a prone position.

"You'll end up meeting them somewhere in the middle," Liz said from the doorway of her mother's room. "This isn't the last word."

"Leave me be," her mother replied. "You've done enough damage."

Chapter 92

AT MR. BENNET'S appointment with his orthopedist, Dr. Facciano said, "You seem to have regained a full range of motion. Any pain?"

"Only the emotional kind, inflicted by my children," Mr. Bennet said.

"Does that mean he can drive again?" Liz asked.

"I don't see why not," Dr. Facciano said.

"Wow," Liz said. "Aren't you thrilled, Dad?"

"I am," Mr. Bennet said. "Because now your last excuse for not returning to New York has been obviated."

"I'm staying until Mom's luncheon," Liz said, and her father rolled his eyes.

He said, "Then for that, you have no one to blame but yourself."

Chapter 93

DURING HER EVENING run, which had replaced her morning run, just before Liz turned from Grandin Road onto Madison Road—which was to say not before she'd begun speculating about whether she'd see Darcy but before she'd reasonably expected that she would—there he was: tall and composed and minimally sweaty, presumably thinking supercilious thoughts but looking so unjustly handsome as he did that all her internal organs lurched a little. His real self, his actual physical body before her, as opposed to the tempting yet irritating idea of him, was somehow a surprise. In as blasé a tone as she could manage, she said, "How are people's brains today?"

"If I'm seeing them, not good." He was running in place, waiting for Liz to catch up to him, and when she had, he began running next to her.

She said, "You know how everyone says, 'It's not brain surgery'—do you and your colleagues say, 'This is kind of hard, but, hey, it *is* brain surgery'?" The look on his face prompted her to add, "Am I the millionth person to ask you that?"

"You aren't the first." As they continued north on Madison Road, he added, "I've been meaning to tell you that my sister is a fan of yours. It turns out she's subscribed to *Mascara* for years, and when I told her I'd met someone who works there, she knew immediately who you were."

"She must have excellent taste."

"Georgie *is* very intelligent. She's a PhD student in history."

"Do you dare tell me where she goes to school, or will I faint?"

"I knew you'd say something like that. She's at Stanford."

Liz pressed the back of one hand to her forehead. "Get my smelling salts!" She glanced at him—he appeared to be only mildly amused, if that—and said, "Seriously, tell her thank you for me. We at *Mascara* love our smart readers. Is your sister planning to be a professor?"

"If she can find a job out there. She's a bit of a homebody."

"Is she younger than you?"

"Significantly—she's only twenty-six."

"And does she literally still live at home? Keep in mind that for once I can't pass judgment, given my own sisters."

"My parents are deceased. Georgie lives in—"

"I'm sorry," Liz interrupted, and rather stiffly, Darcy said, "It's all right." As they crossed Bedford Avenue, he added, "My father was older than my mother and passed away when I was in high school and Georgie was three. Our mother passed away five years ago. Georgie went to Stanford for undergrad, too, and she was living on campus at that point, which she still is. But she's never wanted to give up our parents' house. I don't think she goes there when I'm not in town, but she's very attached to it."

"Do *you* want to sell it?"

"It's on twelve acres, and it's just sitting there. Someone might as well enjoy it."

"You grew up in the Bay Area, right?" Liz tried to sound casual. Had he really just said *twelve* acres?

Matter-of-factly, Darcy said, "In Atherton," and Liz then understood what she previously hadn't bothered to consider. It wasn't astonishing that Darcy came from an affluent family—both his education and bearing had provided clues—but it hadn't occurred to her that his affluence was so extreme. She could hardly guess, in this day and age, at the value of such a property in such a place: Thirty million dollars? Forty? Personality aside, he really was almost freakishly eligible.

She said, "Is there still furniture in the house?"

He nodded. "A couple lives on the grounds in their own cottage, our caretaker, Roger, and his wife. Georgie and I go back a few times a year. It's really a house for entertaining, so unless we're having a bunch of guests, it's kind of depressing. I prefer to sleep on a futon in Georgie's apartment."

How had Liz not googled Darcy prior to this moment? And no wonder Caroline Bingley was pursuing him. Not that his fortune made him more appealing to Liz—if it were only money she was after, she might have reciprocated her cousin's interest. She thought of Darcy's spare apartment, his fondness for seven-dollar meals at Skyline, and then she thought of having divulged to him her family's financial troubles. If she'd known more about his background, she might not have; but since she already had, she said, "My parents got an offer on their house yesterday, from the first people who looked at it."

"Congratulations."

"Well, it's low. But my point is that if they had the choice of holding on to that house forever, they would and so would my sisters."

"You wouldn't?"

"No, but, as my dad told me, I'm cold-blooded."

"It sounds suspiciously like you're bragging."

"Are you working tonight?" Liz asked.

"I go in at eight."

"Then should I come back to your apartment now or what?"

At this, Darcy actually laughed, which was a sound Liz had heard so few times that it was jarring. He said, "You certainly should."

Chapter 94

IN THE DRIVEWAY of the Tudor, the back of Ham's SUV was open, its interior stuffed with boxes topped by several dresses laid flat, still on their hangers. No one was outside, but as Liz stretched in the grass after her return from Darcy's apartment, Lydia emerged carrying a stack of Seven Hills yearbooks and an earring rack, followed by Ham carrying a laundry basket full of folded clothes.

"Are you moving out?" Liz asked Lydia.

"Your ability to pick up on very subtle clues is impressive," Lydia said. "Have you ever thought of being a detective?"

"The way you two bicker," Ham said. "I'm going out on a limb here, because I've never had a sister, but it's got to be an expression of love." Without waiting for Lydia or Liz to respond, Ham added, "Liz, once we get Lydia unpacked, we want to have you over to our place for dinner."

"Great," Liz said. "And good luck with your new roommate, Ham."

Ham smiled. "I believe I'm up to the challenge."

Chapter 95

A WOMEN'S LEAGUE meeting impelled Mrs. Bennet from her bed after a thirty-six-hour period, and while she was up and about, she grudgingly agreed to see a condominium in a twenty-story building that she began disparaging before climbing from the car. "I'd never live so close to the highway," she told Mr. Bennet, Liz, and Shane. "I don't know how anyone sleeps a wink with cars zooming by at all hours."

"The good news," Shane said, "is that every place we see, even if you don't like it, will help us narrow in on what you do want."

Thus, they still toured the unit, and while standing in the master bathroom with her mother, Liz said, "With the influx of money from selling your house, this seems like the perfect time to draw up a budget. You can decide, 'Okay, I'm allotting X dollars per month for ordering stuff from catalogs, and if I exceed that amount before the month ends, I won't buy anything else.'"

Mrs. Bennet gave her daughter a withering look. "I know perfectly well what a budget is, Elizabeth." While gazing at herself in the mirror, Mrs. Bennet added, "I hope Lydia's not making a mistake moving in with Ham. You know what they say about when men get the milk for free."

"Except that he's supporting her. She hasn't even tried to get a job."

Liz's comments seemed to please Mrs. Bennet. "Lydia's such a pretty girl," she said approvingly.

Chapter 96

FITZWILLIAM DARCY ATHERTON, CA, Liz typed into Google, and after reading through the results, she tried, sequentially, *Fitzwilliam Darcy Harvard Medical School, Fitzwilliam Darcy University of Cincinnati Comprehensive Stroke Center,* and, just for the hell of it, *Fitzwilliam Darcy girlfriend.* She determined that he used neither Facebook nor Twitter, and while he wasn't entirely without an online presence, it was a mostly factual one: His bachelor's degree from Stanford was in biochemical sciences and, also from Harvard, he held a PhD in neuroscience. (When had he had time to acquire a PhD?) He'd won a number of obscurely named awards (at the American College of Surgeons' 44th Annual Meeting, the Rothman T. Barnett Resident Prize) and authored or co-authored several even more obscurely titled articles published in medical journals ("Modulation of Brain Stimulation on the Interaction Between Ventral and Dorsal Frontoparietal and Basal Ganglia-Cortical Networks During Expectation and Re-orienting"). In his photo on the stroke center website, he wore both a tie and a white coat.

Rather more titillatingly: His family's estate in Atherton was called Pemberley—it was located at 1813 Pemberley Lane, though Liz guessed the estate name to predate the street name—and its value was estimated at, variously, $55 million, $65 million, or $70 million.

The search for *Fitzwilliam Darcy girlfriend* bore no fruit.

Chapter 97

ADJUSTING TO LIFE in Rhinebeck, Jane reported to Liz by phone, had been nearly seamless: Lydia's assertion notwithstanding, Amanda and Prisha were treating her as a friend rather than an employee; their son, Gideon, was charming; and Jane had discovered a delicious vegan bakery, which, unconstrained by worry about weight gain, she walked to each afternoon for muffins and slices of pie. She felt a lingering sadness about Chip, she conceded, but such melancholy would exist wherever she was and had, if anything, been diminished by the change of scenery. "And meanwhile, you've managed to sell the house in the blink of an eye," she said. "You're amazing."

"It's Shane who sold it, and it's not official until the closing," Liz said.

"Whatever," Jane said. "It's a fantastic house. Have you been in touch with Jasper?"

"He's texted me a few times, but I haven't answered."

"Good for you, Lizzy."

Though it crossed Liz's mind to mention cavorting with Darcy, Jane's mood was too cheerful, and her faith in Liz's strength of character too recently affirmed, to make the disclosure seem appropriate. Instead, Liz said, "Tell Amanda and Prisha hi from me."

Chapter 98

KITTY WAS DOING push-ups on the floor of her room when Liz paused in the doorway. "You and Mary should start looking for an apartment," Liz said. "The inspection of this house is tomorrow."

As Kitty silently continued her push-ups—her form was excellent—a framed photograph set on the mantel of Kitty's fireplace caught Liz's eye. Liz crossed the room to examine it and found that the photo, which was about two by three inches, was of Mervetta and Kitty. The older woman, who was seated, wore a yellow skirt suit and matching yellow straw hat, and Kitty was crouched next to her in a sleeveless dress, both of them smiling.

"When was the picture of you and Mervetta taken?" Liz asked.

From the floor, Kitty said, "Her seventieth birthday."

"Where was it?"

"Her son's house. Bond Hill."

"Did anyone else from our family go?"

"Dad."

How rare it was, Liz thought, to be surprised in a good way by the members of her family.

"Did you and Dad go to Mervetta's funeral?" Liz asked.

Kitty still hadn't looked up. "Of course," she said.

Chapter 99

"THE LEAST HELEN Lucas could do," Mrs. Bennet said as Liz descended the staircase in her running clothes, "is thank me for introducing my nephew to her daughter. I'll tell you what—finding a man willing to date a young lady that size is no easy feat."

Was it possible that in Mrs. Bennet's mind two mutually exclusive narratives coexisted: the belief that Liz had made a dreadful error in spurning Willie *and* the belief that she, Mrs. Bennet, deserved credit for the match between Willie and Charlotte? It appeared so.

Liz had reached the front door and said, "I'm going for a run."

"Did you send a message on the computer to Allen Bausch yet? He'd be so pleased to reconnect with Mary."

"I don't think Mary wants anything to do with him."

"It's worth a try. You just never know."

"No," Liz said. "That's not true. Sometimes you do know."

Chapter 100

"THAT NIGHT WE met," Darcy said, "at the Lucases' house, when I told you the chair next to me was taken, Dr. Lucas had asked me to save a seat for him. He never sat in it, but I couldn't have ignored the request of my host, who also happens to be one of the directors at a hospital where I see patients. I wasn't being rude to you for the sake of being rude."

"I hope that's been weighing on you all summer." Liz was naked, though only recently so, as was Darcy; he was lying on the bed on his back, his head elevated by two pillows, and she was sitting on him, her legs straddling his waist. Again, they had met by semi-coincidence rather than specific plan; they still hadn't exchanged cellphone numbers or email addresses. "When I overheard you trashing me, my family, and Cincinnati," Liz said, "was that also because you didn't want to offend Dr. Lucas? I'm sure you must have been showing your good breeding somehow, because it couldn't have been that you were just acting like an asshole."

"Touché," Darcy said. Both his hands rested on both her hips, and there was something ludicrous and suspenseful—pleasingly ludicrous and suspenseful—about having this conversation unclothed, prior to the main event.

She said, "Anything else you need to clear the air about?"

She'd been kidding, but his expression became serious. "Do you want children?"

"If you're trying to convince me that we shouldn't use a condom, the answer is absolutely not."

He shook his head. "It isn't that. It's a sincere question."

"No," she said. "I don't want children." The ambivalence she usually feigned during such conversations seemed in this instance unnecessary; she was not, after all, trying to endear herself to him. She said, "If you want, I'll give you possible ways to respond and you can choose the one you like best. A) Oh, Liz, you'll change your mind—you just haven't met the right person." Before continuing, she raised her eyebrows and tilted her head with fake earnestness. "B) But who will look after you when you're old?" Switching to a scolding tone, she said, "C) Yeah, I bet you don't want children, you selfish East Coast narcissist." Pretending to be concerned, she said, "D) Wow, your childhood must have *sucked*. Or—" For the last one, she reverted to patronizing: "E) You just have no idea how rich and wonderful parenthood can be. In fact, you haven't really lived until you've wrestled a shrieking four-year-old to the ground at Target. Now, keep in mind, Fitzwilliam Darcy, that you *can* choose all of the above."

"That's quite a list," he said. "Though I think of you as more of a midwestern narcissist than an East Coast one."

"Believe it or not, I do understand why people have kids. For most of my life, I assumed I'd be a mother, and I'm sure it *is* rewarding, when they're not having tantrums. But the older I've gotten, the less I've wanted it for myself. Watching Jane go through her insemination process was the clincher. I like my life now, there's stuff I want to do in the future that isn't compatible with having kids, and it's not even a big, tortured decision. It's a relief."

"What do you want to do that's not compatible with motherhood?"

Liz shrugged. "Travel. Write a book. Run a marathon. Be a super-doting aunt, without having to deal with things like potty training."

"I don't want children, either."

"Really?" She was genuinely surprised.

He smiled slightly. "Which reason do you think applies to me?"

"You'd know better than I would."

"When I went into neurosurgery, I was making a choice that either I'd be the kind of person who lets his partner do ninety-five percent of the parenting or I wouldn't be a parent, period. Anyone who claims that surgeons pull their weight in their own families is lying. The hours make it impossible, and for me, that's before you factor in research. And, yes, I've heard the argument that not having children is selfish, but that's ridiculous. If you really want to do something unselfish, adopt a seven-year-old black boy from foster care. I assume you'll make fun of me for saying this, but I believe the skill set I have means I can contribute the most to society as a scientist and doctor. Any man with a viable sperm count can become a dad, whereas only some people can perform a decompressive craniectomy."

"Why would I make fun of you for that?" Liz grinned. "I already knew you were an egomaniac." The truth, however, was that he did not seem egomaniacal to her; he seemed principled and thoughtful, and she felt a vague embarrassment that she worked for a magazine that recommended anti-aging creams to women in their twenties and he helped people who'd experienced brain trauma. But surely this wasn't the moment to turn obsequious.

Aside from disrobing, they hadn't engaged in any additional pre-liminary activities. Nevertheless, a few minutes earlier, she had wondered if he had an erection, and she was now sure that he did. She rocked her hips forward once. "I think it's time to get this party started," she said, and she leaned down and kissed him on the lips.

Chapter 101

SHANE HAD WARNED Liz that the inspection of the Tudor could take up to six hours, and it was after much deliberation and with much dread that, for the date on which it would occur, Liz had proposed to her parents a day trip to Berea, Kentucky. A town of fourteen thousand just under two hours from Cincinnati, Berea was known for a thriving artistic community that created and sold paintings, sculptures, jewelry, pottery, and weavings. For many reasons, a visit there seemed likely to be a terrible idea—Liz worried that its wares would be too homespun for her mother's taste *and* that her mother would impulsively purchase, say, an enormous and expensive birdbath—but for the length of the inspection, the goal was to transport Mrs. Bennet out of Cincinnati and render her incapable of returning to the Tudor of her own accord.

When Liz broached the topic of Berea with her father, Mr. Bennet said, "I can scarcely imagine a less tempting invitation."

"Right," Liz said. "But your enjoyment is actually irrelevant."

Mr. Bennet chuckled. "Tell me when we leave."

Mrs. Bennet was only slightly more cooperative. "Deb Larsen commissioned a lady in Berea to make a hooked rug that looks like their house in Michigan," she said. "The likeness is amazing." But then a scowl came over her face. "Don't think I don't know exactly what you're doing, Lizzy."

Before departing, Liz emphasized to Kitty and Mary the importance of staying away from the Tudor until she told them that the inspection had concluded. "If you guys are still thinking of getting an apartment together, today would be a good time to look around," Liz said, and Kitty said, "Maybe, but I'm going to a rowing class Ham teaches at eleven."

Liz's contingent used Mrs. Bennet's car: Liz drove, her father rode in front, and her mother sat in back. It was a relief to Liz to take on the role of chauffeur, both because her parents were awful drivers and because Liz had always felt profoundly uncomfortable spending two-on-one time with them. So divided had their attention been for so many years that on the rare occasions when it wasn't, something felt wrong; there was too much opportunity for scrutiny and uninterrupted conversation. In the interest of avoiding both, Liz had checked out of the Hyde Park Branch Library an audiobook she hoped would occupy the narrow overlap of her parents' mutual interests—a nineteen-hour, thirteen-CD biography of a robber baron, published four years earlier and honored with many literary accolades.

The Bennets were approximately six minutes into the first CD when Mrs. Bennet began remarking on topics ranging from the temperature of the car (it was positively icy in the backseat) to the ongoing indignities of selling the Tudor (and besides, what guarantee did any of them have that Shane was trustworthy? Yes, he may have gone to Seven Hills, but there was something about him she didn't care for. She couldn't put her finger on what, but something) to the dullness of the audiobook (for heaven's sake, did the author really expect people to keep track of all those names and who was related to whom and how?) to speculation about whether Ham would propose to Lydia by Christmas (Mrs. Bennet would have preferred Lydia's husband to have a steadier source of income, God only knew if CrossFit was one of those fitness fads that would come and go, but he did seem to have enough of a head on his shoulders that if this business went under, he could find employment elsewhere).

An hour and fifteen minutes in, Mr. Bennet murmured to Liz, "I'll tell you what we're going to do. When we get to Lexington, you'll drop me off at the Art Museum at the University of Kentucky. You'll pick me up three hours later. What you and your mother choose to do in the interregnum is up to you."

Thus Liz and Mrs. Bennet ended up forgoing Berea for a leisurely lunch at a restaurant called Doodles, where Mrs. Bennet expanded upon several of the subjects she'd introduced in the car while also sharing, in depth, the progress of the item solicitation for the Women's League auction. Though Mrs. Bennet conveyed her disappointment at not reaching Berea, her chagrin seemed expressed more than felt.

Liz's phone pinged as she was standing outside the front of Doodles, waiting for her mother to use the restroom. *Call me,* read the text from Shane.

When she did so, he did not mince words. "Your parents have a spider infestation," he said. "We need to get pest control to the house as soon as possible."

Liz winced. "An infestation meaning, like . . . ?" She trailed off. "Like, how is that quantified?"

"That's what pest control will determine, but it doesn't look good."

"Are the buyers still interested?" Liz asked.

"No," Shane said. "But that's not our biggest problem now."

Chapter 102

OFTEN, ON THE last day or two before an issue of *Mascara* shipped to the printer, Liz found herself in extremely frequent contact with her editor: A sentence needed to be added to reflect that the actress Liz had profiled had just entered rehab, or that the member of the women's national soccer team was now pregnant; the additional sentence meant that an equivalent number of words elsewhere in the article needed to be cut. Either in person in the offices of *Mascara* or by text, email, or phone, Liz and her editor would communicate constantly, in an increasingly exhausted and loopy shorthand. And though by the time the article closed, Liz felt utterly sick of whatever it was about— few readers, she believed, had any idea of the amount of work that went into the casual reading experience they enjoyed while riding the subway or taking a bath—when it was all finished, Liz rather missed her editor and their urgent and knowing exchanges.

Later, when Liz looked back on what she thought of as the Week of Fumigation, she felt a similar and perhaps even more surprising nostalgia for her frequent conversations with Ken Weinrich, the proprietor of Weinrich Pest Control & Extermination and the man who steadfastly guided her on a tour into the unsavory and bewildering world of spider infestation. They first spoke when she was still standing outside Doodles in Lexington, Kentucky, and it was the next morning when he parked his truck in the Bennets' driveway. A sturdy, middle-aged white man, Ken Weinrich entered the house wearing a short-sleeved buttondown tan shirt, jeans, and work boots and carrying a flashlight and a clipboard.

The intervening hours had represented, without question, the worst night's sleep of Liz's entire life, even counting elementary school slumber parties, college hookups, and overseas plane flights. For legal reasons pertaining to the former buyers' retraction of their offer on the house, Liz hadn't spoken directly to the person who'd conducted the Tudor's inspection. However, the inspector had told Shane, and Shane had told Liz, that he'd found spiders on every floor, including inside fireplaces, ceiling light fixtures, and showerheads, and that they were most concentrated in the basement and attic. For this reason, Liz slept, or tried to sleep, in Lydia's bed, but every few minutes she awakened convinced that she could feel the tickle of arachnid legs crawling across her skin. The inspector also had told Shane that the violin-shaped spots on the back of dead specimens indicated that the spiders were the brown recluse kind, whose bites were known to cause swelling, nausea, and flesh-eating ulcers. When Ken Weinrich confirmed the species, Liz's first reaction was relief that Jane was gone from the Tudor.

There were probably, Ken Weinrich estimated, thousands of the spiders hiding in the Tudor, though true to their name, they were mostly reclusive. Not *that* reclusive, Liz thought as she recalled her various encounters with them during the past three months. In retrospect, the evidence was plentiful that calling an exterminator was something she ought to have done during her first week at home.

Assuming no rain, the fumigation was scheduled for two days hence and would require tarps to cover the house from the outside; once they were in place, sulfuryl fluoride gas would be released within them, and special fans would circulate the gas. The Bennets would need to be absent from the property for three days. Repeatedly, Ken Weinrich assured Liz that sulfuryl fluoride didn't leave residue, and that not only the Bennets' furniture but even their food would all be safe for future use. The cost of the fumigation was $10,000.

Mr. Bennet seemed resigned, while Mrs. Bennet met news of the infestation with indignation. Much the way they might have had Liz reported the sighting of a single mouse, neither of her parents appeared all that troubled. "I'm sure it's not *thousands* of spiders," Mrs. Bennet said. During the fumigation, they would stay at the country club.

Liz's sisters, by contrast, were horrified, though in Lydia's case the horror contained a rather gleeful undertone only partially compensated for by Ham's immediate offer to let any Bennets bunk at his house in Mount Adams. However, that very day, Mary and Kitty found a two-bedroom apartment—just, as it happened, a few blocks from Darcy's—and Liz was the one to pay the first month's rent and cosign their lease. Not wishing to risk the transport of spiders into this new living space, Mary, Kitty, and Liz drove to the Ikea thirty minutes north of Cincinnati, where Liz bought each sister a bed and, to share, a couch, a kitchen table, and chairs.

She wasn't ignorant of the advantages to her of underwriting their acquisitions: Now beholden, they'd have no choice but to obey the directives she laid out for after her departure from Cincinnati, among them instructions about monitoring their father's diet; keeping the Tudor in a state appropriate to be visited by Shane, other real estate agents, and their clients; and making themselves available to their mother for miscellaneous errands in the forty-eight hours prior to the Women's League luncheon. Though the luncheon itself was little more than two weeks away, Liz had decided not to remain in town for it. She just couldn't stand Cincinnati anymore. She didn't want to spend another night in the now-spidery, soon-to-be-chemical-laden Tudor. She didn't want to sleep for two weeks on Mary and Kitty's couch. And although she appreciated the offer, she didn't want to move in with Ham and Lydia and watch them kiss and coo and drink kale smoothies. With an abrupt urgency, she wanted to be home, in *her* home, which was Brooklyn. She wanted to get saag paneer and samosas delivered from her favorite Indian restaurant and eat them alone on her living room couch while reading a magazine, blasting her air conditioner, and not defending her lack of a husband.

"Do you think it's awful if I go straight back to New York after I interview Kathy de Bourgh in Houston?" she asked Jane over the phone, and Jane said, "I'm not exactly in a position to tell you not to."

Lying on Mary and Kitty's new $500 couch, Liz couldn't decide whether her behavior as a daughter and sister was exemplary or indefensible. On the one hand, she had in recent days exerted herself to an unprecedented degree to ensure the welfare of her family members. On the other, she would not be waiting even until the aeration stage of the fumigation was complete to leave. She'd be in New York in time for Labor Day weekend, and indeed, the main impetus for her flurry of activity was the knowledge of her departure.

Chapter 103

THE WAY LIZ packed her suitcase and purse was to drive them empty in the trunk of her father's Cadillac from the Tudor to the small lawn in front of her sisters' new apartment; also in the trunk were full trash bags containing her clothes, toiletries, digital recorders, and laptop computer. She knelt in the grass and examined each article of clothing, each item from her Dopp kit, to ensure that no spider was clinging to it. She wondered if another resident of the building would complain—it probably looked like she was setting up for a garage sale—but no one did, and she found no spiders. When she'd finished, she carried her full bags into her sisters' apartment, relieved that she would never be any-one's mother and thus would never need to pick through the scalp of a child, searching in just this way for lice eggs.

Chapter 104

HAVING NOT SEEN Darcy for nearly a week, Liz forwent the pretense of a run and simply walked from her sisters' apartment building to his and knocked on the door. He didn't answer, but as she left the building, surly about the lack of gratification, she encountered him on his way in, carrying several plastic grocery bags in both hands.

"I assumed you were working," she said, and he shook his head.

"I go in tonight at six. Is something wrong?" She was deciding how to answer—was he *trying* to make her feel foolish?—when he added, with some degree of awkwardness, "Or did you just come over to, ah—right. Come in. By all means."

"Here." She extended her hand. "Give me a few bags."

As she followed him back up the stairs, she took a perverse delight in sharing the latest news about her family, though instead of mockingly declaring his lack of surprise that the Bennets were harboring an insect plague of biblical proportions, he said, with what bordered on sympathy, "Old houses have a lot of issues. That's a shame the buyers retracted their offer."

"Well, Kitty and Mary are your neighbors now," she said. "They're at the corner of Millsbrae and Atlantic, in case you need to borrow a cup of sugar."

"I'm surprised a landlord would rent to two people without jobs."

"It's my name on the lease."

They had reached the second floor, and Darcy said as he unlocked his door, "You're not worried about destroying your credit?"

"Oh, I assume I will. But I don't see what the alternative is."

Inside, Darcy put away the groceries requiring refrigeration while she sat on a kitchen stool; he offered her beer and water, both of which she declined; and within ten minutes the true reason for her visit had been not only initiated but, for both parties, successfully completed.

"This so-called hate sex," Darcy said then. "Is it the norm for you?" Their latest encounter, like the earlier ones, had been consummated above the sheets, and they were presently positioned near each other but no longer touching; in order to comply with cuddle avoidance, Liz had rolled away from him and lay, as he did, on her back.

Liz laughed. "If you have to ask if someone's slutty, that probably means the answer is yes."

"That's hardly what I was implying. I just wonder if you find it more expedient. Though you did say you recently got out of a relationship, if I remember correctly."

"No, hate sex isn't the norm for me, but neither is living in Cincinnati. And as a matter of fact, I'm about to leave. I go tomorrow afternoon to Houston to interview Kathy de Bourgh, and I'll fly on to New York from there."

"You're leaving town tomorrow?" Darcy seemed surprised.

"Don't be too heartbroken," Liz said. "Have you ever tried online dating? If not, you should."

"Have *you* ever tried online dating?"

"Sure, and I definitely would do it if I lived here."

For a few seconds, Darcy was quiet. Finally, he said, "Is the person you just broke up with Jasper Wick?"

"If it were, that'd be scandalous, wouldn't it? Since he's a married man *and* a Stanford outcast." Liz glanced at her watch. "A part of me is tempted to offer to write your online dating profile, but I'm not sure it's ethical to inflict you on another human woman. It wouldn't be very sisterly, if you know what I mean."

She had been teasing, but the expression on his face seemed to be one of genuine displeasure. He said, "I don't need your help with an online dating profile."

"Fair enough. You do have a PhD, I hear." Liz swung her legs over the side of the bed and reached for her clothes on the floor. She was fastening the clasp of her bra when she heard Darcy say, "That tattoo always surprises me."

It was two inches by one inch, an image of a typewriter on the small of her back. Without turning, she said, "Want to guess how old I was when I got it?"

"Twenty?"

"Even worse. Twenty-three. The irony is that I thought it was much cooler than a flower or a Chinese symbol. I was declaring my serious ambitions as a writer. But somehow, all these years later, it's never been the right moment to show it to any of the people I've interviewed." Liz glanced over her shoulder. "Maybe you should get the Hippocratic oath on your butt."

"Maybe so," he said, and Liz felt a twinge of something. She still didn't particularly like him, but it was hard not to wonder if they'd cross paths again. He tapped his left biceps. "Or the Skyline Chili logo up here."

She had pulled on her shirt and underwear and she stood, turning to face him as she stepped into her jeans. Presumably, it was the last time they'd see each other before she left town, and this unexpected welling of emotion—it was gaining rather than decreasing in intensity. Also, rather bizarrely, there was some chance that a few minutes earlier, during what had appeared to be the height of his pleasure, Darcy had uttered the words, "My darling." If this had indeed happened, Liz was confident the utterance had been accidental, and certainly it had been acknowledged by neither of them. In any case, what was she supposed to do now—hug him goodbye like a co-worker? No, she would not hug him.

"You're way too good for Jasper, if that's who it was," Darcy said. He seemed simultaneously like a stranger and someone she knew extremely well; there was either an enormous amount to say or nothing at all.

She tried to sound lighthearted. "I wouldn't be so sure of that."

Chapter 105

"AFTER I LEAVE town, my parents might tell you they've changed their mind about selling the house," Liz said to Shane. She had met him at Coffee Emporium on Erie Avenue. "My mom especially, but don't trust her. If that happens, call me right away."

"I appreciate the sensitivity of the situation," Shane said. "But this could quickly get beyond the legal scope of what a real estate agent can do."

"They want to sell the house," Liz said. "Or at least my dad recognizes that they have no choice. If they say otherwise, just treat it like static. And the minute you know another agent is planning to show it, call me, I'll call Mary or Kitty, and one of them will make sure it looks okay and get my parents out."

Shane squinted in a way that took Liz a few seconds to recognize as fake casual. "Speaking of Kitty," he said, "how old is she?"

"Twenty-six." Liz felt a mercenary and possibly disloyal temptation to add, *And if you sell our house, she's all yours.* But he hadn't yet asked if she was single; he was wondering, Liz could tell, but he hadn't asked.

Chapter 106

"I FIGURED OUT where Mary goes," Kitty said. "And it's hilarious." Liz had been lying on the Ikea couch in Kitty and Mary's living room, reading a long article on her laptop in the newest issue of the magazine where she and Jasper had once been fact-checkers.

"Where?" Liz asked.

Kitty held up car keys. "Come with me."

"Is it good or bad?"

"Just come," Kitty said. "It's worth it."

They drove through Oakley—this was the route they had followed to the campus of Seven Hills for countless mornings of Liz's life—but instead of continuing to Oaklawn Drive and making a left, Kitty turned right into the parking lot of Madison Bowl.

"She bowls?" Liz said.

"She's in a *league*." Kitty's voice was thick with amusement. "And it's not a hipster league. It's middle-aged fat people."

"That's not against the law."

"Once you see them, you'll think it should be."

As Kitty pulled into a parking space and turned off the car, Liz said, "She's in there now?"

"I followed her here a few weeks ago. I needed to make sure she wasn't in a satanic cult before we became roommates."

"Did you tell her you'd followed her?"

Kitty shook her head.

"So what's your plan? We go inside and yell 'Surprise!' at her?"

"Last time, she changed in her car into a red-and-black uniform," Kitty said. "Don't you think it's weird that she's so secretive about something so dumb?"

"Because she knew this was how you'd act if she told us."

Kitty had parked near a light pole, and in the sallow illumination it provided, the sisters looked at each other. Petulantly, Kitty said, "You're no fun."

"You know what, Kitty? You can decide to be a good person. If you're lucky, you have a long adulthood ahead of you, and you might actually be happier if you're nice instead of mean."

"I *am* a good person," Kitty said. But it was with clear resentment that, to Liz's relief, she started the ignition.

$$Chapter \ 107$$

LIZ CALLED JANE from the Ikea couch, and when she told her sister where she was, Jane said, "I'm sorry your last night in Cincinnati isn't very ceremonious."

"Whatever," Liz said. "This way I'll appreciate the luxury of my Houston hotel room."

"I've been thinking about what the extermination man told you," Jane said, "and the idea of Mom and Dad eating food that was in the house during the fumigation—it makes me nervous. What if you move stuff to Kitty and Mary's place beforehand, or just throw it away? Some of Mom's spices are probably from the eighties anyway."

The annoyance Liz felt—it was because she knew Jane was right, and she also knew that clearing out the many kitchen cabinets, plus the refrigerators on two floors, would not be an insignificant task. And Ken Weinrich's team was supposed to arrive at the Tudor at ten the next morning.

Liz glanced at the closed door of Kitty's bedroom; light shone out from the crack, and she could hear the sound of whatever TV show Kitty was watching on her smartphone. Mary was out, presumably still at the bowling alley. Liz would enlist them both, she thought. To Jane, she said, "Want me to send you a picture of the house when it's tented?"

"No!" Jane sounded dismayed.

"I won't if you don't want me to." Liz lowered her voice. "There's something I haven't told you about Darcy." Her wish to confess stemmed less from a moral awakening than from confusion over the uneasiness she'd experienced leaving Darcy's apartment that afternoon; she needed to discuss the oddness of their final encounter.

"Do you know," Jane said before Liz revealed more, and Jane's tone was equanimous rather than bitter, "if it weren't for Darcy, I have a hunch Chip and I would still be together?"

"What are you talking about?"

"The night he broke up with me, one of the things he said was that Darcy didn't think we made a good couple. Chip also said, as if I didn't know this, how much he respects Darcy."

An unpleasant alertness had come over Liz. "Why would Darcy have disapproved of you and Chip?"

"Who knows? Although I'm sure I could torment myself from now until the end of time guessing." Jane laughed a little, which seemed to Liz a sign of her sister's progress. Indeed, Jane appeared far calmer about what she was describing than Liz felt. "Anyway, it's not like Darcy's low opinion of our family has ever been a secret," Jane said. "What's the thing you haven't told me about him?"

Liz thought miserably of her conclusion—her entirely self-serving conclusion, she realized—that sleeping with Darcy was not wrong. What disloyalty to Jane she'd shown! Surely divulging her trysts to Jane at this juncture, especially when those trysts were now finished, would serve no purpose. Haltingly, Liz said, "That day you fainted, when you were at the hospital—I ran into Darcy outside the ER. He helped me figure out where to go."

Jane was quiet, seemingly waiting for more.

Lamely, Liz added, "I couldn't remember if I'd mentioned that to you."

"I do feel like I can see things more from Chip's perspective than I could at first," Jane said. "What if instead of me telling him I was pregnant, he'd told me that another woman was pregnant with his child? Or if—well, the way Amanda and Prisha had Gideon was using sperm from a friend of theirs, a straight friend. If Chip had donated his sperm to a lesbian couple he was close to, no matter how carefully he'd tried to explain it, it would have seemed weird."

"Not really. This stuff happens now."

"But if you're just getting to know the other person?"

"You're being too easy on him." Liz was, however, unsure if she really thought this or merely wished to deflect attention from herself and what she'd almost disclosed. Then she said, "Kitty solved the mystery of Mary's evening outings. Mary doesn't know we know, but apparently she's in a bowling league."

"Really?" Jane sounded tickled. "That's so cute."

Chapter 108

THE DOORBELL OF the apartment, a sound Liz hadn't previously heard, woke her just before seven in the morning. In the boxer shorts and T-shirt she'd slept in—the shirt was one she'd excavated from her closet at the Tudor, and it read HARVEST FAIR 1991 across the front— she opened the door. Insofar as she was awake enough to have any such expectations, she assumed it would be the building's superintendent, or perhaps the landlord; but to Liz's astonishment, it was Fitzwilliam Darcy. Instinctively, she crossed her arms over her braless chest. "What are you doing here?" she said.

"You told me your sisters' building was at the intersection of Millsbrae and Atlantic." Darcy's countenance was grim: His skin was unusually pale, and there were pronounced bags beneath his eyes. He wore green scrubs, and Liz suspected he'd driven directly from his overnight shift. They looked at each other—was she supposed to invite him in?—and somewhere nearby, an oriole trilled. Darcy said, "I take it you're still planning to leave town this afternoon?"

"Yeah, after the epic fumigation. Or after it starts—it won't be finished for three days."

There was a pause. Then, in a severe voice and without preamble, Darcy said, "I'm in love with you."

"Ha, ha," Liz said.

"It's probably an illusion caused by the release of oxytocin during sex," Darcy continued, "but I *feel* as if I'm in love with you. You're not beautiful, and you aren't nearly as funny as you think you are. You're a gossip fiend who tries to pass off your nosiness as anthropological interest in the human condition. And your family, obviously, is a disgrace. Yet in spite of all common sense, I can't stop thinking about you. The time has come for us to abandon this ridiculous pretense of hate sex and admit that we're a couple." Darcy had delivered this monologue stiffly, while mostly avoiding eye contact, but when he was finished, he looked expectantly at Liz.

If she had ever been so bewildered, she could not recall when. And though she understood that his remarks contained some flattering essence, she had never been more insulted. For several seconds, she searched for words and finally said, "So this isn't—you're not joking? Or are you?"

"I'm not joking at all."

"Darcy, how could we possibly be a couple? We don't even like each other."

"That was at first."

"For you, maybe," Liz said. "I mean, sorry, but I still consider you a jackass. Do you imagine you're doing me some big favor by overlooking how unattractive I am and how much you hate my family and declaring your love anyway?"

Darcy's surprise was apparent in his widened eyes, a surprise, Liz thought, that served as further evidence of his arrogance. Tightly, he said, "I was under the impression that you appreciated candor. It wasn't my intent to offend you."

"How could I possibly want to be with the person who pushed Chip and Jane apart? I know now that you told him to break up with her. And I know you were part of getting Jasper kicked out of Stanford. This idea you have that your judgment is better than everyone else's, that you alone should decide the fates of other people—the only question is if being a surgeon gave you a god complex or if your god complex is what led to your being a surgeon."

"I see," Darcy said. "And you believe that I have not only the will to control people's behavior but also the power?"

"The facts speak for themselves."

"Let me assure you that the idea for Chip to leave medicine and go back on *Eligible* didn't come from me."

"You may not have bought his plane ticket to L.A., but I'm sure you influenced him."

"And when you suggest that I got Jasper expelled from Stanford"—Darcy's expression was haughty—"just so I fully comprehend, was it that he was innocent and I planted evidence on him, or was it that he was guilty but I should have unilaterally decided to let him off the hook?"

"There are worse crimes than writing an idiotic story."

Darcy scrutinized her face before saying, "Yes, there are."

"Even if you hadn't screwed over Jasper and Jane, I'd never want you to be my boyfriend," Liz said. "And even if you hadn't just insulted my looks, my personality, and my family, and blamed your interest in me on sex hormones—even if you'd expressed your attraction like a normal human being, I still wouldn't."

She was experiencing a pleasing anger, a satisfying outrage rare in her daily encounters, and she expected him to be experiencing it, too. But rather than glaring back at her, he seemed wounded, and a small seed of doubt formed within Liz.

"I apologize for misreading the situation so egregiously," he said. Then—it was such a strange, old-fashioned gesture—he basically bowed to her. "Forgive me." He turned, and in a matter of seconds, without further farewell, he was gone. Immediately, Liz began to question whether she'd imagined the whole bizarre exchange.

Still standing on the threshold of the open door, Liz found that she was shaking; her anger was quickly slipping away, replaced with a growing uneasiness. How was it possible that Darcy—*Darcy*—had announced that he was in love with her? If it was at some level gratifying, it was also unthinkable. How thoroughly confused she felt, how rattled and off-kilter.

From behind the closed door of her bedroom, Mary called, "Lizzy, did someone just ring our doorbell?"

Chapter 109

FOR THE REST of the day—while helping her parents settle in at the country club, while dropping off unexpired canned goods from the Tudor at a food pantry, and while discussing final fumigation preparations with Ken Weinrich (yes, Liz had watered the soil the previous day)—through all of it, Liz thought continuously of Darcy. Eating a late lunch on the porch of the country club with Mary and her parents, Liz could hardly follow what anyone was saying, even when the subject changed from Mrs. Bennet's speculation about why things hadn't worked for Jane and Chip to what Kathy de Bourgh would be like. Frowning, Mrs. Bennet said, "I've always found her very strident."

It was Mr. Bennet who was driving Liz to the airport for her flight to Houston, though they stopped first at her sisters' apartment to get her bags. Just outside the door of their unit, set on the floor and leaning against the wall, was a plain business envelope with Liz's first name written on it.

"Who's that from?" Mary asked, and Liz folded it in half, stuffed it into her pants pocket, and said, "Nobody."

Mary made a scoffing sound. "Yeah, apparently."

The envelope practically thrummed as Liz rode to the airport in the passenger seat of her father's car.

"Do you remember when you and Mom are allowed back in the house?" Liz asked as her father merged onto 71 South. "It's one o'clock on Friday. You'll need to dump out the ice that's in the ice maker. Don't make a gin and tonic with it."

"It's remarkable, isn't it," Mr. Bennet said, "that for decades at a time, I've stayed alive without your daily instructions?"

"The fumigation guys will have opened all your drawers and cabinets for air circulation," Liz said. "And the doors and windows, too. But Mary will come over and help close everything. And then, please, will you and Mom both really, really try to keep the house looking presentable for when agents want to show it?"

Without checking his rearview mirror, Mr. Bennet moved over a lane, and a car just behind them honked. "Relax, my dear," he said. "We'll all be just fine."

"Do you realize you almost had an accident right now?"

Mr. Bennet reached out his arm and patted Liz's knee. In an uncharacteristically serious tone, he said, "Lizzy, you've been a voice of reason amid a cacophony of foolishness. It was very good of you to come home this summer."

Chapter 110

AS SOON AS she had checked her suitcase, made it through airport security, and found the gate from which her plane would depart, Liz opened the envelope. The letter filled four pages of notebook paper, and Darcy's handwriting, which she had never seen, was of medium size and no particular beauty; inscribed in black ballpoint ink, it seemed to be that of a person making an effort at legibility:

Dear Liz,

First off, don't worry that I'll try to persuade you here of what I suggested earlier today. The sooner we can both forget my misguided idea, which you obviously found so repulsive, the better for both of us. That said, I'm compelled to clarify a few points regarding Jane and Jasper Wick. I realize that some of what I say might offend you further, and that's not my intent, but if it's a by-product of stating the truth, so be it.

I was, of course, aware that Chip had fallen for your sister. In fact, his feelings for her seemed deeper than for any woman I'd observed him with before. However, although Jane is always a polite person, I wasn't convinced that she reciprocated his interest. The night of Chip's dinner party, I heard Jane tell you that she didn't think she should keep the bike Chip had bought her because of her doubts about their relationship. Granted, I already didn't think your family was the ideal one for Chip to marry into—I know you won't want to hear this, but, beyond your mother's pushiness and preoccupation with social climbing, I find Lydia and Kitty's indifference to basic manners mind-boggling. And remember that I have a sister close in age to them. I didn't think such shallow, pampered egotists existed except on reality television . . . which brings me to my next point. Regardless of my reservations about Jane (reservations Caroline shared, by the way), I couldn't have convinced Chip to leave Cincinnati and join the *Eligible* reunion. Frankly, I assume he used Jane's pregnancy as an excuse to do what he already wanted to, which was take a break from medicine.

You know your sister better than I do, and I'm willing to concede that I may have been wrong about her feelings for Chip. But if she is or was smitten with him, I didn't see the evidence. Nevertheless, I genuinely like Jane, and if I've caused her to suffer, I'm sorry.

As for your accusation that I mistreated Jasper Wick, it's more difficult to refute because I'm not sure precisely what you think I've done. However, I'll tell you the facts, and if you want corroboration, multiple articles ran at the time in the Stanford newspaper.

I knew Jasper only by name for most of our time on campus and didn't have an opinion about him. When we were seniors, he took a creative writing class (again, this is all part of the public record) and he turned in a story written from the perspective of a guy in Sigma Alpha Epsilon. I'm sorry to say that because of the charges eventually

brought against him, and because I was part of the judicial
affairs board, I had the unpleasant experience of reading
this story, and I'm confident it was the worst possible version (if there's any version that's not bad) of frat-boy lit.
Jasper's crimes against the English language weren't the
reason he got into trouble, though. I wasn't in the class (I
suspect you'll be neither surprised nor impressed when you
hear that the only English course I took in college was to
fulfill a requirement), but apparently the discussion of the
story was very acrimonious, and the instructor, who was a
woman named Tricia Randolph, sided with students who
said they found the story offensive.

Ms. Randolph, who had come to Stanford for a two-year
writing fellowship, lived in a ground-floor studio in an on-
campus graduate student complex. That night, she returned
to her apartment to find that a window screen had been
removed and there were puddles of urine all over the papers
on her desk and the keyboard of her laptop computer. People had seen Jasper loitering outside the building, obviously
drunk, and during questioning with campus police, he con-
fessed to being the culprit. It was clearly a case of inten-
tional property damage, and there was question as to
whether, because Ms. Randolph was black, it was also a hate
crime, though that charge was ultimately dismissed. I always had the impression that Jasper saw urinating on Ms.
Randolph's desk as a silly prank and viewed himself as a
victim of rising political correctness, but to me his trans-
gression absolutely had a racial component; whether or not
he himself was aware of it, I doubt he'd have been so bla-
tantly disrespectful to a white instructor. Again, though,
when the judicial panel voted unanimously to expel him, it
was for the property damage charge. Presumably, the sting
of expulsion was exacerbated by the fact that it happened a
couple weeks before our graduation, thus denying him a
college degree, but my take is, if you want to graduate from

Stanford, don't piss on people's desks. Clearly, you and I have different impressions of Jasper, and I hope this will shed light on why I'm not a fan. It would be nice to think a person can evolve, but I'm not sure I believe it. In any case, to reiterate what I told you yesterday: Whatever the parameters of your relationship with Jasper, you're much too good for him. And please don't think that in making such a declaration, I'm suggesting myself as the alternative. Your opinion of me is abundantly clear.

I was tempted to tell you all of this today, but due to the unsettling nature of our conversation, I didn't trust myself to relate the information in a coherent way. While I'm not even sure you'll read this letter, I find the misapprehensions you're under troubling enough that I'm nevertheless moved to try setting them straight.

I wish you luck back in New York.

Best,
Fitzwilliam Darcy

Chapter 111

CONTRARY TO DARCY'S speculation, Liz didn't merely read the letter; she reread it many times and with each round experienced fresh incertitude and distress. His comments about Jane were not particularly convincing. That *he* believed his own version of events was plausible, but she suspected that his antipathy to her family had contributed more to the part he'd played in disrupting Jane and Chip's courtship than his doubts about Jane's enthusiasm for his friend. She was unsurprised to learn that Caroline Bingley also had disapproved of the union.

It was Darcy's description of Jasper Wick that gave Liz pause. Simultaneously so disturbing and so credible, it matched Jasper's own account in many ways. And yet, was Liz really such a poor judge of character? Was Jasper not merely flawed but racist and truly reprobate? Just as their relationship had too closely and obviously resembled a cliché for her to believe it was one, Jasper had alluded too frequently to being a jerk for Liz to interpret his allusions as anything except jokes; wouldn't a true jerk show less self-awareness?

As she'd read the letter for the first time, Liz's stomach had tightened, and when she took her seat on the plane, she realized that the uncomfortable sensation was one of shame. The proof was plain that both her rudeness to Darcy on nearly every occasion and her faith in Jasper had been wrongly directed. Accompanying her shame was, on Jane's behalf, a great regret, because it now seemed that misunderstanding rather than lack of affection from either party had been responsible for the collapse of Jane and Chip's relationship. And yet, with Chip filming in Los Angeles and Jane ever more pregnant in upstate New York, a clarification that could have occurred over coffee in Cincinnati appeared logistically impossible.

That Liz herself had dismissed Darcy's declaration of love was the one decision she didn't regret, for she could no sooner have accepted his entreaty than she could have accepted Cousin Willie's. She and Darcy scarcely knew each other; the entirety of their interactions had been spent either quarreling or having sex and, in one case, on the evening when they'd each wanted the other person to be on top, both. (He had acquiesced.) She wouldn't deny that she'd had fun with Darcy, of a confined, antagonistic, and peculiar sort, but surely fun could not be the basis of a relationship. Could it?

The plane began to accelerate on the runway, and presently, they had lifted off. From her window seat, Liz watched the buildings and rolling hills shrink beneath her, the Ohio River go motionless, the cars on the highways slow to a crawl before vanishing from view. Cincinnati resembled in this moment a miniature model of the sort an architectural firm might create; it didn't seem large enough to contain all the events of the past months. She had wondered, she now realized, if she'd make it out or end up staying forever, trapped by obligation and inertia; yet it was the very act of leaving that cast doubt on the desirability of escape. Or maybe it was nothing as symbolic as doubt, she thought as the pilot curved south; maybe all that was being cast was the shadow of her own plane over the dappled green midwestern afternoon.

Time seemed, as it always does in adulthood after a particular stretch has concluded, no matter how ponderous or unpleasant the stretch was to endure, to have passed quickly indeed.

Part Two

Chapter 112

RIDING IN A taxi from Houston's George Bush Intercontinental Airport to her downtown hotel, Liz called Jane's cellphone. When her sister answered, Liz blurted out, "Jane, I had sex with Darcy four times, and this morning he came to Kitty and Mary's apartment and said he's in love with me."

"Are you serious?"

"I was in my pajamas and didn't even have a bra on."

"What did you tell him?"

"What do you think I told him? He's crazy."

Jane was quiet before saying, "Maybe he's not as bad as we thought, if he recognizes how special you are."

"Actually, he told me I'm not beautiful, I'm not funny, I'm gossipy, and he can't stand Mom—this is *during* his declaration of love. But I still don't think he could imagine any woman, including me, turning down the chance to be his girlfriend."

"Poor guy."

"We're talking about the person who came between you and Chip."

"But think how infatuated with you he must be to swallow his pride, which we all know he has lots of."

"Do you remember that conversation you and I had at Chip's dinner party about how he'd bought a mountain bike for you and you didn't know if you should accept it? Apparently, Darcy overheard us and took your hesitation about the bike as hesitation about Chip in general."

"I can understand that."

"Aren't you mad? Darcy's given me grief for eavesdropping, but at least I do it competently."

"Lizzy, I *did* have reservations about Chip. I expressed them to you more than once. I liked him a lot, but—" Jane paused. "The whole time I was with Chip, I wasn't sure that I was pregnant, but I wasn't sure I wasn't."

"I have something weird to tell you about Jasper, too," Liz said.

"Have you guys been in touch?"

"Not really." He had sent two more texts, neither of which Liz had answered. The first had been another link—this one to a list of unintentionally funny newspaper headlines—and the second had said, *R u ignoring me?* "I didn't know it until recently," Liz said, "but Jasper got expelled from Stanford a few weeks before he was supposed to graduate. Jasper and Darcy were in the same class, and even though Jasper had never mentioned his expulsion, he did admit that it had happened. But the story he told me and the story Darcy told me only sort of match up. Basically, according to Darcy, Jasper was kicked out for—" Liz hesitated out of concern for the taxi driver, who, if listening, had already learned an unseemly amount about her in a few minutes. But really, there were few ways of accurately describing the act. "For peeing on the desk of his creative writing professor," she continued. "And the professor was a black woman."

"He *peed*?" Jane said. "As in going to the bathroom?"

"Yes," Liz said. "That kind of pee."

"On her *desk*?"

"Yes," Liz said. "On the desk in her apartment."

"That's the strangest thing I've ever heard," Jane said.

"It's gross, right? Even if he was twenty-two at the time, and drunk—there's no way it's not gross. Darcy also said Jasper never got a degree. Does that mean he's lied to every employer he's ever had? It makes it even weirder that he wears that Stanford ring."

"Does he?" Jane said. "I hadn't noticed."

"It's gold. I've always thought it looks like what a bond trader from New Jersey would have worn in the 1980s."

"Did Darcy make up the story about Jasper because he's jealous?"

"No, I trust Darcy." The statement felt odd. "But if Jasper peed on his professor's desk, was he standing? Or did he go in a jar, then pour it out?"

"Oh, Lizzy."

"And was it spontaneous, like he has to take a leak and thinks, *I'll do it on her desk*? Or did he decide ahead of time?"

"Jasper has always seemed like a complicated person."

"That's generous." Out the window of Liz's taxi, the other lanes of the highway were packed with cars; to her right, the sun was setting and the sky was tinged pink. "Anyway," she said, "how are you?"

"I'm good," Jane said. "I met with the doctor today, and she was really nice. Was it sad leaving Cincinnati?"

Liz thought of her final view of the Tudor, when the tenting had been almost complete. The tarps Ken Weinrich's crew used had yellow and royal blue stripes, not unlike those for a circus, and this had lent a festive yet undignified mood to the proceedings. Then she thought of Darcy standing just outside her sisters' apartment in his scrubs. "It wasn't sad exactly," Liz said, "but it was different from what I'd expected."

Chapter 113

THOUGH LIZ SOMETIMES went along with the pretense that interviewing celebrities was glamorous, the truth was that she rarely enjoyed it. Arranging the interviews through the celebrity's publicist and
the publicist's assistant was always onerous, with frequent cancellations
or time changes; during the interviews, celebrities often responded to
questions using answers they had given before, which meant Liz's editor wouldn't want them included; publicists tended to sit in, chaperone-
like, on the interviews, thereby dissuading the celebrity from saying
anything ostensibly off-topic; and a general air of urgency attended the
encounters, as if the celebrities were heads of state managing a nuclear
threat rather than, as was usually the case, good-looking people who
appeared onscreen in fictitious stories. Additionally, Liz always worried
that her digital recorders—with celebrities, she used two—would fail
her. These interviews were stressful then, without necessarily being
interesting.

At the same time—and Liz had found this assertion to be displeasing to some people who were not famous, such as her own younger sisters—most celebrities were charismatic, intelligent, and warm. Lydia, Kitty, Mary, and indeed much of the general population clearly wished to hear that celebrities were, in person, rude or moronic or not that attractive, but this had rarely been Liz's experience. Publicists were frequently rude, and celebrities almost never were. Also, the celebrities usually were *more* beautiful in the flesh, emitting a certain glow that made their fame seem inevitable.

That Kathy de Bourgh, while eighty years old and not a Hollywood starlet, possessed this glow was evident to Liz even from halfway back in the vast hotel ballroom where the National Society of Women in Finance keynote speech occurred. The speech began at one-fifteen in the afternoon, before an audience of two thousand; no more than a dozen of them, by Liz's calculation, were men. Two large screens on either side of the stage projected Kathy de Bourgh's image to all corners of the room, and in the first few seconds after Kathy de Bourgh was introduced, Liz noted that she had had Botox, as well as dermal fillers, though after that it was Kathy de Bourgh's poise and the substance of her speech that Liz focused on. Because Liz had read *Revolutions and Rebellions* as well as Kathy de Bourgh's subsequent book of essays and her memoir, much of the advice she dispensed and some of the personal anecdotes she shared were familiar, but her crisp and energetic delivery made everything fresh. Whether citing statistics about the dearth of women in professional leadership roles or recommending the steps individual women could take to command authority, she showed confidence and good humor. Being an icon, it seemed, agreed with her.

At the speech's conclusion, Liz waited in her chair in the ballroom, as directed to do via a text that morning from Kathy de Bourgh's publicist, Valerie. After eight minutes, Valerie texted to say Kathy de Bourgh was on a call but Liz would be escorted to the greenroom imminently.

And then, as they had many times already in the last thirty hours, Darcy's remarks outside her sisters' apartment came back to her. *I'm in love with you. I can't stop thinking about you.* Yes, his confession had contained multiple slights, but those words had flanked them. To re-call such declarations was marvelously bothersome, it was vexing and delectable. *I'm in love with you. I can't stop thinking about you.* They made her feel as if her heart were releasing lava.

She had planned to blithely leave Darcy behind, but it seemed now that matters between them were unresolved. What it was that needed to be settled, however—what she might convey to him—continued to elude her. Surely it was related to the indifference to his feelings, the defiance even, that she'd demonstrated during their final conversation. If on certain topics he'd shown insensitivity, she'd concluded that his misbehavior had been of a less egregious variety than her own. She also couldn't help wondering: Was he *still* in love with her? Had her hostile response immediately nullified his desire? Really, how could it not have?

"Liz?" Approaching from a door near the stage was a young woman in a charcoal pantsuit. "I'm Valerie Wright. Kathy de Bourgh is ready to see you."

Chapter 114

IN THE GREENROOM, Kathy de Bourgh was eating an arugula salad. She stood to firmly shake Liz's hand and said, "I apologize for keeping you waiting, but my dog has keratitis and I was touching base with the vet."

"I'm so sorry," Liz said. She knew that Kathy de Bourgh was the owner of a Pekingese named Button, though Liz did not mention this knowledge because of the fine line between due diligence and creepiness.

As they sat, Kathy de Bourgh smiled and said, "Now that we've both apologized within the first thirty seconds of our conversation about women and power, shall we begin?" While Liz set her two digital recorders on the glass tabletop and turned them on, Kathy de Bourgh added, "You might not know this, but I myself was once a writer for *Mascara*."

"Oh, it's one of our claims to fame," Liz said. She was reassured that Kathy de Bourgh knew what publication she was being interviewed for; regularly, very famous people didn't.

"That was roughly fifteen thousand years ago," Kathy de Bourgh said. "During the Pleistocene epoch."

Liz said, "Knowing you'd worked for the magazine was the main reason I was excited to get a job there."

Kathy de Bourgh laughed. "Liz, flattery will get you everywhere."

As Valerie Wright and two other women whose identities never became clear to Liz sat in chairs against the wall and typed on their smartphones, Liz asked Kathy de Bourgh about feminism's present and past, about whether its current prominence in popular culture struck her as meaningful or fleeting, about reproductive freedom and equal compensation, race and gender, mentoring, ambition, likability, and whether having it all was a realistic possibility or a phrase that ought to be expurgated from the English language. Usually in interviews, every few minutes the subject would say something articulate or insightful enough that Liz knew she could use it in her article, and she'd feel a little lift, or maybe relief; with Kathy de Bourgh, every sentence of every answer was usable. And the responses *weren't* all ones Liz had heard before.

As they reached the end of the allotted twenty minutes, which Liz had high hopes of exceeding, she said, "You didn't marry until you were sixty-seven years old. Was that due to the difficulty of finding a spouse who would treat you as an equal partner?"

Kathy de Bourgh smiled again. "Are you married?" she asked.

Et tu, Kathy de Bourgh? Liz thought and shook her head. She knew that Kathy de Bourgh's husband, a renowned architect, had died of an aneurysm only three years after their wedding.

"I considered getting married many times," Kathy de Bourgh said. "I certainly had my share of suitors. But—" She paused. "How can I describe this?" Liz remained quiet—remaining quiet was the most reliable tool in her interviewing kit—and Kathy de Bourgh said, "With all the men I dated before Benjamin, there was some degree of performance involved. Even when those men and I had a lot of chemistry, or maybe especially then, it was like we were performing our chemistry either for an audience or just for each other. I was engaged once to a very good-looking man"—*Indeed,* Liz thought, *to the attorney general of New York*—"but eventually I realized that when I was with him, I was always trying to present the most cheerful, entertaining, attractive version of myself, instead of just *being* myself. It was a lot of effort, especially over time. Whereas with Benjamin, it never felt like people saw us as a golden couple, and it wasn't how we saw ourselves. We knew each other for ten years before we became involved. During that time, I gradually realized he was easy to be around and easy to talk to. We once traveled together to China as part of a delegation—not just us, but about twenty people—and even when the bus was late or our luggage got lost, he was very unflappable, very considerate of others. That probably doesn't sound romantic, does it? It was *real,* though—we got a clear view of each other. Whereas when I dated other men, whether it was leading protests or attending parties at the White House, there was a fantasy aspect to our time together that I don't think prepared us for some of the mundane daily struggles life has in store."

As Kathy de Bourgh took a sip of water, Liz said, "So the lesson is—?"

Kathy de Bourgh set her glass down. "Benjamin was very nurturing, by which I don't mean that he talked extensively about his feelings. He didn't. But he looked out for me in a steady, ongoing way, and I hope I did the same for him."

"Kathy, you have a three o'clock with George Schiff," Valerie Wright said, standing. "Liz, we need to wrap it up. So glad we could make this happen."

Ignoring Valerie, Kathy de Bourgh said, "There's a belief that to take care of someone else, or to let someone else take care of you—that both are inherently unfeminist. I don't agree. There's no shame in devoting yourself to another person, as long as he devotes himself to you in return."

Within thirty seconds, Liz knew, she'd be back on the other side of the greenroom door. She reached for her recorders but didn't turn them off, in case Kathy de Bourgh was about to share any final pearls of wisdom. Instead, Kathy de Bourgh hugged her, and Liz tried to think who in her life liked her enough that Liz could later make them listen to the barely audible rustle of being embraced by the leader of second-wave feminism. Jane would listen to humor Liz, though she wouldn't really be interested.

"Be well," Kathy de Bourgh said.

Chapter 115

"WOW," JASPER SAID when Liz answered her cellphone. "I'm pleasantly surprised you picked up."

It was evening, and Liz was lying in her hotel room bed in Houston, watching a mediocre movie she'd seen in the theater in high school and thinking, *I'm in love with you. I can't stop thinking about you.*

She said to Jasper, "Did you pee on your writing professor's desk?"

The silence that followed—it lasted for more time than would have been necessary to express reflexive bewilderment. At last, Jasper said, "I assume Darcy has been putting poison in your ear again."

"I have a right to know what really happened."

"If I could go back in time, are there things I'd do differently? Without question."

"What made you think that was okay?"

"Besides ten beers?" Jasper seemed to be waiting for her to laugh, and when she didn't, he said, "It was stupid and juvenile. There's no denying that. But I swear it wasn't racist. Tricia Randolph could have been blue, green, or polka-dotted, and I would have disliked her just the same."

Jasper was reminding her of someone, Liz thought, and after a second, she realized it was her mother. She said, "Did you ruin the professor's computer? You must have." Jasper said nothing, and Liz added, "I can't believe you peed on a writer's computer."

"Don't tell me you never did anything dumb when you were twenty-two."

"I loved you so much." Liz didn't raise her voice; she felt more sad than outraged. "From the time we met—I would have done anything for you. I thought you were so smart and cute and funny, and I was so flattered that you respected me and wanted to be friends. But how could you have strung me along all these years? If my excuse is a misguided crush, what's yours?"

"Nin—" Jasper said, and his pained tone was a reminder that, however he had transgressed, he hadn't done so entirely callously. His affection for her was not fake; it just was partial. Or perhaps it *was* fake, he was faking emotion now, and he had a personality disorder; but between these possibilities, she preferred to see him as inadequate rather than clinically diagnosable. "I'm going to do better," he said. "Starting now, I'm getting my act together. Don't give up on me."

"Oh, Jasper," Liz said. "I already have."

Chapter 116

SHE HAD BEEN asleep for less than an hour when her cellphone rang again, and the sound of it in the dark, in a hotel room, late at night, was sufficiently unsettling that she answered before even looking at the caller ID to make sure it wasn't Jasper again.

"I woke you up," said a female voice. "Sorry. I'll call back tomorrow."

It wasn't Jane; that was the fact Liz was certain of first, but several additional seconds passed before her brain determined who it was.

"Charlotte," she said. "Hi. It's fine. I'm awake."

And then Charlotte Lucas began to sob, and between gulps, she said, "You told me so. You told me, but I moved here anyway, like an idiot."

"Hold on," Liz said. "Slow down. Where are you?"

"I'm at the house. *His* house."

"You're not—he isn't, like, abusive, is he?"

Charlotte sniffled lavishly. "No, he's not abusive. Willie's a sweet, self-centered dork."

"Is he with you right now?"

"He's at work, where he always is." Liz could hear Charlotte swallow, and she sounded slightly calmer when she next spoke. "I'm so dumb."

"Did something happen?"

"I moved to a state where I don't know anyone," Charlotte said. "Including my own boyfriend. That's what happened."

"But did something specific happen? Have you been feeling this way all along?"

"I got a job offer," Charlotte said, and Liz said, "That's great!"

"You'd think. It's a good job, too, with a data analytics company that expects to triple in size in the next year. I'd had a bunch of interviews, but nothing panned out until I got the offer this afternoon. And somehow it made it all real. I've been taking it easy, like going to the gym for an hour and a half in the middle of the day and cooking fancy recipes that we eat at ten o'clock at night. But if I take this job, it means I'm no longer playing house, impersonating a good little 1950s homemaker. I'll really live out here, long-term, with Willie."

"Do you not want that?"

"I don't know what I want!" Charlotte wailed. "Maybe instead of taking the job, I should get pregnant now, and that way, even if Willie and I break up, I'll still be a mom."

"I can see how this feels overwhelming," Liz said, "but I think you're conflating separate issues."

"Have I mentioned that Willie snores like a freight train? And I lie there, thinking, Okay, if I'd dated him for two years before we moved in together, like normal people do—or even for six months—I'd have gotten used to this. Or I'd be deeply in love with him and be like, *Oh, the endearing foibles of my darling boyfriend.* Instead, I feel like I'm a mail-order bride, and he's an annoying stranger robbing me of sleep."

"Nobody thinks snoring is endearing," Liz said. "Does he know he does it?"

"I have no idea!"

"Ask him. If he doesn't know, he should see a doctor in case he has breathing problems. And aren't there special pillows you can buy? But the bigger question is whether you want to make it work. If you'd rather get on a plane and go back to Cincinnati, you're allowed to. I'll bet Procter would hire you again in a heartbeat."

"If I pay for your ticket, will you come out here and tell me what to do with my life?"

"Now?"

"Do you have plans for Labor Day weekend? You're still in Cincinnati, right?"

"I'm in Houston. I interviewed Kathy de Bourgh, who was giving a speech here today, and I was planning to go back to New York in the morning."

"Kathy de Bourgh—oh my God! Was she awesome?"

"Yes," Liz said. "She actually was."

"I know I'm asking a lot," Charlotte said. "But I just need someone else's perspective, someone who knows me well. We have a guest room."

The thought of staying in Willie's house after their last interaction was not enticing to Liz. But she said, "I'll look at flights after we get off the phone, but promise me one thing: Go to a drugstore right now and get earplugs. Or sleep in a different room tonight."

"Earplugs aren't a bad idea," Charlotte said.

"Sleep deprivation makes other problems so much worse."

"You're right. See how crazy I've become? I can't even manage basic self-care."

"You're being too hard on yourself. Just buy some earplugs, relax, and I'll be there tomorrow."

"Thank you, Lizzy," Charlotte said. "I really appreciate this. By the way, if you're worried about things being awkward with Willie, awkwardness doesn't register with him."

"That almost makes me jealous," Liz said.

"I know," Charlotte said. "No kidding."

Chapter 117

WAITING IN THE security line back at Houston's George Bush Intercontinental Airport, Liz found herself indulging in a pointless and perhaps even masochistic imaginative exercise about what it would be like if Darcy were her boyfriend. Given his job, she would need to move to Cincinnati—a possibility that in theory would have seemed distinctly unappealing if not outright prohibitive but, for the reason in question, struck her as potentially manageable. Indeed, the proximity to her family, were she to establish her own life rather than simply facilitate theirs, might be a boon. She could help her parents settle into a new dwelling, keep a closer eye on their finances, and perhaps develop adult relationships with Mary, Kitty, and Lydia (or maybe that was delusional no matter the circumstances). Convincing Talia to allow her to work permanently from Cincinnati would be a challenge, but presumably a juicy profile of Kathy de Bourgh would put Liz's editor in a magnanimous mood.

Then, of course, there was the matter of Darcy himself—of sharing his bed not just for fifteen sweaty minutes at a time but for entire nights, of enjoying the confidence that he was glad she was there, which was such an oddly luxurious notion that it made her feel both swoony and heartbroken. The thought of him as the person with whom she partook of ordinary daily activities—eating soup and grilled cheese together for lunch on a winter Saturday, watching TV dramas or political talk shows at night, holding a palm to each other's forehead or picking up cold medicine when one of them wondered if they were sick—seemed almost inconceivably bizarre. And yet it also filled her with a tender sort of yearning.

If they lived together, she decided as she handed her ticket to the agent at the gate and boarded a plane not to New York but to San Francisco, they'd need to move to a bigger apartment or even a house, so that she could have an office. Though her interest in décor was limited, certainly in comparison to her mother's, she didn't think it would hurt to hang a print or two on the walls and acquire a plant.

Except, of course, that none of this would come to pass. Surely she had destroyed any such eventualities by treating him with rash and unrepentant rudeness; surely his attraction to her had been rescinded.

As it happened, she still possessed neither his phone number nor his email nor even his street address; on all the occasions on which she'd visited his apartment, she'd been more preoccupied with impending events than with the numerals by which his building was identified. But in this day and age, it couldn't be difficult to track him down electronically. She could probably find his email on the University of Cincinnati website. And yet there remained the question of what Liz would say. *I'm sorry* seemed the most obvious option, but perhaps *Hey, how's it going?* was a more casual opener.

Out Liz's plane window, the mountains of northwest Utah were snow-peaked and lunar, even in August. Too preoccupied to read, Liz scrutinized them at length, but they offered no sagacity. At last, she leaned back in her seat and closed her eyes.

Chapter 118

UPON LANDING IN San Francisco, Liz called Ken Weinrich to find out if the fumigation had concluded successfully, and he confirmed that the sulfuryl fluoride levels inside the house had measured at below five parts per million, he had seen no spiders, and his team had removed the tent and fans. Liz then called Mary's cellphone, though it was difficult to hear Mary over the sound of their mother shouting in the background; apparently, they were back at the Tudor, in the kitchen.

"That food was all perfectly good!" Mrs. Bennet was declaring. "Why, I hadn't even opened Bev Wattenberg's peach marmalade!"

"Tell her I'm sure the Wattenbergs will give us more marmalade at Christmas," Liz said, and Mary said, "There's no point."

"The house doesn't smell weird at all?" Liz asked.

"It doesn't smell like anything," Mary said.

"I'll tell you who won't appreciate my tins of smoked trout," Mrs. Bennet was shouting, "and that's a hobo at a shelter."

"I have to go," Mary said.

"Hang in there," Liz said, and Mary said in a churlish tone, "Thanks for the long-distance pep talk."

Chapter 119

OUTSIDE THE DELTA terminal at SFO, Charlotte appeared considerably more tranquil than Liz had expected; this tranquillity was reassuring while casting doubt on the necessity of Liz's presence. But if now they were friends again, then what else mattered?

"Earplugs are the best invention ever," Charlotte said as she merged into the left lane. "I slept for eleven hours last night."

"Congratulations."

"Want to go with me to Nordstrom to buy new work clothes?"

"Does that mean you accepted the job?"

"I called them right before I got in the car to pick you up. I start a week from Labor Day."

"That's great, Charlotte. And I'd be honored to go to Nordstrom with you."

With traffic, it took them almost an hour to reach the Stanford Shopping Center in Palo Alto; they ate lunch at a restaurant before entering the department store.

"Everyone says how casual it is out here, but that's if you're a twenty-five-year-old dude," Charlotte said as she sorted through a rack of plus-size tops.

Inspecting a bra in the adjacent lingerie section, Liz thought, *Would he like this or find it cheesy?* With a jolt, she realized that the *he* in question, for the first time in a long while, was not Jasper.

"I'm trying these." Charlotte held up three hangers, then nodded her chin toward the bra. "Va-va-va-voom."

"It's expensive."

Charlotte looked skeptical. "For a New Yorker?"

Liz held out the price tag, which read $200.

"There's no better investment than your cleavage." Charlotte smirked. "I believe they teach that in business school."

Seventy minutes later, they were in the mall parking lot, walking back toward Charlotte's car with their respective purchases (Liz could not possibly justify buying the bra, and it was in her bag), when Liz said, "So I broke up with Jasper."

"Are you bummed or relieved?"

"Somewhere in between. Mostly I feel stupid for not realizing until now how obnoxious he is, when other people have seen it all along."

"You *were* really young when you met him," Charlotte said. "That should give you some exemption." As she pressed her key to unlock the car, she said, "This morning, Willie made an appointment with an ENT doctor. It turns out he had no idea that he snores. I guess if you've never had a girlfriend, no one's ever told you."

Whether or not it was completely true, Liz was compelled to say, "For the record, I like Willie. I think he's a good guy."

Wryly, but not angrily, Charlotte said, "Which is why you were disgusted when he tried to kiss you?" Liz was on the cusp of saying *He's my cousin,* when Charlotte added, "And don't say it's because you're cousins. We both know you'd have been disgusted no matter what. But that's okay."

"I just don't think he and I had chemistry," Liz said, and Charlotte smiled.

"I hope it's all right that I invited your aunt and uncle for dinner tonight."

"Perfect," Liz said. She had arranged to stay in the Bay Area for three days, then fly to New York on a red-eye. She said to Charlotte, "If you want to take a nap this afternoon, I'm happy to go grocery shopping. Or whatever errands you need—my errand-running muscles have gotten pretty huge this summer."

They had set their bags in the trunk of the car and climbed into the front seat, and Charlotte said, "It's not that I haven't had a bumpy adjustment out here, but I did call you at a low moment last night. Let's do something fun. Have you ever seen the campus of Stanford?"

"Your life changed a lot all at once," Liz said. "It would be weird if you *didn't* have second thoughts. And, no, I've never seen Stanford, although—" How could touring the university make her think of anything except what Jasper had done to his creative writing instructor? "You know what else is around here is Darcy's family's estate."

Charlotte laughed. "His estate? Who is he, the king of England?"

"It's somewhere in Atherton," Liz said. "Okay, don't judge me, but Darcy and I slept together a few times."

Charlotte made a joyous whoop. "I *knew* you two were flirting at Chip's dinner party!"

"That's right," Liz said. "You did call that, didn't you?"

"A *few* times? If you kept going back for more, I take it the sex was halfway decent."

"Yes," Liz said. "You could say so."

"I don't suppose you know the address of this estate?"

As Liz pulled out her phone, her heart thudded. She typed *Darcy estate Atherton,* and a few clicks later, she said, "1813 Pemberley Lane. You'd take Sand Hill Road to El Camino Real."

In a phonily high voice, Charlotte said, "Um, I think Darcy grew up around here? What, go look at it? *Now?* Innocent little me? Why, I wouldn't dream of it!"

Twelve minutes later, Charlotte was making a right from El Camino Real into a residential neighborhood blocked off from the more trafficked throughway by a tall ivy-covered wall. On either side of the entry to the quieter street hung signs that read NO TRESPASSING. RESIDENTS ONLY. "I'd rather not get arrested," Liz said. "I realize we're here because of me, but I'll just put that out there."

"Is the woman who went alone to Saudi Arabia chickening out?"

"I'm not pretending that I'm not interested," Liz said. "It's just that—holy shit, is that it?" A wrought-iron fence that was easily eight feet high enclosed a massive, verdant lawn on which trees and a combination of modern and older sculptures stood at intervals. As Charlotte continued driving, they reached the fence's gate, which was closed. Beyond it, a long gravel driveway led to a brick mansion that in its grandness and symmetry evoked a southern plantation.

Charlotte pointed through the gate to a larger-than-life bronze statue of a nude male. "You think Darcy posed for that?"

"No one lives in the house," Liz said. "Darcy's parents have died, and his sister is a grad student at Stanford. But can you imagine how—" The thought went unexpressed; it was at this moment that a black van with tinted windows approached from the opposite direction and stopped next to them, its driver's-side window descending. A middle-aged man with a crew cut said in a brisk tone, "Can I help you ladies?"

"We're friends of the family who owns this place," Charlotte said. "Friends of Fitzwilliam Darcy."

The man appraised Charlotte, then Liz. "Is one of you Caroline Bingley?"

This wasn't what Liz had expected him to ask, and if she'd thought the situation through, she'd never have uttered what she did next. But she did not think it through. Instead, she raised her hand and said, "I am."

The man's demeanor became marginally friendlier. He said, "Just a minute." He held a phone to his ear, but before they could hear him say anything, his window rose. Charlotte turned and whispered excitedly, "We're on a caper!"

"What's wrong with me?" Liz said. "Why did I tell him that?"

The tinted window descended again, and the man said, "Fitzwilliam will meet us in front of the main house. Follow me." By some invisible mechanism, the hulking doors of the gate opened, and the man drove through.

"Let's get out of here," Liz said.

"I thought Darcy was in Cincinnati," Charlotte said.

"So did I." Panic was quickly overtaking Liz. As Charlotte turned left up the driveway behind the van, Liz said, "What are you doing?"

"I'm not leading that guy on a chase. What if he has a gun?"

"Charlotte, we can't see Darcy. Stop the car. Let me out."

"What are you worried about? You and Darcy know each other biblically now."

"He'll think we're stalking him. Charlotte, right before I left Cincinnati, Darcy told me he was in love with me! Except in this completely weird, unfriendly way, and I was really rude back to him, and the whole thing was bizarre."

Charlotte laughed. "Liz Bennet, you seductress! Is there any man who *hasn't* fallen for you this summer? Besides, we are stalking him. Or at least his land."

In front of the house, though *house* did not seem an adequate descriptor for the gargantuan structure before them, near the steps leading to an enormous front door was a figure that, even from a distance of twenty yards, Liz could tell was Darcy. She thought of the two of them writhing in the bed in his apartment and felt a multifaceted confusion. Near Darcy, the black van made a U-turn and continued back down the driveway, the way they'd come; Charlotte stopped in front of the steps and without warning automatically lowered Liz's window. Darcy walked closer to them, and by the time he recoiled—in surprise, Liz hoped, rather than revulsion—he was truly upon them.

"Liz?" He looked shocked.

Charlotte leaned forward and waved. "Hi, Darcy."

"Charlotte?"

Liz heard Charlotte say, "We were in the area," and it was impossible not to believe that her friend was relishing this encounter.

"That guy," Liz said. "Your bodyguard or whatever—he assumed I was Caroline Bingley, but I'm not."

"No," Darcy said. "You're not." He didn't, as Liz had feared, seem angry; he still seemed simply puzzled. "I thought you'd gone back to New York."

"I came to visit Charlotte."

Darcy glanced at Charlotte. "I understand you've become a Californian."

"Who'd have thunk, huh?" Charlotte said.

"Why are *you* here?" Liz asked Darcy.

"At my own house, do you mean?" But Darcy sounded warm, not mocking—indeed, he seemed to Liz warmer than he ever had in Cincinnati, though perhaps the difference was less his affect than her perception of it. "Georgie and I hold a Labor Day get-together every year," he was saying, "or we host it the years I don't have to work. That's why Roger confused you with Caroline Bingley. She's due here tomorrow."

Liz tried not to demonstrably register this troubling bit of news and instead strove to sound pleasant and breezy. "With Chip?" she asked.

Darcy shook his head. "No, he's still filming, but a few of our classmates from med school are coming from San Francisco, and some friends of Georgie's." Darcy looked between Liz and Charlotte. "As long as you're here, would you two like to see the house?"

"We're actually—" Liz began, and Charlotte said, "We'd love to."

As Charlotte turned off the engine, Darcy said, "I hope Roger wasn't rude. He's the caretaker, not my bodyguard, but he can be overzealous because we sometimes get people snooping around the property."

Chapter 120

FOR ONCE, LIZ wouldn't have asked, but Charlotte did, in a way that somehow seemed as neutral a question a person might pose about an exhibit in a museum, and Darcy answered in kind: The main house at Pemberley was nineteen thousand square feet and contained twelve bedrooms and seventeen bathrooms; there also was a guesthouse, a caretaker's cottage, and a currently unused stable.

They entered through the foyer, made a right into a hallway with a high, arched ceiling, made another right, and found themselves in a ballroom, a vast space with a walnut floor, mostly empty save for two spectacular crystal chandeliers, matching marble fireplaces at either end of the room, and a half dozen murals featuring scenes from what Darcy identified as England's Lake District. He said, "I suspect that my great-great-grandfather thought a veneer of British elegance would distract from his having run away from his home in rural Virginia at the age of thirteen."

"Rags to riches," Charlotte said, and Liz said, "So Pemberley has been in your family all this time?"

"Which is why my sister fears that we'll be letting down all our ancestors by donating it to the National Trust for Historic Preservation, whereas I think the opposite. Neither Georgie nor I will ever have a family big enough to justify this kind of space. *Nobody* has a family big enough."

They walked from the ballroom into a trophy room, then an oak-paneled study with an oil painting over the fireplace of a balding, somber man wearing a black tie, a white shirt with an upturned collar, a black waistcoat, a black jacket, and a pocket watch whose gold chain was visible.

"That's the original Fitzwilliam Darcy, my great-great-grandfather," Darcy said. "He started building Pemberley in 1915, by which point he'd established himself as a railroad and borax-mining magnate. I'm sure you've heard the saying about every fortune being built on a great crime."

Liz, who had spoken little since entering the house, tried to sound normal as she asked, "Should I pretend to know what borax is?"

"Charlotte, I bet you know from Procter & Gamble." To Liz, Darcy said, "Sodium borate. A compound that's in everything from detergent to fiberglass." They were in the library, where scores of leather-bound books sat on built-in shelves, and an enormous Persian rug covered the floor.

"Are the books fake?" Liz asked. "No offense."

"They have pages with words on them, if that's what you're asking. But yes, I'm sure that even when they were first acquired, they were a bit of an affectation. I once read a copy of *Treasure Island* I found in here, but we mostly lived upstairs. The whole first floor, as you can see, has a public feel to it, and my mother was very civically involved. She and my father hosted lots of fundraising events."

"It's like the White House," Charlotte said, and Darcy said, "In a way, I suppose."

From the library, they proceeded through the reception room, which was a sort of mini–living room; the drawing room, which was another sort of mini–living room, this one apparently intended for women to retire to when the men enjoyed their post-dinner cigars and brandy; then the dining room, the butler's pantry, and the kitchen. In the reception room, Darcy had gestured at the doorway, which was framed by columns and a peaked roof, and said to Liz, "All that trim is known as an aedicule—that's a good word for a writer, huh?"

Who *was* this man, this gracious and genial host sharing his time, demonstrating impeccable manners in a context in which he'd have been justified showing the opposite? And how strange it was that he'd grown up in this ludicrous house; truly, it seemed more like the set of a television show about opulence than a home.

The black marble stairwell they ascended was near the trophy room; from the landing, an orchard was visible. On the second floor, the bedrooms all included fireplaces, and most featured televisions from before the flat-screen era. A poster of Larry Bird still hung on the wall of the room that had been Darcy's, and a CD player with a slot for a cassette tape rested on the small desk. There was to Liz something unexpectedly poignant about these items, as well as about the navy blue comforter smoothed over the bed (how many years had elapsed since he'd slept in it?) and the framed photo of his soccer team in perhaps fourth or fifth grade. But doubt overtook her, and she wondered if her surge of tenderness toward Darcy was gold digging in disguise. She didn't consciously yearn to be the mistress of a place like Pemberley, but the wealth it implied was astonishing indeed.

Darcy led them back downstairs and outside. Behind the house, in a fruit and vegetable garden off the kitchen, they sampled one small, ripe tomato each before proceeding through a walled garden; then a sunken garden; then a rose garden; and finally a descending series of terraces, on the lowest of which a reflecting pool shimmered in the midafternoon sun. This wasn't the swimming pool, Darcy explained, though he led them there next. The swimming pool had been added in the 1940s, and adjacent to it was the guesthouse where Darcy told them he and some of his visitors would sleep during the weekend.

As the tour wound down, Liz wished to say something that conveyed her appreciation for his kindness while leading it, a kindness all the more remarkable in light of their last interaction in Cincinnati. What she said, as the three of them approached Charlotte's car without reentering the main house, was "Thanks for showing us around."

Darcy looked at her, and she looked at him, and if not for Charlotte, Liz wondered what sentiments either of them might express. "Of course," he said. "It's funny, both of us being out here this weekend." He stepped forward and kissed Charlotte's cheek. "My knowledge of the area is dated, but if you need any pointers, be in touch."

"Will do," Charlotte said.

"Goodbye, Liz," Darcy said, and when he leaned in to kiss her cheek, she resisted the impulse to cling to him; in an instant, the kiss was finished.

What was there to do but climb into Charlotte's car? Liz did so, and as Charlotte started the engine, Liz felt she might cry. On the other side of the window, Darcy's expression was pensive. As the car pulled away, Liz gave him a small and miserable wave.

"Okay, that was *nuts,*" Charlotte said. "That was totally, completely—"

"Wait, he's saying something. Stop." In her side-view mirror, Liz could see Darcy jogging after them from twenty feet back.

Charlotte braked, and Liz opened her window.

"I don't know why I didn't think of this earlier," Darcy said, and he was only the slightest bit breathless. "You two should come here for dinner tonight. And Willie, too, obviously. Given what a fan of yours my sister is, Liz, she'd be thrilled to meet you."

"Oh—" Liz turned to Charlotte, then turned back to Darcy. "We're supposed to have dinner with my aunt and uncle, Willie's parents. I mean, thank you but—"

"Bring them along. How does six-thirty sound?"

"Six-thirty is great," Charlotte said.

"Any food restrictions for either of you?" Darcy asked. "Georgie doesn't eat meat, so we'll have vegetarian options."

"No restrictions for me," Liz said, and Charlotte said, "Me, either. What can we bring?"

"Just yourselves," Darcy said. "I'll grill something simple. Liz, if you tell me your number, I'll text you now, and when you get here tonight, you can text me to open the front gate."

She recited the digits, and seconds later, her phone buzzed in her pocket. (After all this time, she had Darcy's cellphone number! She had Darcy's number and he had hers, and she felt as giddy as if the cutest boy in seventh grade had slipped a note into her locker.)

"I'm glad this will work," Darcy said.

In a purring tone that made Liz want to slap her friend, Charlotte said, "Darcy, the pleasure is ours."

Chapter 121

SUCH WERE LIZ'S nerves that when she and Charlotte stopped to buy wine to take to Pemberley that evening, Liz purchased an additional bottle of merlot, which she opened as soon as possible in Charlotte's kitchen. "It *is* after five in Cincinnati," Liz said. "And New York."

"Hey," Charlotte said. "Go for it."

"Do you really think he wants to make dinner for a bunch of people, including my aunt and uncle, whom he's never met, when he has all those guests arriving tomorrow?"

Charlotte grinned. "That man is completely in love with you," she said. "I'm sure he'd like nothing better."

Liz took a long swallow from the glass she'd poured. "Join me?"

"Twist my arm," Charlotte said, and Liz poured a second glass.

The one advantage of the new dinner plan, Liz thought, was that her complicated feelings about spending the evening with Darcy so overshadowed her complicated feelings about seeing Cousin Willie as to make the latter set of emotions negligible; her rejection of Willie was no longer the one that preoccupied her.

Liz and Charlotte carried their wineglasses to the front porch of the modest three-bedroom ranch house that Liz knew, because she'd checked online, had cost Willie $1.1 million in 2010. As they sat on Adirondack chairs, the afternoon sky was cerulean with a smattering of cumulus clouds. Palo Alto seemed in this moment an unaffordable yet truly delightful place to live.

"The problem with your theory of Darcy still being into me," Liz said, "is that he invited Caroline up for the weekend. And not even with her brother—just by herself."

"Caroline is odious. There's no way she can compete with you."

"Well, they were involved in the past. They've definitely slept together."

"And that distinguishes Caroline from you how?" Charlotte was leering.

"Did you ever notice in Cincinnati that she was all over him? It's obvious she wants to get back together." Liz felt too jittery to remain seated, and she stood. "Is it okay if I take a shower?"

"Of course. The towels are on the bed."

Before entering the house, Liz said, "Sorry for letting this stuff with Darcy hijack my visit. After we get through dinner, we'll hatch a plan for your life here."

"Lizzy, nothing could bring me greater happiness than to have you staying at my house, freaking out about a boy."

Chapter 122

THEY CARAVANNED BACK to Pemberley: Willie and Charlotte in his Prius, Liz riding with Aunt Margo and Uncle Frank. Willie had greeted Liz by saying in an accusatory tone, "Obviously, a lot has changed since I last saw you," and Liz had replied, with a sincerity that took her by surprise, "I'm so happy for you and Charlotte."

As she rode from Palo Alto to Atherton, Liz offered Aunt Margo updates from Cincinnati: Mr. Bennet's health, Jane's breakup with Chip (Liz provided much less detail than she'd given earlier to Charlotte), Lydia's new beau. Conveniently, describing Ham was helpful in avoiding discussion of the house in which Aunt Margo had grown up being for sale. Shortly, Uncle Frank was turning onto Pemberley Lane; reaching the gates of the estate, he whistled in appreciation. "This must be some friend you've made, Lizzy."

Hi it's Liz, Liz texted Darcy. *We're here.* A few seconds later, the gates opened.

In front of the main house, Liz spotted Darcy and a slender young woman who tucked her straight light brown hair behind her ears and kept her head slightly ducked, as if avoiding the glare of the sunset, though the house faced north. When the cars were parked and their occupants discharged, all seven of them stood in the gravel driveway while introductions were made and handshakes exchanged. Darcy wore high-quality flip-flops, khaki pants, and a white oxford cloth shirt rolled up to the elbows and plain save for a monogram on the left breast pocket—*FCD V*, it said, and Liz knew from looking online that his middle name was Cornelius.

It was immediately obvious to Liz that Georgie was anorexic. More than a decade in the employ of a women's magazine had given her an abundance of experience discerning eating disorders, and made her both sympathetic to their challenges and wary of focusing inordinate attention on them; indeed, before the end of her first year at *Mascara*, she'd privately vowed to cease all conversation about food or exercise with her co-workers, lest she become as obsessive as some of them. She had, of course, broken the vow many times, but she still credited it with helping her retain perspective.

A few inches shorter than Liz, Georgie couldn't have topped a hundred pounds; and though she wore a loose linen shirt along with jeans and flats, the line of her jaw and the prominence of her teeth were clues to her extreme thinness. She seemed far more fragile than Liz had anticipated; Kitty and Lydia were downright husky by comparison.

"We'll eat at the guesthouse." Looking among Uncle Frank, Aunt Margo, and Willie, Darcy added, "I've already subjected Liz and Charlotte to a tour of the main house today, so I'm inclined to spare the rest of you."

Aunt Margo, Liz observed, met this news with disappointment that she quickly concealed, though neither Willie nor Uncle Frank seemed to care. As they all walked past the east wing of the house, Darcy said, "You'll see that the pool is next to the guesthouse, but I have to apologize for not offering you the chance to swim. We haven't opened it in a few years."

Uncle Frank snapped his fingers, as if let down. "And here I'd stashed a Speedo in my glove compartment, just in case."

Everyone chuckled politely at this appetite-spoiling image, and Liz found herself falling into step beside Georgie. "Thank you for having us over on such short notice," Liz said. "I hope you weren't alarmed when your brother said five strangers would be joining you for dinner."

"Oh, the opposite," Georgie said. "Fitzy's talked about you so much, and I think he told you I'm a big *Mascara* reader." Quickly, Georgie added, "At the risk of sounding like a dorky fangirl."

"Ah, but I love dorky fangirls," Liz said. "So Darcy—or I guess you just called him Fitzy—he said you're a graduate student?"

Georgie nodded. "I'm in the middle of my dissertation, which will probably be read by about eight people total, if I ever manage to finish it. I have to ask you this, even though I'm sure everyone does—do you think Hudson Blaise cheated on Jillian Northcutt?"

Forsaking her usual guardedness on the topic, Liz said, "Of course he did!"

"Have you ever interviewed him?" Georgie asked.

Liz shook her head. "Although the word on the street is that he's not big on bathing and smells kind of funky."

Georgie giggled. "Was Jillian nice?"

"She was nice enough. I think it was such a weird time in her life, and, obviously, she was talking about the breakup not because she wanted to but because she had a movie to promote. I felt bad for her, actually. What's your dissertation about?"

"Early-twentieth-century French suffragettes and taxation. Fascinating, huh?"

"Georgie, have you seen the corkscrew?" Darcy called from a few yards ahead. They had reached the guesthouse, and he stood by a two-tiered cart that held an array of wine bottles, glasses, and napkins.

Georgie pointed. "On the lower level."

The pool was covered by a vast green tarp that somehow didn't compromise the loveliness of the setting. Four matching chaise longues were lined up alongside the pool, and a lushly cushioned couch and chairs sat near the entrance to the guesthouse; on either side of the couch, heat lamps stood sentinel. Two additional heat lamps flanked a long iron table set with green plates and matching green cloth napkins, all so elegantly arranged that Liz had a hunch that someone other than Darcy or Georgie—someone with professional expertise—had organized the display. Beyond the far end of the pool lay a lawn of the most deeply green and perfectly manicured grass Liz had ever seen; the expanse begged to be used, and Liz wished she knew how to do backflips, or even just a decent cartwheel. A scent that Liz thought of as distinctly Californian—perhaps it was eucalyptus—became perceptible.

Cousin Willie approached Liz and Georgie with two glasses of red wine and said, "Ladies."

Liz took hers, but Georgie shook her head. "I'll just have water."

When everyone had a drink, Darcy held up his glass. "To family and friends."

Liz's eyes met his briefly, and then they were clinking glasses, as was everyone else. It was difficult to know how to manage her energy, how to manage *herself*, in the company of this version of Darcy. She could see, with a sudden and not entirely welcome clarity, that in Cincinnati, she had cultivated her own rancor toward him; she had made rude and provocative remarks, had searched for offense in his responses, and had relished the slights that may or may not have been delivered. Yet in spite of the culminating acrimony during his confession, he had decided to set aside their ill will. His present behavior wasn't a sarcastic impersonation of good manners; it wasn't meant to count, technically, as kindness, without containing true warmth; it simply *was* kindness. He treated his guests, her included, as if he couldn't imagine a greater pleasure than spending the evening with them, and in doing so he exacerbated Liz's shame about her past pettiness toward him.

At some point during the larger group conversation, when neither of them was interacting with anyone else, Liz turned to Darcy. "When do your other guests get here?"

"Anywhere from late morning tomorrow to early afternoon. You're welcome to come back if you'd like. I'm sure Caroline would enjoy seeing you."

Liz scrutinized Darcy's face and finally said, "Do you not realize that Caroline Bingley and I can't stand each other?"

Darcy looked amused. "Since when?"

"Since about thirty seconds after we met. I suppose it's possible I don't register with her enough for her to dislike me, but I don't like her."

"Do I dare ask why?"

The reason not to criticize Caroline wasn't that she didn't deserve criticism, Liz thought; it was that criticizing her would only make Liz look bad. She said, "If I tell you, you'll think I'm a person who pretends that gossiping shows my anthropological interest in the human condition." Darcy winced a little, and Liz added, "Too soon?"

"No sooner than I deserve. If you'll excuse me, I should start grilling." Had she in fact offended him? He headed inside the guesthouse and emerged a moment later carrying one platter of raw steaks and another of portobello mushrooms and zucchini cut into long strips. Uncle Frank joined him at the grill, and Liz could hear her uncle strike up a conversation about the history of the estate. "It's no secret that property in Atherton is worth a pretty penny," Uncle Frank said, and Darcy said affably, "Yes, times have changed since my great-great-grandfather bought this land for twelve dollars an acre."

Liz rose, looking for a bathroom. On the other side of the guesthouse's glass door, she found herself inside a great room with stainless steel kitchen appliances lining one wall. Passing a first bathroom, she walked down a hall, by three bedrooms—two held twin beds, and one contained an unmade king-sized bed, with an open suitcase on the floor beside it—and, beyond the suitcase, an interior bathroom. As she washed her hands afterward in a sink with a pattern of blue peonies painted across the basin and faucet handles, she was struck, as she occasionally was during a third glass of wine, by how cute she looked in the mirror. Sober, she tended, like most women she knew, toward self-criticism. But tipsy, she could admire her own brightly inquisitive eyes, her shiny hair and game smile, as well as the flattering cut of her jeans and the boost offered by the overpriced bra she'd purchased that afternoon. Even in the presence of her weird cousin and corny uncle, the night had taken on a certain enchanted quality that arose from the splendor of the setting, from the crisp air, the candles they relied on as twilight gathered, and above all from Darcy's solicitousness, which she felt to be directed primarily at her; indeed, she interpreted his attention to all the guests as a personal tribute. But of course she was not certain—she was certain of nothing.

Whether by her own angling or a more mutual stratagem, Liz ended up next to Darcy for dinner; her aunt was on his other side. Complementing the meat and vegetables Darcy had grilled were a loaf of fresh bread, a salad, and more wine, all of them outstanding, though what food and drink wouldn't have tasted delicious beneath a starry sky on a late-summer evening?

"Was your mother a native Californian like your father?" Aunt Margo asked Darcy, and he shook his head.

"She was a proud Yankee who could never quite believe she'd settled here permanently." Darcy looked at his sister. "Wouldn't you say, Georgie?"

The focus of the table shifting to her seemed to make Georgie self-conscious, but she sounded composed as she said, "Our mom grew up in Boston, and she'd lose her voice yelling at the TV during Red Sox games."

"How did your parents meet?" Liz asked.

Darcy said, "Mom was an undergraduate at Radcliffe when our dad was in medical school. She was only nineteen when Dad proposed, and he assumed she'd drop out of school and move here with him. She refused. He joined a practice in San Francisco, but supposedly he kept proposing to her once a month, writing letters. She finally said yes the day after her graduation."

"Your father was a doctor, too?" Aunt Margo said.

"A general practitioner," Darcy said. "I think in another life our mom would have been a landscape architect. When I picture her, it's digging in the gardens here."

"I just realized," Georgie said. "You should all come to our croquet tournament tomorrow." A silence ensued, and Georgie added, "You don't need to wear white or anything. It's informal."

"They probably have plans, Georgie," Darcy said. "Liz, how long are you in town?"

"Till Sunday night."

"I bet we can make it work," Charlotte said. "Don't you think, Liz? What time does the tournament start?"

"Around three," Georgie said. "I mean, don't feel obligated if it sounds boring."

"Margo and I will take a rain check," Uncle Frank said. "We'll be enjoying some R and R on a friend's boat."

"And I need to be at the office," Willie said. "We're in crunch time, and I'm lucky to have gotten away for dinner."

"Then definitely count Liz and me in," Charlotte said. "Darcy, I trust you remember from Charades that Liz is a fierce competitor."

"I remember it well," Darcy said.

Chapter 123

A SIXTY-SOMETHING WOMAN named Alberta materialized before dessert to ask if they needed anything, and Darcy complimented her on the excellence of the food, thereby confirming Liz's impression that he had done little to prepare it. However, it was Darcy himself who loaded the dishwasher, as Liz, Charlotte, and Georgie carried plates into the guesthouse.

Georgie had just taken a hazelnut torte outside—Liz doubted the young woman would be eating any—and Charlotte followed with a pint of vanilla ice cream, leaving Darcy and Liz inside and truly alone together for the first time that evening. As Darcy scrubbed the salad bowl, Liz, who was no more than five feet away, said, "Thank you—" and he turned off the water. "Thank you for everything tonight—" she began again, and, talking over her, he said, "You don't have to come tomorrow just to humor Georgie. Now that I know how you feel about Caroline Bingley, I—"

"No, it's fine." This time, it was her interrupting him. "I mean, I don't want to impose if—"

"You're more than welcome to join us."

Then they just stood there, looking at each other. She wished that kissing him was not impossible. *Was* kissing him impossible? Surely so, with his sister and her aunt and uncle and cousin and friend on the other side of the glass door. It then seemed that maybe they were going to kiss after all, in spite of the lack of privacy and the confused circumstances, because he stepped toward her, and she stepped toward him. He said, "Since you left Cincinnati—" At that moment, Georgie walked in and said, "Did Alberta leave the serving knife in the main house? Oh, sorry."

"It's right here." Darcy turned, opened a drawer, and handed the knife to Georgie.

Both the eye contact and the spell had been broken. And yet Georgie's apology—it was proof to Liz that a spell had existed; she wasn't just imagining it.

She said to Georgie, "I've got the dessert plates." Because Liz didn't wish to increase Georgie's discomfort—also because Liz didn't know what else to do—she followed the other woman out to the patio. A moment later, Darcy emerged after them. It was Aunt Margo who cut the torte.

Since I left Cincinnati what? Liz thought. Though she wasn't alone again with Darcy before they departed, her heart had swollen during that encounter in the kitchen, and it did not shrink again until some hours after she had climbed into the guest bed at Willie and Charlotte's house.

Chapter 124

IN CHARLOTTE'S CAR on El Camino Real, returning to Pemberley the following afternoon, Liz pulled down the sun visor and looked at herself in the mirror, which was something she'd already spent a not inconsiderable amount of time doing at Charlotte and Willie's house, where she'd carefully applied foundation, mascara, and lipstick. In the car, she said, "Is it weird we're going?"

"Liz, the ST between you and Darcy is threatening to engulf Northern California in a fiery ball. It's your duty to save us all by having sex."

"I'm glad this is providing you with so much entertainment." Liz pulled her lipstick from her purse, applied a fresh coat—one of the many tips she had learned during her years at *Mascara* was to begin at the center of her lips and move toward the corners—then rubbed her lips together. "For real, though, I hope Caroline doesn't think we crashed the party."

"Who cares what Caroline thinks?"

Liz slid the cover across the sun visor mirror and folded the visor back into place. "True. Did you wear earplugs again last night?"

"It was like an angel rocked me to sleep. Thank you for suggesting it." Charlotte turned off El Camino Real and said in a more serious tone, "I know Willie isn't dashing like Darcy. But I think he loves me, and I want to make it work."

"I'm *sure* he loves you."

"It's weird," Charlotte said, "because if your dad hadn't had a heart attack, you and Jane wouldn't have come back to Cincinnati this summer, and if you hadn't come back to Cincinnati, Willie wouldn't have visited with Margo, and I'd never have met him. Sometimes it amazes me how much these defining parts of our lives hinge on chance."

"I know. I think about that all the time."

They both were quiet, and the fence of Pemberley came into view. "Are you on the Pill?" Charlotte asked. "Because we can turn around and go buy a condom."

"That won't be necessary," Liz said.

Chapter 125

"WHAT A COINCIDENCE that you happen to be in town the same weekend Darcy is here," Caroline said to Liz by way of greeting. They stood on the lawn near the covered pool, where the croquet equipment had already been set out: the wickets inserted into the grass, the mallets and balls waiting in tidy rows. Along one side of the pool, a buffet lunch still looked vibrant, despite the fact that it was midafternoon: various sandwiches and salads, enormous cookies, lemonade, iced tea, beer, and white wine. Surveying the scene, Liz had the somewhat troubling thought that she was starting to understand Darcy's unfavorable view of Cincinnati; it would be difficult for *any* place to compete with these lush gardens, blue skies, and magnificent spreads of food.

"I'm visiting Charlotte," Liz said to Caroline. "You may have heard that she's dating my cousin Willie."

"I guess beauty really is in the eye of the beholder," Caroline said.

Liz was fairly sure Charlotte didn't overhear the insult, because she was being introduced to the half dozen other guests, but the remark seemed too rude to simply let stand. "Is it my cousin or my oldest friend that you're implying is ugly?" Liz asked.

Caroline shrugged. "Take your pick. When two people like that get together, I never know if I should be happy for them or just pray they don't reproduce."

You're awful, Liz thought. *You're even worse than I remember.*

"Speaking of which," Caroline said, "has Jane reached the swollen-ankles-and-stretch-marks stage yet?"

Liz smiled as warmly as she could manage. "You know how some pregnant women just give off a glow the whole time? Jane's been blessed." Before Caroline could respond, Liz added, "I hear Chip's still shooting the *Eligible* reunion. Is Holly the alligator wrestler part of it? Or it's Gabrielle who has the Celtic cross tattoo on her tongue, right? It always seemed like she and Chip had a lot of chemistry." Liz beamed at Caroline. "Either one would be *so* fun for you to have as a sister-in-law."

Chapter 126

UPON THEIR ARRIVAL, Charlotte and Liz had been welcomed by
Darcy in a gracious but not especially fraught way (Liz was almost disappointed by how not fraught) and introduced to the other guests, all
of whose names Liz promptly forgot: an anesthesiologist and his lawyer wife, a seemingly single male radiologist, a nephrologist (male)
married to an architect (also male), plus two Stanford history PhDs,
both slender young men whom Liz suspected, based on their posture
and inflections around Darcy's sister, to be in love with Georgie.

Though Liz's initial interactions with Darcy were subdued and
matter-of-fact, as the afternoon progressed and the croquet began—
they were playing two separate games simultaneously, both of them the
so-called cutthroat version, in which it was everyone for him- or herself, rather than teams—Liz felt there to be an ever-increasing charge
between herself and her host. She was at all times acutely conscious of
how far he stood from her, of his absence if he stepped away—to bring
out additional bottles of wine from the guesthouse, say, or to greet the

final arrival, a dermatologist, at the front gate—and whom he was talking with. Periodically, it was she who was speaking to him, always in an undramatic fashion. They weren't playing in the same game, but the two courts had been set up on adjacent stretches of grass, and they were sometimes near each other; they'd comment on a shot someone had taken or on the pleasantness of the weather, and while such topics felt faintly ridiculous, so, presumably, would anything else.

When Liz knocked her ball out of bounds, Darcy materialized as she was placing it the prescribed distance from the boundary. "I always have this fantasy of discovering some new skill," she said. "But apparently it's not croquet."

Darcy squinted. "Are you wearing makeup?"

Instinctively, Liz brought a hand to one cheek. "Does it look weird?"

"I guess I'm not used to you in it," Darcy said, and, more defensively than she meant to, Liz said, "It *is* something women often put on their faces."

Without speaking, Darcy patted her right shoulder, as if comforting her; instead, the contact was unsettling, but in a good way.

Eventually, Alberta drove up in a golf cart to clear away the used plates and utensils. Liz had by that point consumed two and a half glasses of wine, three bites of a turkey sandwich, and half a cookie; she was too nervous to eat more. It was Darcy who'd won the first game, and Charlotte the second. Caroline said to Liz, "I take it you're not much of an athlete."

Though Liz had mocked her own croquet skills with Darcy, she couldn't permit such a slight from Caroline. "Well, I run twenty-five miles a week," she said. "And for my job I've tried pretty much every fitness trend out there. But I suppose I'm not athletic besides that."

The two women looked at each other with barely disguised antipathy, and Caroline said, "You leave town tomorrow, right?"

"Is my presence thwarting plans that you had?"

Caroline took a step closer to Liz and lowered her voice. "Just so you know, I see right through you. Your whole laid-back vibe—I can tell it's bullshit."

"Coming from you, I think that might be a compliment."

As Liz finished her third glass of wine, impatience, regret, and tipsiness collected within her. Oh, to get a do-over for that braless, unprepared morning at her sisters' apartment! To be granted just one more run up Madison Road with Darcy, only the two of them and no one else, and then to decamp for his apartment, this time with the awareness that he didn't see the encounter as purely transactional—to know that he *liked* her! But did he still like her, here, today? How long did the sex hormones to which he'd attributed his love linger in the bloodstream?

A short while later, Liz heard herself telling Georgie, as one of Georgie's suitors listened in, "Your brother mentioned that you guys might sell or donate this property at some point. And I hope this isn't too forward, but I want to tell you about something my older sister did. My parents are selling the house they've lived in for a long time, so my sister, who's a yoga instructor, held, like, a ritual farewell where she talked about some of the things we'd done at the house and what she'd miss. And even though I was skeptical, I think it's helped me. Oh, and it only took five minutes."

Georgie looked both interested and confused. She said, "Did someone come and do it for you, or did she do it herself?"

"No, she did it. I can ask if she was following a script or just winging it."

"If you want to learn about moving superstitions, you should talk to my Chinese grandma," Georgie's suitor said. He was still talking when suddenly Darcy was beside Liz; he touched her arm just above the elbow, and again, she felt she might swoon. Instead, in an impossibly normal voice, she said, "Hi."

As Georgie and her suitor continued their conversation, Darcy said, "I wonder if you're free to get breakfast tomorrow."

"Oh," Liz said. "Sure."

"It would have to be early, because there's a group hike planned. Of course, you and Charlotte are welcome to join that, too."

Aware that her friend would probably contradict the statement, Liz said, "I need to give Charlotte some undivided attention, since she's the reason I'm in California, but breakfast sounds great."

"Is eight A.M. uncivilized?"

"It's perfect."

"If you text me Charlotte's address, I'll pick you up."

So he felt it, too. Or he felt, at least, *something*. He wanted to be alone with her, even if, judging from his calmness, he didn't want it as much as she wanted to be alone with him. She yearned to fling her body against his, to smash her face into his shirt, kiss his neck and face, and take him away to where she didn't have to share him.

Blandly, she said, "Charlotte and Willie live in Palo Alto. Their house is really close to here."

Chapter 127

"MY BROTHER," GEORGIE whispered, and she gripped Liz's wrist. It was dusk, and Liz and Charlotte would be leaving momentarily, though Charlotte and the nephrologist were caught up in a heated discussion about earthquakes. "I think he likes you," Georgie continued, still whispering. Liz's buzz had worn off, but she wondered if the other woman was drunk; if so, Liz was surprised, given the caloric content of alcohol. "Seriously," Georgie said. "And it's perfect, because I've always been scared he'll end up with Caroline Bingley, and she sucks."

Yes, Georgie was definitely drunk, which did not mean she wasn't to be trusted. In the fading light, Liz regarded the younger woman. "For what it's worth, I agree with you," she said. "Caroline does suck."

"Do you like Fitzy?"

Liz hesitated only briefly. "Yes," she said. "I do."

"As in *like* him?"

Liz smiled. "I knew what you meant, and the answer is still yes."

Georgie pulled her phone from her pocket. "Give me your number, and next time I'm in New York, you and Jillian Northcutt and I should have coffee."

"Here." Liz reached for the phone and typed the numbers in herself. She wondered if Georgie would recall their conversation in the morning and, if she did, whether she'd repeat it to her brother.

Passing back the phone, Liz said, "I can't speak for Jillian Northcutt, but I'd be delighted to see you anytime."

Chapter 128

HE PICKED HER up on time, in a gray SUV with California license plates; the morning was sunny again but still cool, and Liz had slept even less the previous night than the night before that. Around four A.M., she had decided there was nothing to do but ask him for another chance. As geographically inconvenient and temperamentally implausible as a relationship between them seemed, she wanted it; she wanted it desperately, and she needed to know if he did, too.

Riding to the restaurant he'd selected—the Palo Alto Creamery, though the food was, of course, irrelevant—she felt them inhabiting some simulacrum of coupledom that was both torturous and enticing. His right hand resting on the gear shift near her left knee, his forearm with its brown hair, the almost imperceptible scent of whatever male shampoo or soap or aftershave he used—she could barely stand it. His handsomeness this early in the day was devastating and unmanageable, and so she reverted to small talk. She inquired whether everyone else in the house had been asleep when he'd left, and Darcy confirmed that they had; she asked if a late night had ensued after her and Charlotte's departure, and he again answered in the affirmative; she noted that he must be exhausted, and he said he was accustomed to sleep deprivation.

Turning onto Emerson Street, Darcy said, "Georgie thinks you're great."

"Oh, it's mutual," Liz said. "She's charming."

"I wish you and my mom could have met. You would have gotten a kick out of each other."

Liz's heart squeezed. "I wish I could have met her, too. She sounds very cool."

Darcy glanced across the front seat. "Seeing Georgie—did she look different from how you pictured? Or maybe you didn't picture her a particular way."

A certain giddiness drained out of Liz, which was okay; giddiness was, after all, difficult to sustain. Carefully, she said, "She's very thin, obviously. Is that what you mean?"

"She's been in and out of different treatment centers, which, as far as I can tell, do nothing." Darcy sighed. "But I still wonder if she should go back. She's lost weight again since I last saw her."

"I have a colleague who did a program in North Carolina that really seemed to help, I think at Duke. Has Georgie ever tried that one?"

"Duke doesn't sound familiar. She's been to places in Southern California and Arizona." Darcy smiled sadly. "The one outside San Diego, I think the reason she agreed to check in was that a bunch of celebrities have been patients there, but her stint was celebrity-free. It must have been the off-season."

"I know eating disorders are really hard," Liz said. "I'm sorry."

"I worry that her life is on hold," Darcy said. "And I worry about her heart and kidneys."

He was pulling into a parking space—how inevitable things seemed, how close to him Liz felt—when her phone buzzed with an incoming text. If not for her father's heart attack, she might not have looked at the phone; she might simply have gone into the restaurant and ordered scrambled eggs that she would barely have eaten. Instead, she did look.

Before she read the message, she saw the name of the text's sender, and she said, "Speaking of sisters, this is from Mary." Then she said, "Oh my God."

"Is everything all right?" Darcy asked, but for the first time in two days, Darcy was not foremost in her mind; something else had abruptly pushed him aside, and his voice was background noise.

Lydia & Ham eloped to Chicago, Mary's text read. *Turns out Ham transgender/born female!!!!!! M & D freaking out can u come home?*

Chapter 129

"IS EVERYTHING ALL right?" Darcy asked again.

"Lydia—my youngest sister—I guess she just eloped with her boyfriend. And also—wow." Rapidly, Liz typed, *For real? Not a joke?* Mary hadn't yet responded when Liz sent an additional text: ????

Ham being transgender—it seemed impossible. And Lydia had known? But, Liz thought, he had a goatee!

A few seconds later, Mary's response appeared: *Not a joke.* Shortly there followed: *And Lydia always accused ME of being gay!* And then: *Dad and Kitty driving to Chicago now, mom losing her shit. When can u get here?*

Liz looked at Darcy, who had parked, turned off the ignition, and was watching her with concern. "Sorry," Liz said. "I just—I didn't see this coming. I should talk to Mary. Do you want to get a table and I'll meet you inside?"

Darcy passed her the keys, and as he climbed from the car, Liz was already calling her sister.

"You're sure that Ham is transgender?" Liz said when Mary answered. "And you're sure they eloped? This isn't some prank Lydia's pulling?"

"They—Ham—came out to Mom and Dad last night, and it didn't go well. This morning, there was a note on the kitchen table from Lydia saying they're getting married."

"Does he have a fake penis?" Later, Liz would be relieved that it was only Mary to whom she'd posed this prurient question.

"How should I know?" Mary said. "But Mom is acting crazy. I can't deal with her."

"What are Dad and Kitty planning to do in Chicago? Do they think they can stop the marriage?"

"Lydia and Ham can't do it today because courthouses are closed on Sunday. Then tomorrow is Labor Day. Plus, I checked online and they'll have to wait a day to use their marriage license, unless they already had one before they left, which I doubt. Basically, I don't see how they can make it official until Wednesday at the earliest."

"I'm not in New York," Liz said. "I'm in California. Are you at your apartment or the house?"

"The house, and Mom just popped a bunch of Valium that I think expired ten years ago."

"Hold on." Liz lowered her phone and began typing, searching for flights to Cincinnati; the earliest option she could plausibly make left San Francisco at 11:40 A.M., entailed a layover in Atlanta, and would deliver her to Cincinnati at 9:28 P.M. The cost of this decidedly indirect journey would be $887, which she was pretty sure would deplete the last of her once-respectable-seeming savings.

"I'll go to the airport as soon as I can and text you from there," Liz said.

"It's so typical of Lydia to make us deal with her shit."

"I like Ham, though," Liz said. "Don't you?"

"I don't care about Ham," Mary said. "I have a paper due next week."

Chapter 130

INSIDE THE CREAMERY, Liz spotted Darcy in a booth—a large plastic menu lay open in front of him—and again she was gripped by an awareness of the parallel universe in which they could function as an ordinary couple. This only made it more difficult to say, as she approached the table, "I'm so sorry, but I need to go. Could you—I'm sorry to ask this—could you take me back to Charlotte's to get my stuff, then give me a ride to the airport?"

"What's wrong?"

"The person Lydia eloped with—her boyfriend—he's transgender. I guess my parents are really upset."

Darcy didn't seem shocked, and Liz was reminded of his general disapproval of her family. That the Bennets would find themselves in further turmoil appeared to be no more or less than he expected. He said, "You want me to take you to the airport now?"

"I just think—it sounds like I'm needed at home."

"Why?"

It was a surprisingly difficult question to answer. Haltingly, Liz said, "This isn't the kind of news my parents will respond to well, especially my mom."

"Isn't that their problem? It doesn't seem like Lydia or her boyfriend did anything wrong." Darcy's abruptly condescending tone reminded Liz of when they'd first met.

"Do I think my parents will figure out a way to deal with this if I'm not there?" Liz said. "Of course." She could hear her voice turn wobbly as she said, "But you know what? I didn't really involve myself with stuff at home for twenty years, and during that time, a lot of things went off the rails."

"You think getting on a plane will retroactively assuage your guilt?"

"I'm not trying to convince you I'm right," Liz said. "I just want to know if you'll take me to the airport or if I should call a cab."

Darcy shut his menu. "Fine." But in the same gesture with which he agreed to help her, some goodwill between them officially dissolved; their ST was no longer a fireball threatening to engulf Northern California.

"You won't be dining with us today?" a waiter said as they walked toward the front of the restaurant, and Darcy said brusquely, "No."

"Another time," Liz added with fake brightness.

Back in the car, Darcy was quiet, and so was she. It occurred to her to ask him to simply go straight to the airport, and to have Charlotte send on her belongings, except that Liz didn't wish to risk separation from the digital recorders she'd used to interview Kathy de Bourgh.

She hadn't realized she'd been rehearsing concise explanations of the situation to offer Charlotte and Cousin Willie until she entered the house and found their bedroom door still closed. Liz stuffed her clothes and toiletries into her suitcase and her digital recorders and notebook into her purse and was wondering if she should at least leave a note for her hosts when, passing again by their closed door, she heard female gasps that were unmistakably sexual in nature. She hurried out.

Darcy had never turned off the engine, and after her suitcase was stowed in the backseat, even before she'd fastened her seatbelt, he began driving again. After a prolonged silence, she said, "If you'd told me Lydia had eloped with a cowboy she'd just met in a bar, or with the Bengals' quarterback, sure. But this—I don't know, I've never seen her as having a lot of sympathy for people outside the mainstream."

Darcy said nothing.

"I wonder if my mom even knows what *transgender* means," Liz added. "I guess she does now."

Perhaps ten more minutes passed in silence, and Liz said, "Ham's on the short side for a guy, but—I never would have guessed. He has a goatee, and he's very muscular."

"I'm sure he's on a testosterone regimen." Darcy spoke curtly.

"Have you ever had transgender patients?"

"Yes, but not because they were transgender. For that, they'd see an endocrinologist."

The traffic on the 101 was light—it still was just eight-thirty on the Sunday morning of Labor Day weekend—and Darcy drove in a middle lane. Despite the urgency she felt, sadness billowed in Liz at the first sign for the airport. She could hear the uncertainty in her own voice as she said, "I'm not sure how long I'll be in Cincinnati, but when do you get back?"

"Tuesday morning, but I go straight to work."

"Well, depending on how long I'm in town, maybe I can make this up to you."

Again, he said nothing, and when he pulled up in front of the terminal, she said, "Don't get out. It's faster if I just grab my stuff."

He complied, and after she'd retrieved her suitcase from the backseat, she waved. "Thank you, Darcy."

She'd been afraid he wouldn't get out anyway, that he wouldn't try to hug or kiss her, and that was why she'd told him to stay seated—because she hadn't wanted his nonembrace to be the last thing that happened before she boarded a cross-country flight.

Chapter 131

MR. BENNET HAD found the note from Lydia upon entering the kitchen of the Tudor that morning: *By the time you read this, Ham and I will be on our way to Chicago to get married. Don't try calling because we're not taking our phones. If you make me choose between you and Ham, I pick Ham! from Lydia THE BRIDE.*

As had occurred to Liz, neither Mr. nor Mrs. Bennet had been familiar with the term *transgender* before the previous evening, and having it jointly defined by Lydia and Ham, over cocktails in the living room, had not brought forth the best in them. Why, as Mrs. Bennet told Liz upon her arrival home, she had never *heard* of such a thing! How strange and disgusting that Ham was really a woman, and what could Lydia be thinking to get involved with someone so obviously unbalanced? Though Mr. Bennet had received the news with slightly greater equanimity, he had hardly been a paragon of respect, saying cheerfully to Ham, "If only you'd been born a century ago, you could have been one of Barnum's bearded ladies."

Lydia and Ham hadn't, during that conversation, been seeking Mr. and Mrs. Bennet's approval for their marriage; indeed, there had been no discussion of marriage. Their decision to elope, Mary explained to Liz, seemed to have arisen in reaction to the lack of acceptance or grace with which Mr. and Mrs. Bennet had greeted Ham's disclosure.

Also prior to Liz's return home, Mrs. Bennet had called their long-time lawyer and friend, Landon Reynolds, who'd explained that turning to the police would serve no purpose. Eloping wasn't a violation of the law, and there was nothing to suggest that Ham had taken Lydia to Chicago against her will. While the illegality of same-sex marriage in both Ohio and Illinois could potentially render Lydia and Ham's union void were Ham deemed female, seeking an annulment on Lydia's behalf, given that she was well over the age of consent, would be complicated and costly; and in any case, it seemed likely that the gender listed on Ham's driver's license, if not his birth certificate, was male. His best advice, Mr. Reynolds told Mrs. Bennet, was to buy a bottle of champagne and wait for the newlyweds to return.

Yet so insistent was Mrs. Bennet that twenty minutes later, at her urging, Kitty and Mr. Bennet had begun the almost five-hour drive to Chicago with what Mrs. Bennet chose to believe was the goal of either preventing the couple's nuptials or, if it was too late, of separating them and transporting Lydia back to Cincinnati alone. Mary, in the meantime, had been tasked with calling Chicago hotels to check for reservations under Bennet or Ryan, a search that by late Sunday night remained fruitless.

Shortly after Mr. Bennet and Kitty's departure, Mrs. Bennet had swallowed the expired Valium and retired to bed, and this was where, at ten-thirty P.M., Liz found her. The older woman was weeping with a vigor that appeared unsustainable, yet the voluminous scattering of tissues across the bed, nightstand, and nearby rug suggested that she had been at it for some time; indeed, of the four tissue boxes sitting atop the mattress, two were empty, one was half-empty, and one was as yet unopened but clearly waiting to be deployed. Mrs. Bennet herself was surrounded by flotsam that included a cordless phone, two remote controls (when Liz entered the room, the television was showing an infomercial for a spray-on sealant), a partially consumed three-ounce chocolate bar, a king-sized package of Cheetos reduced to orange crumbs, and a preponderance of throw pillows; on the nightstand were a lowball glass and a bottle of gin. Mary, who had opened the front door of the Tudor and led Liz to their mother's lair, now stood just inside the room with her arms folded. Liz approached the bed and sat, setting her hand on her mother's arm. "Hi, Mom."

Mrs. Bennet shook her head, her cheeks florid and damp. "She's so pretty," she said in a mournful voice. "I don't know why a pretty girl would go and do such a terrible thing."

"I really think Ham is a good person," Liz said. "Remember how he helped me clean out our basement?"

"Are there people like this in New York?"

"There are transgender people everywhere," Liz said. "And there have been throughout history."

Both in the San Francisco airport and then on her layover in Atlanta, Liz had via her smartphone learned about the *kathoey* in Southeast Asia and the *salzikrum* of the ancient Middle East. Also, she now knew to refer to it as a gender reassignment rather than a sex change, she knew that Ham might well not have had "bottom" surgery (based on her own observations, she strongly suspected he'd had top), and, in any case, she knew to be embarrassed for having asked Mary if Ham had a fake penis; it was, apparently, no less rude to speculate about the genitals of a transgender person than about those of a person who was nontransgender, or cisgender.

As far as she was aware, Liz had, prior to meeting Ham, regularly interacted with only one transgender person, a sixty-something woman who was a copy editor at the magazine where Liz and Jasper had been fact-checkers. Surely, if Liz had learned that anybody in her social circle in New York had eloped with someone transgender, she'd have greeted the news with support; she might even have felt that self-congratulatory pride that heterosexual white people are known to experience due to proximate diversity. So why, she decided, should her feelings be any different for Ham? Especially now that she understood and could disregard the slight evasiveness he'd shown the time Liz had asked about his upbringing in Seattle, or Kitty's taunting implication that Liz was ignorant of Ham's true character. Which she didn't believe she had been, Liz thought. In the air over the wheat fields of Kansas, Liz had concluded that if a Cincinnatian could reinvent herself as a New Yorker, if a child who kept a diary and liked to read could ultimately declare that she was a professional writer, then why was gender not also mutable and elective? The enduring mystery of Ham, really, was how he managed to stand Lydia's company and how he now planned to do so for a lifetime.

"Five of you," Mrs. Bennet said, and a fresh wave of tears released themselves. "How is it there are five of you and not one can find a nice, normal, rich man to settle down with?"

"Mom, we're healthy," Liz said. "We aren't drug addicts. Things could be so much worse. And with Dad having been in the hospital, doesn't it put something like this in perspective?"

"Does Ham get up in the morning and say, 'Today I'll wear a dress. No, trousers! No, a dress!'"

"I'm pretty sure he's a guy all the time, Mom. Just think of him like you did before you knew he used to be female." *Used to be female*—Liz had a hunch such a phrase ought not to be uttered by her newly enlightened self, though she'd check online.

"Mom, you should go to sleep," Mary said.

"I'm waiting to hear from your father," Mrs. Bennet said, and Mary said, "He and Kitty are probably going to sleep now, too."

Mrs. Bennet glared between her daughters. "How selfish you all are," she said. "Doing what you like without regard to how it reflects on our family name."

"Okay, I'm done here," Mary said, and Liz stood, too.

"Mary's right, Mom," Liz said. "You should sleep."

Chapter 132

IN THE HALL outside their mother's room, Mary said, "I guess all these years, Lydia has been projecting her secret same-sex attraction onto me."

Liz looked at Mary. "Do you really think that?"

"She has no idea how mean people can be because usually *she's* the mean one." The pleasure in Mary's voice was undisguised. "Living her whole life as this skinny, cutesy blonde—well, she's about to learn."

"I don't think most people who meet Ham have any idea he's transgender," Liz said. "Although it also doesn't seem like either of them is trying to hide it."

"Exactly," Mary said. "Because Lydia doesn't know any better. And trust me, this is the kind of gossip that spreads like wildfire."

"Lydia and Ham are living their truth," Liz said. "More power to them."

Chapter 133

IT WAS DISPLEASING and confusing to be back in her childhood bedroom again so soon after leaving, and especially after its fumigation with chemicals whose ostensible harmlessness Liz was not entirely convinced of. Though she'd been away from Cincinnati for only four nights, Liz also felt a strange envy for the version of herself who had formerly inhabited this room and had, however unwittingly, enchanted Darcy. The net result of her time in California, she feared, had been to decrease his affections. Though moments had seemed promising, something between them had come loose when she'd canceled breakfast and asked him to drive her to the airport.

She thought of texting him to say she'd made it safely back and wished he'd asked her to when he'd dropped her off. But what if, at this very moment, he and Caroline Bingley were sharing a laugh, standing close to each other, with Caroline looking bitchily gorgeous in an expensive frock?

The timing of it all was dreadful yet somehow unsurprising—that on the cusp of finally having an honest conversation with Darcy, an interruption would come from her family, and with the whiff of scandal attached. It was in Liz's opinion a mistake to see symbolism in one's own life, but still, the necessity of her abrupt departure from California felt almost punitive; she wondered if she was being karmically reprimanded for her previous treatment of Darcy.

Sleep overtook her eventually. But even then, woven throughout the night's dreams, her remorse did not abate.

Chapter 134

WHEN LIZ ENTERED her mother's bedroom in the morning after a run and a shower, it was nearly nine o'clock and her mother was on the phone.

"You should check again," Mrs. Bennet was saying. "They might have gotten there right after you left."

It was difficult for Liz to envision her father and Kitty in Chicago. Were they driving up and down Michigan Avenue or wandering on foot around Navy Pier and Grant Park? Were they loitering by the closed courthouse or entering restaurants, showing photos of Ham and Lydia from the screen of Kitty's phone? Or were they simply, as seemed most likely, in a hotel room, watching television?

"For God's sake, Fred, you need to find her," Mrs. Bennet said. "I didn't sleep a wink last night." A few seconds passed before Liz realized that the phone call had ended and her mother's most recent remark was directed at her.

"I'm sorry to hear that," Liz said.

"What's it called when they slip pills into girls' drinks?" Mrs. Bennet said. "They do it at fraternity parties. I wonder if that's how Ham got her to Chicago."

"Mom, I'm sure he didn't give her roofies."

"Here's a question for you: Which locker room does Ham use when he swims? Because no one at the Cincinnati Country Club would want to change into their bathing suit around a person like that."

"Ham can put on a bathing suit at home," Liz said. "There are ways around it. But I bet he uses the men's locker room. Just think of him as a man, Mom."

"Lydia will never be able to have babies." Mrs. Bennet scowled at Liz. "And at the rate you're going, neither will you."

"Lydia and Ham can adopt. Or"—it was impossible not to think of Jane—"there are other options."

Mrs. Bennet shook her head. "When people adopt, God only knows what's in those genes."

"God only knows what's in any of our genes," Liz said, and Mrs. Bennet drew herself up into a haughty posture.

"I beg your pardon," she said. "Your father and I both come from very distinguished families."

Chapter 135

"STILL NO WORD from Lydia?" Jane said.

Liz had brought her laptop and phone to the backyard and was sitting in an ancient patio chair with flaking paint. She said, "Since they didn't take their cellphones, I assume they're not planning to be in touch until they get back to Cincinnati."

What Jane did then was surprising: She laughed. "Lizzy," Jane said. "Of course Lydia took her phone. She'd sooner lose a limb."

As soon as Jane said it, Liz realized her sister was correct. "Wow," she said. "I'm an idiot."

"I feel like I should be there," Jane said. "But Mom would take one look at me and know, and this doesn't seem like the right time for her to find out."

"You don't need to come home. Mom's driving me crazy and Mary's MIA, but I don't know what there would be for you to do."

"It sounds silly, but I keep picturing Ham's goatee."

"He must take testosterone," Liz said, and thought of Darcy.

"What I wonder is," Jane said, "if Ham was choosing from all the male names in the world, why did he pick Ham? I know it's short for Hamilton, but that's still kind of odd. Do you know what his name was when he was female?"

"No," Liz said.

"I wish I knew him better," Jane said. "I guess now I'll get to."

"I shouldn't even tell you this," Liz said, "but there were new unopened Horchow boxes in the front hall when I got home last night, and there's a bunch of raw steak in the refrigerator. Oh, and doughnuts on the counter. Apparently, Mom and Dad are very receptive to our concerns about their physical and financial well-being."

"All we can do is encourage them when they make good choices," Jane said. "We can't micromanage their behavior. So, Lizzy, I think I felt the baby kick."

"Wait, really?"

"It was this flutter that didn't come from my own body."

"That's so exciting."

"I know." Then Jane said, "Promise to call me the minute you hear anything from Chicago."

Chapter 136

ALTHOUGH SHE KNEW she was supposed to be concerned about Lydia, Liz felt more preoccupied with whether she'd hear from Darcy. As she had previously planned to do, he was taking a red-eye, though having seen Pemberley, she suspected he'd be flying first-class. As Labor Day proceeded in a decidedly un-Labor-Day-ish fashion—Mrs. Bennet continued to weep and brood in her bedroom, Mary hadn't yet come to the Tudor, and Liz wasn't sure whether to resent Mary for staying away or be relieved by her absence—Liz imagined Darcy's activities. He wouldn't, presumably, leave for the San Francisco airport until around midnight in Cincinnati, so she pictured him packing his suitcase in the Pemberley guesthouse, perhaps going for a run or playing Scrabble with Georgie. (Liz had no idea if Darcy and Georgie played Scrabble.) Had Caroline Bingley returned yet to Los Angeles? Liz certainly hoped so.

Intermittently, her mother would summon her to unhappily speculate about Ham, sometimes from a new angle and sometimes from

angles previously explored just a short time earlier. Otherwise, Liz bus-
ied herself with tidying the Tudor, as well as with aggressive sniffing in
cabinets and the corners of rooms for lingering traces of sulfuryl fluoride, Ken Weinrich's reassurances notwithstanding.

While she wished that her impatience as she waited to hear from
Darcy would cancel out her impatience as she waited to hear from
Lydia, the opposite proved true; doubly restless, Liz kept experiencing
phantom buzzes in her pocket, incoming texts that turned out not to
exist. She began composing in her head the pseudo-off-the-cuff mis-
sive she'd send when Darcy returned to Cincinnati: *Hey there, wondering if you're free to get coffee/dinner/whatever before I go back to New
York?* Having already changed her plane reservations twice since leaving Cincinnati for Houston, she no longer had a ticket to New York,
but she figured the implication of urgency couldn't hurt.

In the early afternoon, Liz was driving home from the Smoothie
King in Hyde Park Plaza when her phone buzzed with a real and actual
text; it was not, however, from Darcy or Lydia. It was from Georgie.

Liz, the text read, *it was SO great to meet you. I'm sure you've heard
from my brother about him and Caroline and now I feel very awkward
about the conversation you and I had. I really wish I'd bitten my tongue.
I can't wait to read your article about Kathy de Bourgh and I hope we
cross paths again soon!*

Liz's heartbeat sped up unpleasantly, and continued to do so as she
read the text a second time, searching for the part where Georgie specified *what* Liz might have heard about Darcy and Caroline. Really,
though, was specification necessary? Still, it was shocking that exactly
what Liz had feared might happen had happened. Hadn't she been
devoting enough anxious attention to this eventuality to preclude it?
Had discussing the subject with Charlotte not been a sufficient method
of warding it off?

There was nothing to do but change clothes and go for another
run. Although thirty-two ounces of pureed raspberry and mango were
sloshing in her stomach, she couldn't just sit inside the Tudor, knowing that Darcy and Caroline were together. (How could they be together? Was it possible that Liz had imagined all the fraught energy

between herself and Darcy in Atherton, his solicitousness, that moment when they'd almost kissed? Had he invited her to breakfast to tell her that he and Caroline were a couple? To officially retract his affection and establish a more friendly and informal mode, should he and Liz encounter each other in the future?)

Her hands shook as she tied her sneakers. In the second-floor hall, she called, "Mom, I'm going for a run" and left without either waiting for a response or taking a key. Once outside again, she didn't bother stretching in the driveway but simply sprinted off.

For half a mile, adrenaline and bewilderment spurred her on, and her pace was far faster than usual. But sorrow and smoothie gas soon triumphed; she decreased her speed, and tears welled in her eyes. She had been prepared to admit her mistakes to Darcy, to make amends and humble herself. Now Caroline had robbed her of the opportunity, and even worse, Darcy had let Caroline do so.

As Liz reached Madison Road, tears fell down her cheeks, and an undeniable cramp took hold on the right side of her abdomen. And then she was sobbing, she was full-on heaving, in the middle of the day, on a busy street, and instead of making a right, she crossed Torrence Parkway, took a seat on a public bench, and gave in to a combination of regret and sadness that caused her to gasp and shake. She hunched over, her elbows pressed against her thighs, her hands covering her face, and tears and mucus cascaded down as she wept and wept and wept. After an indeterminate amount of time, a tentative voice said, "Honey?" Liz looked up.

It was a slim, middle-aged black woman who also appeared to be exercising; she wore sturdy white walking shoes, shorts, and a T-shirt featuring the University of Cincinnati Bearcat. "Are you okay, honey?"

Liz ran her palm upward over her nostrils. "I'm heartbroken," she said, because it seemed the most succinct way of conveying the facts.

"Oh, honey." The woman shook her head. "Aren't we all?"

Chapter 137

I KNOW U have your phone, Liz typed in a text to Lydia. *I'm not telling u not to marry ham but why don't u reach out to m & d and tell them you're fine?*

No reply was immediately forthcoming. Although she suspected it would achieve little, Liz also looked up the number for Ham's gym and left a message.

She was lying in bed in the dark when, she was almost certain, Darcy's plane took off from San Francisco; there was only one direct red-eye from SFO to Cincinnati. She no longer was waiting to hear from him, but the desolation inflicted by Georgie's text had scarcely decreased. This new development had to be more than just a few stolen, wine-facilitated kisses between Darcy and Caroline, didn't it? Or else Georgie wouldn't have referred to them in such an official way. They, too, wouldn't have eloped, would they? The thought was truly sickening.

During the many years of romantic torment meted out by Jasper

Wick, Liz had routinely cried herself to sleep. But that had been a while ago, and the nocturnal weeping Liz was gripped by in her childhood bed in the Tudor didn't have a recent precedent; it was almost—almost—unfamiliar.

Chapter 138

SEVENTY-TWO HOURS PASSED before Liz received acknowledgment of the text she'd sent Lydia, and when it came, Lydia's response contained no words. It was a photo of herself and Ham standing in front of a white wall, a round blue Cook County seal partially visible behind them. Ham was dapper in a button-down shirt and sport coat, a red rose on his lapel, and Lydia was unforgivably young and stunning in a sleeveless white dress; behind her right ear was tucked a red rose that matched Ham's. Together, the two held out a light blue piece of paper covered with writing too small for Liz to decipher, except that at the top, in capital letters, it said *CERTIFICATION OF MARRIAGE.* They both were beaming.

Congratulations! Liz texted back. *U guys look great!* And then: *When u coming home???*

Again, there was no answer.

Chapter 139

MR. BENNET AND Kitty returned to Cincinnati on Thursday evening, four days after they'd departed and just a few hours after Liz had received the photograph from Lydia; her father and sister had never encountered the newlyweds.

Mrs. Bennet was, as usual, in her bed—the demands of the Women's League luncheon, pressing as they were, had been set aside all week in order for her to devote herself full-time to her shame and distress—and Mr. Bennet and Kitty entered the room to deliver a report devoid of news to her, Liz, and Mary.

"Did you really find out nothing in all that time?" Mrs. Bennet asked her husband.

"I learned that it costs forty-seven dollars a day to park a car at the Hilton." Mr. Bennet seemed extremely weary. "Anything else, Kitty?"

"The Bean is cool."

"I always knew there was something off about Ham," Mrs. Bennet said. "He had a funny look in his eyes, and I didn't trust him."

"They're probably on their honeymoon by now," Mary said with malicious delight.

"Kitty, what do you think?" Liz said. Surely, if Liz had been in touch with Lydia, Kitty had, too. But Kitty merely shrugged.

"We should hire a detective," Mrs. Bennet said. "Fred, remember when the Hoessles were getting divorced and Marilyn hired someone to follow Buddy?"

"Actually," Liz said, "I've heard from Lydia."

"You didn't think to tell us?" Mr. Bennet said.

"It wasn't very long ago, and she didn't say anything. It's a picture." Liz tapped on the message icon on her phone's screen, then on the photo itself: Ham and Lydia in their dressy clothes, holding their marriage certificate, looking jubilant. She showed it to her father first, and his expression seemed to be one of muted amusement.

Kitty said, "Wow, she looks fierce," and Mary said, "Then I guess it's a done deal."

When finally Liz brought the phone to her mother, Mrs. Bennet peered at it with pursed lips and burst once more into tears. "If that's how Lydia wants it, then fine," Mrs. Bennet said. "Fine. But I'll have nothing more to do with either of them."

Chapter 140

LIZ FOUND HER father in his study. She said, "You know when we were talking about if Mary's gay and you said people can do what they want as long as they don't practice it in the street and frighten the horses?"

Mr. Bennet sighed. "It appears your youngest sister is doing everything in her power to call my bluff."

"I realize that being transgender seems weird to you," Liz said. "But the world has changed a lot."

"Indeed."

"I don't want us to be one of those families that has a huge rift and doesn't speak to each other. Do you?"

"What would you have me do?"

"Help Mom get past this. When Lydia and Ham are back in Cincinnati, invite them over for dinner like normal. Or, I don't know, give them a waffle iron. They didn't get married to spite you guys. They're in love."

Mr. Bennet smiled wryly. "I suppose they are," he said. "But that's a condition that's acute, not chronic."

Chapter 141

"WHEN DID YOU know?" Liz asked Kitty. They were in Kitty's car on their way to pick up dinner from Bangkok Bistro. "Did you know as soon as you guys started doing CrossFit?"

"Basically."

"So it's not like Lydia was flirting with the gym owner, *then* found out he was transgender. She knew all along?"

"It's the kind of thing people talk about. It's also, like, Ham is insanely strong. He can do fifty pull-ups in a minute, which is amazing, and when you consider that he was born a girl—" Clearly, Liz thought, Kitty didn't share her concern about using politically incorrect language. Kitty added, "If anything, Ham being trans made Lydia more intrigued."

"I wonder if she'll become an activist for LGBT causes now," Liz said, and Kitty laughed.

"That isn't how she sees herself at all, or how she sees him. She definitely thinks of him as a guy, and she's into the whole chivalry thing. Well, it does sound like his firsthand knowledge of women's bodies is a bonus with sex."

"Ugh." Liz put up a hand, her palm to Kitty, and Kitty laughed again.

"You're such a prude."

"I'm not a prude," Liz said. "Good for them. But I don't need to hear about it."

"Then why are you asking me all these questions?"

Chapter 142

LYDIA'S TEXT ARRIVED in midmorning the next day, sent as a group message to Jane, Liz, Mary, and Kitty: *Were coming back tonite having a party can u guys get some alcohol*

Another text followed: *At our place around 9*

And then a third: *No champagne too sugary but tequila/hard cider not the cheap kinds*

An explosion of sororal texts ensued.

From Kitty: *Congrats!!!!!!!!!!!!!!!!!!!!!*

From Jane: *I wish I could be there, congratulations!*

From Mary: *Are you enjoying being a lesbian?*

From Liz: *I think it's important for you to reach out to M & D*

From Kitty: *Their acting bonkers*

From Liz: *Also tell Ham I look forward to having him as a brother in law*

From Mary: *"Brother" in law*

From Lydia: *Mary trust me ham is more masculine than 99% of dudes out there*

From Lydia: *M & D can think whatever they want*

From Lydia: *We use a 9 inch dildo Mary u should try it some time maybe u wouldn't be so fucking grumpy*

From Lydia: *Isn't it funny I'm the youngest but the 1st to get married???*

Chapter 143

THE REMARKS THAT had previously echoed in Liz's head—*I'm in love with you, I can't stop thinking about you*—had been replaced. As she stood in the shower rinsing shampoo from her hair, as she ate a turkey sandwich, as she drove to Hyde Park Wine & Spirits and compliantly purchased noncheap tequila and hard cider, and then to Joseph-Beth Booksellers, where she acquired a paperback titled *Transgender 101: A Simple Guide to a Complex Issue,* the line that echoed instead was *I'm sure you've heard from my brother about him and Caroline.* Driving along Edwards Road, she thought, *I'm sure you've heard from my brother about him and Caroline. I'm sure you've heard from my brother about him and Caroline. I'm sure you've heard from my brother about him and Caroline.*

Back in her room, Liz looked online and found the location and meeting times of a support group for family members of transgender individuals. She then found the names of three family therapists, copied down the information by hand, folded the piece of paper, inserted it into an envelope on which she wrote *Mom & Dad,* and attached the envelope to *Transgender 101* with a rubber band. Finally, when she could think of no other gestures to convince herself she was a dutiful daughter and sister, Liz booked a ticket on a flight to New York for the following morning.

Chapter 144

LYDIA WORE A short yellow sundress and flats, and she did seem filled with a newlywed bliss Liz had never really believed existed. By way of greeting, the bride held out her left hand to Kitty and Liz (Mary had decided not to attend the party), and an enormous emerald-cut diamond ring atop a diamond-encrusted wedding band caught the light. "We got them at Tiffany's on the Magnificent Mile," Lydia said. "They cost twenty thousand dollars altogether."

"They're pretty," Liz said.

"Did Ham pay in cash?" Kitty asked.

Ham approached then, and though Liz detected in him an underlying wariness as they both leaned in to hug, he, too, seemed genuinely happy. "Congratulations," Liz said. "Welcome to the family."

"I realize this didn't play out in the ideal way," Ham said. "But I hope you know, Liz and Kitty, that I intend to honor and care for your sister."

His earnestness was both touching and embarrassing; also, Liz was aware of scrutinizing his goatee in a way she hadn't in the past. She murmured, "Of course."

"I plan to keep trying with your parents," he said. "I think it's best to let them have some space for now, but I'm not giving up."

"I'm glad to hear that," Liz said, and then a tall, red-haired woman she'd never met embraced Ham and, in doing so, interrupted the conversation.

About three dozen other guests—visibly athletic men and women in their twenties, thirties, and forties, plus a smattering of preppy young women who were childhood friends of Lydia's—milled about. Ham's house was a narrow and immaculate five-story dwelling in Mount Adams with a granite-filled kitchen and a roof deck. Setting her tequila and cider on the dining room table, where a bar had been assembled—there were, in fact, some bottles of champagne, one of which Liz poured from for herself—Liz was accosted by Jenny Teetelbaum, Lydia's best friend from Seven Hills. At a normal volume, Jenny said, "Isn't it crazy about Ham? I would *never* have guessed." In the hope of setting an example, Liz lowered her own voice. "I'm excited for them," she said.

"I hear your parents are freaking out," Jenny said. "Which is so understandable."

"Are you still teaching kindergarten?" Liz asked.

After hearing in detail about the whimsies of five-year-olds, Liz found herself in the living room, at the edge of a conversation about whether clean and jerks or burpee pull-ups were the single best Cross-Fit exercise, when Ham tapped a fork against his glass. He stood in front of the fireplace, Lydia beside him. "Thank you all for joining us tonight," he said, and this remark alone prompted clapping and hoots. "I just want to say, on behalf of Lydia and me, we're thrilled to have you celebrating with us, and we appreciate your support as we enter the next stage of our lives together. And I want to say to Lydia, baby, thank you for making me the happiest guy alive!" They turned their faces to kiss, and the cheering that ensued was positively uproarious. When the embrace ended, Lydia raised both her arms above her head like an Olympic skier who'd completed a victorious run. "Turn on the music!" she cried out, and Liz couldn't tell if the first dance that followed, to Aerosmith's "I Don't Want to Miss a Thing," was planned or impromptu. That Lydia and Ham were in love seemed beyond doubt.

A few minutes later, while Lydia was dancing with Jenny Teetelbaum, Liz tapped her sister on the shoulder. "I'm headed out," she said. "Congratulations again."

Lydia's expression was scornful. "It's not even eleven!"

"I'm going back to New York in the morning. Lydia, I really hope you'll get in touch with Mom and Dad."

"Don't nag me at our party."

"They might be old and weird and narrow-minded, but they're the only parents you have."

"Oh my God, can you even stop for one second?" Lydia reached for Liz's hand, grasped it, and began twirling under their linked arms. "Have you completely forgotten how to enjoy yourself?" Lydia asked, and Liz thought, *Maybe.*

She stepped in and hugged her loathsome, charming younger sister. "Keep me posted," she said.

Chapter 145

OUTSIDE, LIZ WALKED briskly to her father's car and was just a few feet from it when she heard her name. She turned to see Ham jogging after her.

"You slipped out without giving me a chance to say thanks again for coming tonight. Really."

"Thanks for including me," Liz said automatically, and then they both were quiet, and Liz wondered if they would continue to be part of each other's lives for decades to come—if Ham and Lydia would stay married.

"I hope you don't feel"—Ham paused—"I guess, ah, misled."

"I don't care that you're transgender," Liz said. "And even if I did, I realize you don't need my approval. But it'll be a huge bummer if Lydia becomes permanently estranged from our parents."

"No one wants her to have a good relationship with them more than I do," Ham said. "I didn't plan to—she was the one who had the idea of eloping. I could have said no, obviously, but what if I did and your parents succeeded in turning her against me? I couldn't risk losing the love of my life."

To be adored as deeply and inexplicably as Ham adored Lydia—would she herself, Liz wondered, ever experience it?

"I decided the best strategy was to tie the knot now, then spend as long as it takes convincing your mom and dad I'm a good guy," Ham was saying. "That's still my aim, and I welcome your advice."

"So the other stuff you've told me," Liz said, "or your bio on your website—I'd understand if it's not, but is it all true? Were you in the army, and did you grow up in Seattle?"

"It's definitely all true," Ham said. "I was commissioned into the Signal Corps as a female and I had a different name, but yes."

Liz sighed. "Do you think the storage locker with all the stuff from my parents' basement is infested with spiders?"

"That crossed my mind. I can check. Liz, I know that Lydia can be hard on you, but your opinion matters a lot to both of us. I'm really happy we have your blessing, and I promise I'll make things right with your parents."

"I believe you," Liz said. "Now go inside. You're missing your own party." As Ham stepped forward to hug her once more, she said, "Lydia's lucky she found you."

Chapter 146

LIZ'S PLANE LANDED at JFK shortly after eleven A.M., and as it tax-ied toward the gate, she switched the setting on her phone out of air-plane mode. Immediately, three texts popped onto her screen, one of which was from her editor, Talia, a second from Jane, and a third that read, *It's Darcy. Hope things are okay with your family. Can I buy you a drink this weekend?*

Her heart stretched and contracted. Why now? Of course now! *I'm sure you've heard from my brother about him and Caroline,* Liz thought, and the idea of sitting in a bar listening to him describe his renewed romance made her glad she'd left Cincinnati.

She was ready—more than ready—to once again inhabit her life in New York. So it hadn't worked out with Darcy; she was thirty-eight, and it hadn't worked out with plenty of guys. *Actually I'm back in NY,* she typed hastily. *Looks like we're ships passing in the night. Take care.* Then she hit Send, and within a few minutes, she was off the plane and hurrying through the terminal, buoyed, however temporarily, by the relief of resolution.

Part Three

Chapter 147

FOR THE MORNING of the Women's League luncheon, Liz had ordered a large bouquet of pale pink roses, hypericum berries, and sweet peas to be delivered to the Tudor, along with a card bearing her and Jane's names. During the luncheon, she texted Mary and Kitty to ask how it was proceeding.

Fine, Mary texted back. *Almost over.*

Picture a sorority that time traveled 50 years, Kitty texted back. *Except drunker.*

Neither of which exactly answered Liz's question.

The day before, Liz had heard from Shane Williams that another couple was preparing to make an offer on the house, and she had purposely withheld this information prior to the luncheon. Upon calling the Tudor in the late afternoon, she learned from Mr. Bennet that her mother had retired to bed.

"In defeat or triumph?" Liz asked, and her father said, "It's hard to tell sometimes, isn't it?"

Chapter 148

THE INITIAL OFFER was for $899,000; after negotiations, it stalled at $920,000, which Shane told Liz and Mr. Bennet in a conference call he strongly recommended accepting. "Unless you want to take the house off the market, make improvements, and put it up for sale again in the spring," he said. "But with the school year under way, and the holidays on the horizon, now just isn't when most people are looking to move."

The second time around, the inspection did not yield surprises; a closing date was set for October 18, and Liz booked a ticket to Cincinnati accordingly.

Chapter 149

SEPTEMBER IN NEW York was still prone to unpleasant hotness, but by October, which had always been Liz's favorite month, the city was at its best—the leaves in Central Park were changing color, the stylish women who worked at *Mascara* and its sister magazines were wearing belted coats, and her favorite deli was selling pumpkin soup. It had occurred to Liz that her extended stay in Cincinnati might distance her from her New York friends, or even from her own habits there, but in fact, she appreciated the city anew, and the affection appeared reciprocal: She went out often for drinks, dinner, or brunch, in many cases with people she hadn't socialized with for over a year, and there was much to gossip about and discuss. Though she made a point of calling her parents every other evening, and texting her sisters as often if not more so, the absence of constant familial obligations made her feel as if additional hours had been inserted into each day, hours in which she could read novels, attend movies, go for long runs, or visit museum exhibits that she probably, the previous spring, would have intended to see without actually doing so, believing herself to be too busy.

A few weeks had passed before Liz realized that these auxiliary chunks of time were attributable not simply to no longer being at the beck and call of her family but also to the conclusion of her relationship with Jasper. It was in the second week of October, with neither delight nor vengeance, that Liz discarded the red sheer teddy and matching thong underwear, never worn, that he'd sent her in Cincinnati. She also recycled the piece of computer paper on which, over a decade and a half, she had written what she'd once deemed Jasper's best sentences: *I talk way more openly with you than I do with her. Sometimes I think you and I would be a good couple. I love you in my life.* How meager these offerings had come to seem, how provisional their compliments. Yet surely she was as culpable as he was; recalling her casual speculation about when Jasper's wife's grandmother might die and thereby free Jasper and Susan to divorce, Liz wondered if a stronger sign of a relationship's essential corruptness could exist than for its official realization to hinge on the demise of another human being.

In any case, when the autumn nights most filled Liz with yearning—when, as she was leaving work, the smell of candied cashews and fallen leaves wafted through the cool air—the person she thought about wasn't Jasper.

Chapter 150

CONGRATULATIONS, KATHLEEN BENNET! read the email Kitty had forwarded to Liz. *The Kenwood Institute of Cosmetology is pleased to offer you a place in our rigorous and state-of-the-art 16-week Manicuring Program; your session will begin on MONDAY, NOVEMBER 4, 2013.*

Happy now? Kitty had typed above the institute's digital letterhead, and Liz wrote back, *Yes, very. Good for you!*

Chapter 151

MRS. BENNET WAS the one who called Liz, which was unusual, unless there was a sale on bath mats at Gattle's. "Your father has gone to a lecture with that deviant," Mrs. Bennet practically hissed. "Can you imagine?"

"Do you mean Ham?" Liz asked.

"I don't know what your father's thinking."

Liz had been pleased to hear that Mr. Bennet and Lydia had met on more than one occasion for breakfast at the Echo, but as far as she knew, this was the first time since the elopement that he had socialized with Ham.

"What's the lecture about?" she asked.

"That has nothing to do with anything," Mrs. Bennet said.

A modicum of research revealed that the two men had heard a professor at the University of Cincinnati speak on law and politics in ancient Greece.

Are u a history buff? Liz texted Ham.

Whatever it takes, Liz, Ham texted back. *Whatever it takes :)*

Chapter 152

USING A SMARTPHONE matchmaking app that hadn't existed the last time she'd been single, Liz embarked on a series of dates that were neither terrible nor particularly promising. The fifth man she met for a drink turned out to be someone with whom she had gone on one date seven years earlier, though neither of them realized it until they were seated across from each other at a restaurant on East Thirty-sixth Street and had been talking for ten minutes. The man's name was Eric, and he was now living in the suburbs of New Jersey, divorced, and the father of a five-year-old and a two-year-old.

He was a perfectly pleasant person, but as they spoke, all the things that had bothered her the last time around bothered her again, with only the slightest particulars changed. She hadn't been aware of storing this list of Deterrents to Dating Eric Zanti in her brain for seven years, but once it got reactivated, there was no denying that it was there: He didn't read much, he said, because he was too busy. He enjoyed small-game hunting, though on a recent guys' weekend with his buddies, he'd taken down a 150-inch whitetail deer. He thought his ex-wife spent too much time on Facebook.

In her twenties, Liz had lived with a roommate named Asuka who loathed grocery shopping; she said that looking at all the food in the aisles, thinking of the meals she'd need to fix, day after day and year after year, filled her with despair. Parting ways with Eric outside the restaurant—they kissed on the cheek, and Liz stifled the impulse to make a joke about seeing him again seven years hence—Liz understood Asuka's despair, except with men instead of food. Even before she returned to her apartment, she had deleted the matchmaking app from her phone.

Chapter 153

DURING THE FORTY-EIGHT hours she was in Cincinnati for her parents' move from the Tudor and the subsequent closing at the title
company, Liz looked for Darcy. She looked for him running on Madison Road as she drove back and forth—her own trips were staggered
with those of the movers—between the Tudor and the Grasmoor,
which was the building where her parents had, after all, decided to live,
though they were renting a two-bedroom rather than buying a three-
bedroom and using the funds that might have served as the down payment to maintain their country club membership. She looked for
Darcy downtown, when she and her father went to the title company's
office (she had never previously encountered Darcy downtown), and
while she waited at the Dewey's in Oakley to pick up a pizza for her
parents' first dinner in their new dwelling. She looked for him on her
own run the next day, and it would have been a lie to claim she didn't
consider stopping by his apartment, but it was seven-twenty in the
morning and he had a complicated work schedule and a girlfriend.
(I'm sure you've heard from my brother about him and Caroline.)

Before flying out, Liz met Ham and Lydia for lunch at Teller's. "I don't know if Lydia mentioned that I wrote a letter to your mom," Ham said. "Unfortunately, I haven't heard back."

Over pizza the previous night, Liz had inquired about whether her mother had considered breaking the silence between herself and her youngest daughter and her husband. "I certainly haven't," Mrs. Bennet had declared.

"I think she still needs time," Liz said to Ham. "Maybe after they get settled into the new place, she'll be more receptive. But I'm glad you're trying."

"Lizzy, I have a question," Lydia said. "Have you ever gotten your eyebrows threaded?"

The three of them had stood to leave the restaurant when they saw a middle-aged woman Liz recognized as Gretchen Keefe, who decades earlier had been their teenage babysitter and neighbor on Grandin Road. Gretchen was accompanied by another woman, both of them wearing black leggings, recognizably overpriced hooded sweatshirts, and large diamond rings.

"Hey, guys!" Gretchen said warmly. "Is it true that Mary eloped with a transvestite?"

Liz winced as Ham extended his hand and said with equal warmth, "Actually, I'm transgender, not a transvestite, and married to Lydia here, but nice to meet you. Hamilton Ryan."

"Oh my God." Instead of shaking Ham's hand, Gretchen brought her own hand to her mouth; her face had drained of merriment.

"Is it true," Lydia said to Gretchen with feigned brightness, "that you and your husband haven't had sex in fifteen years? Because that's what he told Kitty last summer while she was trying to swim laps."

"I didn't realize—" Gretchen said, and Liz said, too loudly, "Yeah, lots of changes in our family. In fact, our parents moved from Grandin Road yesterday. The house had just gotten too big for them." This was what Mrs. Bennet had explained to Abigail Rycraw, a widow and Women's League member they'd run into in the Grasmoor parking lot, and her mother had said it so convincingly that Liz briefly thought she believed it.

Gretchen looked to be on the cusp of tears, and Liz said, "Anyway, nice to see you!" She glanced at Ham and Lydia and pointed toward the front of the restaurant. "Shall we?"

Outside on the sidewalk, Lydia said, "Gretchen Keefe sucks."

"You need to grow a thicker skin, baby," Ham said. "You'll get there."

"Sorry," Liz said, and Ham shrugged.

"I've heard worse."

Chapter 154

REMEMBER THAT GUY Darcy *who dissed u at the Lucases bbq?* Mary texted Liz on Halloween. *Just saw him at Skyline but he was bizarrely nice.*

Liz was at her desk at *Mascara,* preparing to enter a one o'clock meeting.

Another text arrived from Mary: *Maybe he's bipolar.*

What did you talk about? Liz typed, then deleted.

Was Chip's sister Caroline with him? she typed, then deleted that, too.

Did my name come up? she wrote, and this she also deleted.

Finally, she wrote, *I guess he likes chili,* and that was the text she sent.

Chapter 155

JANE'S FORTIETH BIRTHDAY fell on the first Saturday in November, and Liz traveled by train to Rhinebeck to help set up the dinner party Amanda and Prisha were hosting. Liz had made two earlier trips to Rhinebeck and been reassured both times to see that her sister's coloring was rosy, her demeanor was upbeat, and a small, enchanting bump protruded a little more from her midsection with each visit. By her birthday, Jane was twenty-two weeks pregnant and downright voluptuous. She wore empire-waist shirts that emphasized her full breasts, and jeans whose stretchy belly panels she revealed to Liz with amusement. "You're like a fertility goddess," Liz said, and Jane laughed but didn't seem displeased.

Mr. and Mrs. Bennet called in the afternoon to sing "Happy Birthday"—this was the only duet Liz had ever known her parents to perform—and the guests arrived around seven: friends of Amanda and Prisha's whom Jane had recently come to know, a Barnard classmate and her husband living in nearby Kingston, a pair of yoga studio colleagues who, like Liz, had made the journey from the city. Though Jane didn't drink, Amanda broke out several bottles of what Liz recognized as expensive wine. Liz had brought a cake from a Cobble Hill bakery—on the crowded train, she'd sat with the cake box on her lap like an obedient child, holding above it the book she was reading—and despite the filling meal, no one declined a slice.

Liz shared the double bed in the guest room with Jane and her body pillow, and on Sunday morning, while Amanda and Prisha were still asleep and their son was watching television, the sisters went for a stroll on the woodsy, sidewalkless roads around their hosts' home.

"Does being forty feel fabulous and foxy?" Liz asked.

"More like fatigued and foolish," Jane said, but she sounded cheerful. "Thanks for coming up to celebrate."

"How are you doing on money?"

Jane shook her head. "Amanda won't let me pay for anything, and their friends have been amazing with hand-me-downs. Now I just have to figure out how to break the news to Mom and Dad. Mom still hasn't spoken to Lydia and Ham, has she?"

"I don't think so. Did you hear that Lydia registered? Which, not to sound like Mom, but is that allowed if you elope?"

"I'll have to order her something," Jane said.

"How about dinner china that's $240 a setting? Or perhaps you'd prefer the $650 juicer."

"Are you making those up or are they real?"

"To be fair, the juicer also chops and purées."

Jane laughed. "Maybe I can afford to buy her part of a fork. Lizzy, I don't know what I imagined my financial situation would be when I was forty, but mooching off friends—it wasn't this."

The surprise, Liz thought, wasn't that someone rich would swoop in to subsidize Jane's pregnancy; the surprise was that Jane had arrived at a point where she needed subsidizing. So refined and delicate was Jane, so charming and beloved, that a certain inevitability had surrounded her courtship with Chip, and it was their breakup rather than their coupling that felt like a deviation from the script. Also, Liz wondered, was it indecorous of her to feel relieved that obscenely successful Amanda rather than middling Liz herself was supporting Jane—should Liz insist on taking responsibility, as a family member? Aloud, Liz said, "They seem fine with your so-called mooching."

"*You* would never do it. In fact, the opposite—aren't you paying Kitty and Mary's rent?"

"Only until they finish their classes and get jobs. I have one more thing to tell you about Lydia. She took Ham's last name, so she's Lydia Ryan now."

"Hmm," Jane said. "I guess she's traditional after all."

Chapter 156

IT WASN'T UNEXPECTED to run into Jasper; given the smallness of the Manhattan media world, the only question had been when the encounter would happen. The answer turned out to be a Wednesday evening publication party for a White House memoir by a former national security advisor also known for her magnificently toned calves.

The party occurred at an event space on the twenty-second floor of a building on Columbus Circle. Three other people entered the elevator in the lobby with Liz, and just before the doors closed, an arm shot through them, followed by a male voice saying, "Hold up!" Presently, the rest of Jasper appeared. He and Liz made eye contact, and he smiled. "Hey! It's you."

Guardedly, Liz said, "Hi."

He had always been handsome and still was, but Liz noticed for the first time how old he looked: His curly blond hair was more silver, and the corners of his eyes were marked by crow's-feet. When had this happened? She didn't derive pleasure from her observations; instead, they made her sad.

Everyone disembarked on the twenty-second floor, and Jasper set a hand on the sleeve of her coat to hold her back. He said, "I'm trying to respect your wishes here, but do you really need to starve me out?"

"I'm not starving you out."

"What, then—we're just done? After everything?"

"You had your chance."

"If you're boning some other dude, just promise me it isn't Darcy." She said nothing, and as more guests spilled out of another elevator and passed them, Jasper added, "Can't we at least grab coffee? I miss our conversations."

She pulled her arm away from his grasp. "Then I guess you shouldn't have treated me like you did."

Chapter 157

THE TEXT FROM Kitty arrived while Liz was pulling laundry from the dryer in the basement of her building: *M & D took L & H out for dinner at country club last nite. Thot u want to know.*

Liz called her sister immediately. "This is huge," Liz said. "Don't you think?"

"I guess." Kitty's voice sounded flat, possibly bored.

"Are you painting your nails right now?" Liz asked.

"If I was," Kitty said, "how would I just have texted you?"

Chapter 158

LIZ TELEPHONED HER mother next. "I heard you and Dad had dinner last night with Lydia and Ham."

"There's a new shrimp pasta on the menu," Mrs. Bennet said. "I wasn't in a seafood mood, but I think I'll get it next time. And Lydia had the filet mignon—the club always does a good job with that."

Knowing she should leave well enough alone, Liz said, "Are you okay now with Ham being transgender?"

"Oh, that's a birth defect," Mrs. Bennet said quickly. "It's like a cleft palate. It's not for any of us to question God's plan, but all you need to do is look around to know some people aren't born the way they should have been."

Was this a theory espoused in *Transgender 101: A Simple Guide to a Complex Issue?* Not having read the book, Liz couldn't be sure.

"Ham is thinking of opening a second gym," Mrs. Bennet was saying. "All his classes have wait lists, so expanding would make sense." She sounded, Liz thought, uncannily like the version of herself she had always yearned to be: a mother-in-law bragging about the successful husband of her daughter. Then she added, "Lizzy, I can't find a very nice throw pillow that I bought at the old house. It has a pineapple on it. Do you remember seeing it?"

For a few seconds, Liz froze. Then she said, "Maybe it got mixed up with the donation items for the auction."

Chapter 159

THE TEXT FROM Darcy, which arrived just after ten o'clock on a Thursday night, read: *Hi, Liz, I'll be in NYC next week, and I'd like to take you and Jane out for dinner. Are you free either Tues or Wed? I realize this is short notice.*

How perplexing these few lines were! Why would Darcy wish to have dinner with her *and* Jane? Did he remember that Jane no longer lived in the city? Perhaps, Liz thought, he hoped to avoid issuing an invitation that might otherwise sound like a date.

And then, as sometimes happened, the memory of Darcy's declaration (he'd been *in love* with her, he'd wanted to be her *boyfriend*) flew through Liz's head, followed by that dreadful echo: *I'm sure you've heard from my brother about him and Caroline.*

Yes, there'd been extenuating circumstances; but none, Liz thought with sorrow and regret, had been extenuating enough to absolve her.

Chapter 160

LIZ'S PROFILE OF Kathy de Bourgh appeared in the December issue of *Mascara,* and Jasper's article about Cincinnati's powerhouse squash tradition appeared in the December issue of *Sporty;* the two magazines hit newsstands within a day of each other in early November. By the afternoon, six people had texted or emailed Liz about Jasper's article, four of whom knew she knew him and all of whom knew she was from Cincinnati. She read it that night.

Only after finishing it—the focus switched between the coach and the eleven-year-old boy with the intense father—did she realize that a part of her had expected Jasper's article to morph from a straightforward sports feature into a breaking-the-fourth-wall direct address to Liz herself, a postmodern confession or self-exculpation on Jasper's part. Yet it was none of these things; it was only about squash. Was she disappointed or relieved? She'd have expected the former but instead, without doubt, felt the latter.

The next morning, Liz discovered that after going to bed, she had received a two-sentence email from Kathy de Bourgh: *Dear Liz, Thank you for taking the time to depict me with respect and accuracy. I enjoyed meeting you and am most appreciative. Kathy*

Liz hadn't previously communicated directly with Kathy de Bourgh and was briefly unsure how to address her. Then, decisively, she typed, *Kathy, the pleasure was mine. I'm delighted you enjoyed the article. Liz.* She forwarded Kathy de Bourgh's email to her editor, Talia, prefacing it with the word *Nice* and three exclamation points.

Chapter 161

THROUGH AN EXCHANGE of texts with Darcy that didn't veer in subject from logistics, Liz had agreed that she and Jane would meet him at seven o'clock at a bistro in lower Manhattan. Jane, who was reluctant but obviously sensed Liz's wish for her attendance, arrived in New York via train in the afternoon.

Though Liz wished she could be as indifferent to Darcy as Jane was, an irresistible curiosity gripped her. The evening might leave her bruised or remorseful, but she was compelled to know why he wanted to see them. As they entered the restaurant, Liz's heart pounded and her body pulsed with a jittery energy.

Following the maître d', Liz made eye contact with Darcy from several feet away, and when he stood—without smiling, he held up his right hand—an odd happiness swelled within her.

"Oh my God, Chip's here," Jane said.

It was true—Liz had been so focused on Darcy that she'd failed to notice that Chip was also waiting at the table.

Liz glanced at her sister and said, "I had no idea, I swear." Jane bit her lip, and Liz said, "Is this okay? We can leave."

"It's fine," Jane said quietly.

Even before they reached the table, Liz felt herself oversmiling, talking too loudly and with excess enthusiasm. "Hi!" she said to Darcy and Chip. "Chip! What a surprise!" Chip was now standing, too, and the physical and symbolic intricacies of all of them greeting one another seemed nearly insurmountable. Thus, despite her misgivings, Liz threw her arms around Chip in the friendliest and most midwestern of hugs, and he half-hugged her back while kissing her right cheek. She then hugged Darcy. Had the two of them *ever* hugged? Not, she was pretty sure, while clothed. Even as this thought formed, the hug had concluded, and they were all sitting. She wondered if the men were shocked by the size of Jane's belly.

"What are you doing here?" she said to Chip with great energy, and though she willed herself to turn down both the volume and the chumminess a notch, the strange and ambiguous situation was impelling her to take the reins of the conversation. "Are you in New York for long?"

"I'm not." Though he was considerably more subdued than Liz, his voice contained its usual sincerity and kindness. "But it's really good to see both of you." It was clear that the sentiment was directed at Jane; every molecule of Chip's body seemed turned toward and attuned to her. Was it possible, Liz wondered, that he found this lushly curvy version of Jane to be as beautiful as Liz herself did? When he said to Jane, "I hope you've been well," such depth of feeling infused his tone that the wish did not seem inordinate.

"I've been living up in Rhinebeck, which is very relaxing." Jane removed the napkin from the table in front of her and unfolded it on her lap. "Are you still in California?"

Chip nodded. "We wrapped the *Eligible* shoot in October."

Liz wanted to ask if he'd found love, of either the genuine or the scripted variety, yet posing the question in Jane's presence seemed cruel. Instead, Liz said, "So what's next for you?"

"Funny you should ask. I've gotten an agent, actually, who's talking to some folks about my hosting a medical talk show on cable. It'd be a roundtable thing—me, a nurse-practitioner, an alternative type like an acupuncturist or chiropractor. I'm hoping it's a way to use my expertise without fighting in the trenches like this guy." He gestured with his thumb at Darcy and added cheerfully, "If there was any lingering doubt that I'm a lightweight."

There wasn't, Liz thought, but Jane said, with more force than Liz would have expected, "I think you're being too hard on yourself. If working in an ER isn't what you want to do, you shouldn't be miserable." Was she, Liz wondered, talking only about medicine?

The waiter approached, and Darcy said, "Shall we get a bottle of wine? Jane, I don't know if you're drinking." Both he and Chip already had a cocktail in front of them.

"I'm not," Jane said.

Liz said, "But your doctor self sounded impressively nonjudgmental, Darcy."

The expression on Darcy's face then was hard to read—it might have been irritation—and Liz thought, *You're the one who invited us here.*

"I'm sure Jane knows that she doesn't need to answer to me," Darcy said, but he said it stiffly, and it occurred to Liz for the first time that *he* was not entirely at ease, which was all that was necessary for the last of her own nervousness to vanish. Besides, between them, the two men at this table had broken both her and her sister's hearts. They didn't *deserve* her nervousness!

She said, "Chip, have you ever considered auditioning for that dance competition show?"

"Believe it or not, it's very hard to win a spot. Not to mention, I'm sure I don't have what it takes. No, if I have any self-respect, the *Eligible* reunion will be my reality-TV swan song. If I stay in television, I'd like it to be more service-oriented."

As the four of them selected then received their entrées, Chip spoke the most, Liz the second most, and Darcy and Jane only intermittently. Chip never uttered the words *pregnant* or *pregnancy* but seemingly without discomfort alluded several times to Jane's condition, inquiring about how she was feeling, where she planned to deliver, and whether she envisioned continuing to teach yoga after the baby was born. Darcy paid for the meal—when Liz pulled her wallet from her purse, he shook his head sternly—and after he had passed his credit card to the waiter, Jane went to use the restroom. When she stood, so did both men. In her absence, Chip said to Liz, "She really seems good."

"She is."

"And she's—she's well-settled in Rhinebeck, it sounds like?" Did he wish to be contradicted? During the meal, Liz had concluded that they were all gathered so that Chip and Darcy could officially absolve themselves; they could go forth into the rest of their lives confident that they hadn't wronged the Bennet sisters in any deep or permanent way, assured that they were all on Waspily amicable terms. And this belief that they were entitled to absolution—it seemed the most self-indulgent act of all. But were they gathered instead for Chip to attempt to rekindle the relationship? The possibility was intriguing and alarming.

Carefully, Liz said, "I don't think she's made a concrete plan for after the baby comes."

"I'm glad she—" Chip began, at which point his phone rang. When he checked the screen, he said, "If you'll forgive me, it's Caroline." He stepped away from the table, and Darcy and Liz were alone.

"Do you want to join the call?" The question came out as less joking and more bitter than Liz had been aiming for.

Darcy looked at her curiously.

Liz held up her own phone. "I just downloaded a solitaire app, so I can keep myself entertained." When he still said nothing, she heard herself add, "That sounds like a euphemism for masturbation, doesn't it?" In her head, she thought, *Liz! Stop! I command you to stop at once!* Aloud, she said, "Why are you in New York anyway?"

He nodded once toward the table. "This dinner."

"No, seriously. Why?"

"I flew to New York this afternoon, and I fly back to Cincinnati at six A.M."

A new confusion seized Liz.

"Does Chip leave tomorrow?" she asked.

Darcy shook his head. "He's here for a few days." Then he said, "It sounds like your parents are coming to terms with Lydia's marriage."

Liz squinted. "Who'd you hear that from?"

"It's good news, isn't it?"

"Yes," Liz said. "It is good news."

"You also might be interested to know that Georgie has agreed to donate Pemberley as a historic landmark. She wants us to perform some type of ritual farewell before the handoff, and I understand I have you to thank for that."

"Actually, that's Jane's bailiwick, not mine," Liz said. "I did mention it to Georgie, though." Liz wanted to inquire after Georgie's health, but the enmity between herself and Darcy prevented her. She was grateful when Jane reappeared, and a minute later, so did Chip.

"I hope my manners won't seem lacking if I suggest that just Jane and I go for a little stroll," he said. "Jane, would you consider it?"

Jane flushed radiantly. She glanced at Liz. "Are we expected anywhere else tonight?" Which, Liz knew, her sister was fully aware they were not.

"Nope," Liz said.

Turning back toward Chip, Jane said, "Then I'd love to."

Liz and Chip embraced once more, and Jane somberly thanked Darcy for the meal (again Liz envied the way Jane was compelled to show Darcy neither phony friendliness nor conspicuous derision). Jane and Chip had scarcely left the table when Liz asked, "Is he trying to get back together with her?"

"That's for him to answer," Darcy said.

Liz rolled her eyes. "You put way too much stock in discretion."

He smiled thinly. "Or maybe you put too little."

A silence arose, a silence in which neither of them looked elsewhere or fiddled with their phones; he seemed to be scrutinizing her. If she wasn't careful, Liz felt, she might blurt out, *How could you have picked Caroline Bingley over me?*

Surely, surely, he had to say something. But no. He said nothing at all, and when Liz could withstand it no longer, she said, "I guess you'll be getting up at the crack of dawn, huh?"

"A car is coming to my hotel at four."

"In that case, you shouldn't even go to sleep. You should go on a bender."

"I imagine my patients tomorrow would prefer I didn't."

Did he understand that she had, under the guise of a joke, been putting out a feeler about if he'd like to get an after-dinner drink? She scooted back from the table and reached for her coat. "Then I'll let you get your rest." She pulled her purse onto one shoulder. "Take care, Darcy." It was borderline rude, she knew, not to wait for him and leave the restaurant together; it was borderline cold to wave with false jauntiness rather than exchanging either an Ohio hug or a New York kiss on the cheek. But he was welcome to complain about her manners to Caroline—what did it matter at this point? And anyway, when the tears burst over Liz's eyelids and streamed down her cheeks, she wanted to be away from him, alone on the sidewalk in the cool night.

Chapter 162

LIZ HAD FALLEN asleep on the couch in her living room while waiting for Jane. Thus the lights were on, and the novel Liz had been reading had dropped to the floor, when Jane knocked. Liz was still only partially alert as she opened the apartment door, saying, "I really had no idea Chip would be there. You believe me, right?"

Jane rested one hand atop her belly. "Lizzy, he proposed."

"*What*? Are you serious?"

Jane nodded.

"Holy shit," Liz said. "What did you say?"

Jane was practically whispering. "I said yes."

"Oh my God!" Liz embraced her sister. "This is insane. Start at the beginning."

"Let me get some water. Want any?"

"No thanks." Liz glanced at her watch and saw that it was three-thirty. "Did you guys have sex?" she asked.

Jane moved from the sink in Liz's galley kitchen to the living room.

As gracefully as was possible for a woman twenty-four weeks pregnant, she perched on the arm of the couch, to which Liz had returned. Jane's expression was both bashful and joyous. She said, "I was worried he'd be"—she waved a hand over her midsection—"freaked out. And I think it *was* strange for him at first, but then it was really nice."

"Was this before or after he'd proposed?"

"After. Lizzy, I know you think he acted flaky, but *I* was ambivalent, too. The situation was so confusing, and now we both know what we want."

"I take it he didn't have a ring?"

Jane shook her head. "He had no idea how I'd react." Her brow furrowed. "There's kind of a crazy part to all of this. The *Eligible* reunion will start airing in January, and, obviously, the network wants what happens to be a surprise. For all those shows, they make the contestants sign confidentiality agreements, and the agreements last until the whole season has aired. Even if a couple falls in love during the shoot, they're not really supposed to see each other for months, until after the last episode. If they violate the contract, they're liable for the entire budget of the show, which is something like five million dollars."

Jane took a sip of water, then went on: "The reunion took place at this fancy compound by the ocean in Malibu, and Chip said from the minute he got there, he knew he'd made a mistake—not in leaving medicine but in leaving me. He'd let his doubts about being a doctor, which he'd had for years, cloud his judgment about our relationship, and after he found out about my pregnancy, he was overwhelmed. But when he got to California and was supposed to be in romantic settings with other women, all he could think about was me. He wants to raise my baby as his child. The catch is that because of the contract he signed, we can't be together for at least four months—unless, and this is the crazy part, he thinks that if I'm willing to do it, we can get married now as part of an *Eligible* special. During the reunion, he talked a lot about me with a producer he'd known from his first season, and she tried to convince him to invite me on the show, to come out to Malibu, but he thought that wasn't fair to me, because the whole thing would have been filmed. In fact, he wasn't even planning to reach out to me at all until Darcy suggested it—Chip was worried I hated him. Anyway, he saw this producer last week, and she's pretty sure that if we get married on the air, the network will pay for the wedding, and afterward, before the special runs, they'll rent a house for us somewhere secluded while we wait for the baby."

"That's bonkers," Liz said.

"He's not pressuring me to do it," Jane said. "He said the choice is mine, and if we have to wait until March or April to be together, it's fine. But, Lizzy, by March I'll have a newborn. I'll be in a different place emotionally, and so will Chip. I want us to become parents together. There's no guarantee that if we try to pick up later where we left off tonight, it'll work."

After a few seconds, Liz said, "I wish I didn't agree with you. Here's what I don't get, though—why can't you just move out to L.A., rent an apartment, and see him really discreetly?"

"I asked that, too, and he said he thinks the producers won't allow it. He thinks they're okay with us being together if it's sort of under their control, or if they're benefiting from it, but otherwise, they'll say it's too great a risk. Chip gets recognized much more in L.A. than in other places."

"Jesus," Liz said. "And I thought Mom tried to boss us around." Both sisters were quiet, and Liz added, "Just the idea of you, the sweet yogini, having your wedding nationally televised—it's very weird."

"I know," Jane said. "I used to have such specific opinions about what my wedding would be like. Remember that game we'd play where we'd pick out our bridesmaids? But that was a long time ago. I'm forty, and I'm about to have a kid. I don't care about the ceremony. I'd rather just be married to Chip and get on with our lives." Jane glanced at Liz. "Maybe I've lost my mind."

"Well, I agree that you'd be ratings gold," Liz said. "I'd tune in to see Chip Bingley marry a beautiful pregnant lady. But do you realize what you'd be opening yourself up to? You'd be on the cover of celebrity gossip magazines."

"Really?"

"*Yes,* Jane. Without a doubt. You'd have to sign a contract just like Chip, and one of the things it would require you to do is talk to the media. Plus, tons of trashy websites that you hadn't talked to would say whatever they want about you guys. Did Chip mention compensation?"

"Like money?"

Liz nodded.

"Vaguely," Jane said. "At this point, it's still not definite that *Eligible* wants to do a wedding special with us. The next step is for Chip and me both to sit down with his agent and that producer."

"Has the producer seen a picture of you?"

"I don't know."

"I bet Chip showed her one. Trust me, Jane, they'll want to do it."

"The only way I'll agree to it is if all of you are there," Jane said. "Mom and Dad, obviously, and you and Mary and Kitty and Lydia and now Ham. Do you think they'll go on TV for my wedding?"

Liz laughed. "Some of them."

"Will you?"

"Sure," Liz said. "For you."

"Does this all seem crazy?"

"Yes," Liz said. "But I think you and Chip genuinely love each other." She patted her sister's arm. "I'm glad he wised up."

Chapter 163

ALMOST IMMEDIATELY, A maelstrom of activity was swirling. The following evening, while it was still afternoon in Los Angeles, Liz, Jane, and Chip participated via speakerphone from Liz's apartment in a conversation with both Chip's agent, whose name was David Scanlon, and the *Eligible* producer with whom Chip had discussed Jane, whose name was Anne Lee. It was decided that two days hence, when Chip flew back to Los Angeles, Jane also would journey west, on a different flight. In the meantime, Jane would begin filling out the many forms meant to facilitate her background check.

"Why do they need to do a background check on me if we already know each other?" Jane asked Chip when the call had concluded.

Chip and Liz answered at the same time. "They're being thorough," Chip said as Liz said, "Because they don't want Chip's family to sue them if you turn out to be a psychopath who kills him on your wedding night."

Jane and Chip were seated on the couch, holding hands, and Jane looked at him. "I've never even met your parents," she said. "I hope they're not mad at me."

"How could anyone be mad at you?" Chip said, and he kissed her.

But given that Chip's parents were also the parents of Caroline, Liz thought, who knew what they'd be like? Even if they were genial in the extreme, watching their son marry a pregnant woman they'd never met, on national television, could not be a cherished dream. Then again, since that same son had chosen to appear on two separate seasons of *Eligible*, perhaps his parents would understand how much worse than Jane they might have fared with a daughter-in-law.

As for Caroline herself, spending time in her presence at the wedding filled Liz with a dread exacerbated by the assumption that Darcy would be Caroline's date. For no one other than Jane would Liz have subjected herself to such circumstances.

Chapter 164

IN THE MORNING, Chip and Jane rented a car and drove together to Rhinebeck, where they would stay the night before Jane collected her belongings and bid farewell to Amanda and Prisha.

The following day, Amanda called Liz and said, "This is really what Jane wants? To get married on TV to the guy who dumped her the minute he found out she was pregnant?"

Even under normal circumstances, Liz found Amanda a bit intimidating—if Liz hadn't suspected Amanda would scoff at the idea, she'd have loved to write about her as a Woman Who Dared—and Liz tried not to sound meek or defensive as she said, "I certainly didn't try to talk Jane into it. And if you're upset about her quitting her job, you should talk to her, not me."

"We can find another yoga instructor. But I've always thought Chip Bingley was a total phony."

"Had you met him before yesterday?"

"No, but I swear those were crocodile tears he cried in his season finale." Quickly, Amanda added, "I don't watch the show, but Prisha does. Liz, if Chip leaves Jane again, I'll do him bodily harm."

"I'll do it for you," Liz replied.

"Prisha wants to talk to you," Amanda said. There was a lull as the phone was passed, then Prisha's excited voice. "Do we get to come to the wedding?" she asked.

Chapter 165

WHAT THE PRODUCERS envisioned, Jane explained to Liz over the phone from California, was a three-day event at a resort in Palm Springs. The first night would be separate, simultaneous bachelor and bachelorette parties. The second night would be the rehearsal dinner. The third afternoon would be the wedding. Jane and Chip would be permitted to invite twenty guests total, all of whom would stay at the resort and all of whose travel expenses would be covered. The couple would receive a payment of $200,000, which Chip insisted should be Jane's and which Jane insisted should be equally divided among her family members after Chip's agent—now their shared agent—kept his 10 percent.

"You don't have to pay me to come to your wedding," Liz said. She'd been washing dishes when Jane called, and she turned off the faucet. "It would give me more peace of mind if you opened a secret bank account and put the money there. Are you and Chip signing a prenup?"

"We haven't talked about it," Jane said. "But if we didn't trust each other, we wouldn't be getting married."

Said like a woman blinded by love, Liz thought, but not signing a prenuptial agreement could only be to her sister's advantage.

"They want everything to happen two weeks from now," Jane was saying. "From a Wednesday to a Friday, because that's when they can rent out the whole resort. Do you think that'll work for people?"

"Kitty probably has the most rigid schedule of any of us now that she's in school," Liz said. "But I bet she can miss a few days."

"One of the things the agent negotiated is that the hair and makeup artists will help all of us get ready, not just me," Jane said. "So maybe Kitty can even learn from them."

"And if she doesn't, that's fine, too," Liz said. "Jane, your wedding can be at least a little bit about you."

"I haven't told you the reason the producers want to do it so soon." Jane sounded wry. "The quote from Anne Lee is 'Because you're not getting any smaller, Jane, and the fantasy that American women have of marrying Chip Bingley doesn't include looking like a whale.'"

"Wow," Liz said. "Tactful."

"No, she said it in a funny way," Jane said. "I wasn't offended. The producers are really cool and smart. They remind me of you and your magazine friends."

"They're *not* your friends. Their goal is to make entertaining TV."

"I know." Jane seemed untroubled. "Although they're giving us free rings, too. Did I tell you that?"

"I'm sure some jewelry maker is doing it as part of an advertising deal." But Liz could hear the cynicism in her tone, and, more gently, she added, "What do they look like?"

Jane laughed. "Your guess is as good as mine."

Chapter 166

"I HAVE SOMETHING to tell you all," Jane said into the speaker-phone. "Actually, a few things."

It was Thanksgiving Day, and Jane was back in New York. She and Liz were expected in two hours, along with a dish of marshmallow-topped sweet potatoes, at the Park Slope house of Liz's editor, Talia. In Cincinnati, the Bennets would celebrate the holiday, as they often did, at the Lucases'. It had been after much prodding from Liz as well as Jane that their family members had assembled in advance of the Thanksgiving meal in Mr. and Mrs. Bennet's living room at the Gras-moor.

Jane hesitated, and Mr. Bennet said, "Do go on."

Jane and Liz made eye contact, and Jane bit her lip and furrowed her brows. Liz nodded.

"I'm pregnant," Jane said. There were then several family members exclaiming—it was difficult for Liz to determine if their exclamations were supportive or oppositional—and Jane said, "Wait, there's more.

The way I got pregnant is using an anonymous sperm donor. The baby is due in late February."

In a high, emotional tone, Mrs. Bennet said, "Jane, I didn't have the slightest idea you—"

"No," Jane said. "There's even more. I'm marrying Chip Bingley, and I know it might sound odd, but we've decided to let our wedding be filmed for an *Eligible* special. Even though the special won't air until April, it's supposed to happen very soon—this December eleventh to thirteenth in Palm Springs. The thing I want most in the world is for all of you to be there. Okay, now I'm finished."

There was a cacophony of voices, and at last, Liz said, "It's really hard to understand you guys unless you speak one at a time."

"I thought Chip was back in Los Angeles, and you were living with those ladies in the country," Mrs. Bennet said.

"He is," Jane said. "And I have been, although I'm moving to L.A. But Chip came here to visit."

"I wonder if they can film you just from the neck up," Mrs. Bennet said. "Or they can do what they did when that curly-haired gal on the sitcom got pregnant, and you can carry a grocery bag in front of you."

"My pregnancy won't be a secret," Jane said. "They'll definitely show it."

"Can they tell people the baby is Chip's?" Mrs. Bennet asked.

"Aren't you guys excited to be grandparents?" Liz said. "And aunts?"

"Jane, now that you mention it, your tits did get kind of huge before you left Cincinnati," Lydia said.

"There's no way I'm going on *Eligible*," Mary said. "And why would you want to marry Chip? He has no backbone."

"Mary, men get confused," Mrs. Bennet said. "Chip comes from a lovely family, and he'll make a devoted husband."

Deploying a strategy she and Liz had discussed in advance, Jane said, "Mary, I was hoping you'd read a poem during the ceremony."

"No," Mary said.

"Jane, congratulations," Ham said. "This is fantastic news." Until he'd spoken, Liz hadn't been certain he was present.

"As long as we're making announcements," Kitty said, "then I have one, too. I'm dating Shane now, so he should come with me."

Simultaneously, Mr. Bennet said, "The realtor?" and Mrs. Bennet said, "The black man?"

"We're expanding your horizons," Kitty replied. "Welcome to the twenty-first century."

"Then I also have an announcement," Lydia said, and her voice sounded more tentative than usual. "Mary, I still don't like you, but I shouldn't have tried to force you out of the closet. Your gayness is your business."

Snippily, Mary said, "I'm not gay."

"She bowls," Kitty said. "That's what she does."

In a shaky voice, Mrs. Bennet said, "Now what on earth is bowls?"

"As in bowling balls," Kitty said. "The sport."

"How do you know?" Mary asked, and Kitty said, "Mary, I'm your roommate now."

Mr. Bennet cleared his throat. "Anyone else with a confession?" he said. "Lizzy?"

"Not today," Liz said.

Mrs. Bennet said, "Jane, we'll need to invite the Lucases and Hickmans and Nesbits to your wedding. Oh, and the Hoffs. They'd all be very hurt otherwise."

"They're only letting us invite twenty people," Jane said.

"Everyone will know it was just immediate family, Mom," Liz said. "The proof will be on TV."

"You'll all need to sign nondisclosure agreements, and the producers are very serious about them," Jane said. "That means you can't talk about the wedding before it airs. Especially not on social media, Kitty and Lydia. But something fun is that there'll be wardrobe and makeup people to help us look great. Isn't that neat?"

"Tell them my look is contemporary but classic," Mrs. Bennet said. "And I don't care for navy blue."

"I'm not wearing makeup," Mary said. "The texture of foundation disgusts me."

"Dad, what do you think?" Jane asked. "You've been quiet."

Before Mr. Bennet could reply, Mrs. Bennet said, "Why don't they come here and film at Knox Church? Knox does an elegant service."

"I think it's easier for them to shoot in California," Jane said. "Dad?"

"You're forty years old, Jane. If you want to make a spectacle of yourself, I can hardly stop you."

"Fred, Chip is a Harvard-educated doctor whose family started Bingley Manufacturing," Mrs. Bennet said. "He's very distinguished."

"Is that really what you think, Dad?" Jane sounded distraught.

"Jane, let them get used to the idea," Liz said. "You can't expect them all to be jumping for joy right away."

"You do realize we can hear you, right?" Mary said.

"Tell them the last thing," Liz said to Jane, and Mr. Bennet said, "To top what's come so far, it had better have to do with alien abduction or bestiality."

"You'll each get paid about thirty thousand dollars," Jane said. "Sorry, Ham, not you. But the rest of you."

"Ha," Kitty said. "Do you still not like the texture of foundation, Mary?"

"In that case," Mr. Bennet said, "this sounds like an excellent opportunity for our entire family."

Chapter 167

TWELVE DAYS LATER, on the plane to Phoenix, where they'd board a second plane for Palm Springs—for both flights Liz was disappointed but unsurprised to find they were flying coach—Jane said, "In all the hubbub, I haven't even formally asked, but I've been assuming you'll be my maid of honor. Will you?"

"Of course," Liz said.

"Just so you know, Darcy will be Chip's best man. You're okay with that, right? You and Darcy seemed very civil at the restaurant."

That Darcy would attend the wedding was a likelihood to which Liz had reconciled herself; after all, as Chip's friend and Caroline's beau, he was doubly connected to the Bingleys. She had considered the possibility that what she presumed was his disdain for reality television, combined with his inflexible schedule, would result in his absence, but she'd recognized that such a conclusion was probably wishful thinking. However, that he would be the best man was not an eventuality she'd entertained.

"Chip feels indebted to Darcy," Jane continued. "We wouldn't be getting married if not for him making that dinner happen."

"Or maybe if not for him you wouldn't have broken up in the first place," Liz said.

"But I still would have been pregnant." A look of worry crossed Jane's pretty features. "Lizzy, the media stuff will blow over quickly, don't you think? When people appear in tabloids all the time, aren't they in cahoots with the reporters?"

"Kind of," Liz said. "But with the baby born by the time your wedding airs, I'm sure there'll be a bounty for pictures of the *Eligible* offspring."

Jane shuddered.

"Does Chip expect that Caroline will be your manager now, too?" Liz asked. "Do they want you to shill for, like, a diaper company?"

Jane shook her head. "He told me the night he proposed that I'm the only person he's met since he appeared on TV who loves him for him and isn't trying to ride his coattails. He knows I have no desire for fame. He wouldn't say it, but, Lizzy, I think he even wonders if Caroline is using him a little."

"A little?" Liz repeated. "He wonders?"

"The house we'll live in after the wedding is in a gated community in Burbank," Jane said. "I hope it's not weird being so isolated. I'm actually excited about L.A., but I'll be happy when everything with *Eligible* is finished."

"I know you will," Liz said, though what she thought was *Everything with* Eligible *hasn't even started*.

Chapter 168

LIZ, JANE, AND Chip had arrived in Palm Springs a day earlier than their families in order for Jane and Chip to attend to various obligations, including fittings for their wedding clothes, on-camera interviews, and filming of B-roll footage (Jane walked pensively and alone on the resort's golf course, and then they both sat by the pool gazing at the sunset, his hands placed protectively on her belly). A team of six from the national jewelry chain that was indeed a sponsor of the show held a consultation in which the couple chose from an array of rings; this meeting was also, of course, caught on camera.

Liz had expected the Hermoso Desert Lodge to be mostly empty upon their arrival, but after being met at the airport luggage carousel by Anne Lee—who proved to be a poised, unpretentious woman with stylishly cut black hair and a quick laugh—as well as a driver who hefted their suitcases into his white van, Liz discovered that the resort was already abuzz with a production crew of perhaps eighty. Indeed, the entire grounds—the main lodge, with its pink stucco exterior and

Spanish-tiled roof; the elegant courtyard featuring a slate hot tub and a heated infinity pool; the lush eighteen-hole golf course dotted with palm trees, beyond which stood the scrubby beige mountains—resembled a small but busy village. Men and women, though mostly men, wore dark T-shirts and cargo pants, moved about briskly, and spoke into walkie-talkies; trucks and vans came and went from the parking lot, around the perimeter of which trailers and tents had been set up; collapsed ladders, large black plastic buckets, coils of thick orange extension cords, and mysterious equipment inside stacked black suitcases were transported on large dollies; long tables of craft services food appeared at intervals in the parking lot, crew members flocked to them, and then just as quickly both the people and the food disappeared again. Eventually, Liz deduced that some sort of control room was being set up in a first-floor guest suite that opened onto the courtyard; black twill fabric was unrolled to cover the windows from the inside, and people seemed to enter and exit with particular urgency.

The room Liz and Jane were sharing included two double beds, a balcony (Liz's point of observation for outdoor activity), and a fireplace. On the desk, a gift basket contained a fat white scented candle, two pairs of pearl earrings, hair-removal cream, razors, mini-bottles of rum and vodka, and three string bikinis with padded breast cups. The attached card read, *Liz and Jane, welcome to Palm Springs from all your* Eligible *friends!*

Liz held up the bikini top. "Is this meant for me?"

Jane smiled. "It's not for me, obviously."

In her other hand, Liz held up the package of pink razors. "Very subtle."

Much wasn't quite as Liz had expected: Her cellphone would not be confiscated, nor had the television been removed from their hotel room. "That's just for the longer shoots," Anne Lee had explained when she'd escorted them upstairs, before pointing out what she referred to as a Pelco camera—it looked to Liz like a security camera—hanging in one corner of the room near the ceiling. "Just to catch any fun, casual conversations you guys might have," Anne said in a lighthearted tone, and for Jane's sake, Liz refrained from jokes about Communist surveillance.

The hair and makeup artists Jane had mentioned would be working with guests besides Jane and Chip only for the wedding itself—Jane seemed surprised to learn this, and apologetic—so otherwise, Liz was responsible for her own appearance. And though, as the sister whose wedding wasn't imminent, Liz had anticipated having time to enjoy the lodge's amenities—perhaps by booking a massage or, before she realized how public it was, soaking in the hot tub—she, too, was kept busy.

Her own sit-down interview occurred the first evening, while Jane and Chip enjoyed an "intimate" dinner in the hotel restaurant that Jane subsequently told Liz had been filmed by two camera crews of three men each. (Upon discovering that prior to the wedding, she and Jane rather than Jane and Chip were sharing a room, Liz had assumed Jane would sneak out during the night to see her fiancé. But if she did, Liz realized, the Pelco camera would alert the producers, and a camera crew would likely materialize.)

It was Anne Lee who conducted Liz's interview, in the living room of a first-floor suite. A man stood behind a camera set on a tripod. Two panel lights were mounted on separate tripods, and there was much adjusting of the lights, the furniture, and even of Liz's posture. She sat in a brocade-covered chair, and Anne sat off-camera in an identical chair facing her. "We're so excited for this amazing love story between your sister and Chip," Anne said warmly. "And America will be so excited, too."

Since the initial conference call, Anne had been Jane's primary contact; when Jane spoke positively about the *Eligible* people she'd met, she mostly meant Anne, and indeed, it was Anne and a crew of four who had flown to Cincinnati the week prior to interview assorted Bennets. An impulse to travel there herself for purposes of supervision and possible intervention had arisen in Liz, but she'd been scheduled to conduct two *Mascara* interviews of her own on back-to-back days in New York; plus, wasn't all this *Eligible* stuff not in her jurisdiction? Still, she had been unsettled rather than reassured by her family members' universal praise of Anne Lee (or, as Mrs. Bennet referred to her, "that nice Chinese girl," though Liz suspected Anne was of Korean descent). The more favorable everyone else's opinion, the more suspicious of Anne Liz had become, and meeting in person hadn't allayed Liz's concerns. It was that Anne was so upbeat, so easy to talk to, so reassuring about what a nutty situation this was, and above all so totally not fake-seeming that Liz distrusted her primarily on the basis of her very trustworthiness; it was no wonder that, at this woman's behest, hundreds of Americans had gotten inebriated, fought, stripped, canoodled, and divulged secrets, all with cameras rolling.

"What I need you to do," Anne was saying, "is talk in complete sentences, which should be no problem since you're obviously supersmart. But if I say, 'What's your favorite color?' I need you to say, 'My favorite color is blue,' as opposed to just 'Blue.' Is that cool?"

"You might already know that I'm a journalist," Liz said. "I'm the writer-at-large for *Mascara*. So I'm definitely familiar with how interviews work, although I'm accustomed to being on the other side."

"Fantastic." Anne beamed. "Now, TV is a different medium, and I won't be saying 'uh-huh' or laughing, even if you say the most hilarious thing ever, because I don't want to make noise while you're talking. If you lose your train of thought, no worries. Just pause and start over. And you don't need to censor yourself—talk how you normally talk, and if you drop an F-bomb, we'll bleep it out. This isn't live."

"Just please don't Frankenbite me," Liz said, and Anne looked at her blankly. "Isn't that what it's called?" Liz said. "When you take one word I said here and one word there and put them together into a sentence that you use as a voiceover?"

"I've never heard that term." Anne was still smiling. "You're funny, though. Okay, to get us going, how about if you tell me your name, your relationship to Jane, your age, and where you're from?"

Bullshit, Liz thought. *Bullshit you've never heard it*. Aloud, she said, "I'm Liz Bennet. I'm Jane's sister, the sister closest in age to her. I'm thirty-eight years old, and I live in New York."

The interview lasted for an hour, and Anne was, Liz had to admit, highly competent—she asked all the questions Liz herself would have—and also skilled at disguising her attempts to look for points of tension or vulnerability. The bulk of the questions were about Jane— her "journey" as a single woman, her "love story" with Chip—though Anne also inquired about alliances and discord within the Bennet family and about Liz's own love life. (On this front, Liz was graciously tight-lipped.) Liz learned with relief that Anne was aware of Ham's transgender status, and thus it was not up to Liz to divulge or conceal it; but on one topic, Liz was unhappy with her own lack of discretion.

"You know Chip's sister Caroline, don't you?" Anne asked near the end of the hour, and Liz said, "Yes, I know Caroline Bingley."

"What's your opinion of her?"

Liz was tired, both from traveling—it was midnight Eastern time— and from answering Anne's questions.

"She's fine," Liz said.

"You sound kind of tepid," Anne said, and, as ever, her tone was friendly. "Are you sure that's how you feel?"

"Caroline Bingley is *charming*," Liz said in a jokingly posh voice. "She's *delightful*." Then she looked directly at the camera guy and said, "Don't use that."

"Why don't you want him to use it?" Anne asked. "Are you being sarcastic?"

Simultaneously, Liz felt regret surge through her, and she felt a desire to speak candidly to Anne—to say, *I'm exhausted. I need to go back to my room and sleep. I don't like Caroline Bingley, but surely you can understand how publicly disparaging my sister's new sister-in-law will only create problems that will long outlast your television special. As one professional woman to another, let's strike that from the record.*

"Did something happen between you and Caroline?" Anne said.

Liz shook her head. "I do like Caroline," she said. "I'm kidding around."

"Do you find her bitchy?" Anne asked. "I've heard that some people find her bitchy."

Liz laughed. She couldn't help it. She said, "Which people?"

"It's just the word on the street."

Again, Liz was tempted to acknowledge the preposterousness of the conversation, to say, *I understand exactly what you're trying to do.* Instead, firmly, she said, "Well, *I've* always gotten along well with Caroline."

On returning to her room, Liz looked up Frankenbiting online. There were many search results, they went back as far as 2004, and the term meant exactly what she'd thought it did.

Chapter 169

"LIZZY, I DON'T know why you never got married," Lydia said. "It's really fun. I make steak for Ham when he's finished teaching at night and I totally feel like a grown-up."

Shortly after the Cincinnati contingent's arrival at the Hermoso Desert Lodge—they were a party of seven, counting not only the Bennets but also Ham and Shane—Lydia and Kitty had come to inspect their sisters' quarters. On the same hall, Lydia and Ham were sharing a room, as were Kitty and Shane; Mary had been assigned her own room, which made Liz wonder why she herself hadn't, until she recalled Anne Lee's remark about the Pelco camera capturing her and Jane's "fun, casual" conversations. Liz was newly determined to provide no such thing.

Jane was away, but Lydia and Kitty had made themselves at home on her bed, in spite of the fact that Liz was sitting at the desk, laptop open, trying to finish writing the toast she would deliver at the reception.

Without looking up, Liz said, "When I started working full-time and paying my rent is when I felt like a grown-up. And that was, hmm . . ." She pretended to calculate "Sixteen years ago."

"Don't you want someone to come home to at night?" Lydia said. "I'd be so bored living alone."

"Then I guess it's a good thing you don't."

"If Jane's baby turns out cute," Lydia said, "maybe Ham and I will use the same sperm donor she did."

"Your kids will be doubly related," Kitty said. "That's weird."

"It's just some dude's jizz," Lydia said. "He won't be part of their lives. Anyway, sometimes two brothers marry two sisters, and their kids are double cousins. Jessica and Rachel Finholt married brothers."

"I hate Jessica Finholt," Kitty said. "In kindergarten, she stole my Raggedy Ann out of my cubby." Kitty was paging through a brochure that had been lying on the nightstand. "Do we have to pay for spa services here?"

Liz glanced over her shoulder. "I'm sure."

"It's such a waste that Jane is getting married on *Eligible* when she doesn't even watch it," Lydia said. "Don't you think Ham and I would make a good reality-TV show?"

She wasn't wrong, which wasn't the same as the idea being a wise one. Mildly, so as not to encourage Lydia, Liz said, "I bet living with all those cameras would annoy you guys." She stood. "Both of you follow me." She walked into the bathroom, and Lydia and Kitty looked quizzically at each other. Lydia said, "Are you going to teach us how to do monthly self-exams of our boobs?"

"Just come here," Liz said.

When they'd joined her, she closed the door and lowered her voice to a whisper. "Did you notice that camera hanging in the corner of the room?" she said. "Don't say anything the whole time you're here that you don't want to be on TV. I'm serious."

"Like what?" Lydia asked.

The lecture was probably, at best, useless; at worst, it could promote the opposite of the behavior Liz hoped to encourage.

"The producers don't care if we look good or bad," Liz said. "All they're trying to do is create TV that people want to watch. Just don't say anything nasty about anyone else, and don't pick fights." It was hard not to think of the intemperate remarks she herself had made the night before about Caroline Bingley. "They'll be looking for conflict."

Lydia laughed. "I doubt they'll have to look that hard."

Liz sighed. "Fine," she said. "Do what you want. But I warned you."

Chapter 170

IN HER PARENTS' room, Liz found her mother bustling about and her father sitting in an armchair, an enormous hardcover book about the Renaissance open on his lap. The room contained just one king-sized bed; surely, Liz thought, it would be the first time in years her parents had slept beneath the same sheets.

From the bathroom, her mother said, "I can't find the hair dryer. When I called the front desk, they said it's here, but, Lizzy, they forgot to give us one."

Liz entered the bathroom and pointed to the shelf below the sink. "It's right there, Mom."

Irritably, Mrs. Bennet said, "Well, it wasn't there before." As she picked it up, she added, "I think it's much better if they say Jane's baby is Chip's. People who are watching will be confused otherwise."

"Have you seen Jane yet?" Liz asked. "She looks good, doesn't she?"

With great confidence, Mrs. Bennet said, "She's carrying low. That means a boy." In the hushed tone she used for delicate matters, Mrs. Bennet said, "Liz, I don't know if Kitty and Shane are serious, but life can be very hard for mulatto children."

Liz winced. "I wouldn't say that to either of them."

"Fitzwilliam Darcy is Chip's best man." Mrs. Bennet now sounded oddly approving, even before she added, "It speaks well of Chip that he has such high-quality friends. Is Fitzwilliam single?"

When, and why, had her mother developed a favorable opinion of Darcy? Back in July, at the Lucases' party, Mrs. Bennet had been offended by him on Liz's behalf. "He's going out with Chip's sister," Liz said.

"What a shame." Mrs. Bennet frowned. "Now we also need to make sure the Chinese girl knows to say on the show that Ham's situation is a birth defect. People might think it's disgusting otherwise, but if they know it's a birth defect, they'll understand."

Her mother's belief that she could, via Anne Lee, control the narrative of the *Eligible* special—it was, Liz thought, so utterly wrong that there was no point in trying to correct it. As if sensing Liz's disloyal musings, Mrs. Bennet looked intently at her. "Don't *you* think it's confusing if they say Jane got pregnant from a man she doesn't know?"

"Mom, that's not the way anyone would describe donor insemination. And, no, I don't think it's a difficult concept to grasp."

"I think it's nicer if they say the baby is Chip's."

"But it's not true."

"Oh, for heaven's sake," Mrs. Bennet said. "That doesn't matter."

Chapter 171

AS WHEN SHE'D returned to Cincinnati for the closing of the Tudor, Liz was constantly alert to the possibility of encountering Darcy. With the bachelor and bachelorette parties just hours away that evening, surely he'd arrived on the property, but even by standing on the balcony and surveying the grounds at regular intervals, she hadn't spotted him. Though, she reflected, perhaps not seeing him at all was better than spying him and Caroline strolling arm in arm on the golf course.

The balcony did afford Liz a bird's-eye view of the courtyard meeting between Mr. and Mrs. Bennet and Mr. and Mrs. Bingley, which of course was also attended by Jane and Chip. This summit took place around a table on which was set a handsome flower arrangement, champagne flutes, and no food. Though Liz couldn't hear the conversation, there was no doubt it would exist for posterity; a man held a boom mic a few feet above the heads of the family members, two more men with cameras on their shoulders stood just behind the families, and freestanding lights illuminated the proceedings as dusk fell.

Mrs. Bingley was a slim woman with a classic blond bob, wearing beige capri pants, a matching beige jacket, beige flats, a pale purple silk scarf, and no smile; she was recognizable to Liz as the sort of woman who played tennis at the Cincinnati Country Club, who was rather like certain friends of the plumper and frumpier Mrs. Bennet. Mr. Bingley looked like an older version of Chip, with gray hair parted on one side; he wore a dark blue suit, a white oxford cloth shirt, and a green bow tie. Liz felt too much anxiety on Jane's behalf to observe the interaction in its entirety, and she soon went back inside to shower and dress for the evening.

Jane returned to the room an hour later, accompanied by Anne Lee, two makeup artists, and a wardrobe stylist. "How'd it go with the Bingleys?" Liz asked, and Jane said, "Great. His mom does a lot of yoga." Jane was visibly mic'd—the mic pack was behind her back, and the actual mic was clipped to the inside collar of her shirt—but if there was some coded, contradictory message she wished to send Liz, Liz saw no evidence of it; Jane's happiness seemed genuine.

While her sister's makeup was retouched in the bedroom, Liz applied her own in the bathroom, with the door closed, before rejoining the others. Jane's beautification process was still under way when, as scheduled, a production assistant and an audio guy knocked on the door. The audio guy mic'd Liz, and the assistant escorted her to the entrance of the lodge. Two film crews and a black limousine waited in the driveway, and when Liz entered the limo—she was purposely wearing fancy jeans rather than a skirt—she took care to angle herself into the car in the least buttocks-displaying manner possible. Inside the limo, she discovered yet another camera crew waiting, though she was the first guest. Addressing the man holding the camera—he was a forty-something guy with gray stubble and a baseball cap—she said, "Are we going to a restaurant tonight or more of a nightclub?"

After a pause, the guy said, "We're not supposed to talk about the show with you. If you have questions, ask a producer."

The production assistant who'd escorted Liz from her room had vanished. Glancing among the camera guy, a guy who wore thick black headphones, and a third guy whose role seemed to be related to lighting, Liz said, "Do you all work for *Eligible* full-time?"

"I do," the camera guy said. He nodded toward the other men. "They don't."

"How long have you—" Liz began, but she didn't finish the question because Caroline Bingley was climbing into the limo. In those first few seconds of their seeing each other, Liz could have sworn Caroline's nostrils flared with distaste. "Hello, Liz," she said in a cool tone.

"Hi, Caroline." Liz was highly conscious of both the camera crew and her mic pack; she could feel the pack between her back and the seat. She said, "I guess none of us would have found ourselves here if you hadn't nominated Chip to be on *Eligible* way back when, huh?"

"Your family must be thrilled," Caroline said, and Liz tried to infuse her voice with extra friendliness as she replied, "And yours even more so."

Liz's acting experience had begun and ended with a chorus role in a Seven Hills Middle School production of *Oliver!* And yet as the evening proceeded, Liz had the odd sense of once again participating in a play, of being obliged above all not to break character, with her character in this case the kind and supportive sister of the bride. Caroline and Liz were next joined by Mary, then Kitty and Lydia appeared together, then Chip's older sister, Brooke, whose existence Liz had been unaware of until the moment she entered the limousine. (She was the eldest of the three siblings, apparently, the married mother of an eight-year-old and a ten-year-old, all of whom lived near Mr. and Mrs. Bingley in the suburbs of Philadelphia.) At last Jane materialized, to applause that at least on Liz's part was heartfelt. As the limousine pulled away from the lodge, the tinted window separating the driver from the passengers descended, and Anne Lee grinned and held up two bottles of champagne. (Of course Anne Lee was there, and of course she was holding up two bottles of champagne.) "Who's ready for the best bachelorette party ever?" she called out.

Chapter 172

THEY ATE DINNER in the private room of a restaurant, where at first the conversation was highly stilted; when Liz went to use the restroom, Anne Lee, who'd been standing behind a camera, intercepted her and asked in her untrustworthily normal way, "How do you think it's going?"

"Fine," Liz said.

"You don't feel like things are awkward?"

"We don't know Chip's sisters that well," Liz said. "I just met Brooke tonight."

"And there's that tension between you and Caroline." Anne's expression was one of eminent sympathy. "Maybe it's better to speak your mind to her before the wedding. Like, clear the air and come out closer, you know?"

Liz had decided in advance that she'd consume no more than two drinks; after champagne in the limo, a vodka cocktail upon arrival at the restaurant, and a glass of wine with the meal, she'd already exceeded this limit. But she still found Anne far from convincing. She smiled with her mouth closed. "I told you I have no problem with Caroline."

It was shortly after the entrées had been cleared that a knock sounded on the door of the private room; Liz guessed it would be Chip, but when the door opened, it was a cop and a firefighter, or, as Liz soon discerned through her fourth drink, male strippers wearing cop and firefighter uniforms. Liz wouldn't soon forget the sight of them gyrating around pregnant, sober Jane—she was the only one not drinking—their oiled pecs displayed as they removed their clothing, save for a pair of briefs each plus, in the firefighter's case, a helmet, suspenders, and boots, and in the cop's case, a peaked blue cap and handcuffs that dangled from one wrist. The strippers proceeded to dance with some of the other women to Beyoncé's "Single Ladies": Lydia and Kitty swiveled their hips and wiggled their bottoms with particular enthusiasm, Liz shimmied around enough to seem (she hoped) like a good sport, and even Brooke took a turn grinding the firefighter, which made Liz like her significantly more; but both Mary and Caroline watched with disdain and shook their heads when beckoned to join.

The strippers had just left when there was another knock on the door, which, once again, was not Chip; this time, it was Rick Price, *Eligible*'s host. Among the women, a spontaneous cheer went up, which Liz was surprised to find herself joining, and this was when (she was on her fifth drink) she realized both that she was completely drunk—not just tipsy, not merely buzzed—and also that she was much happier than she'd been an hour or two before. She felt a retroactive remorse for all the *Eligible* contestants she'd deemed trashy and idiotic from the comfort of her living room; apparently, like teriyaki pizza and bee venom facials, getting wasted on a reality-TV show was not to be knocked until tried.

"I hear there's been lots of craziness going on," Rick Price said in a teasing tone, and the women cheered again. "I've just come from seeing the guys, and they've issued you a challenge. They want you to join them at this super-cool club for a game we're calling the Not-Yet-Wed

Game. Are you girls in?" There was even more cheering, and as it wound down, Liz heard Mary say, "Can I go back to the hotel?"

When they were all in the limo again, however, Mary was next to Liz. "This sucks," Mary said. "It's exactly how I thought it would be."

"At least you're getting paid."

Presumably, the acknowledgment that money was changing hands would never be aired; but in case there was any doubt, and also just for kicks, Liz looked directly at the camera and smiled grandly.

The club was empty except for Chip's entourage. The game was to occur in a lounge area that contained orange and red sofas and chairs; even before she'd entered the lounge proper, Liz saw Darcy sitting between Shane and Chip, holding a glass of what looked like Scotch, his expression grim. The other men present were Ham and Chip's brother-in-law, whose name was Nick, and Liz abruptly thought that if the women's dinner had been awkward, the men's must have been almost unendurable. Because truly, Shane and Ham were practically strangers to everyone present, including each other.

It was disagreeable to observe Caroline heading straight for Darcy. The two of them spoke, and as they did, Darcy's eyes met Liz's. Was Caroline denigrating her? Liz looked away.

The game required Jane's and Chip's respective wedding parties to take turns guessing how the bride and groom would complete sentences such as "I first knew I was in love when ——"

Rick Price, who was asking the questions, stood at the front of the room; Jane and Chip sat in thronelike chairs on either side of him; the male and female teams faced each other; and on a low table between them were lined up what Liz estimated to be no fewer than a hundred shot glasses filled with liquids of varied hues. Initially, she was under the impression that you did a shot for getting the answer wrong, but it seemed perhaps you took one for getting the answer right as well.

Was it surprising, or not surprising, that the game was tremendous fun? Certainly it compared favorably to Charades in Cincinnati, or maybe it was just that this time around, Liz was the best player. Whether it was "Our first date was at ——" or "The place we got engaged was

——" Liz hardly hesitated. Although Rick Price encouraged her to confer with her teammates, she was soon simply shouting out answers, but by then a general chaos had taken over: Lydia was sitting on Ham's lap, and Brooke had vomited in the corner, then wiped her mouth with the back of her hand and cheerfully rejoined the group. ("You guys are awesome!" she'd said to Liz, and Liz had barely restrained herself from saying, *I'm so glad you're not horrible like Caroline!*) Rick Price frequently reminded them all not to interrupt one another, and for a few questions, the camera guys had to do additional takes because too many people had been talking at once. As, for the fourth time, Liz called out, "Their first date was at Orchids!" she wondered if it was possible she deserved a Best Supporting Actress Oscar.

Then she was in a different part of the club, and she and Kitty were dancing to a rap song they both knew all the words to, and Kitty was wearing a thin plastic headband with antennae off of which wobbled life-sized sparkly pink penises. How marvelous this headband was! Even more marvelously, Kitty pointed out that Liz was wearing an identical one. Truly, it was a magical night. Liz had lost track of Darcy—he wasn't dancing—but she couldn't remember a time when she'd more thoroughly enjoyed the company of her sisters.

As Lydia joined her and Kitty on the dance floor, Lydia put her mouth close to Liz's ear and yelled over the music, "Do you know who Chip's best man is?" Though their faces were inches apart, Liz could only just make out what her sister was saying.

"It's Darcy!" Liz yelled back.

"It's Darcy!" Lydia yelled. "I hate him! He's the one who told Mom that stupid shit about transpeople and birth defects."

"You mean the stuff she keeps saying about cleft palates?" Liz yelled. "That's from Darcy?"

Lydia nodded. "He just left, but when I see him tomorrow, I'm telling him to stay out of other people's business."

"But you have to admit—" For multiple reasons, a dance floor didn't seem like the place for this conversation; nevertheless, Liz forged ahead at the highest volume she could manage. "Don't you think that gave Mom a framework for understanding Ham?"

"Mom understanding Ham is her problem!" Lydia yelled. "He's not asking for her permission to exist!"

"But isn't life better when you're on speaking terms with your mother?"

Lydia smirked. "Hard to say."

"*Why* did Darcy talk to Mom?" Liz yelled.

"Because he thinks he's the smartest man in the world and he likes when other people listen to him."

"No!" Liz yelled. "I mean, how did he know there was a need for him to intervene?"

"Exactly!" Lydia yelled back. "There wasn't!"

Chapter 173

LESS THAN AN hour later, Liz lay in her spinning hotel room bed in the dark while poor Jane stood in the courtyard below, still being interviewed in front of blinding lights; although Liz had experienced one of the superlative nights of her life, surely by now Jane had to feel some doubt about the manner in which she'd decided to get married. Abruptly, and somewhat nausea-inducingly, Liz sat up, turned on the nightstand lamp, rose from bed, grabbed the plastic card that was her room key, and hurried down the hall.

After Liz had knocked on the door, Mary opened it with a toothbrush in her mouth, a foamy outline of toothpaste around her lips. "What?" she said.

"That time you ran into Darcy at Skyline," Liz said, "did you tell him Mom still wasn't speaking to Lydia?"

Suspiciously, Mary said, "Why?"

"I think he ended up talking to her afterward."

"Oh," Mary said in a slightly friendlier tone. "He did." She turned and walked toward the bathroom, and Liz followed her. Mary spat into the sink and rinsed off the toothbrush's bristles. "At Skyline, he asked if he should. Because of his job, he thought he could explain the trans stuff in terms of Ham's brain."

"So he told her it's like a birth defect?"

"I wasn't there for the conversation, but that seems to be Mom's one and only talking point."

Meaning Darcy had salvaged her family's happiness in not one but two ways; in addition to bringing Jane and Chip back together, he had facilitated the reconciliation between Lydia and Mrs. Bennet. But why? For whose benefit? Neither situation affected him directly, and in neither case had he sought credit—indeed, Liz suddenly recalled Darcy deflecting the question when she'd asked at their dinner in New York how he knew Mrs. Bennet and Lydia were no longer estranged—yet his efforts far exceeded basic kindness.

Mary turned off the faucet, and the sisters made eye contact in the mirror. "In case you don't realize it," Mary said, "you got superdrunk tonight, and you reek right now."

Chapter 174

HAM LED A CrossFit workout in the courtyard at nine in the morning; he had told Liz the night before that anyone was welcome, including parents, and that he'd modify the exercises to be compatible with the participants' current fitness regimes or lack thereof. But no workout could have been modified enough to accommodate the dry-mouthed, head-pounding state in which Liz awakened. She didn't attend the class; she didn't attend the midday lunch for the two families; and it was only a short while before the rehearsal dinner, which also was to happen in the courtyard, that she forced herself out of bed. The rehearsal dinner was supposed to be casual; even bathing suits, the producers had mentioned a number of times, were acceptable.

Liz applied makeup, drank a cup of black coffee she brewed in the bathroom, and was visited by the same production assistant and a different sound guy from the previous night.

That the rehearsal dinner functioned both as a real rehearsal for the wedding and as an event that was itself being recorded for the entertainment of an audience represented a brain-hurting conundrum, but Liz's brain hurt for other reasons, and she was mostly preoccupied with which hair-of-the-dog beverage she'd consume as soon as the walk-through of the ceremony concluded. While making chitchat with Mr. Bingley, she acquired from a passing tray a glass of white wine. Having learned of her job, Mr. Bingley was confiding that he'd always yearned to write a novel. With wine in hand, Liz's prospects for the evening improved greatly.

Though Liz wore a sundress rather than a bathing suit, Lydia, Kitty, Ham, Shane, and Caroline all swam. (Liz attempted not to stare at Ham's chest, but insofar as she did, she noted that it was impressively, masculinely defined; a trail of hair ran above and below his navel, and the only evidence of his previously female body were two thin red scars beneath male-looking nipples.) The women all wore bikinis that Liz assumed were courtesy of their own welcome baskets; Caroline's was white, and at one point, she emerged from the water, approached Darcy—he wore khaki pants and a long-sleeved button-down shirt open at the collar—and was clearly trying to convince him to join her in the pool. He shook his head; she shivered sexily; he still shook his head.

Jane, who was standing next to Liz, said, "Are you planning to go in?"

"I'm afraid I'd accidentally become the role model for American women who shouldn't wear bikinis but do."

Jane pointed at her belly. "Then heaven help me."

"Oh, please," Liz said. "You get a free pass."

There was a multitude of topics Liz wished to discuss with Jane, and no way of broaching them with any confidence that they wouldn't later be broadcast. Was Jane having a horrible time or did she find this whole spectacle funny? Did she actually like the Bingleys or was she just pretending? Were their parents behaving, and had their mother yet delivered any on-camera rants? To Liz's amusement, Mr. Bennet and Mr. Bingley had discovered a shared fondness for cribbage and cigars and apparently had spent most of the day at a table in the courtyard, puffing and playing.

A chicken fight commenced, with Lydia on Ham's shoulders and Kitty on Shane's, as Liz said to Jane, "Are you nervous about tomorrow?"

Jane smiled. "I'm ready to start living the rest of my life."

Because she found it difficult not to, Liz again looked directly at the camera and audio guys standing five feet from them. "You're welcome," she said.

Chapter 175

SHE WAS CROSSING the lobby with Mary and Mr. Bennet, all of them headed toward the elevators to return to their rooms after the rehearsal dinner's conclusion, when Liz heard her name being called. As she turned, she was surprised to see Caroline Bingley walking briskly behind her. "Go ahead," Liz said to her father and sister, and, warily, she waited for Caroline. The other woman had changed from her white bikini into dark jeans and a fitted gray hoodie sweatshirt that looked to be cashmere.

When Caroline was still a few feet away, Liz said, "What do you want?"

"You're completely wrong for Darcy," Caroline said.

"I beg your pardon?"

"Don't play dumb with me, Liz. It's obvious you've had your sights set on him since that awful Fourth of July barbecue. But he wasn't available then, and he's not now."

"Okay." What on earth, Liz wondered, had inspired this confrontation?

"Your sister is lucky to be marrying Chip," Caroline said. "Very lucky. Don't let it give you any ideas. I know your family thinks of itself as, like"—Caroline made air quotes—"'Cincinnati high society.' But that's an oxymoron. And Darcy and I go way back. There's always been an understanding that we'd end up together. We have this intense chemistry, and the moment is finally right for us to be serious."

Liz smiled in as nasty a way as she could manage. "How wonderful for both of you."

"If Darcy goes for you, it'll only be because he's lost perspective living in Ohio. It's like when people start sympathizing with their kidnappers."

If Darcy goes for you—were Darcy and Caroline not a couple? Because if they were, then this display was even more unhinged than if they weren't. *I'm sure you've heard from my brother about him and Caroline*, Liz thought, and the revelation of her own foolishness was like a clap of thunder in her brain. Upon receiving that text from Georgie, she had, of course, wondered, *Heard what?* But she'd quickly gone from wondering to suspecting that she knew to being certain. Never would she have leapt to a conclusion this way when writing an article, never would she have allowed a fact to be alluded to without clarification. Trust but verify—that's what she'd have done. Yet not once in the past three months had she even attempted verification. How sloppily, and with what slim evidence, she had embraced the disappointment of her own desires. Why on earth had she been so ready for, so complicit in, the denial of what she most wanted?

"But if Darcy goes for you," Liz said slowly to Caroline, "would that be a more suitable match? No one would be embarrassing themselves?"

"Listen," Caroline said. "It's not a secret that your dad bankrupted your family. Your mom and your sisters are idiots, and now you have a tranny brother-in-law. You're not girlfriend material for Fitzwilliam Darcy."

"Let me see if I understand. Your brother is a reality-TV star, which you set in motion. But *my* family is too tacky for Darcy?"

"The TV stuff is business. *Eligible* has just been a way of establishing Chip's brand and setting him up for his own projects."

"In your defense," Liz said, "I can tell that you believe what you're saying, even if it's completely illogical. But either way, Darcy is a grown man who makes his own decisions."

Caroline's eyes narrowed. "Are you guys already together?"

Liz laughed. "How could we be when it would be such a breach of propriety? It would almost be worse than wearing linen after Labor Day. Maybe as bad as using a salad fork for your main course."

"You find yourself very clever," Caroline said. "We all know that about you."

"I'm going to bed now," Liz said. "Good night, Caroline." But Liz had taken only a few steps toward the elevators when she turned back. "By the way," she said, "we're delighted to have Ham join our family, and no one uses the word *tranny* anymore. Or at least no one with good breeding does."

It was inside the elevator, during the short ride up to the third floor, that Liz remembered that she had been mic'd for the entire conversation.

Chapter 176

IN THE HOTEL room, Liz grabbed her cellphone from the bureau where she'd left it before the rehearsal dinner and searched frantically for the text from Georgie. After rereading it (*I'm sure you've heard from my brother about him and Caroline and now I feel very awkward about the conversation you and I had. I really wish I'd bitten my tongue*), Liz typed hastily.

Georgie so sorry I never responded to this. It was great to meet u too. I know this is random but what did u mean when u said u were sure I'd heard from your brother about him & Caroline?

During the next ten minutes, Liz was so addled and impatient that she began doing jumping jacks to distract herself; after a few, as a courtesy to whoever was staying in the room under hers, she switched to sit-ups. Although she hadn't smoked in years, she was considering trying to find a cigarette when, at last, Georgie's response arrived: *I meant the car accident. Your Kathy de Bourgh article was awesome! I knew it would be.*

What car accident? Liz replied. *Thanks about article!*

Georgie's subsequent response came in three separate bubbles.

Not sure how much you already know, the first one read, *but coming back from hike that day, another driver hit my brother's car in foothills and Caroline's collarbone fractured.*

The second text read, *It wasn't Fitzy's fault but he felt responsible since he was driving. Caroline NOT happy the rest of the weekend. I think she is better by now!*

The third text read, *You're all at Chip and your sister's wedding, right? So funny to think Fitzy will be on eligible. I told him to get a selfie w/ Rick Price. He will probably "forget" so pls remind him!*

Did the fact of Caroline having sustained an injury mean, Liz wondered, that she herself ought to feel more compassion and less loathing for the other woman?

Just to confirm, Liz wrote, *your brother & Caroline aren't a couple now & haven't been since we were all in Atherton?*

Nope! Georgie responded.

This, Liz decided, was the reason she shouldn't loathe Caroline: not because she wasn't loathsome but because she wasn't Darcy's. And then Liz understood with an abrupt urgency what she needed to tell Darcy and—even more important—what she needed to ask him. Indeed, the urgency was so great that she considered texting him immediately, or just figuring out which room he was staying in and knocking on the door. But surely such a conversation ought not to be initiated impulsively.

Thanks Georgie, she wrote. *I'll see what I can do to get a pic of Rick & your brother.*

Chapter 177

THOUGH CHIP'S TEARS during the exchange of vows weren't a surprise, their duration and magnitude was a spectacle unlike any Liz had ever witnessed. They began the moment Jane appeared, following the procession of her sisters and soon-to-be sisters-in-law: She was resplendent in an ivory silk organza gown; her blond hair was pulled into a loose chignon; she wore a tulle veil delicately dotted with freshwater pearls; and she carried a bouquet of white roses. On her feet were gold satin peep-toe pumps whose heels, Liz thought with some consternation, hadn't been designed to support someone in Jane's current condition, though it was undeniable that they contributed to an overall presentation of exquisite and even magical beauty; Jane resembled nothing so much as a pregnant angel.

She was accompanied down the aisle by Mr. Bennet, in a new tuxedo. In his suitcase, he had brought to California the Brooks Brothers one he'd acquired in 1968 as the Cincinnati Bachelors Cotillion escort of a debutante named Peggy Isborne, and inducements from various young and attractive members of *Eligible*'s wardrobe department had been required to convince him that he'd be even more dashing were his formal wear updated. The bridesmaids wore lavender chiffon dresses with plum-colored sashes, and though Liz remained generally wary of *Eligible,* she appreciated that the wardrobe department had chosen different cuts of the dress to most flatter each woman's body; hers was sleeveless, with a V-neck and a knee-length skirt.

The ceremony occurred in the courtyard; during the night, rather miraculously, the pool had been overlaid with a clear acrylic cover on which rested the guests' chairs, divided into two clusters to create the aisle. At the pool's far end stood a wooden altar off which hung yards of gauzy white fabric adorned with freshwater pearls in a pattern that echoed Jane's veil, and around which coiled white roses that echoed Jane's bouquet. Six camera crews were present, one of whom was responsible for the large jib camera on a crane. Also on a crane was a thin rectangular lighting panel that measured perhaps six by ten feet. The officiant was Rick Price.

From his first sighting of Jane, Chip's face crumpled; and the subsequent gush from his eyes would surely have been sufficient to bathe a medium-sized dog: a corgi or, perhaps, a border collie. As maid of honor, Liz stood just behind Jane and had the best view of anyone of the storm twisting Chip's features. When Jane and Mr. Bennet had made their way down the aisle, Mr. Bennet had lifted her veil, kissed her on the cheek, then taken her right hand and held it out for Chip to grasp with his own. (If only, Liz thought as this sequence then occurred twice more for the cameras, she were a person who could see the tradition as charming rather than queasily patriarchal.) As Mr. Bennet sat, Chip squeaked out to Jane the words "You're so beaut—" but was unable to finish, interrupted by a fresh torrent of emotion. Jane set her hand on his upper arm, patting gently, and though Liz could not see her sister's expression, she felt confident it was one of enormous affection.

"Greetings," Rick Price intoned. "We have gathered here today for a truly blessed event, a celebration that is the pinnacle of life and love. Chip and Jane, before your families, God, and the world, you'll affirm your commitment to each other." He paused and winked toward the guests. "Now, who's ready to have some fun?"

A confusing pause ensued, and then Jane said, "I am." Chip tried to speak, couldn't, sniffled even as new tears fell, and simply nodded.

"Rick, let's do that again without the wink," a bearded producer standing behind one of the film crews interjected, and the ceremony proceeded thusly: a progression of do-overs and tears that made what likely would have been a ten-minute rite last over an hour. At intervals, makeup was reapplied, particularly to Jane but also to Chip, Rick Price, and the rest of the wedding party; a break was taken while Jane, accompanied by Liz and three members of the wardrobe department, went to urinate; and for multiple minutes at a time, everyone simply waited as Chip tried to collect himself, with Jane murmuring reassurances that were in fact audible to all.

Yet Liz was never bored; the entire ceremony was a surreal and delicious purgatory that she could have contentedly existed in forever, making uninterpretable but possibly flirtatious eye contact with Fitzwilliam Darcy. Liz had walked down the aisle as the final bridesmaid before Jane and had by some trick of vision managed to ignore both Chip and Rick Price standing before her and seen only Darcy: impossibly tall and serious and handsome. His handsomeness, still, was astonishing. But it was the import of what she wanted to say to him combined with her uncertainty about how he'd respond that left her in no hurry for the ceremony's conclusion. Given that Darcy was not Caroline's boyfriend, and given also the rumor that Darcy still had feelings for *her*—the swoon-inducing rumor unwittingly propagated by Caroline—Liz felt some degree of optimism. But optimism could always be quashed, and her heart could be broken once again.

Eventually, even with Chip's voluminous tears, the ceremony finished. The couple made their victorious promenade down the aisle as husband and wife, to great applause; then, so as to ensure that the cameras didn't miss a single angle, they circled back and made the same promenade two additional times. At this point, the guests were free to mingle, though Liz knew there was much more to endure, including her own toast. Presumably, the documentation of both the first dance and the slicing of the wedding cake would also require extra patience. But champagne was being served, appetizers were being passed—stuffed mushrooms, crostini smeared with goat cheese—and there was for at least a few minutes an interlude of comparative freedom. Darcy stood by the hot tub talking to Shane, and as Liz hurried toward them, she was intercepted by Lydia.

"This is the most boring day of my life," Lydia said with her mouth full of stuffed mushroom. "Aren't you bored?"

"I guess you're not cut out for reality TV," Liz said. "Which is good to know, right?"

"Does Jane get to keep that dress?" Lydia asked, and Liz said, "There's something I have to do. I'll be back in a second." As she pushed past Jane, Chip, and the small throng encircling them to issue congratulations, she turned off the microphone discreetly clipped to the inside of her dress, near her collarbone. At the edge of the hot tub, she tapped Darcy on the arm. When he looked at her, she said, "Hi. Hi, Shane. Can I steal Darcy for a second?" Up close, she could unmistakably see the makeup Darcy wore—base and powder, it appeared—which might have been disconcerting if she had not felt so preoccupied with the mission she had assigned herself.

"You look great, Liz," Shane said. He lifted his champagne glass. "Cheers."

Liz held no glass, but she repeated, "Cheers." To Darcy, she said, "Will you come with me?"

"Where?" He said it without particular warmth.

She had decided on a spot beside the path that led around the side of the lodge. She pointed. "That way. And can you turn off your mic?"

"Can I what?"

It was easier to do than to explain—she stood on tiptoe, reached up to his lapel, and switched it off herself. Turning, she walked quickly toward the path, still carrying her bouquet, avoiding eye contact with family and crew members alike and hoping that Darcy and no one else was following her; surely some audio guy, perhaps someone in the control room, had already taken note of having lost sound for the maid of honor and the best man and was en route to rectify the situation.

She glanced over her shoulder—Darcy *was* following her—then stepped off the path and behind a large boulder bordered by desert grasses and bleached, sandy soil. He joined her, his expression quizzical, and they stood facing each other.

"You talked to my mom about Ham, didn't you?" Liz said. He looked surprised, and Liz added, "Lydia and Mary both mentioned it."

Darcy scanned Liz's face before saying, "I'm afraid the birth defect explanation isn't politically correct, but I was trying to find terms that would be understandable to someone of her generation."

"Did you talk to her over the phone or in person?" Liz hadn't planned to ask, but she found herself wondering.

Darcy smiled. "That's a very Liz Bennet–ish question. I took both your parents to lunch."

"That was brave." After a pause, she said, "Is a Liz Bennet–ish question a good or bad thing?"

Darcy said, "Actually, that's a very Liz Bennet–ish question, too."

"You guys didn't go to Skyline, did you?"

"We went to Teller's. Would you like to know what we ordered?"

But there was growing affection in his tone, not sarcasm. And the thought of him inviting her mother and father to lunch, sitting with them at a table in Teller's, helping them, with the authority conferred by his medical degree, to understand that having a transgender son-in-law wasn't a terrible thing—it was very moving. Liz said, "Thank you. And thank you also for getting Jane and Chip back together—for making the dinner in New York happen."

"I'm glad you feel that way after the paces we've been put through in the last few days." He grazed his jaw with his fingers. "And me standing here like a fool in makeup."

"It kind of suits you. Is the stroke center okay with you taking time off?"

"I'll be working Christmas and New Year's, which is fine. Georgie's flying to Cincinnati for the holidays." Their eyes met again, and he said, "Georgie called me last night. She's worried that she sent you a confusing text on Labor Day."

"It wasn't Georgie's fault. It just—" Liz swallowed. "I jumped to conclusions. I didn't know you and Caroline had been in a car accident, and I thought you'd gotten together, like as a couple. It didn't seem that far-fetched, because I could tell I'd annoyed you by interrupting our breakfast and flying to Cincinnati when Lydia eloped. Then when you texted me right after I got back to New York—I wish now that I hadn't responded so coldly, but that's why I did. And it's why I didn't behave very well at the dinner with Jane and Chip."

"Yes, it was clear that night that I'd done something to displease you," Darcy said. "Even if I wasn't sure what."

"I actually wanted to ask you in New York how Georgie is doing," Liz said.

"Much better," Darcy said. "Thanks."

There was a brief silence, and Liz gathered her courage. "I'm sorry," she said. "I'm sorry because I've been rude, and you haven't deserved my rudeness. In Atherton, I felt like things between us were good in a way they hadn't been before. I really enjoyed being around you, and even though I'd been obnoxious in Cincinnati, I thought maybe you'd forgiven me. But after Lydia eloped, it seemed like I'd ruined any shot you and I had."

"I wasn't annoyed that morning. I was disappointed. And later kicked myself for taking too long to follow up, but you were so consumed with your family that at the time it seemed better to give you space."

"Well, you were right about my family being a disaster, as the rest of America will soon learn. And about my being gossipy and not as funny as I think I am."

"Liz." Darcy reached a hand out and set it on her bare forearm, and the gesture made her heart volcanic. "I hope you know that your talent for gossip is a large part of why I enjoy your company." He was regarding her with an expression that was both appraising and tender. "I've never met anyone with your interest in other people. Even when you're judging them, you do it with such care and attention. I can never predict who you'll like or dislike, but I always know your reasons will be very specific and you'll express them with great passion. I've also never known anyone more loyal to her family."

"Are you kidding? I don't even like all my sisters. Or both of my parents."

"Yet you think nothing of hopping on a plane or running through the midday heat to help them the minute they need you." Darcy looked away, though his hand remained, electrically, on her forearm. He said, "If it's not obvious, I was wrong about a lot of things, too. That morning at your sisters' apartment, I guess I thought—" He paused. "I thought I needed to be rude to overcompensate for being in love with you. I was afraid that I was chasing you like a schoolboy, and you'd find me corny. But I went much too far in the other direction."

Simultaneously, Liz felt a rapturous hope at his reference to having been in love with her and a panic that he no longer was. Couldn't he indicate one way or the other, to put her out of her suffering? It was difficult to speak, but she said slowly, "Caroline told me last night that I'm not allowed to be your girlfriend. Because of my tacky family and all that. But it made me wonder—" Liz hesitated. "It made me wonder if she was mixed up. If she thought you were planning to tell me you were interested in me because she didn't know you already had."

Darcy was looking at her with seriousness. He said, "If I told you again that I was interested in you—do you think it would be a good idea?"

Liz nodded. She tried to keep her voice steady as she said, "I'm old enough to know that sometimes you don't get a second chance."

"My darling—" Darcy lifted his palm from her arm to her cheek, and she leaned into it; she thought she might weep, and closed her eyes. "I would—I will—give you as many chances as you need. My feelings for you have never changed. And all the mushy things I was too cowardly to say before, they're just as true now. You're different from any woman I've ever met. Even when you're arguing with me, you're easy to be around. And those times you came over to my apartment—those were the most fun I've ever had."

Liz opened her eyes. "You look at diseased brains all day. No offense, but your bar for fun might be kind of low."

"No," Darcy said. "It's not. I used to watch from the window as you left in your running clothes, and I'd think, *One of the times she leaves will be the last time I see her.* It destroyed me. I didn't want us to have a last time, and that was how I realized I'd fallen in love with you."

Such compliments—they were thrilling but almost impossible to absorb in this quantity, at this pace. It was like she was being pelted with a magnificent hail, and she wished she could save the individual stones to examine later, but they'd exist with such potency only now, in this moment. And in any case, the clock was ticking.

She still was holding her bouquet, and in her plum-colored silk pumps, she crouched, setting the flowers on the uneven ground; then she stood again and extended both her arms toward him. After a very brief hesitation, during which Liz silently summoned the guiding spirit of Kathy de Bourgh, he took her hands in his.

"Darcy," she said. "Fitzwilliam Cornelius Darcy the Fifth. I know your middle name because I googled you. Is that creepy or impressive?"

"Will it hurt your feelings if I say neither?"

She grinned. "Fitzwilliam Cornelius Darcy, I admire you so much. The work you do, the way you literally save lives, how principled you are—you're the most principled person I know. Even if it means you're insulting sometimes, you're the only person I know, me included, who never lies. And you're amazingly smart, and when you're not telling harsh truths, you're incredibly gracious and kind and decent. I love you, Darcy—I ardently love you. And I want to know—" One of them was, or maybe both of them were, shaking; their clasped hands trembled, and inside her chest, her heart thudded. She gazed up at him and said, "I want to know, will you marry me? Will you do me the honor of becoming my husband?"

She hadn't known he could smile so broadly. He said, "I thought you'd never ask."

"I don't have a ring," she said, "but here." She bent her head and kissed the lower part of the ring finger of his left hand, which was still joined to her right one.

He was leaning his face down to her, and she was lifting hers to him, when she said, "Oh, and I'll totally sign a prenup. Obviously, your family has millions of dollars, and mine is borderline destitute, but that has nothing to do with why I want to marry you."

"How romantic. I think we can figure out those details down the line."

"And I realize I'll need to move to Cincinnati. I can't believe I'm saying this, but I don't even mind. The irony, huh?"

"Liz?"

"Yes?"

"Will you stop talking for a second so I can kiss you properly?"

Liz smirked. "As long as you're not afraid of messing up both our lipstick."

"That's actually the one cosmetic I seem not to be wearing right now," he said, and then—outside the lodge, behind the boulder, he in a tuxedo and she in a lavender bridesmaid dress—their faces met and they kissed at such length that the kiss contained multiple phases, including the one in which they both were smiling, practically laughing, and the one in which she forgot where she was.

When at last they paused, he said, "I guess it would be a violation of our *Eligible* contracts to go to my room right now."

They were eyeing each other, silently conferring, as Anne Lee came around the side of the boulder, followed closely by a camera crew. Darcy and Liz instinctively stepped apart.

"You guys, your mics are down," Anne said in a brisk tone. "We need to fix them." Already, a sound guy was reaching inside the top of Liz's dress; he was doing it as professionally as possible, which still didn't eliminate the weirdness. "Did you disconnect your mics on purpose?" Anne asked.

Liz said, "No," just as Darcy said, "Yes."

Anne looked between them. "Why'd you disconnect them?"

"We wanted privacy," Liz said.

"Are you two involved?" Anne asked.

After another pause, Darcy said, "That hardly seems relevant."

"I know you are," Anne said. "I just saw you making out."

Was she bluffing?

Liz said, "Then I guess that answers your question."

"How long have you been hooking up?"

Yet again, there was a silence, and with undisguised irritation, Anne said, "Fine. We need you both at the reception right now."

As they followed the path back to the courtyard, Liz could sense Darcy behind her, and her body quivered with joy. *Hate sex,* she thought gleefully. *Hate sex! Except without the hate!*

The reception lasted until well past midnight, and during that time, she and Darcy were frequently near each other and rarely spoke, except to sometimes exchange banal pleasantries. "Are you having a good time?" he asked her at one point, with the utmost politeness, and she replied in kind, "I am. Are you?"

"I am, too," he said. They danced just once—apparently, Darcy would only slow-dance, and even then he was a bit awkward, neither of which surprised her—and they hardly talked; but she rested her head against his chest, and the solidity of him felt like the promise of their future together.

As the various reception rituals were enacted and filmed, including Liz's toast (ironically, her distraction seemed to make for a smoother delivery), Liz knew that the *Eligible* crew was only doing what they were supposed to do, what the Bennet and Bingley families had agreed to allow. But still, Liz was unwilling to grant them access to her new and wondrous romance; she loved Darcy too much to try to prove her love to anyone except him.

Four Months Later

Chapter 178

INCONCLUSIVE DISCUSSIONS HAD occurred about the circumstances under which the Bennets would watch the *Eligible* wedding special when it aired, and the likeliest option seemed to be that Ham and Lydia would host dinner and a viewing in their living room. Liz and Darcy were still sharing his Madison Road apartment—she had left New York in February, and they had purchased but not yet moved into a recently renovated loft in downtown's Over-the-Rhine neighborhood—and Liz was frankly wary of watching with her family members. The injuries to their vanity could, she worried, be so extensive as to require triage on her part.

As it turned out, all of the Cincinnati Bennets were caught by surprise when Jane's first appearance came not on *Eligible: Chip & Jane's Road to the Altar* but, rather, two weeks prior to the special's debut, on *Eligible: Fan Favorites' Reunion*. Though Liz had expected to need to avert her eyes as Chip kissed his way through the reunion season, he had thus far paired off only once. And while the heavy petting that had transpired in a hammock between him and Rachelle B. (not to be confused with Rachelle T.) had seemed in every way consensual, the next morning, Chip had with great sorrow told Rachelle B. that his heart was somewhere else. In the next episode, he mentioned Jane by name during a confessional, yet still neither Liz nor any other Bennets were prepared for Jane herself to show up onscreen the following week in the reunion's penultimate episode.

In the hot tub at the Malibu compound, the contestants were recuperating from a nude obstacle-course competition when a phone rang audibly. A contestant named Lulu sprang from the hot tub and ran inside in her dripping bikini. From a table in the living room of the main house, she lifted the receiver of a black rotary phone that Liz felt confident was a prop; she was nearly certain that, up to that point, there had been no phone anywhere on the compound. "Chip," Lulu called. "It's for you!"

Chip answered, and then the screen split and Jane appeared. She lay in a bed recognizable to Liz from their room at the Hermoso Desert Lodge.

"It's Jane," Jane said. "I have some news. I know we broke up, but—" The shot widened to include her belly, which she patted. "I'm pregnant." Chip's jaw dropped in astonishment, and the show cut to a commercial.

Clearly, Jane and Chip were complicit in the charade, though Liz hesitated to call Jane and ask about it because Adelaide Bennet Bingley, born three weeks before at seven pounds, two ounces, was fussy in the early evenings, and it was presently six-thirty P.M. in Los Angeles. In additional scenes, Jane and Chip declared by phone their enduring affection for each other, and Chip embarked on a long walk on the beach, an excursion marked by either (to judge from his expression) moody contemplation or gastrointestinal distress. Liz's phone was abuzz with texts from Lydia and Kitty, who were watching with their mother at the Grasmoor (*WTF! Did u know about this? Jane wasn't really there for reunion right?*). At the next commercial break, Liz could resist no longer and texted Jane: *Do u know you're on Eligible reunion right now?*

A moment later, Liz's phone rang. "The producers wanted to introduce me during the reunion so the audience would get invested in Chip and me ending up together," Jane said. "Are they making it convincing?

"Actually, yes."

In the background, Liz could hear Adelaide's bleat. Three days after her birth, Liz had journeyed to Los Angeles to meet her; she was a miraculous and tiny human whom Liz felt immediate devotion toward and was relieved not to be the mother of. Over the phone, Liz asked Jane, "How's my niece?"

"She doesn't want to sleep unless someone's holding her, and maybe not even then." Jane's voice had gone high and singsongy; she sounded blissful. "Right, Addie?" she said. "Right, baby girl? Why would anyone want to close their eyes when there's so much to learn about the world?"

"Here," Liz heard Chip say. "Give her to me. And tell Liz I say hi."

"Are you guys watching?" Liz said.

"We weren't planning on it." Jane laughed. "I mean, we already know what happens."

Chapter 179

"FRED, COME QUICK!" Mrs. Bennet had shouted when she spotted her eldest daughter onscreen. "Goodness gracious, Lydia, tell your father to come at once."

"Dad!" Lydia shouted without rising from the sofa. "It's an emergency."

Mr. Bennet wandered out of his bedroom looking unconcerned.

"It's Jane!" Mrs. Bennet pointed at the television. "Right there."

Mrs. Bennet continued exclaiming through the commercial break and into the show's resumption, at which point Kitty said, "Mom, I can't hear if you're talking."

"I would never have left town if I'd known," Chip was telling Jane over the phone. "Jane, I'm not the kind of man who abandons the mother of his child. I always loved you, and I always wanted to make it work."

"Oh!" Mrs. Bennet clapped her hands. "They're saying it's his! I knew they would, I just knew it! It makes so much more sense this way!"

"It's bullshit, though," Kitty said, and Lydia said, "Kitty, it's called *reality* TV. It's not called *true* TV."

Neither Ham nor Shane had accompanied the sisters to the Grasmoor; after bonding amid the strangeness of Palm Springs, Shane had joined Ham's gym and the two men had taken to going out for Korean barbecue after the Thursday night class Ham taught.

"Isn't it funny," Mrs. Bennet said, "that the very first episode of *Eligible* I've ever seen has my own daughter in it?"

Mr. Bennet snorted. "It's past time to lay that canard to rest, Sally."

"I don't know what you mean."

"Mom, you watch with us every week," Kitty said.

"Well, I've seen bits here and there but not a whole show." Kitty, Lydia, and Mr. Bennet exchanged glances, and Mrs. Bennet said, "I haven't! You know me, always popping up and down."

In fact, as usual, she had been seated for the entire episode, which was well into its second hour; she had been perusing her housewares catalogs but mostly during commercials.

"I've never really been a TV watcher," Mrs. Bennet said, and whether or not anyone else believed her, it was abundantly clear that she believed herself; she spoke with confidence and pleasure. She said, "I've always far preferred a good book."

Two Weeks Later

Chapter 180

"I WAS UNDER the impression that this was a terrible show," Darcy said seven minutes into *Eligible: Chip & Jane's Road to the Altar.* "But it's literally unwatchable."

"Not literally," Liz said. "Your eyeballs aren't melting."

They were curled into each other on the couch, a blanket spread over them; it was early April and still cool in Cincinnati.

With his fingertips, Darcy pulled down the skin around the sockets of his eyes. "Are you sure?"

"I'll make you a deal," Liz said. "If you promise to stick with it for the next three nights, I'll never try to get you to watch *Eligible* ever again."

Darcy grinned. "Do you think that's tempting? It's not like I'm obligated to watch anyway."

"You kind of are," Liz said. "Because you're in it, and so am I, and we're the loves of each other's lives."

Darcy leaned in and kissed her. "We are the loves of each other's lives," he said. "But that has nothing to do with *Eligible.*"

What Liz didn't yet know, but would discover imminently, was that the humiliation of *Eligible: Chip & Jane's Road to the Altar* belonged primarily to her. She, her sisters, and Chip's sisters would all appear onscreen with chyrons showing not only their names but also—perhaps in the interest of distinguishing this bevy of women—their identities, or some stereotypical version of their identities bestowed with minimal regard for fact. Brooke Bingley was "The Stay-at-Home Mom," which was accurate enough, but Caroline Bingley was "The Romantic." Lydia Bennet was "The Free Spirit," Kitty was "The Entrepreneur," Mary was "The Scholar," and Liz (oh, how this stung!) was "The Party Girl." Shortly after a clip in which Kitty declared, "What I'm really interested in long-term is opening a chain of salons that cater not just to physical beauty but also to inner well-being," Liz showed up saying, "I'd describe myself as a focused, down-to-earth person," and there ensued a montage of her gulping wine, pounding shots, and at one point not just holding but drinking from two separate champagne flutes. Which had actually happened at the wedding reception, but only because she'd picked up a glass for her mother as well as herself, her mother's had been excessively full, and Liz had been trying to prevent it from spilling.

Naturally, the confrontation she'd had with Caroline appeared in its entirety, contextualized in advance by Caroline trashing Liz during multiple interviews and describing with surprising frankness, if a delusion could ever be called frank, her belief that she and Darcy were meant to be together. A camera crew had, albeit without sound and from a distance of perhaps forty feet, caught Liz's proposal to Darcy and their subsequent embrace; both were interspersed with Caroline crying furiously, as if she were observing the scene firsthand, which Liz strongly doubted had happened. But maybe weeping on-camera had been the price Caroline was required to pay in order to become the star of the next season of *Eligible;* the announcement of her role, reflecting the first time in *Eligible* history that a sibling pair had starred one after the other, would come the following week.

Liz had assumed she wasn't interesting enough to warrant a prominent role in the wedding special, given that she was pushing forty, was

in neither a transgender nor even an interracial relationship, and didn't
don a bikini. That she'd been mistaken might have been flattering if it
weren't so embarrassing.

"I don't think I can ever leave this apartment again," she would tell
Darcy. "Aren't you mortified that people will know you're engaged to
the Party Girl?" (They were to marry in August at Knox Church.
They'd considered holding the ceremony at Pemberley, just before the
estate was passed off to the National Trust for Historic Preservation,
but Liz had reasoned that it was her mother who cared most about the
proceedings, and due to a once-unimaginable confluence of circumstances, Liz found herself the daughter best suited to making Mrs.
Bennet's every wedding dream come true. So why not?)

Darcy would look amused. He'd say, "Who cares what anyone
thinks?" He'd kiss Liz's forehead and add, "Besides, who wouldn't
want to marry the Party Girl?"

Chapter 181

IT WAS MARY'S firm belief that any woman capable of satisfying her own desires—which, though not all of them knew it, was any woman anywhere—would never need to disgrace herself in the pursuit of a man. The nine-inch dildo Lydia had boasted of sounded garish, but after experimenting over the years, Mary had settled upon a sleek and ergonomic vibrator with five modes of stimulation, powered by an almost silent motor. She used it nightly before bed, and sometimes in the morning as well, after her alarm went off for her job as a sales account manager at Procter & Gamble.

For her undergraduate degree, Mary had attended Macalester College, where she had been involved, sequentially, with two men and one woman, and the collective lesson she had learned from them was that she cared little for sex and even less for sharing a bed. Back then, before hookup websites became common, physical intimacy involved such rigmarole—you might start on meals and conversations with someone weeks or months prior to them providing you with any true gratification, and even then, gratification wasn't guaranteed; it was all incredibly inefficient. As for sharing a bed, the other person's snores and blanket hogging, the small talk you needed to make when going to sleep or waking up—really, what was the point? Mary preferred to spread out alone on a mattress, turning the light off or on when she pleased.

Explaining her view to her sisters, or to anyone else, was out of the question. Everyone she knew was preoccupied with coupling, either for themselves or for others, and Mary understood that trying to persuade them would be an exercise not only in futility but also in tedium. (And with regard to exercising: That was something else Mary didn't do, nor did she diet, shave her legs or underarms, pluck her eyebrows, or wear makeup. She showered daily, brushed her teeth, and applied deodorant, a routine she deemed more than adequate in terms of holding up her end of society's hygiene bargain.)

Though Mary knew that her sisters considered her strange, and would consider her more so were she to articulate her true outlook, she observed with a nearly anthropological derision their elaborate fitness rituals and fakely scented lotions and the hours—nay, years—they devoted to making some man see them in a particular way; they reminded her of plastic ballerinas inside music boxes, twirling in their private orbits of narcissism.

She did not detest her sisters, she did not consider them evil—certainly shallow, but not evil—and yet if she weren't related to them, she wouldn't spend time in their company. Then again, she wouldn't spend time in the company of most people.

Even the members of her bowling league, who were the closest approximation Mary came to a community, weren't individuals she saw except on Tuesday nights. Mary's team consisted of two other women and two men, and the next youngest person after her was eighteen years her senior. Among their appealing qualities was that Mary stood no chance of encountering any of them at the Cincinnati Country Club.

Really, it was the sport rather than the people that drew Mary week in and week out to Madison Bowl. Every time she entered the build-

ing, with its scent of gymnasium and french fries, its rhythmic knocking of heavy polyurethane against wood, excitement activated her
salivary glands.

If the first episode of *Eligible: Chip & Jane's Road to the Altar* had
fallen on a night other than Tuesday, Mary might have watched it or
she might not have; the decision would have depended on what else
she had in the way of P & G deadlines or pleasure reading. As it was,
the first episode did air on a Tuesday, and Mary didn't for a moment
consider skipping bowling. Thus, at the exact moment her image first
flashed on screens all over the country ("Mary Bennet: 'The Scholar' "),
she was waiting her turn in lane 10. When Felicia, who was Mary's
teammate and a fifty-seven-year-old special education teacher, moved
out of the way, Mary walked to the ball return, inserted her fingers into
her ball (she used one that weighed fourteen pounds), lifted it from
the rack, purposefully approached the foul line while extending her
right arm behind her, kept her gaze on the pins, and released. The ball
surged down the oiled wood lane. In the seconds just before it collided
with the pins, Mary knew that a strike would occur, and then it happened: All the pins fell, and when they did, it was so, so satisfying. As
the pinsetter descended, Mary balled her right hand, bent her arm, and
pulled it back in fist-pumping victory. Her sisters, she thought, could
have their crushes and courtships, their histrionics and reconciliations.
For Mary, this was heaven.

Acknowledgments

I'm incredibly lucky to work closely with a trio of strong, smart, funny women: my agent, Jennifer Rudolph Walsh; my editor, Jennifer Hershey; and my publicist, Maria Braeckel.

For advocating on my behalf, and for being people with whom it's always a pleasure to interact, I'm thankful to many others at WME, including Cathryn Summerhayes, Raffaella DeAngelis, Tracy Fisher, Alicia Gordon, Erin Conroy, Suzanne Gluck, Eve Attermann, Eric Zohn, Maggie Shapiro, Katie Giarla, and Elizabeth Goodstein.

At Random House, I have benefited enormously from the support and wisdom of Gina Centrello, Avideh Bashirrad, Theresa Zoro, Sally Marvin, Leigh Marchant, Susan Kamil, Tom Perry, Sanyu Dillon, Caitlin McCaskey, Anastasia Whalen, Anne Speyer, Allyson Lord, Christine Mykityshyn, Janet Wygal, Bonnie Thompson, Alaina Waagner, Maggie Oberrender, Paolo Pepe, Robbin Schiff, and Liz Eno.

In the U.K., I'm indebted to Louisa Joyner and Katie Espiner, who approached me with the idea for this book, as well as to Kate Elton, Jaime Frost, Suzie Dooré, Cassie Brown, and Charlotte Cray at Borough Press, who saw it through to the end. I am appreciative of my friends at Transworld, among them Marianne Velmans and Patsy Irwin, who permitted a professional excursion.

My generous-hearted early readers include Emily Miller, Susanna Daniel, Samuel Park, Jynne Dilling Martin, Sheena Cook, Eric Bennett, Rory Evans, Anne Morriss, Susan Marrs, Tiernan Sittenfeld, Jo Sittenfeld, and, for being my go-to expert on all things Cincinnati, P.G. Sittenfeld. My parents, Paul and Betsy Sittenfeld, are not (thank goodness) to be confused with Fred and Sally Bennet, though I'm pretty sure they've all encountered one another at a cocktail party. My husband, Matt, and our children are my favorite midwesterners.

I enjoyed entertaining conversations and tasty snacks with my Austen book club: Hillary Sale, Maggie Penn, Becky Patel, Stephanie Park Zwicker, Jane Price, Susan Appleton, Susan Stiritz, and Kristin Maher.

I feel great fondness for the people who know more about certain subjects than I do, and who let me pick their brains, often in extensive detail: Ben Hatta, Jute Ramsay, Elizabeth Randolph, Liz Rohrbaugh, Mariagiovanna Baccara, Bruce Hall, Wyman Morriss, Cynthia Wichelman, Craig Zaidman, Stephanie Park Zwicker (again!), Maurizio Corbetta, John Stewart, Jarek Steele, Kris Kleindienst, and Tricia Sanders.

In terms of research, I also want to acknowledge my use of the website for Filoli, in Woodside, California, and of an October 2014 *St. Louis Post-Dispatch* article about spiders by Susan Weich. *Transgender 101: A Simple Guide to a Complex Issue* is in fact a real book by Nicholas M. Teich.

Finally, I hope it goes without saying, but I'll say it anyway: I am very grateful to Jane Austen, whose books have brought delight to many readers, including me.

About the Author

CURTIS SITTENFELD is the bestselling author of the novels *Prep, The Man of My Dreams, American Wife,* and *Sisterland,* which have been translated into twenty-five languages. Her nonfiction has been published widely, including in *The New York Times, The Atlantic, Time, Vanity Fair,* and *Glamour* and broadcast on public radio's *This American Life.* A native of Cincinnati, she currently lives with her family in St. Louis.

curtissittenfeld.com
@csittenfeld
Find Curtis Sittenfeld on Facebook.

About the Type

This book was set in Galliard, a typeface designed in 1978 by Matthew Carter (b. 1937) for the Mergenthaler Linotype Company. Galliard is based on the sixteenth-century typefaces of Robert Granjon (1513–89).